FROM
THE
ASHES

ALSO BY DAMIEN BOYD

A DI Nick Dixon Novel

FROM THE ASHES

DAMIEN BOYD

THOMAS & MERCER

Text copyright © Damien Boyd 2024
All rights reserved.

Published by Thomas & Mercer, Seattle

www.apub.com

Amazon, the Amazon logo, and Thomas & Mercer are trademarks of Amazon.com, Inc., or its affiliates.

ISBN-13: 9781662507373
eISBN: 9781662507366

Cover design by @blacksheep-uk.com
Cover images: © MaciekArt © Ilya Andriyanov / Shutterstock; © Roberto Ouro Tubio / Arcangel; © markhonosvitaly / Getty Images

Printed in the United States of America

For Rod

Prologue

He liked to watch.

From a safe distance, in the shadows, away from prying eyes.

It had become a habit, an addiction even; the urge almost irresistible.

It was his creation and he felt responsible for it somehow. Not just legally, that was an occupational hazard; more like a parent.

Parental responsibility, that was it. He had given it life, loved it, cherished it, watched it finding its way in the world. Blossoming, even.

That first flicker of flame.

He always left when the fire engines arrived. No sympathy, no mercy, no pause to marvel at the beauty of it. They'd just set about killing it, as quickly and efficiently as they could.

He couldn't bring himself to watch that.

The pain would last for days, the sense of loss – a bereavement, almost. Until he gave it life again, somewhere else.

Oxidation was the key.

He'd tried to understand the science of it, but that stripped away the magic, the mystical element.

It was almost spiritual. It really was.

Never erotic, despite what that psychiatrist had said. That had been a close shave all the same – sentencing adjourned for psychiatric reports. He'd told them what they wanted to hear and walked away with probation.

Who gave a crap about a thatched bus shelter anyway? It was just begging for someone to light it up.

And he still had the photos: flames climbing into a starry sky, dancing; alive, almost – living and breathing. But they were just for him.

No Instagramming those. No way.

It had been hard work, that one, come to think of it, the thatch tightly packed, stopping the oxygen getting to it.

There we go, oxidation again.

Understanding a little of the science helped, oddly enough.

It had been a bit too busy on the seafront as well, the fire hardly going before some do-gooder was on their phone, dialling 999. There'd been no real chance to savour it in peace, to watch it grow, even at that time in the morning. Still, the fire brigade had taken twenty minutes to get there, so it wasn't all bad.

And he'd got those photos.

Tonight would be very different. He'd teach them a lesson: never sack an arsonist if you don't want your hotel burned down. It was as good a lesson as any.

Whoever heard of a waiter being sacked for eating leftovers? The job was seasonal anyway, and there'd only been a few weeks to go.

He'd had to improvise too, and it would be fun seeing if it worked. His preferred method was the filter of a Jin Ling cigarette wrapped in Swan Vesta matches. The few minutes it took to burn down gave him a chance to get clear, get his camera ready. It had been a stroke of luck finding them at that car boot sale; none of that reduced-ignition nonsense you get with shop-bought cigarettes to have to deal with.

He stepped back into the trees, his eyes fixed on the kitchen area at the back of the ballroom, and waited. Not long to go now, surely?

Tonight would be a tribute to Jason Bourne, although in the film he'd stuffed a magazine in the toaster. All he could find was yesterday's Torbay Gazette. Still, that was all it was good for, really.

Yes, tonight would be very different.

The gas bottles would see to that.

Chapter One

'I'll do the talking.' Police Constable Nigel Cole rang the bell, even though the front door of the bungalow was standing open, a shaft of light illuminating the garden path. 'Better wipe your feet before we go in as well.'

PC Sarah Loveday had beaten him to it, and was already brushing her boots off in the long wet grass by the metal gate that had slammed behind her on a spring. The farmyard muck was taking some shifting. 'Shouldn't we take them off?' she asked. 'My nan would do her nut if we traipsed this lot through her flat.'

'I think this old bird's past caring.' Cole was trying to stay patient. A probationer in the Rural Crimes team was all well and good, but this one was too keen by half – young and irritatingly bright; she'd been running rings around him for weeks. Much more of it and he'd wring her bloody neck.

Cole stepped into the hall just as a woman in a blue carer's uniform appeared at the far end of the corridor. 'You're not coming in here like that, are you?' she asked, glaring at his boots.

'We've just come from a farm at East Brent; bloke's had his tractor pinched.'

'Stay where you are and I'll put some newspaper down.' The woman picked up a copy of the *Burnham and Highbridge Weekly News* from a pile by the phone, and backed away towards the open living room door, covering the hall carpet with sheets of newspaper as she went. 'No point in treading mud everywhere.'

'Is the doctor still here?' asked Cole.

'Through here,' she replied. 'With Deirdre. Just make sure you stay on the paper.'

The doctor was sitting on the arm of the sofa, idly scrolling through pictures on a smartphone. Instagram probably; the app swiped away and the phone dropped into an inside jacket pocket in one well-rehearsed movement. 'Ah, you're here,' he said, standing up. 'She's dead, obviously, but there's no real reason for it that I can see. Nothing in her medical records that might explain it either, but I'm not her GP, so it's one for the coroner, I'm afraid. Unexplained.'

'Who found her?' asked Cole.

'I did,' replied the carer, hovering in the doorway. 'I came in just after six, as usual, and there she was. She'd had her hair done today, as well.'

'How old is she?'

'Eighty-eight.'

The old lady looked peaceful, asleep even. Eyes closed, head resting in the corner of the winged armchair, a pen and a crossword book in her lap. She was sitting in front of an electric fire, a single bar glowing orange, her legs covered by a blanket.

It was a familiar scene: a small table on one side of her with a copy of the *TV Times* and the remote control, an open box of chocolates, a pair of glasses, the telephone handset and an empty mug. A walking frame was carefully positioned on the other side, if needed.

'She looks like my nan,' said Sarah. 'Her hair looks nice too.'

A single curl of grey had slipped out of place and fallen across the old lady's forehead.

'Trish somebody does it for her,' offered the carer. 'Her details are in Deirdre's address book. Does the rounds, you know.'

'So, you can't give a cause of death?' asked Cole, turning to the doctor.

'I'm afraid not.' He was shuffling his way towards the door. 'I've got no idea what it is, but she's not seen her GP in the last twenty-eight days, so it needs to be referred to the coroner anyway.'

'Any idea of the time of death?' asked Sarah.

'I'm a doctor not a pathologist, I'm afraid.' Two steps towards the door this time. 'Well, if there's nothing else?'

'Who closed her eyes?'

'Nobody, if she died in her sleep.'

'I think we can let the doctor go now,' said Cole, stifling a sigh. 'Sorry.' He listened to the footsteps on the newspaper in the hall, then the front door slammed shut. 'When did you last see Mrs Baxter?' he asked, the carer now following Sarah around the living room, placing newspaper in front of her.

'I see to Deirdre twice a day. Half an hour in the morning, nine till nine-thirty. I get her up and do her breakfast, make sure she takes her tablets, that sort of thing. Then I come in at six for an hour, cook her supper and get her ready for bed. Trish was cutting her hair late morning, so she must've died this afternoon, I suppose.'

'Tablets?' Cole again – he was supposed to be in charge, after all.

'She took a statin and one for her blood pressure. Apart from that she was fine, really. She had a few mobility issues, but that was it.'

'Would the television usually have been on?' asked Sarah. She was looking at the family photos on the mantelpiece now. 'My nan's is always on.'

'It's always on when I come in at six.' The carer smiled to herself. 'Deirdre never missed *Countdown*. She loved watching the golf too; she could tell you who all the players were. Used to be quite a good player herself, apparently. Ladies club champion at Burnham and Berrow back in the day. There are some trophies in the corner cabinet.'

Sarah was standing in front of Deirdre Baxter now, staring down at her body. It wasn't her first dead body, so Cole wasn't entirely sure he could understand the fascination.

The carer looked at him and raised her eyebrows, waving what was left of the newspaper in his direction.

'Miss Marple,' whispered Cole, with a smirk.

'Who's the duty detective inspector?' asked Sarah.

She had heard his Marple remark, and either blushed with embarrassment or flushed with anger, he couldn't tell, but he suddenly felt guilty for having said it. 'Oh, come on, what makes you think CID are going to want to have a look?' Cole was scrolling though the contacts on his phone, about to ring the coroner's office.

Sarah opened her mouth to reply, but he didn't give her a chance.

'And you know very well who the duty SIO is this weekend. It's me you have to impress, not him,' he said, tapping his chest with his phone. 'I'm the one they'll ask for a report at the end of your probation.'

'When was the last time you looked at the intranet?'

'A couple of weeks ago, maybe.'

'A couple of months, more like.'

'There's never anything on it about rural crimes.' The sudden realisation she knew something he didn't washed over him, much like the time that child had thrown up in front of him on the rollercoaster. 'Let's hear it then,' he said, with an air of resignation.

'Be on the lookout for elderly persons dying alone in unexplained circumstances in their own homes, and refer to CID.'

◆ ◆ ◆

'You don't even like cider.'

'Yes, I do.' Detective Chief Inspector Nick Dixon sniffed the mulled cider in the plastic cup that had been thrust into his hand by Home Office pathologist Dr Roger Poland. The pungent waft of mixed herbs and spices was rising in the steam from the hot drink, the warmth from the cup just about making it through his thick gloves. Cinnamon certainly, but God knows what else. Dixon held it up to the light from the fire pit, trying to work out what it was that was floating on the top. Cloves, bits of apple, a twig of some sort. It was best not to look too closely.

'Try it then,' said Detective Sergeant Jane Winter, clearly determined not to let him off the hook.

Poland was pushing through the small crowd at the bar, a drink in each hand. 'Here's an orange juice for you. It was either that or lemonade,' he said, offering it to Jane. 'How far gone are you now?'

'Six months.'

'Not long to go then.' Poland grinned. 'Think of all those sleepless nights you've got to look forward to.'

'We're used to them, Roger,' replied Dixon, still summoning up the courage to try the mulled cider that was rapidly cooling in the cold night air.

'Good, isn't it? I got a pint.' Poland took a swig from the large plastic cup in his right hand. Clearly a connoisseur of mulled cider, he looked as if he was about to gargle with it.

Dixon had taken the glove off his left hand, passed it to Jane, and was now trying to fish a piece of apple from his cup without burning his fingers.

'Stop mucking about and drink the bloody stuff,' she muttered. 'At least you can have a drink.'

'It smells like mouthwash,' whispered Dixon.

'Don't expect any sympathy from me,' she said. 'I wanted a quiet night in, but you insisted. Let's go wassailing, you said.'

'It was Roger's idea, and we're staying at his house tonight, Sergeant, in case you'd forgotten. He's doing us a curry.'

'I am. Prawn and chicken, all the trimmings.' Poland chuckled. 'You know you're in trouble when he's calling you "sergeant". I used to call my fiancée "darling".'

'You're divorced, Roger.'

'True enough. Maybe I'd have been better off if I'd called her Cruella de Vi—' He was interrupted by the jangling of a host of small bells. 'Ah, jolly good, the Morris dancers are here.'

'Fuck me, that's all we need,' grumbled Jane.

A loudhailer crackled into life. 'Right then, ladies and gents, welcome to Oake Cider Farm. My name is Malcolm Hope-Bruce and I'll be your master of ceremonies this evening. As you know, Oake is very much a family affair, and you've met my sister-in-law, Diana, and my nephew, Jos, at the bar. I hope everyone's enjoying the mulled cider?'

A cheer from the crowd.

'Let's go wassailing!'

Dixon joined in, half-heartedly, if only to drown out Jane's sigh; that and delay drinking the mulled cider a little longer.

'We're almost ready for the procession out to the orchards,' continued Malcolm. He was carrying a shotgun over his shoulder, the barrel glinting in the light from the flaming torches being held aloft by the crowd behind him. 'Has everyone got a copy of the incantation so you can join in? For those of you who don't know, the idea is to ward off evil spirits so we get a good crop of apples for next year's cider making.'

'The bloody Morris dancers will do that on their own,' said Jane.

'We all sing the incantation, then when I've fired the shotgun, rattle your pots and pans if you've got them and hit the trees with

9

your sticks. After that, we welcome the good spirits with offerings of burnt toast soaked in cider.'

Dixon put his arm around Jane's waist and pulled her towards him. 'Don't. Say. It.' Then he kissed her on the lips. 'Just keep thinking about Roger's curry. And if it's horrible, we can feed it to Monty under the table.' He looked down at their feet, where a large white Staffordshire terrier was sitting patiently. The dog's nose was twitching, his eyes fixed firmly on the person carrying the toast.

'Everyone is welcome to have a go,' continued Malcolm, still shouting into his loudhailer. 'We just hang the toast in the branches of the trees, drink from the wassail cup, then there'll be a display from the Mendip Morris dancers.'

'Oh no you don't.' Jane reached out and took hold of the fur-lined hood of the coat in front of her, stopping her half-sister, Lucy, in her tracks as she made a beeline for the bar. 'You're coming with us. If I can't get out of it, neither can you. And besides, you're sixteen.'

'It's only cider,' protested Lucy.

'You won't get past that dragon at the bar, anyway,' said Poland. 'I thought she was going to ask *me* for ID.'

Dixon offered the girl his plastic cup. 'Here, have this.'

'No fear, that's the mulled stuff. I think I'd puke.'

'I'm getting another one,' said Poland. 'She can have a half of the plain stuff, surely? Then I thought we'd just tag on the end of the procession.'

'A half then,' said Jane, a frown appearing from underneath her bobble hat.

The procession started to move off in the direction of the apple orchard, lanterns hanging in the trees lining the track. The crowd was following a couple of folk musicians, one playing a frame drum, the other a piccolo.

'It dates back a thousand years,' Poland said over his shoulder as he waited at the back of the queue for the bar.

'They had nothing else to do back then,' said Jane. 'And they certainly didn't have a curry waiting for them.'

'It guarantees a good crop of apples.'

'So does fertiliser.' Dixon had given up on his mulled cider and was busy tipping it down a drain.

'Peasants.' Poland turned back to the bar. 'I got us some copies of the incantation, so we can sing along,' he said, appearing seconds later with a plastic cup in each hand and several bits of paper between his teeth.

'He's your friend, you deal with him,' Jane said, watching Dixon rummaging in his inside coat pocket. 'Oh, that's bloody marvellous, that is. Please tell me that's not your phone buzzing?'

'I am duty SIO tonight. I did warn you.'

'Knowing your luck you'll have to drop everything and go.'

'Funny you should say that,' Dixon replied, with a consolatory shrug. 'Save me some of the prawn stuff.'

Chapter Two

'Sorry, Sir.' Cole had been watching Dixon park his Land Rover on the pavement opposite the bungalow, and opened the garden gate.

'Don't be,' replied Dixon, with a shake of his head. 'I was wassailing.'

'Oh, that's great fun,' said Sarah, from the porch. 'I love the mulled cider too.'

Cole gritted his teeth. 'She's driving me round the bend,' he hissed. 'Too bloody keen by half; I feel like I'm caught in her slipstream.'

'Just go with the flow, Nige, and take the credit when your protégé becomes the next chief constable.'

'Yeah, right.'

'What've we got?' Dixon stopped at the front door, noticing the muddy footprints on the newspaper in the hall, then he looked down at Cole's boots.

'We were at a pig farm over at East Brent,' Cole said, the impatient edge to his voice all but gone. 'We thought it best to preserve the scene, just in case.'

'The scene?'

'The intranet says we're to notify CID if we come across an unexplained death – an elderly person in their own home.'

Dixon knew Cole better than that. 'You've looked at the intranet?'

'She did.'

Sarah was standing on the doormat, her boots off and placed neatly on a piece of newspaper in the porch.

'Well done, Constable.'

'Thank you, Sir.'

He was tempted to ask if the intranet mentioned why CID should be alerted, but thought better of it. Perhaps reading it himself in future might be an idea? 'Who is she?' he asked, changing the subject.

'Deirdre Baxter,' replied Sarah, her notebook already open. 'Aged eighty-eight. She was found by her carer, Christine MacBride, just after six. She called the duty doctor, but he couldn't find any obvious cause and there's nothing in Deirdre's medical records. She's not seen her GP in the last twenty-eight days, so it needs to be referred to the coroner anyway.'

'See what I mean?' muttered Cole.

'Is Christine still here?'

'She had other clients to see to, so we let her go,' replied Cole. 'She said she can pop back after ten if we need her.'

'The armchair opposite Deirdre has been moved, Sir.' Sarah stood to one side when Dixon stepped into the hall. 'It's not sitting in the indentations on the carpet. The TV was off too. Christine said it was usually on all day; Deirdre liked the company. The voices, you know.'

'And that's it, is it?'

'It's all we could see,' replied Cole.

'I'll go and have a look then,' said Dixon. 'While I'm doing that, you go and have a word with that nosy bugger opposite. Lights on, curtains open, you can bet he's got chapter and verse on comings and goings.'

'I'll do it.' Sarah was hastily putting on her boots, and set off down the garden path with the laces still undone.

'She's going to be the death of me,' said Cole, under his breath. 'D'you want me to go with her?'

'You stay there, Nige.'

Dixon walked on the newspaper, careful to avoid the muddy boot prints. An alert to be on the lookout for unexplained deaths among the elderly meant there had been others – with, at the very least, a suspicion of foul play. Where, though? Certainly not on his patch. Someone would have mentioned it.

Looking for anything that might be remotely suspicious explained Sarah noticing the wandering armchair too. A bright kid.

The newspaper in front of the electric fire was well trodden, but even the warmth from the single bar was welcome on a cold January night; not quite the same as the fire pit at the cider farm, but better than nothing. Dixon looked down at Deirdre Baxter. The colour had drained from her face some time ago, replaced by the pallid grey of death.

Eyes closed. Died in her sleep, possibly, but then how many people slept with their fists clenched?

A pair of reading glasses on a cord around her neck, folded flat so you had to look carefully to notice one arm was missing.

A personal alarm was on the floor under the small table to her left, the elasticated wrist strap still intact. Dixon slid a pen out of his inside jacket pocket, squatted down and pressed the button.

'Hello Deirdre, it's Ruth from Taking Care. Are you all right?' The voice was coming from a base unit on the sideboard.

'Ruth, this is Detective Chief Inspector Dixon of Avon and Somerset Police. I'm afraid Mrs Baxter is deceased. Can you tell me whether you've received any other calls from this alarm today, please?'

'Oh, I am sorry to hear that. No; no calls. It would be on the system if we had.'

'When was the last one?'

'Boxing Day, it says here. Deirdre pressed the button by mistake. It happens a lot at Christmas. Sometimes they just want someone to talk to.'

'All right, thank you,' replied Dixon. 'Someone will be in touch in due course.'

He turned back to Deirdre and stared at her. Something wasn't quite right, he knew that much, but as for what it was . . .

Sarah was right, the armchair had been moved, but not by much; maybe six inches nearer the fire. And nearer Deirdre. The indentations in the carpet were deep and there were no other marks, so the chair was rarely moved, if ever. That was the best Dixon could come up with, no matter how hard he stared at it.

The wrist strap was tight, so maybe she'd taken off her alarm and put it on the table, from where it had fallen on the floor? Then she'd died peacefully in her sleep.

No, it was her face, something forced about it.

'Sir, Sir.' There was an urgency in Sarah's voice and her footsteps on the newspaper in the hall. 'You need to come and hear this. That bloke opposite.'

Sleet was falling as they crossed the road, which would have put paid to Jane's wassailing and given her the perfect excuse to head for the safety of Roger's house, and the curry. Dixon checked his phone and there was the text message:

Pissing down. Gone back to Roger's Jx

'This is Mr Hardy,' said Sarah, making the introductions on the doorstep over the yapping of a small terrier in the window. Unshaven, balding; the unmistakeable whiff of beer, although the can of Stella in his right hand might have had something to do with it. 'DCI Dixon. Tell him what you told me.'

'I don't want you to think I'm some sort of nosy neighbour or anything.'

'We don't,' said Sarah.

Can lie convincingly too, thought Dixon. She'll go far.

'I leave the curtains open so Parsnip can look out. There's a window seat. I watch the telly and he watches the world go by.'

Barks at it, too, for all he's worth. Still, Monty did his fair share of that, so who was Dixon to criticise?

'I've known Deirdre for years and sort of keep an eye on her. She's got carers and stuff, but I've done odd jobs, fixed her fence, cleared the snow off her path a couple of years ago. Not for money, you understand. Anyway, she's got a routine, you can set your watch by it: carers, the hairdresser today, postie.'

'And . . .' Sarah looked as if she was going to burst.

'Today there was someone else. About five o'clock. Well, I say *about* five o'clock; it was three minutes to, I checked. I thought it was her carer arriving a bit early, but then she turned up as usual at six.'

'Who was it?' asked Dixon.

'No idea. It was dark, mind, and the streetlights are down there' – pointing along the lane. 'They parked across the drive, used the key safe and went in, so they must've known the code.'

'Male or female?'

'It's difficult to tell, these days. And we're not supposed to judge, are we? How do I know how they identify?'

Dixon ignored the sarcasm. 'Could you see any features?'

'No, they had their back to me; coat with a hood up.'

'How long were they in there for?'

'Twenty-two minutes.'

'You checked?'

'And he wrote it down, Sir,' said Sarah.

'You got a full statement?'

'Yes, Sir.'

'Good.' Dixon didn't want to spend any more time on the doorstep in the sleet than he had to. 'When this person came out, they'd have been walking towards you,' he said, turning back to Hardy. 'Could you see what they were wearing then?'

'Yeah, the coat was open. A white top, like what the nurses wear. Down to here.' Hardy was drawing a line across the tops of his thighs with his fingers. 'Had a pass dangling on a lanyard too, and dark trousers; I thought green, but I might be wrong.'

Sarah was scribbling notes in her notebook. Not a *full* statement then. 'That's an OT's uniform, Sir,' she said. 'An occupational therapist. White tunic and green trousers.'

'Show him a picture.'

Dixon waited as patiently as he could for Sarah to do a Google Image search on her phone. 'OT uniform' did the trick.

'Yeah, that looks like it,' said Hardy.

'And you still couldn't tell whether they were male or female?'

'No, sorry. The coat was open, but the hood was up. Seemed in a hurry too.'

'Any cameras covering the front of your property?'

'No, sorry.'

'Motion activated dashcam on your car, perhaps?'

'Forward facing only, so it's looking straight at my garage door.'

'Thank you, Mr Hardy,' Dixon said. 'We may need to speak to you again.'

'Of course, mate. Any time.'

'Let's have that carer back here,' said Dixon, as he passed Cole in the porch of Deirdre Baxter's bungalow.

'She said she could come back at ten, Sir.'

'Now, please.'

17

Sarah had followed and was standing on a piece of newspaper in the doorway of the living room, watching Dixon stare at Deirdre's body.

'Check with the local hospitals, will you?' he said. 'See if an OT visit was scheduled for today. The medical centre too.'

'Yes, Sir.'

An occupational therapist wasn't an unusual visitor for an elderly person to have in their own home. Deirdre had a walking frame; the legs of her armchair were on risers. He'd glanced in the lavatory on the way past and there were handles on the wall and a folding seat in the shower, so she must've had visits in the past, and she'd certainly been supplied with equipment to help her manage in her own home.

'Carer's on her way now, Sir,' said Cole, leaning around the door.

'What d'you think, Nige?' asked Dixon.

'I'm happy to leave that to you, Sir,' he replied, nodding in the direction of the hall, where Sarah was on the phone to one of the local hospitals. 'And her.'

Strengths and weaknesses. Cole knew his own, which itself took a certain wisdom. And, either way, there was nobody Dixon would rather have by his side when confronted by a crossbow-wielding killer.

'The medical centre doesn't have an OT, Sir,' said Sarah, squeezing past Cole's large frame in the doorway. 'I rang the emergency line. They say they'd have made a referral and there's nothing in her records. No record of a visit either, not from Weston, Taunton or Burnham.'

Something wasn't quite right, the eyes possibly. Dixon leaned over and examined Deirdre's eyelids. It had only been a few short weeks since he had closed the eyes of a colleague killed in the line of duty. It gave an air of peace to the dead, but not quite. It looked forced.

It did then and it did now.

'Her glasses are broken.' Sarah had managed to fit on to the same piece of newspaper as Dixon and was looking over his shoulder. 'I didn't spot that before.'

'Could have happened any time,' said Cole.

He was right, of course, but it was about gut feeling.

'Hello?'

'Through here.' Cole turned back into the hallway.

'That's the carer, Sir,' said Sarah. 'Christine MacBride.'

Christine looked nervous when she walked into the living room. 'A detective chief inspector?'

'It's an unexplained death and we're just trying to rule out anything else,' replied Dixon, with his best disarming smile. 'Did Deirdre take off her personal alarm often?' he asked.

'Never. Why, where is it?'

'Under the table.'

'Oh, yes.' Christine leaned over and reached out to pick it up.

'Don't touch it, please. Here, put these on,' Dixon said, handing her a pair of latex gloves.

'Of course. Sorry.'

'What about her glasses? They're broken.'

'Are they?' Christine frowned. 'She never mentioned it. I'd have dropped them into the opticians for her, if she'd said.'

Dixon stepped back on to a piece of newspaper further away from Deirdre, allowing Christine to step closer. 'Is there anything else you can see that's out of place or unusual in any way?' he asked.

The lid was open on the box of chocolates, so Christine picked it up in her gloved hand. 'Someone's eaten the nut ones. Deirdre hated them; they always went in the bin. Soft centres only.'

'What about the hairdresser?'

19

'She may have done, I suppose.'

Cole turned out into the hall, reaching for his phone.

'What was she wearing when you saw Mrs Baxter this morning?' asked Dixon.

'Not that top, now you come to mention it. She had a blouse and cardigan on, with a low neck because she was having her hair done later.'

'And what lady would pull on a roll neck sweater after she'd had her hair done?' said Sarah. 'My nan would rather freeze to death than ruin her hair.'

It was all still circumstantial. Someone else might have eaten the chocolates – the OT even, there for a perfectly innocent reason. And Deirdre could very well have felt cold and changed her top, sat on her glasses and taken off her own personal alarm.

'Could she have changed without help?'

'Just about,' replied Christine. 'It would have been a bit of an effort, mind you, but she could've done it.'

'I've spoken to the hairdresser, Sir,' said Cole, reappearing in the doorway. 'Blouse and cardigan and she doesn't eat chocolate.'

Dixon had options: an unexplained death with a recommendation to the coroner that Deirdre be referred for post mortem, or the nuclear option that would involve the crime scene manager, Scientific Services and tearing Poland away from his curry. 'Thank you, Christine,' he said, gesturing to Cole, who ushered her to the front door. Then Dixon leaned over Deirdre, taking hold of the roll neck collar of her sweater lightly between the latex-gloved thumb and index finger of each hand, rolling it back slowly to reveal her neck.

Everything he had seen in Deirdre's bungalow up to that point was capable of perfectly innocent explanation.

But not that.

'She's been strangled,' he said, rolling the collar gently back into position. 'Call it in, will you, Sarah?'

Chapter Three

'Newspaper? Which bright spark thought that would be a good idea?'

Dixon recognised the voice. Harinder – 'call me Hari' – Patel, the frighteningly efficient crime scene manager. It was no surprise he had arrived, clipboard in hand, before anyone else, even beating the traffic officers summoned to close the road.

Cole and Sarah were knocking on the doors of the immediate neighbours, looking for anyone who might have seen anything; dashcam and doorbell camera footage too. The sleet had turned to rain and Dixon was sheltering in the porch of Deirdre Baxter's bungalow, replying to a text message from Jane.

> *Roger's not happy with you. He was just about to sit down*
> *to eat :-) Jx*

He dropped his phone in his coat pocket, looking up to see Hari standing on the doorstep, taking a photograph of the line of soggy newspaper in the hall.

'Uniform attended an unexplained death,' said Dixon. 'The deceased's carer put the paper down to protect the carpets.'

'An unexplained death?'

'They, quite properly, referred it to CID, and it was my decision to treat it as a crime scene.'

'Oh, right.' Hari softened. 'I'll bag it up in that case. You never know, there might be something on it.' He had already put on a hazmat suit and a very fetching hairnet. He was leaning on the front door frame, stretching a pair of latex overshoes over his white wellington boots. 'You decided to stay then?' he asked. 'Rumour had it you were on your toes.'

'I decided to stay.'

'Pleased to hear it.' Gloves now, his clipboard tucked under his arm. 'I had a call from a CSM in Warwickshire; wanted to know how I got on with the dipstick of a DCI who likes to trample all over crime scenes.'

'And what did you tell him?'

'Get there first in future and lock the door.'

'Good advice.'

'I'm going to need to ask you to step outside so I can secure the perimeter.' Hari had unrolled a length of blue tape – 'Crime Scene Do Not Cross' – and was waiting to stick it across the door. 'This is now a controlled area.'

'Even the porch?' Dixon sighed. 'It's pissing down with rain.'

'I've got a brolly you can borrow.'

Both ends of the road had now been blocked by patrol cars – more uniformed officers arriving to help with the house to house enquiries. It was late, but not that late, and most of the houses in the lane had lights on behind the twitching curtains anyway.

Dixon watched the patrol car at the top end reversing out of the way to allow a Volvo through the roadblock. This was going to cost him a trip to the Zalshah.

'Nice curry, was it?' he asked, approaching the back of Poland's car, the boot already up. Mercifully, he caught the hazmat suit that came spinning towards him through the air like a frisbee. 'Thanks,' he said, ripping open the plastic bag.

'I never got to eat a bloody thing.'

'It'll warm up when you get home.'

'This is going to cost you a biriani,' said Poland, his head appearing around the side of the car fleetingly before ducking back inside.

'I thought as much.' Dixon had dropped his coat on the back seat of Poland's car and was putting on the one-piece white suit, which seemed to glow in the streetlights. 'Did you stay for the end of the wassailing?' he asked.

'Pretty much. Jane insisted on leaving before the Morris dancers got going, though.'

'She shouldn't be out in the rain in her condition.'

'That's what she said.' Poland was leaning on the back of the car now, trying to wriggle his large frame into a hazmat suit. 'The message said it was suspected strangulation?'

'*Unexplained*, according to the duty doctor, but there are red marks on her neck, Roger.'

'Could be any number of reasons for that, but then you'll tell me that's why I'm here.'

Scientific Services had arrived and two officers were carrying arc lamps into the bungalow, a line of stepping plates replacing the newspaper that was now bagged up and in a plastic crate on the garden path, under a gazebo to keep it out of the rain. Hari had been busy.

He was standing under cover, presumably to keep his clipboard dry. 'Dr Poland, you may go in,' he said, ticking the box with a flourish. 'And DCI Dixon. Time is twenty-two-seventeen.'

Dixon followed Poland along the stepping plates and into the living room.

'Well?'

'Her alarm is on the floor under the table, there.' Dixon watched a suited and booted Scientific Services officer lean over and take a photograph of it. 'That chair is pulled forward,' continued Dixon. 'And someone's eaten the nut centres. She only liked the soft.'

'Fuck me, is that it?' The Scientific Services officer clearly couldn't help himself.

'No, it isn't,' snapped Dixon. 'And where's Donald Watson?'

'On his way, Sir. He said we should make a start.'

'There's something not right about her face, Roger,' Dixon said, turning back to Deirdre Baxter.

'The eyes have been closed after death.' Roger was leaning over the body. 'The mouth too, by the looks of things. The lips aren't sitting naturally, but it's hardly conclusive.'

'Look at her neck.'

Exactly as Dixon had done, Poland took hold of the roll neck collar of Deirdre's sweater gently between thumb and index finger, and rolled it down. 'Ah,' he said. 'I see what you mean.'

Red marks on the sagging skin of her painfully thin neck.

'They're low down,' said Poland. 'Presumably to avoid fracturing the hyoid bone. I'm not surprised the doctor missed it. Crafty.'

'The last person to see her alive was the hairdresser, just before lunch, and she says Deirdre was wearing a blouse and cardigan. So, my guess is someone's killed her and then put the roll neck sweater on her in the hope of hiding any bruising. An elderly person in her own home; the coroner could be forgiven for not ordering a post mortem. The body gets cremated and . . .' Dixon didn't feel the need to finish his sentence.

'A killer gets away scot-free.' The Scientific Services officer finished it for him.

'I won't know for sure until I open her up, but that is what I would call a *good spot*.' Poland seemed impressed.

'I was looking out for it,' replied Dixon. 'There was an alert on the system: the elderly dying alone in their homes, otherwise unexplained. She was quite fit, apparently, and it certainly wasn't expected.'

'I'll get her medical records and have a good look,' said Poland. 'Usual drill.'

'Her glasses are broken and we need to find the missing arm. It might be down the side of the chair.'

'We'll have a rummage when we've moved the body,' replied the Scientific Services officer.

'Time of death?' asked Dixon.

'Four to six hours,' replied Poland. 'If that fire's been on since then.'

'It has.'

'Between four and six o'clock, I'd say, in that case.'

'That fits.'

'What with?'

'She was visited by someone dressed as an occupational therapist about an hour before she was found by her carer at six.'

Poland straightened up. 'An OT killing old people in their own homes. What have you stumbled on?'

'We've got some doorbell camera footage a few doors down, Sir,' said Sarah, running along the pavement. 'It might have picked up the car, but it'll be sideways on, so we won't get a number plate.'

Dixon was standing under the gazebo, trying to wriggle out of his hazmat suit.

'It was dark by four-thirty,' said Cole, arriving from the opposite direction. 'So, most of them had their curtains closed and the telly on. Didn't see or hear a thing. Apart from matey-boy over there' – gesturing over his shoulder to Hardy's house opposite.

'We'll need the footage from the nearest traffic cameras.' Dixon had got his arms out of the suit and was rummaging in his inside jacket pocket for his phone. 'That's all I need.' A deep breath. 'Yes, Sir,' he said, putting his phone to his ear.

'Well done, Nick,' said Assistant Chief Constable David Charlesworth.

It was not what Dixon had been expecting at all. 'Thank you, Sir,' he said. There was bound to be a catch, the ACC phoning him at this time of night.

'Who spotted it?'

'The Rural Crimes team, Sir. Nigel Cole and Sarah Loveday.'

'Has Roger Poland confirmed it?'

'He's in there now, but yes, subject to a full post mortem.'

'That's the second then. The first was an elderly man in Sidmouth. The Devon and Cornwall lot didn't spot it and strangulation was only picked up on routine post mortem a few days later. They've lost the crime scene as a result; the victim's daughter went in cleaning everything, apparently.'

'When was this, Sir?' asked Dixon.

'A couple of weeks ago. They've got a live investigation ongoing and a Superintendent Small will be coming up to Express Park tomorrow, to liaise.'

Stick his nose in, more like.

'I've spoken to Deborah Potter,' continued Charlesworth, 'and there'll need to be a major investigation team, of course, but we'll talk further in the morning. Say, eight o'clock sharp?'

'Yes, Sir.'

'Good work. It's nice to know we didn't drop the ball, unlike Devon and Cornwall. The press are going to have a field day at their expense. Poor sods.' Charlesworth rang off.

'We're going to move her to the mortuary in a minute,' said Poland. 'While everyone's got their curtains shut.' He was standing behind Dixon, under the gazebo, his case in one hand, car keys in the other. 'Post mortem at ten suit?'

'Yes, fine.'

'Don't forget your coat is on the back seat of my car.'

'Did you find the arm of her glasses?'

'Down the side of the chair; snapped off, possibly when she was being . . .' Poland's voice tailed off, conscious that he was outside and people might be listening. 'You've got a key; just let yourself in. If I get home first I'll leave you a bowl of the prawn stuff in the microwave.'

'Thanks very much.' Dixon dropped his hazmat suit in a plastic crate on the lawn and ran across the road, managing to snatch his coat off the back seat of Poland's car just before he accelerated off down the lane towards the roadblock at the bottom.

'There's been another,' had been Charlesworth's words. Which makes two that we know about, thought Dixon. And how many more that we don't?

'What have we stumbled on?' he said, out loud as it turned out.

'Does that mean there are others, Sir?' asked Sarah.

'What time is it?' Jane was sitting on the edge of the sofa in Poland's living room, wiping the back of her hand across her mouth. Monty looked pleased with himself, tail wagging. 'Yes, I know you're a handsome prince,' she said, reaching down and scratching him behind his ears. 'But there's no need to kiss me to wake me up.'

'Works for me,' said Dixon.

'You're different,' Jane said, through a yawn. She was following him through to the kitchen. 'I know where you've been. Have you eaten?'

'Not yet.' Dixon was looking in the microwave, then started taking the cling film off a bowl of curry. 'What time did Roger get home?'

'About an hour ago; went straight to bed,' replied Jane. 'Here, I'll do that. I'll need to boil some fresh rice. You go and sit down.' She took a beer from the door of the fridge and handed it to him. 'Take that with you.'

'Thanks.'

Jane glanced at the clock on the wall. 'It's two o'clock! Where have you been?'

'Express Park. Mark came in and we've got some doorbell camera footage he's working on – checking the traffic cameras. I've lined up house to house for tomorrow. Scientific are still at the scene so I can't get in; thought I'd come and get a few hours' sleep.'

Jane dropped a handful of dog biscuits in Monty's tin bowl, then raised her voice over the sound of it being pushed around the kitchen floor. 'Tell me about it then.'

Dixon leaned forwards, his elbows on the kitchen table, and closed his eyes. 'Who would want to strangle an eighty-eight-year-old woman in her own home?'

'Not unexplained then?'

'Sadly not.' A swig of beer. 'It was Sarah who spotted it. There was something on the intranet, apparently.'

'I read that. There was one in Sidmouth and they missed it. Uniform put two and two together, assumed the old codger had died in his sleep and just referred it straight to the coroner. Turned out it was foul play.'

'I've got a superintendent from Devon coming up in the morning to stick his nose in.'

'You'll need to stick your nose into his case too, don't forget. And you'll have to watch they don't put a regional task force in place. You'll love that; a superintendent outranks you.'

It was a point that had occurred to him, and might explain Charlesworth's unusual interest in the case. It wasn't often he came down to Express Park at all, thankfully, and rarely at that time in the morning. The delivery of bad news could account for it.

'I reckon he'll want us to take the lead if that happens,' continued Jane. 'So you should be all right. It'd be good publicity, and you know how much he loves that.'

'The last thing we need is publicity. If word gets out there's someone going round – in an NHS uniform – killing old people in their own homes, you can just imagine the panic.'

'Is that what happened in Sidmouth?' asked Jane. She was leaning against the worktop in the kitchen, her hands resting on her bump.

'I don't know yet,' replied Dixon. 'But I've got a horrible feeling this is just the start of it.'

Chapter Four

'I wouldn't hold your breath.'

The streetlights had gone off in the lane outside Deirdre's bungalow just after midnight, and it was still dark when Dixon was let through the cordon the following morning, the front garden lit only by the arc lamp set up by Scientific Services. He had squeezed past the line of plastic crates on the path and was standing under the gazebo, tearing open the plastic wrapper of yet another hazmat suit.

'I reckon your killer is forensically aware,' continued Donald Watson, the senior Scientific Services officer. 'There are plenty of fingerprints, but none where you'd expect to find them. The arms of that chair, for example.' He pulled his face mask below his chin and gave an exaggerated wince. 'Wooden, but not a single print. Wiped clean.'

'Haven't you found anything?'

'We've taken the usual tapings and scrapings. There are fingerprints, but plenty of people to eliminate: Mrs Baxter, the carer, the hairdresser, a stepson and his wife. Even her bloody solicitor had been in there. Uniform were at least wearing latex gloves. Like I say, I wouldn't hold your breath.'

'Can I go in? I've got a couple of hours before I need to be at Express Park.'

'Yes, might as well.' Watson turned back into the hall. 'Can't do any harm now.'

Jane had left before Dixon had woken up, but he knew where she'd be. No doubt an incident room would be up and running by the time he got to Express Park; if a major investigation team was in the offing, she'd be making damn sure she was on it.

It explained why Detective Constable Mark Pearce had come in to work the night before too. At a bit of loose end these days, was Mark, and a murder investigation would give him a sense of purpose, perhaps.

It was a small team, what was left of it.

A double-fronted bungalow, with a bay window either side of the front door, a dining room on the left that looked as though it hadn't been used in years. Dark oak furniture, a layer of dust on the oval table; oil paintings on the wall, a sideboard with several decanters on a silver tray – all of them empty; photographs in sterling silver frames, slightly tarnished. Black and white pictures of Deirdre on her wedding day; a more recent photograph of husband and wife holding a trophy. Golf probably – she'd been good at that, according to her carer.

Someone played the piano too, an upright gathering dust against the wall behind the door.

'I've had a quick look, but we haven't done in there yet, so be careful,' said Watson, when Dixon turned to the room opposite. 'It's used for storage, like the old-fashioned lumber room. I reckon they must've downsized at some point and dumped the furniture they didn't need in there.'

Dixon opened the door, Watson following him in.

'There's some nice stuff,' he continued. 'That card table, for a start. Walnut inlay, envelope top. Maybe eight hundred in the right auction. The felt underneath is in good condition too.'

Dixon puffed out his cheeks. Still, being trapped in an episode of *Antiques Roadshow* made a pleasant change from *Homes Under the Hammer*.

'That bureau in the bay window is nineteenth-century French walnut. Four and a half grand's worth that.'

Two single beds were hidden under boxes and suitcases; a folding wheelchair leaning up against the wardrobe, much the same as the one in the porch, apart from the missing wheel. A set of golf clubs had been slotted in between the wardrobe and the wall, an old exercise bike gathering dust between the beds, a set of pine chairs stacked on the far side. A pair of filing cabinets completed the picture of a spare bedroom no one had slept in for years.

'We'll get that old computer off to High Tech,' continued Watson. 'Probably her late husband's, so . . .'

'I won't hold my breath, don't worry.'

Piles of magazines dating back to 2008, a combination lock briefcase.

'We're going to have to break that open,' said Watson. 'Don't know the code.'

Dixon had seen enough for the time being and headed for the hall.

'We've finished in her bedroom. Round to the right.' Watson was gesturing to an open door. 'Found her jewellery in a divan drawer, so robbery's not the motive.'

'Never thought it was.' Three hundred and twenty pounds in cash and her bank cards still in Deirdre's open handbag on the floor by her chair had been enough to confirm that.

Grab rails had been fitted either side of Deirdre's bed, the divan base lifted on risers, a commode next to the bedside table.

Dixon was reminded of a line from a song by The Who, although getting old wasn't the problem. It was getting *too* old.

He followed the stepping plates into the living room, Deirdre's chair now empty, apart from her iPad sitting in an evidence bag on the cushion.

'It's not locked, but there are no banking apps installed on it. She doesn't shop online by the looks of things, either; just web browsing – news sites, mainly – and playing bridge. She seems to spend a lot of time playing bridge.' Watson shrugged. 'Keeps the mind sharp, I suppose. My late mother did crosswords every day.'

Dixon opened the drawers in the sideboard one by one, recognising a long thin brown envelope, the end sticking out from under a pile of greetings cards. Solicitors were creatures of habit, the client's copy of their will invariably sent in a brown envelope with the words 'last will and testament of . . .' printed in some fancy font. Still, it helped the family, who would no doubt be looking. And police officers.

'When was this solicitor's visit you mentioned?' he asked.

'Tuesday. It's on the calendar in the kitchen. Doesn't say what it was about, before you ask.'

The will was two years old, so Deirdre was either updating that or doing a power of attorney, perhaps. Equity release was another possibility.

'How much money has she got?'

'All her financial papers are in that red case. There's a civil service pension and then about eighty grand in cash ISAs and savings accounts. There's a copy of her late husband's will and it looks like he owned this place, left it to her for life, then it goes to his son.'

A stepson, keen to get his hands on his inheritance a bit early. If only everything in life was that easy, thought Dixon.

It ruled out equity release, though.

'Where's her address book?'

'He lives in Kingsbury Episcopi, out on the Levels.'

Knowing Jane, she'd have his photo on a board in the incident room already.

Several watercolours of Lake District scenes Dixon knew well were on the wall opposite Deirdre's chair. Borrowdale, Coniston Water, Little Langdale, the name 'D Baxter' scribbled in the bottom right corner in spidery writing. A complete set of Wainwright guides to the fells, the dust jackets long gone, on the built-in shelves to the left of the fireplace, and a packet of Kendal Mint Cake that had passed its 'best before' date twenty years ago, bought on her last trip to the mountains, probably.

It was a sobering thought, that one day he'd be making his last trip to the mountains.

Too much of life revolved around death; too much of his, anyway. He had plenty of time.

Everybody does, until suddenly they don't.

He stood in the window, the bottom end of the back garden emerging from the darkness in the first glow of dawn, the sun still not up. High hedges, a rotary washing line leaning with the prevailing wind in the middle of the lawn. The patio was lit by the bright light from the arc lamps in the living room: weeds growing in the cracks in the cement; a white plastic table and chairs, stained green with algae.

'Have you been in the garage?' asked Dixon.

'I don't think anyone's been in there for yonks,' replied Watson. 'There's an old Fiesta and a lawnmower, but I'm guessing the gardener brings his own.'

'There's a gardener?'

'Once a week, for a couple of hours, that's all.'

Nice work if you can get it.

Jane had been busy and the incident room on the second floor was already up and running by the time Dixon arrived at Express Park just before eight. The only thing missing was the major investigation team. Louise Willmott and Mark Pearce were there, sitting at workstations, but that was it.

Sarah Loveday was there too, hovering nervously at the back even though her shift didn't start until two o'clock; 'too keen by half', Cole had said.

Two detective constables and a probationary PC.

A picture of Deirdre Baxter had been stuck on the whiteboard, a line across to a picture of her stepson, the name 'Lawrence Baxter' scribbled underneath in Jane's handwriting. Dixon had seen the same photograph in a frame on the sideboard, tucked away behind several pictures of West Highland White Terriers.

Mark had managed to extract a cleanish image of the car from the doorbell camera footage. Sideways on, so no number plate and no real view of the driver. 'That's it for the moment, I'm afraid, Sir,' he said, when he saw Dixon looking at it. 'There are a couple of PCSOs downstairs on the traffic cameras.'

Two detective constables, a probationer and two community support officers. Deirdre Baxter deserved better.

A second whiteboard next to Deirdre's was empty; that is until Jane appeared and stuck a photograph top middle. 'Michael Allam,' she said. 'He's the Sidmouth victim. Strangled in his own home; it was a couple of days before they found him. He was a widower, with two daughters, one living in Sunderland, the other in America.'

'Making yourself indispensable, I see,' said Dixon.

'Don't I always?' Jane handed him a piece of paper. 'He was ninety-one, but in good health. That photo was taken a couple of years ago.' Wearing a panama hat, sitting on the deck of a cruise ship. 'He had a lady friend,' continued Jane. 'Val Rose. She took the photo. Found him too. Poor sod.'

Sarah had finally summoned up the courage and was now standing right behind Dixon, not that he had heard her creeping up on him. 'I was wondering if I could help, Sir,' she said, hesitantly.

'You're on lates, aren't you?'

'Yes, Sir.'

'You should be in bed.' Dixon shook his head. 'So, you thought if there was going to be a major investigation team, you were going to try to get on it?'

Sarah blushed.

'There's a lot of it about,' said Dixon, with a sideways glance at Jane. 'What makes you think you wouldn't be on it?'

'I don't know, Sir.'

'If it wasn't for you, Deirdre would have gone off to the coroner and we'd have lost the crime scene.'

'Ah, you *are* here.' Charlesworth was standing at the top of the stairs, his hands on his hips. 'It said on the system you weren't in yet.'

'I'm sure I swiped my pass when I came in, Sir,' said Dixon, sure that he hadn't done anything of the sort. He preferred to slip in unnoticed when someone else used their pass to open the security door, and never had to wait more than a couple of minutes for someone to come along.

'Well, no harm done. We're in meeting room two.'

Detective Chief Superintendent Deborah Potter was sitting on the far side of the circular pine table, a pair of reading glasses perched on the end of her nose, her head bowed, staring at the screen of her phone. The press officer – or head of corporate communications, to use her full comedy title – Vicky Thomas, was doing the same, only with no glasses on the end of her sharp nose. Both placed their phones face down on the table when Charlesworth closed the door behind Dixon.

'Sit down, Nick,' he said.

It felt like bad news was coming, but then Charlesworth's job, more often than not, was to tell people what couldn't be done, rather than what could. A thankless task was management, as Dixon had found out during his weeks as managing DCI at Express Park.

'I've just got off the phone with my opposite number at Devon and Cornwall.' Charlesworth paused while Dixon pulled a chair out from under the table and sat down. 'There's going to be a regional task force, Nick, given that we've got victims in both force areas. The feeling is there are likely to be others we don't know about as well. It's going to be a big team and it enables us to pool our resources. As you know, collaboration is the buzz word at the moment.'

Pool our resources and save a few quid. It really was amazing how Charlesworth managed to gloss over the real motive.

'There's a Superintendent Small on his way from Exeter now. He'll be attending the post mortem with you at ten and would like to go to the crime scene after that. Please see to it he's given every cooperation and courtesy.'

'Of course, Sir.'

'He will then brief the Devon team, who will be joining your RTF.'

Dixon hesitated. RTF was regional task force. No, more confusing was the *your* RTF.

Charlesworth had spotted his surprise. 'The RTF is to be based here, given that we're the ones with the live crime scene. Devon and Cornwall's only stipulation was that it be led by a superintendent.'

Dixon glanced at Potter, who seemed amused at his irritation. 'Not me,' she said.

'Who then?' Dixon was trying not to bristle.

37

'You,' said Charlesworth. 'We are all in agreement, and I've cleared it with the chief con, so you are now acting detective superintendent, with immediate effect. I know the ladies present will forgive my language when I say' – he smiled, all too fleetingly – 'just don't fuck it up.'

'Yes, Sir.'

'It'll be great publicity for us,' said Vicky Thomas. 'I was thinking of a press conference later on today.'

Dixon had known that one was coming. 'Can you imagine the panic if we tell people there's a killer out there wearing an NHS uniform targeting the elderly in their own homes?'

'We need to say something,' said Potter.

'No mention of the murders. I agree.' Charlesworth had the bridge of his nose between his thumb and index finger, his horn-rimmed glasses bouncing up and down as he rubbed. 'We need to alert people to someone in an NHS uniform up to no good; a doorstep burglar, perhaps?'

'We'll be misleading the press again.'

'You can deal with it, Vicky. Tell them you didn't know, if you have to.'

'Now for the bad news.' Potter sighed. 'You knew there'd be some, Nick.'

He nodded, slowly.

'Personnel, or rather the lack of it.'

'We're already stretched tighter than I don't know what,' said Charlesworth. 'And the idea of assigning a large team to a task force for the duration is just—'

'Impossible.' Potter completing Charlesworth's sentence for him. 'Devon and Cornwall are sending eight, so we have to match that. There's you and Mark Pearce. I'm guessing you'll want Sergeant Winter to run the incident room. I'll continue to do her pregnancy risk assessments. Who else?'

'Louise Willmott.'

'Really?' Charlesworth frowned. 'I had understood DC Willmott was questioning your judgement on the graffiti thing.'

'That's precisely why I want her,' replied Dixon. 'Someone who agrees with everything I say is no use to me.'

'That's four so far then.' Potter was chewing the arm of her reading glasses. 'Including you.'

'I'll have the probationer too, Sarah Loveday. She's a bright kid and it's down to her we've got anything at all.'

'Won't that leave the Rural Crimes team short-handed?' asked Charlesworth.

'No more than it is already,' replied Dixon. 'And I'm guessing you'll get no objection from Nigel Cole.'

'We need to find three more then.'

'We can take them from the Portishead major crime team,' offered Potter. 'Won't be till the start of the week, though.'

'Call on uniform in the meantime, Nick,' said Charlesworth. 'For cameras and stuff like that. I imagine you've got a few of them doing house to house this morning?'

'Twelve, Sir. And a couple of PCSOs watching the cameras. A neighbour's doorbell camera picked up a car at the right time and we're trying to track that.'

'Press conference at five,' said Vicky Thomas. 'Then we can catch the evening news.'

Chapter Five

'He's setting you up to fail.'

It wasn't long since Dixon had crossed swords with Charlesworth, and both of them had been on their best behaviour in the weeks since. The confrontation had come in the yard behind Dixon's cottage, Jane watching from the upstairs window as words were exchanged. She had occasionally tried to ask him what it had been about, but he always dodged the question. She knew something had been said, but had no idea what. No one did.

'You do know that,' continued Jane.

'"Congratulations on your promotion" would be traditional, dear,' said Dixon.

'Of course, congratu-bloody-lations.' Jane pecked him on the cheek. 'Just be careful, that's all I'm saying.'

'Where's Sarah?'

'Here, Sir.'

'You're not on the major investigation team, I'm afraid.'

'Oh.' She looked crestfallen.

'You're on the regional task force. Go and get changed out of that uniform. You'll be working with Mark for the duration.'

'What about Nige?'

'I'll clear it with Nigel, don't you worry.'

'What about me, Sir?' asked Louise, hesitantly. She had put on her coat and was sitting on the edge of her chair, ready to leave by the looks of things.

The last case had tested their partnership, Dixon knew that. He had still been raging after his arrest for murder, even though the charge had been dropped, and Louise had borne the brunt of it. To her credit, it hadn't stopped her questioning his judgement when she thought he had got it wrong. 'Barking up the wrong tree' was the phrase she had used.

'You look like you're going somewhere,' he said.

'Well, I just thought you'd—'

'Superintendent Small and a colleague from Devon and Cornwall are down in reception, if you'd like to go and get them. Then we've got the PM at ten. All right?'

◆ ◆ ◆

It was a feeble attempt at hiding surprise. Dixon could imagine the cogs going round, the thought plain for all to see: *God, even the superintendents are getting younger.* Louise noticed it, managing to stifle a chuckle.

'Superintendent Dixon?' asked Small, his hand outstretched while he glanced around the room, looking for someone older, presumably.

'Nick, please.'

Then Small spotted Sarah Loveday, sitting at a workstation. He turned to his sidekick to see if he had noticed, the exchange of glances saying it all. *It's like a bloody kindergarten in here.*

'Most people *look* but they don't *see*,' said Dixon, quietly. 'She may be young, but she has an enquiring mind way beyond her years. She's keen, too; worth any five clock-watchers. What's more, she doesn't know how good she is.'

'Lucky you,' said Small. Now he was staring at Jane's bump.

'This is Detective Sergeant Winter,' said Dixon, before Small could say anything from the Stone Age. 'Jane will be running the incident room.'

'Does your partner know you're working a murder investigation?'

'My fiancé does,' replied Jane.

'And what does he think of that?'

'He's fine with it, not that he has a lot of choice.' There was mischief in Jane's voice, and her glance at Dixon.

'Right, well, you've got a crime scene, which is one-up to you,' said Small. 'Who have you got to thank for that?'

'Sarah,' replied Dixon. 'Come and meet Superintendent Small, a colleague from Devon and Cornwall.'

Small cleared his throat; introductions over, he turned to Dixon and whispered, 'A bright kid.'

'That's what we think.'

It didn't take long to brief Small on the death of Deirdre Baxter. He took a copy of the image of the mystery car from the doorbell camera and a photograph of Deirdre, but it was still early days and there were no results yet from Forensics to get excited about.

Dixon was far more interested in finding out from Small about the death of Michael Allam in Sidmouth.

'He hadn't been seen for a couple of days and a neighbour rang us, so a couple of PCSOs did a welfare check. They saw nothing, so a constable tried again the next day. Usual story, really.' Small looked around ineffectually, trying to hide his embarrassment. 'Happens any number of times a day. The neighbour was there saying she saw him most days, so that was it, in went the door and there he was slumped in his armchair. The doctor spotted nothing untoward and off went the body to the coroner. We notified the daughter and she came down from Sunderland, started clearing the place and cleaning. Then we got the results of the post mortem.'

'Strangulation?'

Small was still avoiding eye contact. 'It wouldn't have taken much. Michael was frail and old. We stopped the daughter cleaning, obviously, and have alibied everyone we can think of. House to house turned up nothing; neither did doorbell cameras in the vicinity. It's all high walls and long drives. You'll see for yourself when you come down.'

'Any visits from an OT in the previous days?' asked Dixon.

'We're checking that now. We've got a team on it at Exeter, although they'll be coming up here tomorrow to join your RTF.'

'And who was Michael Allam?'

'A retired teacher, from a private school in Burnham-on-Sea, oddly enough. St Joseph's, although I believe it's closed down now.'

Jane had been standing at the whiteboard and spun round, marker pen in hand. 'Deirdre Baxter was a retired teacher,' she said. 'St Christopher's, also in Burnham-on-Sea, also long since closed down.'

'Could be a coincidence,' Small said, dismissively.

'We don't believe in those, do we, Sir?' said Sarah, turning to Dixon.

'No, we don't.'

'There's no fracture of the hyoid bone.' Poland was waving a scalpel like a conductor's baton. 'I've read the PM report on your Mr Allam and his wasn't broken either.'

'Do you know Superintendent Small, Roger?' asked Dixon.

'We've met,' replied Small.

Introductions would've been all but impossible anyway, given that Poland was covered in blood – gloves, apron, sleeves; there was even some on his wellington boots.

Louise had opted to wait in the anteroom with Small's sidekick, who still hadn't said a word.

Deirdre Baxter was laid out on the slab, a green sheet covering her from just below the shoulders down to her feet. Her head was tilted back, the skin of her neck cut vertically from just below her chin to the top of her sternum, the flaps peeled back and held in place by clamps.

Dixon watched Poland's mortuary assistant leaning over and taking close-up photographs of Deirdre's windpipe.

'You don't always get a fractured hyoid bone with strangulation anyway, and not where the pressure has been applied low on the neck, as in this case. Donald Watson said he reckoned the killer was forensically aware and I reckon they're anatomically aware as well.' Poland paused while his assistant took a last photograph and then stepped back. 'Here's the hyoid bone,' he continued, pointing with the scalpel. 'It's shaped a bit like a horseshoe and sits just below the jaw, protecting the windpipe, so you can see why it's often broken in these cases. But here it's perfectly intact, look.'

Small leaned over and did as he was told, Dixon thinking better of it.

'In fact, a break of the hyoid is more likely in the elderly, if anything, because it becomes brittle with age. All bones do.'

'But you can tell she was strangled, surely?' asked Dixon, trying to hide his impatience.

Poland's eyes gave away his smile, his mouth covered by a face mask. 'Oh yes. Beneath the hyoid bone, you've got the thyroid cartilage, although it's more of a bone by this age – it ossifies, the older we get. Also known as the Adam's apple in men. Women have it too, it's just smaller.'

Dixon drew breath, but was silenced by a wave of the scalpel.

'Then beneath that you've got the cricoid cartilage, which again ossifies as we get older and so becomes more of a bone. And it's Mrs Baxter's cricoid *bone*, we'll call it, that's broken.'

'And that corresponds with the bruising I saw on her neck?' asked Dixon.

'Most certainly.' Poland peeled off his gloves and pulled his face mask below his chin. 'Cause of death, strangulation. Pretty much identical to your Mr Allam,' he said, turning to Small.

'How long would it have taken?' asked Small.

'Not long in a person of this age,' replied Poland. 'She'd have been unconscious in a matter of seconds, dead in a couple of minutes.' Poland reached over and turned back the sheet covering Deirdre's body. 'She may have died quicker of heart failure, of course. I haven't got that far yet, but it would still be murder, either way.'

It was difficult to reconcile the body lying on the slab with the photograph of Deirdre on her wedding day. Ageing is a cruel business, thought Dixon.

'Your Mr Allam had prostate cancer,' continued Poland, turning to Small. 'Although there's no mention of it in his medical records, so he almost certainly didn't know. It moves fairly slowly at that age anyway, and if he'd seen a doctor, he'd probably have been told something else would get him first.'

'And it did,' muttered Small.

'Would it require much strength?' asked Dixon.

'Ordinarily, yes, but look at her.' Poland looked sombre. 'Hardly going to put up much resistance, is she? And her neck's painfully thin.'

'What about the bruising?'

'There are several small bruises on the left side, which could be fingertips; a larger one on the right side, the killer's thumb, possibly – probably. The pressure to the front of her windpipe is narrow, so I suspect the killer used the base of their thumb, rather than the flat of the palm.'

'One hand or two?'

'If you're asking whether I can tell from the bruising, the short answer is I can't. It could've been one large hand or two small ones, or maybe even one hand on top of the other. The best I can say is there's more damage to the left side of her neck, but that's hardly conclusive either way.'

'So, you can't tell if it was a man or a woman?'

'No. Sorry.' Poland was sucking his teeth. 'One thing I can say is this: there's no more up close and personal way of killing someone. You're there, right in front of them, looking into their eyes as they lose consciousness. Then you keep squeezing, and you keep squeezing. This is no mad slash with a knife, or pull of a trigger. You're right in their face, watching the life drain out of them. And it takes time.'

'Time for second thoughts,' said Dixon.

'Plenty. It's just about as deliberate as it gets.'

Dixon was standing under the gazebo outside Deirdre Baxter's bungalow, watching through the front window as Small and his sidekick walked around the dining room. Small picked up Deirdre's wedding photograph, then the picture of her and her husband holding the large trophy, before setting them back down. Scientific Services had finished inside the house, so it was latex gloves only. Even the stepping plates had gone.

'Small seems all right,' said Louise. 'But I hardly got two words out of DS Wevill. Had a charisma bypass, I think. I hope they don't find something we've missed.'

'They won't.'

The garage was standing open, the bonnet of a red Ford Fiesta poking out from underneath a bedsheet. One careful lady owner from new no doubt, low mileage; it probably hadn't moved for twenty years. Dixon took a step closer and looked at the tax disc: August 2004, and there were at least five or six more discs slotted into the holder behind it. Late nineties then, which corresponded with the number plate.

'There's nothing in here,' said Watson. 'The key was in a drawer in the kitchen and it doesn't look like anyone's been in here for ages. All the gardening stuff is in the shed, so not even the gardener comes in here.'

'It'll make someone a nice runaround,' Dixon said, gesturing to the car.

'Needs to be scrapped,' replied Watson, dismantling the last arc lamp. 'Cars need to be driven, and that one'll be buggered; all the hoses perished, the electrics shot. Cost you more to fix it than it's worth.'

Dixon pulled back the sheet and tried the driver's door, which was open. Someone had wound down the windows, but the seat and dashboard were still covered with small spots of mould. The door pocket was empty apart from two Shirley Bassey cassettes, a few car park tickets and a chocolate bar wrapper Dixon didn't recognise.

Louise had followed him into the garage and opened the passenger door. 'Smells damp,' she said, turning up her nose.

'Nice low mileage example,' said Dixon.

'How many miles has it done?'

'Seventeen thousand,' he replied. 'But it's only a five-digit counter, so I suppose it could be one hundred and seventeen thousand.'

'The MOT records would confirm it.' Louise tried the glovebox, which contained several damp invoices, the last coming from

Kwik Fit, and a mouldy leather document wallet. 'She's still got the owner's manual. Had a new tyre on the front in July 2003 too. Kwik Fit Torquay that was.'

'What about the last MOT?' asked Dixon.

'August 2003. Sixteen thousand eight hundred and eighty-one miles. Ugh. Fancy a twenty-year-old Murray Mint?'

'No, thanks.'

'I wonder why she stopped driving?' Louise was trying a biro on the palm of her hand. 'That's it, apart from a packet of tissues, a small first aid kit, a pen that doesn't work and a baby's dummy.'

'She married again, so maybe her husband had a car,' replied Dixon. 'What about the boot?'

'There's nothing in the boot,' shouted Watson, from outside on the lawn. 'I looked.'

The internal door opened. 'Ah, there you are,' said Small, stepping into the garage. 'Where to now? We've seen enough here, I think.'

Chapter Six

'This is posh.' Louise was leaning over and looking out of the driver's side window of Dixon's Land Rover as they followed Small along the Bickwell Valley Road in Sidmouth. 'I dread to think what that one's worth. One-point-five maybe?'

On the nearside it was high hedges and walls, with gates and garages at unusually long intervals. The houses on the right were set on the side of the hill, with perfectly manicured front lawns and long drives; far too far for a doorbell camera to pick up any footage of the road.

'Even a flat would be worth half a million,' continued Louise, in full *Homes Under the Hammer* mode. 'Sorry, *apartment*.' She was rummaging in her pocket for her phone. 'That one's for sale, let me have a look on Rightmove.'

'Don't bother on my account,' replied Dixon.

'What's the postcode?'

He stayed silent, hoping it might shut down the conversation.

'One-point-seven-five. Seven bedrooms, gym and an indoor pool. The garden backs on to the golf course.'

'And what would you do with all of that?' he asked. 'There's only you, your husband and Katie.'

'I'm not saying I'd want it. I'm just interested, that's all.'

'Why?'

Louise hesitated, clearly having to think about an answer. 'I don't know really. Everybody's interested in houses, aren't they? Especially other people's houses.'

'Nosy, then.'

'Yeah, I suppose.'

Hopefully that would put an end to the tedious property speculation; for a while anyway. Dixon had forgotten just how irritating the whole process of buying a house was. Six months spent in the conveyancing department as a trainee solicitor had been bad enough, but now he was experiencing it for himself, from the other end – buying the small cottage opposite the Red Cow that he and Jane rented.

If the bloody solicitors take too much longer, interest rates will have gone up again.

'How's your purchase going?' asked Louise.

'Slowly.'

Dixon followed Small into a driveway on the right, the front garden gravelled over for parking. He counted seven cars.

'There are eight flats, which tells you how big the place is.' Louise hadn't got the message. 'Upstairs would've been for the staff. Someone's holiday home back in the day, I expect.'

Bay windows, two balconies; loft conversions, judging by the dormer windows.

Small had parked his car and appeared at the driver's door of the Land Rover just as Dixon climbed out. 'Michael Allam had one of the garden flats, with its own entrance around the side. I'll show you.'

They followed Small along the path at the side of the building, past flowerbeds packed with neatly pruned roses.

'I dread to think what the service charges are,' said Louise.

Small stopped in front of a door and began sorting through a set of keys. 'There's a bit of bad news, I'm afraid,' he said, inserting a key in the lock. 'We rang the daughter to let her know what's been going on and she's driving down from Sunderland, apparently; wants to speak to the man in charge.' He turned the key and the door swung open. 'Don't envy you that one, I'm afraid. She's a right pain in the arse, complaining about this and that. She's even threatened to make a formal complaint to the IOPC.'

Things were looking up. Another run-in with the Independent Office for Police Conduct.

'The poor old bugger moved down here from Somerset to be near his daughter,' continued Small, 'and she promptly ups sticks and moves to Sunderland.'

Four large bin liners, each tied at the top, were lined up along the wall in the hall.

'Then, he's only been dead a couple of days and she's down here clearing out his stuff and cleaning the place. She'd already been on to an estate agent, as well. It would serve her bloody well right if he'd changed his will and left it all to the cats' home.'

A nice thought. Dixon had drafted a few wills like that in his time as a trainee solicitor.

'Have you seen his will?'

'A copy. It's just a straight split between his two daughters. The other one married an American and lives in Atlanta.'

'What's in these bags?' Dixon asked.

'That's the daughter tidying up. His clothes had already gone to a local charity shop. These are just rubbish that we retrieved from the recycling bin. Forensics went through them and it's all in their report,' replied Small. 'I'm arranging for you to have system access.' He picked up some junk mail off the doormat and left it on the radiator cover. 'It'll be done by the time you get back to Express Park.'

Dixon handed Louise a pair of latex gloves.

'You won't need those,' said Small. 'We've finished in here.'

'Force of habit,' said Dixon, snapping on the gloves anyway. 'There's no key safe.'

'He was able to answer the door, according to his daughter. It took him a while, but he got there in the end.'

'So, he answered the door to whoever killed him.'

'He did.'

'Living room's through here.' Small pushed open the door with his foot, both hands thrust deep into his pockets. 'This is where he was found. That chair over there.'

An L-shaped room, the back windows looking out over a patio, a white painted metal table and chairs just beyond the patio doors. A television in the corner, three armchairs and a sofa; oddly tidy, but then the daughter had seen to that.

'He had a table by his chair, but it's gone back to the mobility people already,' said Small. 'A walking frame too, and there were other bits and pieces: a grab rail for the bed, stuff like that. A bit like your Mrs Baxter.'

'She wouldn't have wanted them in the estate agent's photographs, Sir,' said Louise.

'How long was it between Mr Allam being found and the post mortem?' asked Dixon. It was an embarrassing question for Small, possibly, but that was just tough.

'Five days.' Small sighed his answer. 'And then another two days before it was acted upon.'

'The daughter had been in here a week?'

'I know, I know.' Small held up his hands in abject surrender, nothing 'mock' about it. 'She came down the day after he was found and stayed here for six nights. Then, when we broke the news to her, she went to the Victoria Hotel on the seafront.'

'Not an easy conversation.'

'I've had better days. She even got the bloody chief constable involved, and the PCC.'

That was going some. Complaints about Dixon had got as far as the chief con, but not the police and crime commissioner. Not yet, anyway.

'He was sitting in this chair,' said Small, trying a change of subject. 'It's one of those electric recliners. There was a blanket over the back and a waterproof liner on the seat cover in case he . . .'

A nod from Dixon assured Small he needn't explain further.

'Of course, he'd been dead for two days before he was found, so—'

'That explains the air fresheners,' said Louise.

There were several around the room – one on the mantelpiece, one by the television and another two plugged into electrical sockets.

Lavender.

'There are some photographs attached to the post mortem report,' said Small. 'The old boy just looked as if he was asleep. He had one of those alarm things, but it's already gone back. He never rang it, though.'

'Where's the phone?' asked Dixon.

'The landline is in the bedroom, but he had the handset next to him on the little table,' replied Small.

'He had a mobile too, Guv,' said Wevill. 'It was on a charging cradle on the table in the hall. We checked it and the SIM was a pay-as-you-go one that had expired; battery was dead too.'

It was the first time Wevill had spoken; he just seemed to follow Small around like a lost puppy.

'No router?' asked Dixon.

'He didn't have the internet, Sir,' replied Wevill. 'His daughter didn't want him getting scammed.'

It hadn't taken the daughter long to declutter the whole flat – Dixon winced to himself, grateful he hadn't said that word out loud, *declutter*; Louise would think he'd been watching daytime TV.

Even her late father's books had been boxed up and were sitting on the bed in the spare room, waiting to go to the charity shop, presumably. Medieval English and military history, mainly, with a few crime novels thrown in for good measure.

'He taught history, in case you were wondering,' said Small.

The master bedroom had been cleared, the wardrobe empty; drawers too, except for new drawer liners – lavender scented. Even in the en-suite, not so much as a towel on the rail, let alone a toothbrush.

'Seen enough?' asked Small.

'Not yet.'

'Oh, right.' Small made no effort to hide his disappointment. 'What else is there? There's nothing here.'

'Has there been any local press coverage?' asked Dixon.

'We kept it out of the press, for obvious reasons.'

Can't blame them for that, thought Dixon. Charlesworth would have done exactly the same.

Small was getting impatient, motioning towards the front door. 'Look, I'll brief my team and then they'll be up to Bridgwater tomorrow to join your task force.'

'Sergeant Winter is running the incident room and will be able to help with local B&Bs,' replied Dixon. He had followed Small out into the corridor and was staring at the bin liners.

'She's the pregnant one, Deano,' said Small to Wevill, with a grin. 'So don't you go getting any ideas.'

'I wouldn't recommend it.' Louise only just managed to stifle a chuckle.

'Husband-to-be a bit of a handful, is he?'

'I can be.' Dixon leaned over and picked up a bin liner in each hand. 'Bring the other two, will you, Lou.'

The bags had been tied loosely. Dixon undid the first one and upended it on the double bed in the master bedroom. Then he began sifting through the contents.

'This one's dry food, tins, stuff like that, Sir,' said Louise. She had opened a bag and was shining the torch on her phone at the contents.

'That can go to the food bank, in that case,' he said.

Junk mail, freebie local newspapers, a couple of crossword books, old copies of *The Times*.

'That's what she'd bunged in the recycling,' said Wevill. 'Scientific went through the grey bin too, but there was nothing, just food waste.'

Several copies of the *Radio Times*, a couple of flattened Amazon delivery boxes, the daughter's name – Mrs C Woodard – and the father's address; cleaning stuff, probably. A calendar had been torn in half and thrown in the bag, although there were no entries for January, except on the ninth: 'gas fire service, 2.30pm, Grandisson'.

'What was the date of death?'

'Sometime on the eleventh, according to the pathologist. The old boy was found on the thirteenth,' replied Small.

'Has anyone spoken to Grandisson?'

'Not yet, Sir,' said Wevill after a short pause, during which Small had glared at him, no doubt. Not that Dixon could see them standing behind him – hands on hips, probably.

The writing on the calendar entry was hardly the sort of spidery writing you'd expect from a ninety-one-year-old man. 'What about carers?'

'He used the agency along the way there; a hundred yards down the road. They'd sent three in the last few weeks and we've got statements from them. You'll find them on the system.' There was more than a measure of frustration in Small's voice now; much more petulant and he'd be stamping his foot. 'We're checking with them about a visit from an OT.'

'We've re-run the house to house this morning asking the same thing,' offered Wevill. 'Nothing.'

'You see what I mean about the road, though,' said Small. 'No one would notice a marching band, let alone a medic.'

Dixon was still sifting through the pile of rubbish on the bed, before gesturing to Louise to tip the contents of the third bag on top.

More copies of *The Times*, mainly just the Mind Games section, the crosswords and other puzzles done, some more than others. Michael Allam had been good at cryptic crosswords, but hadn't seemed to have got the hang of sudoku. Not that Dixon would criticise him for that; he couldn't even understand some of the puzzles, particularly the maths problems. It was why he had trained as a lawyer, not an accountant.

'Puzzles seem to be the order of the day,' he said, handing a crumpled piece of newspaper to Louise, letters and numbers scribbled all over it. 'He's got all the history questions right in the quiz too.'

'Kept him busy, I suppose,' she said. 'Deirdre Baxter had a puzzle book and played games on her iPad.'

'Something to look forward to,' said Small. 'I'm only eighteen months off retiring, myself.'

Dixon had moved on to the last bag that had been tied at the top and labelled 'for shredding'. Utility bills, old bank statements, investment valuations; it explained why it had not gone in the recycling, perhaps. 'We'll keep this lot,' he said, stuffing the papers back into the bag.

'We went through his bank statements,' said Small. 'There was nothing untoward.' He tapped Wevill on the arm and gestured to the bag, the surly DS doing the honours. 'I'll tell my team – well, what was my team – to get to you for eight o'clock sharp. Is that all right?'

'Fine.'

'I'll tell them to be on their best behaviour too.'

Chapter Seven

Dixon was sitting in the corner of the canteen at Express Park. He bit into a soggy baguette, brushing away the grated cheese that fell down his front.

'Ah, there you are,' said Jane. 'I saw Lou, so I knew you were back. Is that an early supper or a late lunch?'

'Late lunch,' he replied, spraying more cheese everywhere. 'Who puts grated cheese in a baguette, for heaven's sake?'

Either Jane recognised the rhetorical question or she chose to ignore it. 'If you missed lunch, then you must've kept your blood sugar levels up with fruit pastilles, I suppose?'

Dixon braced himself for the lecture.

'I've had Michael Allam's daughter on the phone and you're going to love this,' she said, surprising him with the sudden change of subject. 'Cynthia Woodard. She's on her way down from Sunderland, hopes to get here about seven, and *expects* the senior investigating officer to make himself available to speak to her.'

'I would anyway.'

'Of course you would, and I told her that, but she's just so bloody rude. You'll need to take a deep breath and count to ten.'

'Anything else?' he asked, through a mouthful of baguette.

'We're still a bit thin on the ground upstairs. Mark's on the traffic cameras with a couple of PCSOs. Sarah's come up with something though, but I'll leave her to brief you on that.'

'More bad news, I take it.'

'It's not all bad,' replied Jane. 'There are fairly active Facebook groups for old pupils of both schools, so we should be able to find out if Michael Allam and Deirdre Baxter knew each other. I've even traced a couple of their teaching colleagues who are still alive.'

'But there's no obvious connection between the two?' Dixon knew the answer to that one but asked it anyway.

'No, sorry.'

That would have been too easy.

'It's going to be a long day for Monty, poor sod.'

'I nipped home at lunchtime; gave him a run in the field, don't worry. And Lucy's going to be there later. She's not going back to Manchester until the morning. I'll drop her at the railway station first thing.'

'He'll have to come with me tomorrow.' Dixon stuffed the last of the baguette back inside the wrapper and left it on the plate. 'We've got eight coming from Devon.'

'Yes, I know. I emailed over an accommodation list for them, so they'll have to take pot luck. Some might commute too; it's only an hour down the motorway.'

'Not even that.' Dixon stood up.

'What did you find at Sidmouth?' Jane asked, following him along the landing.

'Not a lot. It was a full week before the post mortem confirmed it was murder, and his flat looks like a show home now. Poor bloke's hardly cold and the daughter's getting his place ready to go on the market.'

'Doesn't surprise me, having spoken to her on the phone.'

Once at the top of the stairs, Dixon made a beeline for Sarah's workstation. 'I gather you have some news for me,' he said.

'Yes, Sir,' she replied, nervously. 'I was doing a trawl for other similar cases and there is one, I'm afraid.'

'Go on.' He pulled a chair out from under the adjacent desk and sat down.

Sarah picked up her notebook. 'Thomas Fowler. He was eighty-nine, found dead on the fourth of December last year. The doctor certified the cause of death as old age. He hadn't seen him within the last twenty-eight days though, so there was a referral to the coroner – that's how I was able to find out about it. There were no suspicious circumstances, no further investigations, no post mortem, and he was buried in the family plot at Bradford Abbas church just before Christmas.'

'What do we know about him?'

'Nothing yet, Sir.'

'Is there any family?'

'A son who lives locally – I've got an address in Yeovil, but I haven't spoken to him yet.'

'Is it consecrated ground?'

'Is what consecrated ground?'

'The churchyard,' replied Dixon. 'Not all of them are.'

Sarah looked puzzled. 'How would I find that out?'

'Ring the churchwarden or the vicar. There should be a webpage somewhere with their contact details. Otherwise, Bradford Abbas is in Dorset, so you could contact the Bishop of Sherborne's office.'

'Then what?'

'We dig him up. Better set up a meeting with the son for tomorrow.'

◆ ◆ ◆

A vacant workstation in a quiet corner of the incident room. It sounded better than it was; most of the workstations were vacant and you could hear a pin drop.

Dixon had spent a couple of hours going through the Devon and Cornwall file into Michael Allam's death. Witness statements from the carers, neighbours and his doctor; the post mortem report, which recorded identical fractures of the cricoid bone, although the pathologist referred to it as 'ossified cricoid cartilage'.

Several supplemental statements had been added to the system that day. The doctor confirmed there had been no referral to an OT or to Sidmouth or Exeter hospital. The carers confirmed they had not seen or been expecting an OT visit, and the immediate neighbour had heard and seen nothing.

The report from Devon Scientific Services made grim reading too. Several sets of fingerprints had been eliminated, as had the DNA samples. Apart from that, there was nothing.

The only really interesting photographs were those attached to the post mortem, taken by the paramedics of his body slumped in the armchair. If nothing else, they showed that the daughter must be suffering from some form of obsessive compulsive disorder. Jane made sure the shower gel was facing the right way and Dixon pulled her leg about OCD, but this was something else entirely.

The pile of newspapers by the old man's chair must have been a foot high; more of them on the small table. Dixon had found some in the bin liner at Michael Allam's flat, but not this many, surely?

Dirty mugs, sweet wrappers, the TV remote, plates stacked on the floor.

A retired teacher.

There would be a connection with Deirdre Baxter. It was just a matter of finding it.

And now a connection with Thomas Fowler as well, possibly.

Dixon looked up to find Jane and Sarah standing over him. Sarah was the one looking anxious, Jane there for moral support more than anything.

'It is consecrated ground, Sir,' said Sarah. 'St Mary's at Bradford Abbas.'

'Ecclesiastical law.' He sighed. 'You'll need to write this down.'

'Is it bad?' asked Jane.

'As bad as it gets. I made the mistake of doing the module in the second year of my degree.' Dixon rolled his eyes. 'Seemed like a good idea at the time. Ready?'

Sarah nodded.

'We're going to need to petition the consistory court of the diocese of Salisbury for a faculty for exhumation. It can be done on paper, without an oral hearing. I'll need to swear an affidavit, but that's about all I can remember, to be honest. You'll need to get the legal department at Portishead to help you. We'll need the Dorset coroner's say-so too, and the next of kin's permission. Did you ring the son?'

'Tomorrow at two,' replied Sarah. 'We're meeting him at his father's house in Bradford Abbas.'

Dixon spotted Charlesworth weaving his way between the workstations towards him. 'Oh, shit, the press conference.'

'It's all right, Nick, we went ahead without you,' said Charlesworth, when Dixon checked his phone. Three missed calls, but no messages. 'I was ringing to tell you not to bother racing back for it. Deborah and I dealt with it.'

'Thank you, Sir.'

'We went for a generic reminder to be on the alert for doorstep fraudsters, as there'd been reports of them masquerading as NHS employees. Check identification carefully before allowing anyone into your home, that sort of thing. We didn't think we should be worrying people any more than that at this stage, although I gather there's been a third?'

'Sarah's come up with a possible in Bradford Abbas,' replied Dixon.

'A genuinely *regional* task force.' Charlesworth could hardly contain his relief. 'It means the Dorset lot can help out. The more, the merrier. People, I mean; not murders.'

'Of course, Sir.'

'I'll put a call out to my opposite number in Dorset. Has there been a post mortem?'

'No, Sir.'

'There'll need to be one sharpish then. Where is he or she?'

'Buried in consecrated ground at St Mary's, Bradford Abbas.'

'Sod's Law, I think they call that.' Charlesworth turned on his heel. 'Well, keep me posted.'

'Got off lightly,' said Dixon, when Charlesworth was halfway down the stairs.

'You won't now,' replied Jane, sliding her phone back into her pocket. 'Michael Allam's daughter is down in reception.'

'I am not stupid, Richard.'

It was an animated whisper that carried across the reception area when Dixon appeared through the security door at the bottom of the stairs. Mrs Woodard's husband reminding her not to be rude, probably.

Jane had done exactly the same at the top of the stairs.

Cynthia – frighteningly close to Hyacinth, although in name only, it seemed.

Mid-fifties, perhaps, greying hair tied back tightly in a bun; dressed for battle in a two-piece trouser suit. She stood up when she noticed Dixon and Louise walking towards them, grabbing her husband's elbow to ensure he did the same.

The husband had an apologetic look on his face, but then he had the bearing of a man who spent his life apologising.

'Superintendent Dixon?' demanded Mrs Woodard.

'Yes.'

'I want to know what you're doing about the murder of my father.'

'Let's take this in an interview room, shall we?' he said, offering his best welcoming smile. 'My colleague, Detective Constable Willmott, will be making notes, if that's all right.'

'Why wouldn't it be?'

Not rising to the bait was going to be the challenge. The obvious answer to that one was, 'I don't know, you tell me,' but that was just inviting confrontation. There was a time for that, but not now, unless she pushed him too far, of course. 'You'll be Mr Woodard,' he said, turning to the husband in the open doorway.

'Richard,' he replied, offering his hand, despite the disapproving glance from his wife.

'Sit down, please.' Dixon waited until they had both sat down before doing the same.

'I take it you've read our witness statements?'

'I have.'

'Well, that's a start. I just hope to God you're not as incompetent as those idiots from Devon.' Mrs Woodard was gathering steam. 'You're certainly very young to be a superintendent.'

Dixon could imagine the response the poor sod who had taken their statements had got when they'd asked her for her whereabouts at the time of her father's death. At least he was spared that, although there were difficult questions to come.

'Look, I'm not here to defend Devon and Cornwall Police, but in fairness to them the attending doctor gave the cause of death as old age. It was only referred to the coroner because your father hadn't seen his own GP within twenty-eight days of his death.'

'You spotted the second victim straight away,' protested Mrs Woodard, 'and preserved the crime scene.'

'Yes, but we were on the lookout for elderly people dying alone in their own homes, precisely because of what happened to your father.'

'That doesn't explain the delay between the post mortem and Devon and Cornwall getting off their arses and doing something about it. By then I'd nearly finished clearing out Dad's flat.'

Dixon couldn't argue with that one, so thought it best not to try.

'We've put in place a regional task force, consisting of officers from both Avon and Somerset and the Devon and Cornwall force. We'll be collaborating closely to find your late father's killer.'

'Platitudes. Collaboration, blah blah. Do you have a suspect?'

'We are pursuing a number of lines of enquiry—'

'Another platitude. That's a no then.' Mrs Woodard folded her arms. 'It would be nice to think you took the murders of old people seriously, but that's hardly the impression I get from the appointment of someone so young to lead the so-called *regional task force*.'

'Look, let's be clear right from the outset,' said Dixon, firmly. 'There are things that I can tell you and things that I can't, and no amount of shouting is going to change that.'

Mrs Woodard looked surprised, in stark contrast to her husband's look of amusement, although that was quickly wiped from his face when she glared at him.

'Who is the second victim?' she asked, changing tack.

'A retired teacher living in Berrow.'

'A colleague of my father's?'

'Not as far as we can tell. She taught at St Christopher's, retiring when the school closed down in the nineties.'

'What's her name? I was at St Christopher's.'

'We'll come on to that in a minute, if that's all right.'

'There must be some connection though, surely.'

'That's one of the lines of enquiry we're pursuing,' replied Dixon.

'What are the others?'

Dixon admired her persistence, but it was time to shut down the jousting. 'I find that these meetings work best when I ask the questions.'

Mrs Woodard drew breath, but thought better of it.

'Tell me about your mother,' Dixon said.

'She died three years ago.' Mrs Woodard softened at the memory. 'Alzheimer's. Late onset, mercifully, and Dad kept her at home until near the end. It wasn't easy, mark you. She'd wander off, given half the chance, and they'd find her down on the beach in her nightdress.'

'When did they marry?'

'1961. Then I came along in 1963.'

'And your father taught at St Joseph's throughout his career?'

'He did.'

'Even towards the end when it became co-educational, or had he retired by then?'

Mrs Woodard turned an alarming shade of crimson, visible even under her make-up. 'Oh, I see where this is going.' She turned to her husband, her mouth pinched in fury. 'I told you. My father teaches at a boys' boarding school, is murdered, and suddenly he's being suspected of interfering with the pupils.'

'We're just trying to establish a motive,' said Dixon. His smile was beginning to feel strained, and probably looked it too.

'And I suppose this other teacher is suspected of interfering with the girls at St Christopher's?' She sneered. 'You people.'

'This isn't getting us anywhere, is it,' Dixon said. 'Either you want to help us find who killed your father, or you don't. It's that simple.'

'How dare you—'

'For heaven's sake, Cynthia,' said her husband, placing his hand on her arm. 'Just tell him what he needs to know.'

'How do I know what went on? I was just a child.'

'Where were you living?' asked Dixon.

'We had a flat in Grove Road when the school was based there. It occupied most of the buildings on the right, as you walk up to the beach. Then it moved to Rectory Road and we had a house in the grounds. Dad was deputy head by then.'

'And you said you went to St Christopher's?'

'I was there from 1974 to 1979. Then I went to St Joseph's when it went co-ed.'

'What about your mother, did she work?'

'She taught French.' Mrs Woodard shrugged. 'She was French, so it made sense.'

'Was there any infidelity in the marriage that you're aware of?'

Dixon watched Mrs Woodard bridling at the question and was waiting for the indignation, but it never came. Just sadness. 'My mother had an affair, or so I found out years later. It was with a young science teacher. He was only there for a couple of years and then moved on, or was moved on, when it became public knowledge. I think he went to Allhallows, but that's closed down now as well.'

'Do you remember his name?'

'Newsom.'

Dixon braced himself. 'Let's go back to the difficult question then. Were any allegations ever made about your father's conduct arising from his time at St Joseph's?'

'No. Absolutely not. In fact, I don't recall any allegations of a sexual nature – that's what you mean, isn't it – ever being made against any of the teaching staff there.'

'What about St Christopher's?'

'The same.' Mrs Woodard pursed her lips. 'I guess that makes us lucky, compared to what you read about these days.'

'Would your sister say the same thing?'

'Angela. We don't speak.' Mrs Woodard crumpled, the anger that had been keeping her going all but gone. 'She buggered off to America years ago. She's a couple of years younger than me; followed me through the same schools, then met an American at Oxford and was gone. Hardly seen her since. We weren't even invited to her wedding. None of us were.'

'When was the last time she saw your father?'

'She saw him once in the last twelve years of his life, and that was at our mother's funeral.'

'Does the name Deirdre Baxter mean anything to you?'

'Mrs Baxter taught me maths. God, she's not the other victim, is she?'

Dixon remained impassive.

'She was lovely, bless her.'

'Did your father know Mrs Baxter?'

'I really don't know. I expect so.'

'What about Thomas Fowler?'

'Is there another one?' Her husband this time, unable to contain his curiosity. 'That makes three.'

Mrs Woodard had clearly got the message, even if her husband hadn't. 'No, I'm afraid that name doesn't mean anything to me.'

'Where was your father living before he moved to Sidmouth?'

'My parents retired to Brean. A bungalow on Coast Road. You got straight out on to the beach from the end of the garden and the dogs loved it. Wire-haired Dachshunds; he had three, but the last died not long after Mum. He only moved to Sidmouth after my mother died, then you got that job up north,' she said, turning to her husband again. 'I felt awful about that, but we had to go and that was that. Dad didn't want to come with us, so . . .'

'How did he spend his time?'

'Watching TV, doing puzzles. His eyesight was becoming a problem for him and we'd been talking about a care home, but he was stubborn. He used to read a lot, used a magnifying glass and tried audiobooks when the macular degeneration started to get worse.'

'Did he have a computer?'

'No. Never wanted one. No internet connection either.'

'Well, please rest assured we're going to be doing everything we can to find your father's killer.'

'I know, young man,' replied Mrs Woodard. 'Thank you.' She stood up.

'You've still not told him, have you,' said her husband, staying put. 'And I'm not leaving this place until you do.'

Dixon had been rising from his chair but sat back down, glancing at Louise, who was opening her notebook again.

'It's got nothing to do with his murder,' said Mrs Woodard, with a heavy sigh. 'It can't possibly have. It was so long ago – that's if it even happened at all. I've always thought it was more of a legend than fact; one of those stories that goes around schools, like chicken pox.'

Dixon gestured to the chair Mrs Woodard had vacated.

'You need to understand, my father never confirmed any of this – I did ask him about it, but he always changed the subject, never would discuss it. He just said it was rubbish and I should forget about it, so it might very well not be true at all,' she said, sitting back down. 'There was supposed to have been a school play, a pantomime; a joint production between St Joseph's and St

Christopher's, boys and girls. *Old King Cole*, I think it might have been. It would have been long before I was there in the seventies, so it might even have been the sixties, I really don't know. Anyway, one of the girls is supposed to have fallen off the stage and broken her neck.'

'No name, I suppose?'

'No. Look, us kids told it more as a ghost story to scare the younger kids, so I really wouldn't waste any time on it.'

'Who would have been directing the pantomime?'

'My father, possibly. I know he directed some of the school plays.'

'And there's nothing else you can remember about it?'

'No. It was just a ghost story. Really.'

'Well, that wasn't as bad as I thought it was going to be,' said Louise, locking the front door behind Mr and Mrs Woodard. 'You had her eating out of the palm of your hand by the end.'

'She's bound to be angry with the Devon lot.'

'I'd be fuming.'

'We'll start with the teachers, anyone who knew Michael Allam or Deirdre Baxter; hopefully we'll find one who knew both.'

'Where does Thomas Fowler fit in, I wonder?'

'We'll worry about that if and when he's exhumed and a post mortem confirms he was murdered.'

'What about the ghost story?' asked Louise, her voice loaded with mischief.

'Stranger things have happened, but we won't waste too much time on it.' Dixon was punching the code into the lock at the bottom of the stairs. 'Check and see if the coroner's records go back that far. Otherwise, we'll ask if anyone else remembers it. We've got to speak to them anyway.'

'Deirdre and Michael must've known each other.'

'It would be odd if they didn't, I suppose. Deirdre was teaching Michael's daughter maths, for a start.'

'I don't know all of Katie's teachers.'

'My parents didn't know all of mine,' replied Dixon. 'Some, but not all.'

Chapter Eight

'Where is he?' asked Dixon, his voice hushed. Louise turned away, her phone clamped to her ear.

They were standing on the doorstep of a converted barn on the edge of Kingsbury Episcopi, Dixon watching two horses, their heads over the stable doors, munching hay. More horse power in the carport opposite, although it was under a car cover, whatever it was. Suitably low to the ground, the familiar Ferrari logo over the middle of the bonnet and a cat curled up on the roof, out of the rain.

An outside light over the door – Dixon wasn't sure whether it was the front or the back – illuminated a doorbell camera, so he was watching them, wherever he was. He'd known they were coming too.

'He's in the Rose and Crown at East Lambrook,' said Louise.

'His stepmother's been murdered and he's gone to the bloody pub?'

Louise knew a rhetorical question when she heard one. 'He wants to know whether you want him to come home,' she said, the phone pressed to her shoulder.

'Tell him it's either that or we come down to the pub and have our little chat in front of everybody.'

'Yes, Sir, that would be most helpful,' Louise said, into her phone. 'We are waiting, so if you could come now that would be appreciated.' She rang off. 'He said he's five minutes away; apologised profusely.'

'He did know we were coming?'

'He wasn't given a time, apparently.'

'Oh, well, that's all right then.'

'He probably heard every word you said through the doorbell camera. They have microphones on them.'

Louise walked across the gravel to the carport and looked under the cover. 'An F355 Berlinetta, with cream leather. It should be in an air-conditioned garage, really.'

Dixon sighed. Next she'd be telling him how much the house was worth.

'It's my husband who's the car nut,' continued Louise. 'I get dragged around classic car shows and motor museums, but you have to do your bit, don't you?'

'And how much is the house worth?' asked Dixon. It might not be totally useless information, after all.

'Depends how much land it's got. Maybe eight-fifty with a couple of acres?'

Dixon was standing under the carport now, watching Louise straightening the car cover. It was either that or shelter under the canopy over the front door, but that was too close to the doorbell camera and its microphone.

'Remind me what he does for a living.'

'Windows and doors, conservatories, that sort of stuff. He's got a company based over at Yeovil.'

'Have we done a company search?'

'It's on my list of things to do.'

Car headlights turning into the drive announced the arrival of Deirdre Baxter's stepson, Lawrence. He parked behind Dixon's

Land Rover, a woman jumping out of the passenger seat of the Jaguar SUV and running across to the door. She opened it and disappeared inside, leaving it standing open.

Lawrence Baxter slammed the driver's door and walked over to the carport. 'I'm sorry about that,' he said – half-heartedly, thought Dixon. 'We were meeting friends; a long-standing arrangement, you know how it is.'

Dixon opened his mouth to speak, but Baxter beat him to it.

'I know what you're thinking, but I'm not going to lie. I never liked Deirdre and she never liked me, so I'm not going to be shedding any tears now she's gone. And I'm certainly not going to miss dinner with friends.' His voice reduced to a whisper, as if he suddenly thought better of being so blunt. 'Or at least I wasn't until you rang.'

A dismal night in late January, the rain had turned to sleet, and Dixon was buggered if he was going to conduct an interview in a carport. 'Shall we go inside?' he asked. Besides, he wanted to have a look around.

'Er, yes, of course,' replied Baxter. 'How long is this going to take? Only we said we'd try to get back to the pub, and our friends are waiting for us.'

'We'll try to get you back in time for last orders, Sir,' replied Dixon, following Baxter across the gravel.

'Through here,' said Baxter. 'Would you like a coffee or something?'

'No, thank you, Sir.'

The woman who had run into the house was leaning back against the worktop in the kitchen, pouring herself a glass of white wine.

'This is my partner, Samantha,' said Baxter. 'I was with Sam most of the day yesterday. That's what you're going ask me, isn't it?'

'Would you mind?' asked Dixon, turning to Samantha.

73

'Give us the room, Sam,' said Baxter. 'That's what the Americans say, I think.'

Louise sat down at the kitchen table and took out her notebook while they waited for Samantha to leave.

'I went into the office in the morning,' continued Baxter. 'Came home for lunch and then we spent the afternoon in the field. The fence was down on the far side and the horses were getting out, so we fixed it. After that, a shower – together – how much detail do you want?'

Dixon ignored the question.

'Then we went into Yeovil about six and met some friends for a bite to eat. We're fairly social animals, if you hadn't guessed already.'

'The friends?'

'Oh God, you're not going to pester them, are you?' Baxter was allowing his impatience to creep in. 'I know, I know, most people are killed by someone they know. Neil and Kelly Wood. He's a property developer and I'm after the contract to supply the windows and doors. He's got a development over at Stembridge.'

'When did Deirdre meet your father?' asked Dixon. He was standing in front of the fridge, looking at the various magnets. A travelogue, of sorts.

'My mother died in 2002 and they married in 2005, I think it was. It was a second marriage for both of them. I was an only child and Deirdre had no children.'

'How did they meet?'

'They started out as bridge partners before becoming husband and wife.' Baxter snapped open a can of Coke that he'd taken out of the fridge when Dixon had moved on. 'Look, I was twenty-six when they married, and had flown the nest, so to speak, so it wasn't as if it made much difference to me.'

'Why the tension between you?' asked Dixon. 'You said you didn't get on.'

'We got on all right to begin with, but it was the same old story: jealousy and suspicion creeps in. She could be difficult, cantankerous even, and I thought she was just after Dad's money. She was on her uppers and he was well off. She's had his pension and been living in his house ever since he died.'

'When was that?'

'2019. Prostate cancer. She did look after him when he was ill, though, nursed him at home despite her age. I'll give her that.'

'What about you?'

'Divorced. I've got two boys, aged fifteen and eighteen. The younger one's at Blundell's, the other's just started at uni. Their mother still lives in our old house at Martock.'

'And is Samantha just after your money?'

Louise looked up from her notebook, surprised at the question, but not as surprised as Baxter.

'Of course not!' Indignant now.

'Perhaps your children think she is?'

'They don't think that at all. They get on well with her.'

'Are you planning to marry?'

'Maybe one day.'

'So, if Samantha's not after your money, what makes you think Deirdre was after your father's money?'

Dixon watched Baxter soften as the realisation began to hit home. 'I don't know, when you put it like that.'

'Have you seen a copy of her will?'

'We never talked about things like that.'

'She left her entire estate to you.'

'Really?' The surprise seemed genuine. 'I thought she'd have left it to charity or something like that. Maybe I've been a bit hard on her?'

'Maybe you have.'

'I get the house anyway, though, but you probably know that already.' Baxter dropped his empty can into a bag hanging on the back door handle. 'The house was in my father's name and Deirdre got to live there until she died, then it comes to me.' He shook his head. 'I suppose you think that gives me a motive to kill her?'

'It's something we have to rule out, Sir.'

'Yeah.'

'How often did you see Deirdre?' Dixon knew it was a question to embarrass Baxter, but he asked it all the same.

'Not often. We used to invite her at Christmas, but she never came, so we stopped. I feel awful now.'

And so you should.

'How is your business doing?'

'Fine, thank you,' replied Baxter, the question snapping him out of a moment's reflection. 'We've got our share of debts, but it's under control. Cash flow is good.' Spelling it out now. 'I don't need the money.'

Dixon was looking at the photographs on the exposed brick-work above the fireplace, a double-sided wood-burning stove heating the kitchen and the adjacent TV room. Leather sofas and oak furniture, a huge television mounted on the wall.

Two boys at various ages, playing cricket and rugby; a school photograph, the pupils lined up in rows, so no doubt Baxter's boys would be in there somewhere.

'You pay their fees, I'm guessing?' he asked.

'Of course. School and university. I don't want Roly saddled with student debt, and I'll be doing the same for Marcus as well.'

Dixon tapped Louise on the shoulder. 'My colleague here will just go and have a word with Samantha, if that's all right.'

'Check my alibi, you mean.'

'That's exactly what I mean, Sir,' replied Dixon. 'We have questions we have to ask, boxes we have to tick.'

'Of course you do.' Baxter opened the door of the utility room, letting two black Labradors into the kitchen. 'I might as well let them out for a few minutes, while we're here,' he said, the dogs jumping up at him. 'Am I allowed to ask how Deirdre was killed?'

'She was strangled. It wouldn't have taken long in a person of that age.'

'That's something, I suppose.' Baxter opened the back door and let the dogs out into the darkness, a motion-activated light coming on outside.

'Does the name Michael Allam mean anything to you?' asked Dixon.

Baxter was standing in the doorway, trying to keep track of his dogs in the gloom, occasionally waving his hand to flick the outside light back on. 'I'm afraid not. Who is he?'

'Another elderly person killed in his own home.'

'Sounds like you've got your hands full.' A whistle and the dogs came running back into the kitchen, Baxter managing to throw an old towel over one of them before it shook water everywhere. 'Listen, I don't suppose you happen to know who Deirdre's executor is?'

'It's you, as it happens, Sir.'

'Really? You do surprise me. When will I be able to get into the house, do you know?'

'It's a crime scene, so it's unlikely to be for a while,' replied Dixon. 'We'll let you know.'

'Thank you.'

The door on the far side of the TV room opened, Louise appearing, closely followed by Samantha.

'Right, well, we'll leave you to it,' said Dixon. 'You can get back to the pub.'

'We might give it a miss,' replied Baxter, turning to Samantha. 'I'll give Neil a ring.'

'One last question, Sir, while I think of it,' said Dixon, just as Baxter was showing them out into the rain.

'Of course.'

'Where did you go to school?'

◆ ◆ ◆

'What do you think?' asked Louise, as Dixon turned out into the lane.

'We'll see what the company search says, and check with his bank, but we can rule him out if he hasn't got any financial worries.'

'Doesn't look as though he has, does it?'

'He could be mortgaged up to his armpits, and with interest rates going up . . .' Dixon flicked his lights to full beam, accelerating along the foggy lane, deep rhynes on either side. 'How did you get on with Samantha?'

'Her story matches his. I even got chapter and verse of what they got up to in the shower, which I could've done without, to be honest.'

'I shouldn't think for a minute someone like that would get his hands dirty anyway, so an alibi is fairly meaningless.' Dixon was staring into the fog, flicking his lights between dimmed and full beam. 'What's more important is that there's nothing on the face of it to connect him to Michael Allam. Baxter went to the wrong school.'

'Or the right one,' said Louise.

'I'll drop you back to your car, then go home, Lou. Get some sleep.'

'Yeah.'

◆ ◆ ◆

It was just after ten when the rattle of Dixon's diesel engine started Monty barking.

The lights were on in the living room at the cottage and the curtains open, the dog sitting on the window seat. He spent most days sitting there, when he wasn't out and about with Dixon, waiting patiently for someone to come home, although he was just about old enough now to realise that someone always would.

Jane was standing in the open kitchen door when Dixon slid out of the driver's seat of his Land Rover.

'How'd you get on?' she asked.

'The stepson's a bit of a pillock, but I don't think he killed Deirdre and there seems to be no obvious connection between him and Michael Allam, even if he did.'

'Have you eaten?'

'Not since that baguette.'

'I'll bung a fish pie in the microwave.'

'Has he been out?' asked Dixon, the dog jumping up at him.

'Just round the field.'

'I might take him up the hill in a bit then.'

'Take that,' Jane said, gesturing to a can of beer on the worktop. 'And go and sit down.'

Dixon sat down on the sofa, leaned back and closed his eyes. 'What did Sarah find out about the other one, Thomas Fowler?'

'Not a lot,' replied Jane, raising her voice over the noise of the microwave. 'And the legal department is closed until tomorrow. She tried the emergency number, but was told an exhumation wasn't urgent and could wait.'

'Was she, indeed?' A swig of beer. 'Deirdre's stepson was in the pub, would you believe it? Lucky for him they didn't go back, otherwise I'd have had uniform waiting for him at closing time with their breathalyser.'

'They didn't get on?'

'Actually, he was a bit sheepish about it, I think. We'll do the usual checks, but unless he's in deep trouble financially, I can't really see a motive.'

'It may be that there's no connection between Deirdre and Michael Allam.' Jane placed a tray on Dixon's lap, the fish pie still in the plastic container, which had buckled in the heat. Not that he could say anything, mind you, having an equally relaxed attitude towards food presentation.

'No-added-sugar ketchup.'

'There's none of the other stuff.' Jane was lying, and knew that he knew she was lying, but there was no hint of an apology. 'You shouldn't be having it with fish pie anyway.'

'There must be a connection between them,' said Dixon. 'The alternative is that the killings are random and that's just too horrible to contemplate.' He was watching a wisp of steam rising from the mashed potato, half an eye on Monty, who was inching closer. 'Yes, they were both teachers at schools in Burnham, at the same sort of time, but there must be more to it than that.'

'Thomas Fowler was a retired lift engineer and there were no lifts at either school. We checked.' Jane had sat down on the arm of the sofa. 'He retired twenty-five years ago, but we've got employment details from his son. Sarah's going to check which area he covered, but you're seeing the son at two anyway.' She smiled. 'Maybe wassailing wasn't so bad after all?'

'At least we get the team from Devon tomorrow.' Dixon was breathing in sharply, trying to cool the mouthful of fish pie.

'I don't think they can be short of a bob or two, down there,' said Jane. 'They've all gone to the Premier Inn on expenses.'

'You never know, we might get some help from Dorset too, if Thomas Fowler turns out to be another victim.'

'That'll please you-know-who.'

'Oh shit, I didn't do my jab.' Dixon dropped his fork and began fumbling in his inside jacket pocket for his insulin pen.

'How are you getting on with that thing in your arm?'

'Completely forgot about it, to be honest.'

'Give me your phone.' Jane held out her hand in front of him, not giving Dixon much choice in the matter. Then she entered the passcode and held it to the sensor on the back of his arm. 'Ten-point-one, going up. You've been at the fruit pastilles again. And you've switched off the alerts.'

'I can't have the thing bleeping at me all day.'

'It's supposed to alert you if your blood sugar level is going too low.'

'I can feel it, don't worry,' he said, with a dismissive wave of his fork.

'I'm going to install the app on my phone, then I can creep up behind you and check your blood for myself.'

'It'll only pair with one device.'

'You need to take this seriously. You're going to be a father – and my husband, if we ever get round to sorting it out.'

'Sooner rather than later, please,' said a voice from the top of the stairs, Jane's sister Lucy leaning over the banister. 'I'm still waiting to be a bridesmaid. I've got the dress and everything.'

'What time's your train in the morning?'

'Twenty past eight.'

'Go to bed.'

'After this investigation.' The mouthful of fish pie hid the tiredness in Dixon's reply, mercifully.

'You said that last time, and the time before that. Then, when you finally set a date, it got cancelled.'

'Postponed,' snapped Jane. 'And you know why that was.'

Dixon reached over and put his hand on Jane's knee. Lucy was a good kid who had been pushed from pillar to post: from one foster home to another, back to her drug-addicted mother, then back into care. Jane had been spared that, by parents who adopted her at birth. Her father, Rod, was waiting patiently to walk her down the aisle too.

It was a conversation they'd had many times, Dixon reminding Jane that Lucy needed a friend first and foremost; a sister, not yet another mother figure.

'I'll speak to Jonathan.' He was holding the empty plastic tray for Monty to lick the last of the fish sauce.

'You've got until the end of the week,' said Lucy. 'Then I'll text him.'

'All ri—' Dixon was stopped mid-sentence by the slam of Lucy's bedroom door.

'It's your fault,' Jane said, airily. 'You wanted Jonathan to marry us. And he's practically part of the family now.'

Jonathan was the vicar of Westonzoyland and godfather to Lucy's boyfriend, Billy. It was close enough.

Jane had taken the tray into the kitchen and was standing in the open back door, looking out at the rain. 'Are you sure you're going to take him out?'

Monty took one look out into the darkness and turned tail for the warmth of the sofa.

Dixon smiled. 'Apparently not.'

Chapter Nine

The incident room was buzzing when Dixon arrived just before eight the following morning. Jane was already there, having left Lucy at Highbridge railway station suitably early for her train, despite protests.

'I'll be waiting forty minutes!'

'Tough.'

The team from Devon had arrived and were sitting together at the back, apart from three of the younger ones who were crowded around Sarah Loveday's workstation, being a little too attentive, perhaps.

'Gentlemen,' said Dixon, with a clap of his hands. 'This is a major crime regional task force, not a speed-dating agency.'

'Yes, Sir.'

He felt sure he heard a 'You're a fine one to talk,' but decided to let it pass.

Detective Sergeant Wevill was there, in an animated conversation with a female officer, clearly more talkative now he was out of Superintendent Small's shadow. Dixon wasn't entirely sure whether that was a good thing or a bad thing, but would reserve judgement for now.

'First of all, welcome to our colleagues from Devon and Cornwall Police,' he said. It was tempting to ask their names, but he'd almost certainly forget them anyway and time was short. 'We'll do introductions as we go along, if you don't mind. I'm hoping you've found the canteen on the first floor. Just avoid the cheese baguette, would be my advice.'

'And the flapjack.'

'Thank you, Mark.' It was good to hear Mark Pearce chiming in, and to see him smile. It had been a while.

The Devon team was matched in number by the new faces from Portishead that Dixon had been promised. He only recognised one of them, and that was from his time on the cold case unit while he waited for a disciplinary hearing. Happy days.

'Devon team will stay on the murder of Michael Allam in Sidmouth, please. You know the ground. We need to revisit the witnesses in light of the new information we have from Deirdre Baxter's murder. There are images of a car and grainy images of someone who appears to be dressed as an occupational therapist. I know doorbell cameras are difficult in that location, but we need to see if we can pick up the same car on traffic cameras in the area.'

'We've got people on that at Middlemoor, Sir,' said Wevill.

'One of Allam's neighbours – a Mrs Stanton – said she was out walking her dog and thought she saw a car turning out of the car park.'

'We're doing the house to house again and we've got officers stopping traffic in the area as well.'

'Our focus has to be on finding a connection between Michael Allam and Deirdre Baxter.'

'Nothing yet, Sir,' said Jane. She was standing by the two whiteboards, a third one at the far end blank, ready for the next victim. And there would be one, Dixon was in no doubt about that. The only question was whether it would be Thomas Fowler or somebody else's grandmother or grandfather.

'There is a possible third victim. How far have we got with the exhumation, Sarah?'

'The legal team at Portishead are already on it and will have the papers drafted by early afternoon. They want you to speak to the chancellor of the diocese, just to put him in the picture and impress upon him the urgency. He's some senior lawyer from London, the Worshipful somebody-or-other, with letters after his name. The guy at Portishead was most anxious the SIO speaks to him.'

'We can find a quiet lay-by somewhere,' said Dixon.

'He's in court until four,' continued Sarah. 'So you're to ring him at his chambers after that. I've spoken to his clerk and he'll be expecting your call.'

'Both confirmed victims were retired teachers who taught at private schools in Burnham-on-Sea, so we may find our connection there. We need to find old pupils who remember them and get statements, so we've got our work cut out.'

'There are active Facebook groups,' offered Jane. 'And we've made contact with some already.'

'Devon team will focus on old boys and girls from St Joseph's. Michael Allam taught there for almost his entire career, until the school closed down. Find out what interaction there was with St Christopher's – whether the teachers might have known each other. I'm teaching you to suck eggs now.'

'Yes, Sir.' Wevill hid his sarcasm. Almost.

'We'll be focusing on St Christopher's, which is where Deirdre Baxter taught,' continued Dixon, turning to the group down from Portishead.

'The Facebook group for St Christopher's has ninety-three members,' said Jane.

'How many for St Joseph's?' asked Wevill.

'One hundred and twenty-one.'

'I'm sure there'll be others who are not on Facebook,' said Dixon. 'I spoke to Michael Allam's daughter yesterday.'

'Rather you than me.' Wevill again.

'She said there was a joint pantomime, in the sixties possibly, with kids from both schools – she thought it might have been *Old King Cole* – and a girl is supposed to have fallen off the stage and broken her neck. The daughter said it was more of a ghost story than anything, but there may be some truth in it. We're checking with the coroner, but ask the question anyway. Who directed it, produced it, who was in it. Anything.'

'What about Deirdre's stepson?' asked Mark.

'Lou and I spoke to him last night,' replied Dixon. 'We're checking his finances, but my feeling is we can rule him out. On the face of it, he's got an alibi and no connection whatsoever with Michael Allam.'

'How does Thomas Fowler fit in?' asked Wevill. 'Assuming it's confirmed he's a victim.'

'He doesn't. He's a lift engineer from Dorset and neither school had a lift. If he is a victim then we're likely to find ourselves back to square one. We've got the press conference at ten, so we'll see if anything comes of that.'

'What if there's no connection between any of them?' Wevill again.

'Then we're dealing with something entirely different. A killer picking his or her elderly victims at random, and it doesn't bear thinking about.'

◆　◆　◆

'Just to be clear,' said Charlesworth, turning to Dixon in the corridor behind the media suite, 'there's to be no mention of the third victim – the third *possible* victim. Three makes it a serial killer and we really don't want those words being bandied about.'

'I haven't spoken to the son yet, anyway, Sir,' said Dixon.

Vicky Thomas was hovering behind Charlesworth. 'I thought a family member had agreed to appear at the press conference?' she asked.

'Michael Allam's daughter did offer, but I decided against it,' replied Dixon.

'Why, may I ask?'

'It took a week for Devon and Cornwall to spot her father had been murdered, and she's pretty hot under the collar about it. I didn't want to risk the press conference becoming about police incompetence. After all, as far as the general public are concerned, the police are the police, they don't care about county boundaries and chains of command.'

'Bravo, Nick,' said Charlesworth.

'The press are expecting a family member, though, so I'll need to let them know before you go in.' Vicky disappeared through the door behind Charlesworth.

The visitors' car park had been empty when Dixon arrived at Express Park, but a glance out of the floor to ceiling windows upstairs had told him the media suite would be full. The BBC and Sky, satellite dishes on top of the vans, not that there was much he could tell them at this stage. Less than forty-eight hours ago he'd been walking his dog on the beach and looking forward to going wassailing, blissfully unaware there was a serial killer on his patch.

And there was. He was in no doubt about that.

'I've got a prepared statement to read, then we'll take questions,' said Charlesworth. 'You still haven't done your media training, have you?'

'No, Sir.'

'We must sort that out, then you won't need me to hold your hand at these things.'

And there was me thinking you did it just to get on the telly.

Television cameras guaranteed a slot on the evening news, half-hourly on the rolling news channels if it went national, and it probably would. Someone killing old people in their own homes was suitably grim. It might even make Netflix one day, not that Dixon would appear in the documentary.

Charlesworth's prepared statement laid out the bare facts – those that could be made public anyway. It was short, even allowing for the request for members of the public to keep an eye on elderly neighbours and the appeal for information at the end, two doorbell camera images from Deirdre Baxter's neighbour projected on to a screen behind him.

'We are anxious to eliminate this person from our enquiries . . .'

Dixon let his mind wander. There was a connection between Deirdre Baxter and Michael Allam, he felt sure of it; finding it was another matter. Sometimes it was just a question of realising the significance of something he'd already seen. But what? Nothing had really struck him as odd, or out of place. Except perhaps a baby's dummy in the glovebox of Deirdre's car. There wasn't one in his glovebox; not yet, anyway.

'We'll now take questions.' Charlesworth's words dragged Dixon back to the press conference.

Reluctantly.

'I have a question for the acting detective superintendent.'

The voice came from the local hack, a mischief-maker from the *Bridgwater Mercury* who'd got Dixon into trouble before with his blunt questions.

'Is there a serial killer on the loose?'

And there it was again. Dixon could feel Charlesworth's eyes burning into the side of his head.

'We are aware of two victims at the present time, so the answer to that question would be no, a serial killer is not *on the loose*.' It was a lie, and Dixon knew it in his gut.

'Is there any connection between the two victims, other than the manner in which they were killed?' A woman down at the front, a handheld recorder at full stretch.

'We're exploring a number of lines of enquiry. Both victims were retired teachers at schools in Burnham-on-Sea, so we're asking any pupils and colleagues who may remember them to get in touch. Deirdre Baxter taught at St Christopher's and Michael Allam at St Joseph's. Any memories you may have of them, however trivial they seem, might just hold the key.'

'Is there any suggestion of abuse at either or both schools? They were boarding schools, weren't they?'

'None whatsoever, and that sort of speculation is unhelpful.' Dixon was bridling now; he shifted in his seat, trying to hide his unease. 'Both victims were long-serving and dedicated members of the teaching staff, but if evidence of abuse comes to light then it will be taken seriously and dealt with accordingly.'

Charlesworth wound up the press conference, much to Dixon's relief.

'They're going to do exactly what we've done,' Charlesworth said, once in the sanctuary of the corridor behind the media suite. 'They'll trawl through the records of the coroner's court looking for elderly people dying alone in their own homes. And there's nothing we can do to stop them.'

'They won't check Dorset,' replied Dixon. 'So I'd be surprised if there was a welcoming committee waiting for us when we pitch up at the graveyard to exhume Thomas Fowler.'

'When is that likely to be?'

'Later on today, Sir, if I can arrange it. I've got everybody on standby and I'm meeting the son this afternoon. The coroner will give his direction today, then it's just a matter for the ecclesiastical court. I'm hoping the chancellor will make the order without a hearing.'

'A hearing?'

'It's consecrated ground.'

'Would be, wouldn't it. What about the post mortem?'

'We'll bring the body to Taunton and Roger Poland will do it straight away. It'll cost me another curry, but it'll be worth it.'

Chapter Ten

'I've never been to Somerton before,' said Louise, staring out of the passenger window of Dixon's Land Rover as they crept along Pesters Lane.

'Really,' replied Dixon, idly. 'What are the house prices like around here?'

'You're being sarcastic now. I can tell.'

'It's that one down there.' Dixon was pointing to a driveway that sloped down to a bungalow, the roof level with the lane.

'Jane said that Mrs Rosser knew Deirdre and Michael Allam, so it should be interesting.' Louise had noticed the estate agent's 'For Sale' board attached to the fence with cable ties, but must have thought better of mentioning it. That didn't stop her sliding her phone out of her pocket and googling it, though.

Dixon glanced over at the screen as he parked the Land Rover across the drive, not bothering to turn in. 'I'd go for five-fifty.'

'How the . . . you checked before we came, didn't you?'

'Jane did.'

'Must have a big garden out the back.'

A ramp gave wheelchair access up the steps to the front door, railings bolted to the wall and a key safe mounted on the door frame. 'It said on the Rightmove listing there's no chain, so my guess is she's going into a care home.'

'Well, she is ninety-four,' replied Louise. 'She's done well to stay in her own home this long.'

Dixon rang the doorbell, at the same time peering through the frosted glass. Then a wheelchair appeared from the door on the far side of the inner hall.

'It's open.' A weak voice, struggling for volume.

He pushed open the door.

'I got Alison to leave it unlocked when I knew you were coming, dear.'

It was an electric wheelchair, mercifully; the old lady would never have had the strength to move it.

'Mrs Rosser, I'm Detective Superintendent Dixon,' he said, warrant card in hand.

'Come in, come in. I know who you are.'

They followed her into the living room, Mrs Rosser expertly positioning her wheelchair next to the fire, just where an armchair would have been. 'Let me switch that off,' she said, reaching for the TV remote control on the table next to her.

Everything within reach; apart from the wheelchair, it was a mirror image of Deirdre Baxter's front room. And Michael Allam's for that matter.

'Poor old Deirdre.' Mrs Rosser dropped the TV remote into her lap and gave a sad smile. 'Living in Berrow; not gone far from the old place then. Not that it's there any more. They knocked it down and put houses on it. Lovely old building. Such memories.'

'You're selling up?'

'Going into a care home near my daughter in Tavistock. Funny isn't it, I spend my entire working life in a boarding school, and now, at the end, I'm going back to a boarding school. That's what it feels like anyway.'

Louise was perched on the edge of the sofa, her notebook open on her knee.

'I just hope there's someone to talk to,' continued Mrs Rosser. 'You worry that everyone's got dementia in these places.'

'You've been to see it, presumably?' asked Dixon.

'My daughter has.' There was resignation in the old lady's voice – to her fate.

Dixon decided that a change of subject was called for. 'Tell me about Deirdre Baxter.'

'Deirdre was lovely. We worked together for . . . must be thirty-five years. Thirty certainly. Right up until St C's closed down in 1992. She was maths and science and I was English and history. She did hockey, and I was netball. We were roughly the same age, had a lot in common, but lost touch eventually, you know how it is.' She was rummaging for a paper handkerchief stuffed up her sleeve. 'We met for lunch occasionally, then it was Christmas cards, then we got too old for that even. You can live too long,' she said, dabbing the corner of her eye with the tissue.

It was a thought that had occurred to Dixon.

'You're still at that age when you think it'll never happen to you. I thought that.' She sighed. 'Then you wake up one day and, all of a sudden, it has. Still, at least I can look back on my working life and feel nothing but happiness. Will you be able to say the same?' She fixed Dixon with a steely glare, the fire still burning brightly in her eyes.

'It's not a question to which I have applied my mind.' A rehearsed answer for batting away awkward questions, but Dixon hesitated. 'And I dread to think what might happen if I did.'

'You were telling us about Mrs Baxter,' said Louise, clearly feeling that her intervention was necessary.

And it was.

'Yes, of course. Like I say, maths and science. Then there was the ballroom dancing. That's how she knew Mr Allam.'

'Ballroom dancing?'

'It sounds a bit daft now, I know, but we used to organise dancing lessons in the gym at Naish House. Mr Allam would bring the boys over from St Joseph's and there'd be an hour of waltzing and what have you. It was a life skill, useful for them to learn. And the thinking at the time was that it would be good for the boys and girls to mix a bit, under supervision, you understand. These were ten- and eleven-year-olds, remember.'

'How often was this?'

'Weekly, I think. We'd see them at church too. Every Sunday morning we'd take the girls down to St Andrew's and the boys from St Joseph's would be there, sometimes with Mr Allam. You'd see them walking crocodile-fashion along Berrow Road.'

The whole of the wall behind the television was taken up with framed photographs, some black and white, but mostly colour; grainy all the same, which gave away their age. Various school photographs, the girls lined up outside the school; several of hockey matches on the beach, netball in a gym, school plays.

'The older you get, the more time you have to spend thinking about the past,' said Mrs Rosser, watching Dixon examining the pictures.

Time for another change of subject. 'How well did you know Michael Allam?'

'Not very well. He was always "Mr", never "Michael". It was a professional relationship. Nothing more.'

'What about Deirdre Baxter?'

'The same, as far as I'm aware. He was married anyway, I think, if that's what you're asking?'

'And there's no possibility that Deirdre and Michael had a relationship without you knowing?'

'Yes, it's possible, I suppose.'

'Would she have told you if they were seeing each other?'

'Possibly; possibly not. Maybe we weren't as close as I thought? Who knows, after all this time?'

'But you never saw anything that gave you reason to think they might have been?'

'No. I'd have asked her outright, if I had.' Mrs Rosser gave an embarrassed grin. 'I could be a bit of a nosy devil, back then.'

'Where were you living at the time?'

'I started off in rooms in the school, but when I got married we lived in a house on the Berrow Road.'

Dixon lifted a framed picture off the wall, a black and white photograph of the cast of what looked like a pantomime, judging by the costumes. Boys and girls in it too, definitely.

'That was a joint production of *Aladdin*,' said Mrs Rosser.

He checked the picture again, noticing the lamp this time.

'Maybe 1978, or something like that. The date will be on the back of the photograph, if it's important,' continued Mrs Rosser. 'I directed it – jointly with their English teacher, Brian Laparge, from memory.'

'Do you recall a production of *Old King Cole*?'

'No.' Mrs Rosser shook her head. 'I started at St C's in 1964, so it might have been before my time, I suppose.'

Dixon was hanging the picture back on the wall. 'A girl is said to have fallen off the stage and broken her neck.'

'That's a myth,' replied Mrs Rosser. 'It was supposed to have been the stage in the old gym at St Joseph's – it's a care home now and the gym was knocked down to make way for more accommodation. I heard the story several times, but it wasn't true.'

'A ghost story?'

'The older children used to tell it to the younger ones, just to scare them. This was St Joseph's, you understand, not St C's, but I heard it when we were there for *Aladdin*. St Joseph's hadn't gone co-ed by then, so if it happened it would have been one of our girls and I would certainly have heard about it, even if it was before my time. We had one girl, many years before I got there, die in a horse riding accident, and I knew about that.'

'And there were no rumours about Deirdre and Michael Allam.'

'There were certainly no rumours at St C's that Deirdre was having an affair. There may have been at St Joseph's that *he* was having an affair, for all I know.'

Dixon looked at Louise and nodded in the direction of the door.

'Can I ask a question before you go?' asked Mrs Rosser.

'Of course.'

'How were they killed? It didn't say on the television news and your colleague didn't mention it when she rang.'

'They were both strangled, I'm sorry to say,' replied Dixon.

'Am I in danger?'

'We've certainly got no reason to believe so, but then I would have said the same about Deirdre and Michael Allam if you'd asked me forty-eight hours ago.'

'I'll get my daughter to come and fetch me, in that case. She did offer.'

◆　◆　◆

'Doing well for ninety-four,' said Louise, as they walked up the short drive to Dixon's Land Rover. 'Mind is still sharp. I'm not sure how much further her evidence takes us, though.'

'It tells us that Deirdre and Michael did know each other, and quite well over a long period of time.'

'Yeah, but she was adamant the relationship was purely professional.'

'And how would she have known if it wasn't?' replied Dixon. 'If they were determined to keep it a secret.'

'I'm glad she's got somewhere to go. I'll get uniform to keep an eye on her this afternoon, till her daughter gets here. Did you notice she had no puzzle books or crosswords?'

'Mind seems sharp enough without them,' said Dixon, opening the Land Rover door. 'Let's get over to Bradford Abbas. Sarah's meeting us there with the notice Thomas Fowler's son needs to sign for the exhumation.'

Chapter Eleven

Sarah was waiting for them when Dixon and Louise arrived outside Thomas Fowler's house in Bradford Abbas, her silver Fiesta parked in the middle of two spaces in the residential street.

'Shall I get her to move forward a bit?' asked Louise.

'Don't bother.' Dixon pulled on the handbrake, leaving the back end of the Land Rover sticking out of the drive, blocking the pavement.

'This is the notice of application and a copy of the petition,' Sarah said, hardly giving Dixon a chance to get out of the driver's seat, which was difficult enough being hemmed in by a hedge. 'There's a second copy for him to sign to confirm he's happy with the exhumation. The drafts have gone to the chancellor by email as well.'

'Shall I wait here?' asked Louise, leaning across from the passenger seat.

'The more, the merrier,' replied Dixon. He flicked through the papers before slotting them back in the envelope.

'You've come mob-handed.' Thomas Fowler's son was a small man, balding with long hair at the sides. He looked as if there was a strong wind behind him; either that or he'd just stuck his fingers in an electrical socket. He was holding the front door open. 'Are you here to arrest me?'

'I didn't mention why we needed to see him, I'm afraid, Sir,' whispered Sarah.

'Shall we talk inside, Mr Fowler,' said Dixon.

'Yes, of course,' replied Fowler, although it hadn't been a question.

'You've driven down from Maidenhead?'

'Yes, but I'll stay a couple of days now I'm here, and use the opportunity to clear some more junk to the tip. Pops was bit of a hoarder, as you can see.'

A small cottage, but it looked more like the inside of a removal van – a full one.

'There's room in here.' Fowler turned sideways and squeezed through a gap that turned out to be a door.

Dixon followed, Louise and Sarah behind him, finding Fowler leaning back against the kitchen sink.

'I started with the kitchen and the spare bedroom,' he said. 'Gives me somewhere to eat and sleep when I'm staying here. Now' – he folded his arms – 'what's this all about?'

'It's your father we need to talk to you about,' said Dixon.

'I saw you on the news, didn't I? Do you think my father was another victim of this . . .' Fowler was sucking his teeth. 'That's impossible.'

'Difficult,' replied Dixon. 'But not impossible. When did he go into the care home?'

Louise and Sarah frowned at each other.

'End of September. He had one last summer here, but it was getting too much for him really, so we got him into Lower Ham House. The garden was all over the place. I had to get people in.'

'Tell me about his death.'

'I got a call from the care home one night to say they'd found him. Someone had been in earlier to check on him, but they'd thought he was asleep and just left him. It wasn't until he didn't go down to have supper that they checked him again, and that wasn't until about nine or so. Useless bloody lot, and you wouldn't believe how much it cost.' Fowler looked up sharply. 'God, you're asking to dig him up, aren't you?'

'There was no post mortem done.'

'He was nearly ninety.'

'But otherwise in good health?'

'I suppose. I saw him the weekend before and he seemed fine. My wife and I came down on the Sunday and took him out for lunch. He wasn't on any medication, which is pretty damn good for someone of that age; a bit forgetful, perhaps, and frail. He was starting to lose his balance and then he'd topple over, hit things on the way down. I'd got called to Yeovil Hospital a couple of times, so we decided enough was enough.'

'So, it's fair to say his death wasn't expected.'

'Not imminently, no.'

Dixon tried a comforting smile. 'His body will be taken to Musgrove Park Hospital, where a Home Office pathologist will perform a post mortem.'

'And then he'll be reburied?'

'If no evidence of foul play is found then he'll be reinterred at the earliest opportunity in the family plot.'

'What if he was murdered?'

'Then his body will need to be retained, pending a prosecution. There may need to be a further post mortem too, if the defence insists.'

'Hardly resting in peace, is it?'

'All I can say is, if my father had been murdered, I'd want justice for him,' replied Dixon. 'I'd want to know who did it and why.'

'And you'll be able to tell me that?'

'At the moment we have two victims, both retired teachers from schools in Burnham-on-Sea, one from St Joseph's and the other from St Christopher's. There's evidence they knew each other and we're exploring various lines of enquiry on that basis. If your father was a victim, Mr Fowler, then it changes everything – *possibly* changes everything.'

'I don't think Pops ever went to Burnham.'

'How long was he a lift engineer?'

'He was in the army for a while, got to regimental sergeant major, left when he was about forty or so, then got the job with Kone. Stayed there until he retired, so twenty-plus years.'

'Did he know a Deirdre Baxter or a Michael Allam?'

'They're not names I ever heard him mention. Let me check his address book, it's in the other room.'

Sarah looked puzzled, but waited until Fowler had left the kitchen. 'How did you know he'd gone into a care home, Sir?' she asked.

'It's on the death certificate, under "place of death".'

'There's nothing in his address book under B or A,' said Fowler, thumbing through the pages of a small red book when he reappeared in the kitchen.

'May we?' asked Dixon, his hand outstretched, passing the book to Louise in one motion when Fowler placed it in his hand.

'Can we keep it?' she asked.

'I will get it back?'

'Yes,' replied Dixon.

'I'm guessing you need my permission for this exhumation then?' asked Fowler.

'Your father is buried in the churchyard at St Mary's, which is consecrated ground. We have to apply for a faculty under ecclesiastical law, and notice has to be given to the next of kin.' Nothing like a bit of legal jargon to move the subject on quickly.

'There's only me,' said Fowler. 'I just can't believe anyone would want to kill my old man.' Tears were collecting in the corner of his eyes as the full realisation that his father might have been murdered hit home. 'Why?'

'We don't know, Sir. Yet.'

Fowler's back straightened – by resolve hopefully, thought Dixon.

'Do I have to sign something?'

'A copy of the notice of petition. My colleague has the papers,' replied Dixon, turning to Louise. 'While you're doing that, could I see your father's belongings, perhaps the stuff he took with him to the care home?'

'It's mostly gone, I'm afraid. His clothes weren't even good enough for the charity so they went in the bin. There were puzzle books and magazines, but they went in the recycling.'

'Any photographs?'

'I've got the family albums at home. Sorry.'

'You've got to ring that bloke in London after four o'clock, don't forget, Sir,' Sarah had said, just before she had sped off in her Fiesta. 'I'll text you his name and number when I get back to Express Park.'

Now Dixon and Louise were sitting in his Land Rover in the gravel car park in front of Lower Ham House, lights on inside even though it wasn't quite dark yet.

A concrete ramp up to the front door; another one to a side entrance to what looked like a new annexe. Dixon could just about make out piano music and singing as he slid out of his Land Rover into the drizzle.

'Something to look forward to, hey, Sir,' said Louise.

A wave of his warrant card got them through the locked front door when a carer finally answered the doorbell, Dixon flicking back through the pages of the visitors' book while he waited for the manager. There were several entries for the fourth of December, none visiting Thomas Fowler.

'Can I help you?' The voice sounded nervous, but then perhaps it was just his new rank. Dixon had noticed that – the higher his rank, the more nervous people became.

'We're making enquiries into the death of Thomas Fowler,' he said.

'He wasn't with us long, sadly.'

The faint smell of stale urine reached him as he followed the manager along the corridor to her office, formal introductions along the way. Jenny, as she insisted on being called, was wearing a red sweatshirt over her carer's uniform, a large iPhone sticking out of her back pocket.

'Who found Mr Fowler?'

'Elena. She's from Romania. She came and got me and we called the doctor.' Jenny closed the door of her small office. 'It's not an altogether unusual event in a place like this.'

Dixon handed her the visitors' book. 'Can you account for all these visitors on the fourth of December?'

'No one came to see Thomas. Er, that's Lynn, she was visiting her mother. That's Mr Fellows visiting John Jackson. I know Mr Fellows, he's a local solicitor. I don't know who that is.' She turned the book to face Dixon and pointed at an entry. 'I don't know who April Smith is. It says she's visiting Doris, but she's certainly not a relative or friend – that I know of anyway.'

'Can you find out who let this person in?' asked Dixon. 'They must've rung the bell and been let in by someone.'

'I'll check the duty roster for the day, see who was in,' said Jenny, stepping back to open a filing cabinet.

'Do residents ever answer the door?'

'Some do. Some have dementia, which is why we keep it locked, but we have a few who are able to do it. We ask them not to, but they still do it,' she said, with a shrug. 'Here we are. Yeah, we've got a couple who aren't in today.'

'Leave it for now,' said Dixon. 'We'll confirm if we need the information.'

'Which room was he in?' asked Louise.

'Top of the stairs, on the right.' Jenny frowned. 'Sorry, are you saying someone came in here and killed Tom?'

'Possibly, yes,' replied Dixon. 'We'll be exhuming his body for a post mortem, although that is highly confidential.'

'I understand,' said Jenny, taking a deep breath. 'But no one signed in to see Thomas that day.'

'Would a member of staff check what a visitor had written in the book?'

'No, almost certainly not. They'd just tell them to sign in and then point them in the right direction.'

'What about asking for ID?'

'No, not if they explained who they were and who they were visiting.'

'So, they could write any old rubbish in the book, pick a name at random from other visits further up the page – Doris, for example – and they're in.' Dixon sighed. 'Does anyone show them out?'

'No. There's a code to get out, but it's on the wall. It's just to stop the dementia patients, really.'

'What about CCTV?'

'There's some in the entrance lobby, but we only keep it for thirty days, I'm afraid.'

◆ ◆ ◆

'You drive, Lou,' Dixon said, lobbing his car keys to her over the bonnet. 'I've got to ring the Worshipful Raymond Lodge KC.'

'Where to?'

'Express Park.' He managed to put his telephone call off ten minutes by flicking through Thomas Fowler's address book, not that he recognised any of the names. Some of the phone numbers were disguised pin numbers – obvious even to the untrained eye – unless he really did know people called Lloyd and Barclay. It was possible.

Dixon checked his phone; a full signal, so it was now or never.

'You want a faculty for exhumation, I gather?' said Lodge, introductions having been made by the telephone receptionist.

'Yes, Sir,' replied Dixon.

'There's a presumption that a Christian burial is permanent, the final resting place; it's a high hurdle to get over and you need to satisfy the court there are special circumstances giving me a good and proper reason to make an exception. Usually—'

'Usually you wouldn't have two confirmed murder victims, if I may say so, Sir,' interrupted Dixon. 'You also wouldn't have a potential serial killer on the loose and a senior police officer telling you that the deceased might very well be the first victim.' If ever there was a time to be bandying those words about, it was now. 'I need to catch whoever is killing these elderly people, and I need to do it before I find myself having to explain to another family that their beloved grandmother or grandfather is dead.'

'I've seen a draft of the petition. He was in a care home, this chap, according to the death certificate.'

'He was, Sir, but the eyewitness evidence we have at the moment is that the last person to see Deirdre Baxter in her own home was dressed in an occupational therapist's uniform. I'm sure you will appreciate that if that is right, he or she would have had no difficulty gaining access to a care home.'

'The cause of death is given as old age.'

'That just means the doctor had no real idea what killed Thomas.'

'Somewhat harsh, perhaps.'

'There were no suspicious circumstances, Sir. No one had any reason to believe anything untoward had gone on and, consequently, no referral was made to the coroner.'

'Explain to me the urgency. In the ordinary course of events we'd have a hearing, although I couldn't fit that in until the end of next month.'

'We're trying to find a serial killer, Sir.' Dixon's voice was taut, trying to hide his rising frustration. 'We need to stop him or her before they kill again. It really is as simple as that.'

'Yes, of course. Has the son consented?'

'He has, Sir. A copy of the notice duly endorsed will be sent over to you with the petition.'

'And the coroner's direction, I hope.'

'Yes, Sir.'

'When do you plan to perform the exhumation, assuming I grant the faculty?'

'Immediately, if we can. As soon as it gets dark.'

'All right. There clearly is a need to establish the true cause of the deceased's death; necessary in justice to the deceased and his family. Get the completed papers to me straight away and you can take it that I've granted the faculty based on this telephone call and the emailed drafts.'

'Thank you, Sir.'

Chapter Twelve

'That's all we need.'

They were sitting in the corner of the Rose and Crown in Bradford Abbas, the half an hour spent on the phone, lining up the various teams for the exhumation, coinciding with opening time. They had already been standing by, but it would be at least another hour until everybody arrived: Scientific Services, Roger Poland and the mortuary van, the gravediggers, the vicar too – prayers were an essential requirement, apparently.

Dixon was scrolling through local news reports of the investigation, the phrase 'serial killer' cropping up several times, despite it having been denied at the press briefing.

'Journalist at three o'clock,' continued Louise. 'Standing at the bar. It's that tosser from the *Bridgwater Mercury*. And he's got a photographer with him.'

The foot-long zoom lens slung over a shoulder was a bit of a giveaway. That and the huge flash mounted on top of the camera.

'He'll flog the story to the nationals.'

'Someone's tipped him off,' said Dixon. He took a swig of beer and stood up. 'Let's go and see what he's got to say for himself.'

Warren Hugget, whose every question at press conferences seemed designed to embarrass the police in general, and Dixon in particular. An old green waxed jacket, the pockets torn open, matching waxed flat cap, jeans and wellington boots. The photographer was wearing what looked like golf waterproofs and a wide-brimmed leather hat. They kept their backs to Dixon as he approached, but they knew full well he was there.

'You're a long way from home,' said Dixon, placing his pint on the bar next to them. He didn't use Hugget's name for the simple reason he didn't want him to think he knew it. 'What's the going rate for a story like this?'

Smug grins from the pair of them. 'Now, Inspector – sorry, *Superintendent*,' replied Hugget, 'you don't expect me to give up my source.'

'No. I just asked how much it cost you.'

'Thinking of getting in on the act?'

Dixon waited.

'Five hundred quid, if you must know.'

'If you'd asked, I'd have told you free of charge.'

'Really?' Hugget thought he'd try his luck. 'Whose body is it you're exhuming then?'

'I'm not going to reveal that unless and until foul play has been confirmed,' replied Dixon. 'What I can tell you is we suspect the deceased is indeed a third victim, but we won't know for sure until a post mortem has been carried out overnight. Until then you'll just be publishing speculation.'

'We do that all the time, mate. Ah, right on cue.' Hugget was watching Roger Poland shaking off his umbrella in the entrance lobby. 'What about his age, can you tell me that?'

'No.'

'So, you're not actually going to tell me anything I don't already know, are you?'

'Beer, Roger?' Dixon asked, turning to Poland.

'What about the threats?' demanded Hugget. 'The "publish and I'll run you out of town" stuff I usually get from you lot.'

'Would it make a difference?'

'No, it bloody well wouldn't.'

'Thought not.'

'Let's go over to the graveyard, Warren,' said the photographer. 'It's bound to be a recent burial and there can't be that many.'

Hugget finished his drink in one gulp and slammed his glass down on the bar. 'Good idea, mate.'

Actually, it wasn't, thought Dixon, but he wasn't going to tell them there was no gravestone in place yet. 'Are you serving food?' he asked the barman, when Poland's pint was placed on the bar.

◆ ◆ ◆

'No bloody gravestone,' muttered Hugget. 'Ha-bloody-ha.'

Dixon was standing under the lychgate at the entrance to the graveyard and hadn't noticed Hugget sidling up to him until it was too late.

'You never asked,' he said.

'The questions I have asked, you haven't answered.'

'Occupational hazard. You get used to it.' Dixon was watching the photographer leaning on the wall, filming video footage on his camera, not that it would show much from that range, apart from a Scientific Services tent lit from the inside by arc lamps, the gravestones in the vicinity covered in bubble wrap. Uniformed officers had arrived and were keeping spectators, and the press, at a suitable distance.

Poland was still in the pub. After all, there was no point getting wet until the gravediggers had done their bit.

'Well, we're going to run with the story anyway,' said Hugget. 'And if it's not another victim you're going to look a bit of a wally, aren't you?'

Dixon spun round, but that turned out to be Hugget's parting shot, the journalist now jogging across the road to his car.

The grass was long and wet, Dixon using the light on his phone as he weaved his way through the gravestones from the sanctuary of the tarmac path. Lights were on in the windows of the houses that backed on to the graveyard, several people visible, one looking through a pair of binoculars, his view partially obscured by a large weeping willow that stood guard over the dead.

Rain was falling, the drops visible in the glow from the tent, the sound of digging just carrying over the rain as Dixon approached.

It was his first exhumation and there was a lot at stake – not just the risk of looking like a bit of a wally, as Hugget had put it. If Thomas Fowler really was another victim, then all lines of enquiry thus far had been red herrings. All bets were off; it was back to square one and any other cliché Dixon could think of.

He stepped inside the tent, Louise watching the gravediggers at work, a large and growing pile of earth on a tarpaulin next to Thomas Fowler's grave.

Donald Watson, the senior Scientific Services officer, was there, sitting on an aluminium box. 'It'll suit you better if he's not a victim, I suppose, otherwise it's back to the drawing board, isn't it.'

And there was another.

'Where's the vicar?' Dixon asked.

'Been and gone,' replied Watson. 'Said a prayer before these lads started work and then legged it. He was only here a couple of minutes.'

One of the gravediggers stopped for a rest, leaning on his spade. 'Do you want us to fill it in when you've got him out or shall we leave it?'

'Leave it a couple of days,' replied Watson. 'Depending on the results of the post mortem, we may be releasing him for reburial straight away, or we may not.'

'Oh, right.'

'We'll let you know one way or the other tomorrow.'

The rain was falling harder now if anything, a trickle running under the side of the tent and into the grave. The noise of the water on the outside of the tent was louder too, punctuated by drips from the overhanging branches of an oak tree. And the spade cutting into the soil.

Dixon's phone buzzed in his pocket; a text from Poland.

How much longer?

He was tapping out a reply, only to be interrupted abruptly by the hollow thud of a spade hitting wood.

'That's him.' The gravedigger straightened up, one hand in the small of his back. 'Wasn't too deep, because his wife's underneath him.'

The gravestone plinth was still there, at the head of the grave, but the stone had gone, presumably to have Thomas Fowler's name added to his wife's.

Dixon deleted the message and tapped out another:

Reached coffin

Then watched the speech bubble, Poland typing something.

on way

Dixon stepped out into the rain and listened to the sounds all around him, the peace of the graveyard shattered by spades scraping the mud from a coffin lid, a mortuary trolley rattling along the path, phones ringing.

Someone was filming now from an upstairs window of one of the houses backing on to the graveyard, so he gestured to a uniformed officer.

'Yes, Sir.'

It turned out that pointing at the cameraman was enough, the curtains snapping shut.

'We'll open the coffin at Musgrove Park,' said Poland, striding along the path. 'No point in doing it here.'

'When will you do the post mortem?' asked Dixon.

'Straight away. That's what you want, isn't it?'

The gravediggers were using hand trowels to clear the earth away at both ends of the coffin as Dixon followed Poland back inside the tent. Then they placed straps underneath it and climbed out.

Dixon hesitated long enough to allow the mortuary assistants who had arrived to step forward and pick up the other ends of the straps.

'It's not been two months yet,' said Poland, his voice hushed as the coffin was slowly lifted out of the grave. 'So he shouldn't be too bad.'

It was placed in an even larger wooden box, then covered in a black sheet before being carried across to the trolley that had been left out on the path.

Dixon looked into the grave expecting to see the wife's coffin, but there was just bare earth.

'The wife's collapsed ages ago,' said the gravedigger, spotting his curiosity. 'So we dig down far enough, but not too far, if you know what I mean.'

'If a journalist contacts you—'

'He already has,' interrupted the gravedigger, with a mischievous grin. 'We told him to get stuffed.'

◆ ◆ ◆

Dixon spotted the silver Ford Fiesta parked on the street when the convoy of vehicles turned into the car park at Musgrove Park Hospital. It pulled out behind him, and followed them round to the pathology department.

'Are we being followed?' asked Louise. She was looking over her shoulder, having spotted Dixon watching something in his rear view mirror.

'It's Sarah,' he said.

'Anxious to know whether she was right about Thomas Fowler, I suppose.'

'I'd have rung her.'

The mortuary van continued around to the back of the lab, Dixon parking next to Poland in his Volvo. Sarah parked on the other side of the car park, trying to keep out of the way, probably.

Louise shook her head. 'I'll go and get her.'

'We'll be a few minutes getting ready,' said Poland. 'We've got to get the coffin open and do the usual checks. I'll switch the coffee machine on for you.'

'What are you doing here?' Dixon asked, when Sarah appeared, hiding behind Louise almost.

'I wanted to come to the PM, if that's all right, Sir. I feel sort of *responsible* for him, really.'

'Of course you can come,' said Poland, smiling. 'The more, the merrier; keep the old boy company. We'll go this way, follow me.'

A side door, keys jangling.

Poland switched on the lights and then leaned over behind two vending machines, flicking switches on both.

'Coffee and nibbles,' he said. 'Give me ten minutes and I'll come and get you.'

'Did you get the papers off to the chancellor of the diocese?'

'The legal department did,' replied Sarah. 'Email and the originals by courier.'

Dixon was rummaging in his pockets for some change.

'I've got some cash,' offered Louise. 'Three coffees?'

Sarah was still looking sheepish. 'Mark went home at eight, Sir,' she said, trying not to blush. 'So I thought I'd come here.'

'Did he find anything on the cameras?'

'Nothing, I'm afraid. We've found lots of people who knew Deirdre Baxter and Michael Allam, but nothing to indicate why they've been murdered. Most people seem to have fond memories of them. Wish I could say the same about my teachers.'

'What about the ghost story?'

'Lots of former pupils at both schools remember that – remember being told that, I should say. One said he thought it happened in the nineteen-thirties, but couldn't tell us why he thought that.'

'So, we're no further forward.' Dixon was blowing the steam off a coffee Louise had handed him, trying to ignore a thin film of God knows what floating on the surface. Suddenly, mulled cider didn't seem quite so bad.

'We might end up further back, if Thomas Fowler really is a victim,' said Louise, handing a coffee to Sarah, the whirr of the machine behind her.

'I prefer to think of that as a step forward.' Dixon took a sip; the coffee really was as bad as it looked. 'Anything from Scientific?'

'Nothing yet, Sir,' replied Sarah.

'Did Jane go home and feed Monty?'

'She went about four.'

'Good.'

'Then came back about six.' Sarah grinned. 'Brought him with her and he's been asleep under her workstation in the incident room since then. Even growled at the ACC when he came for a nose around.'

'I trained him myself,' said Dixon, proudly.

'Ready when you are.' Poland was standing in the door leading to the pathology lab, dressed from head to toe in dark green, although his plastic apron was white, as were his wellington boots. 'We've got him on the slab, ready to go. Masks will be the order of the day, and there's a tub of Vicks VapoRub in the top drawer of the filing cabinet.'

Sarah looked nervously at Louise.

'Put a blob on your top lip, under your mask,' said Louise. 'It's for the smell.'

'Oh, right.'

'He's been embalmed, so he's not too bad,' said Poland, clearly trying to be helpful. 'Best to be on the safe side, though.'

Thomas Fowler was lying on his back, his body covered in a green sheet from his shoulders down. His face had a waxy sheen, a blackened nose, with red and purple blotches on his skin. Eyes closed, his mouth was open, the gums receding from his teeth.

'I thought we'd start with the bit you're interested in,' said Poland. 'I can do the rest of the PM after that.'

'Thank you.' Dixon was standing behind Louise and Sarah now, figuring it was his turn to use them as a shield.

Poland took hold of the very edge of Thomas Fowler's eyelid with a pair of tweezers and rolled it back, examining the underside with a magnifying glass. 'There's petechial haemorrhaging. Not much, but enough.'

'That means he's been strangled,' ventured Sarah.

'Not necessarily,' replied Poland. 'It means there's been a build-up of pressure in the head and the tiny little blood vessels burst. Strangulation is often the cause, but not everyone who exhibits petechial haemorrhaging has been strangled. And, as we know from

Deirdre Baxter, not everyone who has been strangled exhibits pete-chial haemorrhaging.'

'So, he hasn't been strangled?' Sarah again.

'Let's see, shall we?' Poland picked up a scalpel.

Dixon had seen the same incision on Deirdre Baxter's body and knew what was coming, turning away when Poland tilted Thomas Fowler's head back.

'Oh, shit,' mumbled Sarah, under her breath.

'The cartilage in the neck is ossified, as you would expect in a person of this age,' said Poland. He was attaching clips to the flaps of skin either side. 'The hyoid bone is intact, just as it was with the other two victims.'

Dixon waited.

'Cricoid bone is cracked; front and sides, just like the other two.' Poland straightened up. 'He was strangled. Nearly got away with this one, too. Well done, you,' he said, pointing at Sarah with the scalpel.

'Thanks, Roger,' said Dixon. He was already opening the door of the lab. 'I owe you a curry.'

'It's nearly midnight, for heaven's sake. I thought at least two!'

An exchange of text messages had saved Dixon a visit to Express Park and he got home just before one in the morning to find Jane asleep on the sofa. He had parked in the pub car park and crept across the road, managing to get his key in the back door lock before Monty woke up.

No barking this time, though; it was as if the dog didn't want to wake Jane up either.

Dixon opened the back door and slipped on the dog's lead before tiptoeing into the living room and standing over Jane. A black and white movie was still on pause – *Mrs Miniver*, by the looks of things – the light from the screen enough to illuminate Jane's chest rising and falling as she slept.

Her skin looked pale, or perhaps it was just the light?

A police officer, doing her duty, working long hours. Exhausting for most, Dixon included, but Jane was six months pregnant.

She was eligible to go on maternity leave; they'd talked about it before and would do so again, first thing in the morning. And this time, she'd bloody well have to listen.

Would she, bollocks.

He closed the back door as silently as he could and set off along the road. It had stopped raining and Monty was running ahead, off the lead, but the dog knew which way to go, turning left up the narrow lane to the knoll, every now and then stopping to sniff something on the grass verge or in the hedge.

Three dead.

No nearer finding a motive.

A headline plastered across the homepage of the *Bridgwater Mercury* website – *Police Exhume Possible Third Victim.*

No doubt it had gone national by now, although Dixon hadn't checked.

He'd had better days.

And he'd need to be updating the Policy Log in the morning, documenting the senior investigating officer's decision-making process. Charlesworth was probably checking it hourly.

He looked to the west as he climbed the knoll, the lights of the vast building site at Hinkley Point twinkling through the gloom.

Actually, it wasn't all bad news. Perhaps Sarah finding Thomas Fowler was a good thing? There were so many connections between Deirdre Baxter and Michael Allam, even a regional task force could disappear up its own backside investigating them all.

But what was their connection to Thomas Fowler?

That could narrow it down a bit, and be the key to unlocking the whole thing.

Possibly.

Hopefully.

Dixon had his phone in his hand, using the light to inspect what was left of something Monty had been eating, when Jane's text arrived.

> *Where are you? Jx*

> An easy one to answer: *Up the lane. Monty's been eating horse shit. Go to bed. Nx*

> *Is Fowler another victim? Jx*

> *Yes.*

> *Fuck.*

> *We need to talk about maternity leave in the morning*

He added a smiley face to that one, not that it would do any good.

> *Yeah, right*

Chapter Thirteen

'No Jane?'

'We were going to have a chat about maternity leave this morning and, as you can see, she's buggered off.'

Louise was standing in the kitchen at Dixon's cottage, watching him eat a bowl of cereal. 'She won't go with all this going on. I wouldn't.'

'It's not all bad news, though,' he said, with a cheeky grin. 'It means I can have a sprinkle of sugar on my cornflakes, with the diabetes police safely out of the way.'

'She'll probably dust the bowl for prints if you leave i☺n the dishwasher.'

'I'll wash it up before we go.'

There was a reason Louise was standing in his kitchen at seven-thirty in the morning, and no doubt she would get round to telling him what it w☺ in her own time. Dixon flicked on the kettle. 'Coffee?' he asked, through a mouthful of cornflakes.

'We haven't really got time, Sir,' replied Louise. 'You have seen your messages, haven't you?'

Perhaps he should have checked his phone? It was still in the pocket of his jacket, hanging over the back of the dining chair, and had been there since he'd got back from his walk with Monty at two in the morning.

Louise took the hint. 'A care home over at Shepton Mallet had an unusual visitor yesterday, early evening. A person claiming to be an occupational therapist visited one of their residents; signed the visitors' book as June Jones. The night duty manager rang late last night, said she'd hang on for us this morning.'

'Someone has a sense of humour,' said Dixon, rinsing his bowl under the tap. 'April Smith when she visited Thomas Fowler and June Jones this time. *Alias Smith and Jones*.'

'I've heard of *Alas Smith and Jones*, but not *Alias*.'

'It was an American TV series in the seventies. Wild West. Do we have another victim?'

'That's the funny thing. She visited a Mr George Sampson, aged eighty-seven, and didn't kill him.'

'Let's go and find out why then, shall we?'

'Lucerne House, it is.' Louise was following the satnav on her phone. 'Up here on the right.'

'There's CCTV covering the car park,' said Dixon, spotting the camera as he turned into the gravelled entrance. He parked next to the patrol car, two uniformed officers visible in the lobby of the care home. 'Are Scientific standing by?'

'Donald Watson said he could get here for about ten, if we need him.'

One of the uniformed officers saw them walking up the ramp to the front door and pressed the buzzer, the door opening automatically.

'We've preserved the CCTV images, Sir,' she said. 'And this is the duty manager, Tammy Davies.'

'I saw it on the telly, then Faith said she'd let someone in, so I thought I'd better let you know. Everyone's fine, though, so I'm probably wasting your time.'

'Is Faith still here?' asked Dixon. The door had closed behind him, taking the fresh air with it, leaving only the faint smell of urine and bleach.

'She's stayed, in case you wanted to speak to her. She was on duty all night, so is probably having a nap in the staff room.'

The entrance lobby opened into a television lounge, various elderly people slumped in chairs; some asleep, none actually watching the film. It was a good one too – *A Night to Remember* – far better than the remake.

An upright piano was standing against the far wall, double doors leading out into the garden via another ramp; a large noticeboard covered in pictures of the residents with party hats on.

That lyric again. Dixon could hear the line, see Roger Daltrey belting it out even, but couldn't remember the name of the song.

Tammy noticed him looking all around. 'The only camera is the one outside, I'm afraid.'

'Can I see the footage?'

Black and white; grainy. The same car. A night vision camera, maybe, but it was not a good one, even with the light streaming from the care home windows. That said, whoever it was had the hood of their coat up anyway, so a view of the face was not going to happen, but it was raining so that was to be expected, perhaps.

'Faith's your best bet,' said Tammy. 'She actually spoke to her. The staff room's just here.'

Slightly bleary-eyed, but that was to be expected as well. Faith had changed into jeans and a pullover after her shift and was clinging on to a mug of strong black coffee as if her life depended on it. Straggly dark hair, pale complexion, bags under her eyes; it must've been a long night.

'I didn't get your names,' said Tammy, intending to make the introductions, but realising she couldn't.

121

'That's the one that was on the telly, Tam,' said Faith. 'You wanted to give him a good—'

'Yes, thank you.' Tammy blushed.

'Tell me about this visitor, June Jones,' said Dixon, glaring at Louise, who was chuckling to herself.

'It was about seven, I suppose. The doorbell went and there was this OT standing under the canopy.'

'She said she was an OT?'

'Not as such, but she had the uniform on under her coat. And an ID card on a lanyard. It looked legit, so I let her in.'

'What did she look like?'

'Dark hair, curly, short. She put her hood back when I let her in. Black glasses. A bit of make-up, maybe. I didn't take too much notice, I'm afraid. She said she was here to see George, signed in the visitors' book, then I pointed her in the direction of his room and left her to it.'

'And nothing about it struck you as odd?'

Faith was standing in the doorway of Tammy's office, elderly residents walking past in the corridor behind her. 'I thought a visit from an OT was unusual, because we provide whatever a resident needs, but apart from that, not really.'

'Would you be able to identify this person again?'

'Maybe.'

Dixon turned to Louise. 'Let's get a sketch artist over here to see Faith.'

'Can I go home and get some sleep first?' asked Faith, over a long yawn.

'We've got three dead and whoever is doing it clearly has no intention of stopping.'

'I'll make myself another coffee.'

George Sampson's room was in the ground floor annexe. A long corridor with rooms either side, those at the front with bay windows looking out over the car park, the ones at the back with doors out to private patios and more expensive, no doubt.

All of the doors were open, giving the residents no privacy, but it meant that Dixon could see through to the back garden. Well maintained, a raised pond in the middle, the fountain switched off.

Tammy stopped outside an open door, 'George Sampson' inscribed on a small nameplate.

'He's a lovely man,' she said. 'Some of them get angry, violent even, and you wouldn't believe the language, but he just sits there quiet as a mouse, watching his television.'

'He has dementia?' asked Dixon.

Tammy gave a sad smile. 'George?' She tiptoed into his room, looking around the corner of the bathroom. 'There's someone to see you.'

The old man was sitting in an armchair on the other side of the bed, the television mounted on the wall above a chest of drawers opposite. Corduroys, a shirt open at the neck and a cardigan, a blanket sliding off his knees on to the floor.

He appeared fascinated by what was on the TV, watching it intently.

'He loves the crime dramas,' whispered Tammy. 'And when you've got dementia, there's no such thing as repeats.' She picked up the remote control and paused the programme just as Hercule Poirot was about to reveal the killer's identity. George looked up, bemused rather than cross. 'There's someone here to see you, George.'

'My daughter came to see me yesterday,' he said.

Tammy turned to Dixon and mouthed, 'His daughter lives in New Zealand.'

'Who are you?'

'They're police officers, George.'

The old man reached out and took Louise's hand. 'Are you Alison?'

'Your daughter's not here today,' said Tammy. 'This is a police officer.'

'What's Alison been up to?'

'It's not Alison. She's fine.' Tammy gave a beaming smile, trying to reassure the old man. 'She's coming to see you next month. Remember?'

A blank look.

'These officers want to talk to you about someone who came to see you yesterday.'

'I never get any visitors. I do wish my wife would come to see me more often.'

Dixon was standing at the chest of drawers, looking at the selection of family photographs on the top. And the small pile of DVDs, mostly old British war films: *The Cruel Sea*, *Sink the Bismarck!* and *The Bridge on the River Kwai* among them.

'Your wife died, George.' Tammy was holding the old man's hand now. 'She died before you came to live with us.'

'She could do more to help, but she's probably busy with the baby.'

Tammy reached across George and took a small photo album off the table next to him, where a cup of tea had long since gone cold. 'Who's this?' she asked, holding the album open at the first picture and pointing at a black and white image of a small boy in school uniform.

'Is it him?' George was pointing at Dixon.

'No, it's you, George,' said Tammy. 'When you were a boy.'

The old man squinted at the photograph, running the tip of his index finger softly over the image. 'Me?'

Dixon took the photograph album from Tammy and sat down on the edge of George's bed, next to the old man. 'You said your daughter came to see you yesterday.'

'She did.'

'Can you remember what she was wearing?'

The old man hesitated, his eyes welling up with tears of frustration.

'What did you talk about?'

'The old days. We always talk about the old days.'

'He doesn't remember the old days,' said Tammy, softly to Louise.

'Did you ever know a woman called Deirdre Baxter?'

'Is she my wife?' George was looking at Tammy quizzically.

'No, George, your wife's name was Edith,' Tammy said.

'What about Michael Allam?' asked Dixon.

'Is he my doctor?'

'That's Dr Morgan, George,' said Tammy, calmly.

'One last question then, George,' said Dixon. 'Does the name Thomas Fowler mean anything to you?'

The old man's eyes glazed over, the connection lost. Dixon watched him looking around the room, his gaze settling on the television, where Hercule Poirot was frozen in mid-sentence. 'Bridge,' George mumbled.

'That'll be *The Bridge on the River Kwai*. It's his favourite film. I'll put it on now for you, George.' Tammy opened a DVD case and took out a disc. 'Although he'll probably fall asleep in front of it, he usually does.'

'It was lovely to meet you, Mr Sampson,' said Dixon, shaking the old man's hand. 'Thank you for your help.'

'What shall I tell Scientific?' asked Louise, once they were back out in the corridor.

'There might be fingerprints, I suppose,' replied Dixon.

'There won't.' Faith had been hovering in the doorway while they spoke to George and was now loitering in the corridor. 'She was wearing latex gloves, which I thought was odd, come to think of it. She came in wearing them.'

'See what I mean about George?' Tammy spoke softly, anxious that the old man shouldn't hear. 'He's probably forgotten all about it already. Sometimes I can get him to recognise the people in those photographs. He'll say things like "That's my wife," but when you ask him her name, he can't remember. It's so sad.'

'Is his daughter really coming next month?' asked Louise.

'Oh yes. We never lie to them,' replied Tammy. 'She's a trooper, she really is. Comes for three weeks every year, even though she knows full well her father will have no idea who she is.'

'We'll need to take your visitors' book, please,' said Dixon, following Tammy along the corridor towards the front door.

'We will get it back?'

'In due course.'

Louise was on the phone behind him, ringing off as they turned the corner into the entrance lobby. 'I've told Scientific they're free to go elsewhere and the sketch artist will be here in half an hour.'

'We'll need statements from you, and Faith as well,' said Dixon.

'So you think it was the serial killer. Here, in my care home?' asked Tammy.

'I do,' replied Dixon.

'Why didn't she kill George, in that case?'

'There's no need, is there? Not if she's killing to keep a secret he can't remember anyway.'

126

Chapter Fourteen

The morning briefing had been put back to midday, the staff car park at Express Park almost full when Dixon arrived on the top floor just before eleven-thirty. He'd spotted Charlesworth's car in the visitors' car park and suspected an ambush. They waited, hoping for someone else to open the security door, but in the end Louise needed the loo and that was that.

If Louise was in, then so was Dixon, and Charlesworth would be on the prowl.

He got as far as the canteen.

'Ah, there you are, Nick.'

Dixon pretended not to hear.

'You haven't updated the Policy Log for quite some time. It's supposed to be an active record of the SIO's decision-making process.'

And that was the point. Dixon hadn't made any decisions. Yet.

'Would you like a cup of tea, Sir?' he asked, arriving at the front of the queue just as Charlesworth appeared at his elbow.

'No, thank you.' Charlesworth cleared his throat. 'Give it to him in a takeaway cup, please,' he said to the assistant pouring Dixon's tea. 'I'll be in meeting room two.'

'Yes, Sir.'

No Deborah Potter this time, although the press officer was there. Dixon sometimes wondered if Charlesworth and Vicky Thomas were joined at the hip.

'You had a journalist sniffing around the exhumation last night, I gather,' said Charlesworth, when Dixon sat down. 'Tipped off, I suppose. Not by one of us, I trust.'

'Certainly not by one of my team.'

'And the body is another murder victim?'

'Roger Poland has confirmed strangulation as the cause of death.'

'And three makes a serial killer,' said Vicky Thomas. 'It's not a good visual, someone running around killing old people in their own homes, and even care homes.'

'Look, Nick, I've spoken to my opposite number at Dorset. He has every confidence in you and your regional task force to clear this up.'

Dixon waited. He was enjoying watching Charlesworth squirm far too much to give him an easy way out.

'They're stretched as it is, in Dorset.'

'Aren't we all, Sir.'

'Well, quite. But the reality is there's going to be no reinforcements, not from that quarter anyway.'

'From which quarter then, Sir?'

'None, as it happens.' Charlesworth gave an apologetic shrug. 'I know, sixteen people is not where we'd like to be on an investigation of this size, but we are where we are.'

'And it is what it is, Sir,' said Dixon, with just a hint of sarcasm.

'Tell me about this morning.' Charlesworth had clearly decided a change of subject would get him off the hook.

'An old man with dementia at a care home in Shepton Mallet. She got in and left without killing him. She was wearing gloves, so there's nothing for Scientific and there'll be God knows how many people's DNA all over the place, so we can forget that.'

'Nothing to learn from that then,' said Vicky Thomas.

'On the contrary, we've learned a great deal. These victims are not being selected at random; they're being killed for a specific reason – a secret they share, a secret they're dying for. Except George Sampson, who can't remember it anyway.'

'So, his dementia saved his life,' said Charlesworth.

'Some might say it took it long ago, Sir,' muttered Dixon.

The briefing had not gone well, Dixon left wondering which groan was louder: the one that came when he told those assembled there'd be no help coming from Dorset, or the one that greeted the news that all of the witnesses would need to be reinterviewed, looking for a connection between Deirdre Baxter, Michael Allam, and now Thomas Fowler and George Sampson.

Mark Pearce wasn't a happy bunny either, another set of traffic cameras in Shepton Mallet to search, but at least the footage of the car outside the care home gave him a starting point. A couple more community support officers had come forward to offer their help too.

'There's only sixteen of us!'

Dixon wasn't entirely sure he recognised the voice, but he appreciated the sentiment. And it would be down to fifteen if and when he found the leak. One of the Devon lot had tipped Warren Hugget off that there was an exhumation going on, and he was going to make damn sure he found out who it was.

He was standing in front of the whiteboards, his arms folded tightly across his chest, when Jane appeared next to him.

'Where did you get to this morning?' he asked.

'Incident rooms don't run themselves, you know.'

'We need to have that chat about you going on maternity leave.'

'I can't yet.'

'Yes, you can. We checked the rules, remember? You get fifteen months in total, but a maximum of twelve after the baby's born, so you're supposed to go three months before your due date, which is now. The longer you leave it, the less time you'll get.'

'All right, all right. I'll go at the end of this case.'

'It might go on for months.'

'Then we'll take it a day at a time.'

Dixon was pushing his luck, he knew that. Jane could be stubborn and her fuse had been getting shorter the deeper she had got into her pregnancy. Not that they had ever fallen out. He knew the line, and that it kept moving.

'Just promise me you'll go home early today. Four o'clock at the latest. And get some sleep.'

'I will.'

'I'll put Monty in your car when I go off with Lou, then you'll have to take him home and feed him.'

'Where are you going with Lou?'

He could've thrown a dart at the whiteboards, blindfolded, for all the good it would do him. 'Do you know what, I have absolutely no idea. None whatsoever.'

'You'll get there,' said Jane. She had moved closer to him and was squeezing his hand, out of view of prying eyes. 'You always do.'

◆ ◆ ◆

'Just dropping my dog off at home, then I'll be back' had been a little white lie for the benefit of the Devon team. The rest of the regional task force had known exactly where he was going and it was his lunch hour, after all, if anyone was going to get all *jobsworth* about it.

Charlesworth was still on the prowl, although Dixon had managed to slip out of the security door when someone else had been coming in.

The tide was rolling in, but there was still enough beach, Monty out of the car in a flash and off down the steps before Dixon had even closed the back door of the Land Rover.

The water was lapping against the sea wall at Burnham but there was still bare sand to be had to the north, towards the lighthouse. Monty had gone that way anyway, never overly keen on getting his paws wet. Nobody about either, which was a bonus. There was usually a scream from at least one dog walker when they saw a large white Staffie charging down the steps.

A cold and wet day in late January, the only thing keeping Dixon's hands warm was the bag of chips. Lashings of salt and vinegar; grease and carbohydrate to keep his blood sugar levels up.

Three dead, and one spared because he had dementia.

The killer a woman.

The pace accelerating, the visit to George Sampson coming the evening after the second press conference, and no doubt there'd be more to come.

If she'd stopped at number one, she would, quite literally, have got away with murder. Thomas Fowler, murdered almost two months ago in his care home, buried without anyone even realising there had been foul play.

Old, so it was to be expected.

Dixon would have a quiet word with the doctor who had certified Fowler's cause of death, when this was all over. Or maybe it would be better coming from the coroner? Either way, someone needed to give his backside a bloody good kicking.

Never even touched Fowler's body. 'Nothing obvious. I'll put "old age",' with a dismissive shrug. Signed the certificate, left it on the bedside table and was in and out in under five minutes, according to the duty manager at the care home.

The duty doctor who'd gone to see Deirdre Baxter hadn't been much better, although he had waited for uniformed officers to arrive.

Dixon lobbed Monty's tennis ball along the sand, watching it roll down towards the water that was gradually filling up the muddy channel, the dog showing no interest in it whatsoever. Maybe this tennis ball launcher Jane had bought wasn't such a waste of time after all? At least he could pick up the ball without touching it. Always useful when you're eating your lunch at the same time, he thought, tucking the plastic thrower under his arm, the tennis ball safely in the cup, dripping mud and slime as he walked.

Jane was being a pain about her maternity leave. If she left it any longer she wouldn't get her full entitlement. There had been no argument this time when Dixon had told her she was running the incident room, so that was progress, perhaps, although Deborah Potter had just raised her eyebrows when Dixon discreetly enquired how Jane's last pregnancy risk assessment had gone.

He was getting quite good at interpreting what Jane meant when she said something, though, which was making life a little easier.

'We'll take it a day at a time,' actually meant: *If you think I'm going on maternity leave while there's a serial killer out there targeting old people in their own homes, then you can piss off.*

Life would be so much easier if people said what they really meant; there'd be nothing to interpret.

Or misinterpret.

He turned for the steps and started to run, Monty running alongside him, thinking it was a game.

Chapter Fifteen

Five missed calls and several text messages. One from Louise – *where are you* – in the middle of several from Jane asking much the same thing, but with the odd expletive thrown in for good measure.

Dixon was standing on the doorstep of Lucerne House, waiting for someone to come and let him in, Monty standing on the driver's seat of the Land Rover, his front paws up on the steering wheel, getting sand everywhere. Dixon had rung the doorbell twice and was tapping out a reply to Jane. It was either that or ring the bell again.

> *There are two bags of recycling on the bed in the spare room at Michael Allam's flat in Sidmouth. They need to be at Express Park when I get back pls Nx*
>
> *Get back from where?*
>
> *Shepton Mallet*

Jane was typing another message, he could tell that from the speech bubble, something along the lines of *what the bloody hell are you doing in Shepton Mallet*, probably, but the duty manager was opening the front door now, so Dixon dropped his phone into his inside jacket pocket.

'I need to see George Sampson again, please.'

'Er, yes, that's fine,' replied Tammy, quizzically. 'He's in his room, if you wouldn't mind signing in. You pinched the visitors' book, though, so you'll have to make do with that.'

Dixon had asked for the leather-bound visitors' book the day before, and it had been replaced by sheets of paper on a clipboard. 'Sorry about that,' he said. 'I'm guessing the dining room's empty at this time of day?'

'They'll all be back in their rooms by now.'

'Then if I could have him seated at a table for four, that would be ideal. And I'll need you and one other person as well.'

Tammy hesitated, turning away then back before thinking better of asking the obvious question. 'It's through there,' she said, pointing to an open door at the bottom of the stairs. 'I'll go and get him. And one other person?'

'Yes, please.'

It had the look of a school dining room, tables and chairs evenly spaced out, a tray of salt and pepper pots on a sideboard; a pile of board games on the large windowsill overlooking the front garden. Something with pastry and gravy had been lunch, judging by the splodges on the table, and the crumbs. It didn't smell half bad, either.

A woman wearing an apron was spraying, wiping down and laying the tables, ready for the evening meal.

'Not this one if you don't mind,' said Dixon. He had picked the table nearest the door, taking a chair from an adjacent table to make up the four. Then he sat down and waited.

'Let me just give it a wipe for you,' said the woman, sending the crumbs on to the carpet. 'I'll hoover when you've gone – don't worry, love.'

'Thank you.'

The television in the adjacent lounge was on, nice and loud, *The Ladykillers* entertaining the two elderly residents who weren't asleep in their armchairs. Dixon recognised the voices, Alec Guinness, Peter Sellers. Maybe a care home isn't so bad, he thought, if you get to sit around and watch old films all day?

Then George Sampson appeared at the far end of the corridor, walking with a frame, Tammy on one side of him, another carer Dixon didn't recognise on the other, holding the old man's elbow.

One step at a time; shuffling.

Dixon checked his phone, to hide his impatience more than anything, swiping away the text from Jane.

What are you doing in Shepton Mallet?

It was a good question, and the best answer he could come up with at the moment was clutching at straws. Not that he'd tell her that, he thought. Best to ignore the question, and if it turned out to be a dead end, no one need ever know.

'Sorry it took so long,' said Tammy. 'We had to change him.'

Dixon nodded his understanding, anxious not to embarrass George, although the exchange seemed to pass him by anyway.

'We could've used a wheelchair, I suppose, but the walking is good exercise for him.'

'It's fine.'

'Is it supper time?' asked the old man.

'No, George,' replied Tammy. 'This man has come to see you.'

'I haven't had my lunch yet.'

'Yes, you have, George. You had steak and kidney pie. Remember?'

George didn't. 'They don't feed you enough in here,' he said to Dixon. 'And what they do feed you is disgusting. I'd go to another restaurant, if you can. I won't be eating here again, I can assure you.'

They sat him down on the dining chair opposite Dixon, then Tammy sat down to Dixon's left, the other carer to his right.

'This is Jodie,' said Tammy.

George was looking at Dixon, a blank expression on his face; no hint of recognition or curiosity even. A clean pair of blue trousers, neatly ironed into a crease down the middle, a clean shirt, but the same cardigan, the pockets bulging with paper handkerchiefs. They'd even brushed his white hair.

'Do you need reading glasses, George?' asked Dixon.

'He doesn't,' said Tammy, her frown growing deeper by the second.

Dixon took a pack of playing cards from his pocket, placed it on the table in front of him and then slid it across to the old man.

'You deal, George.'

Tammy looked at Dixon and shook her head. 'I really don't think we should be putting him through—'

George reached out slowly, picked up the pack and opened it, pulling the cards out of the box gently. Then he discarded the jokers and began shuffling the deck, quickly gaining momentum, familiarity bringing a glint to his eyes.

Jodie had to stifle a chuckle, but managed it – just – although George was interested only in the cards.

He started dealing, a small pile soon appearing in front of each of them sitting around the table.

George was first to pick his up, quickly sorting them into a neat fan in his hand, his eyes fixed on the cards in front of him, a glimmer of excitement and recognition, his eyes darting from side to side.

'He's actually—'

Tammy shut down Jodie with a glare. 'What now?' she asked.

'Pick up your cards and hold them up, just as he is,' replied Dixon. 'You open the bidding, George.'

'One spade,' said the old man, without even the slightest hesitation.

'What happens now?' mouthed Tammy.

Dixon looked at Jodie and whispered, 'Say one no trump.'

Jodie did as she was told.

'Two spades,' said Dixon, with an air of confidence and authority, although he was pretending he knew what he was doing. He had a few spades in his hand, in amongst the other suits, but whether it was the right bid was a mystery to him. It sounded right. Then he turned to Tammy and mouthed, 'No bid.'

'No bid,' said Tammy.

'Three spades.' George was on a roll now, still tinkering with the cards in his left hand, organising them into suits, seeing to it that they were properly lined up in a neat fan.

'I just don't believe it,' said Jodie. 'Look at him. He's smiling. I've never seen him do that before.'

Dixon was sure he saw Tammy wiping away a tear. He pointed at Jodie discreetly. 'Two no trumps.'

'Two no trumps,' she said.

'Four spades.'

George scowled at Dixon. 'You should've passed.'

Dixon knew that bridge partners occasionally kicked each other under the table, and no doubt George would have kicked him then, if he could have reached.

'Pass, Tammy,' Dixon whispered.

'Pass.' She managed to get the word out, despite struggling to keep her composure.

George passed immediately.

Tammy leaned across and placed her left hand softly on George's forearm. 'George, who is this?' she asked, pointing at Dixon with her right.

'That's Tom, my bridge partner,' he replied, without looking up from his cards. 'Thomas Fowler. He's hopeless at bidding. Never knows when to pass.'

Chapter Sixteen

'I can't thank you enough,' Tammy had said, as Dixon was leaving Lucerne House. 'I'll get some of the ladies from the WI to come in and play bridge with him. He'll love that, and it'll do him the power of good.'

'He's helped me more than I've helped him,' Dixon had said.

Now he was waiting on the ramp at Express Park, the electric gates to the staff car park taking longer than usual to open, or so it seemed.

Several figures had appeared in the floor to ceiling windows, gone when he took a sly glance in his wing mirror. A welcoming committee, no doubt.

The building manager was first, waiting behind the security door when Dixon opened it.

'You can't bring that in here.'

'*That?*'

'That dog.'

Back to the car, old chap, thought Dixon, knowing full well the jobsworth twerp would be gone by five-thirty.

'And there's a bag of food in the incident room.'

'I was just going to mention that, Sir,' said Louise, who was next in line. 'They brought all three bags up from Sidmouth, but I'm guessing it's the recycling you want?'

'Thank you.'

'I'll get it sent down to the foodbank in that case.'

Jane was next in line, and mercifully the only one who followed him back out to the Land Rover on the top floor of the car park. 'We've got a full house,' she said. 'Everyone's back for a briefing at five, just like you said. Charlesworth and Deborah Potter are here too, so I expect they'll be loitering at the back.'

Dixon opened the back door of the Land Rover, allowing Monty to jump up into his bed. Then he looked at Jane and winked.

'I know that look,' she said.

'Where are those bin bags?'

There were two left, sitting on a table at the back of the incident room. All eyes followed Dixon as he weaved his way between the workstations.

Someone had opened both bags and had a look, although he or she would have had no idea what they were looking for. Dixon did, reaching in and producing a handful of old newspapers, *The Times*, all of them folded open at the Mind Games section.

He spread them out across the adjacent table. 'What do you see?' he asked.

'Not a lot,' replied Jane. 'He's had a go at the Killer Sudoku, and the Polygon, that word thing, but that's it as far as I can see.'

'Me too.' Sarah was standing behind Jane, peering over her shoulder.

'That's what I thought when I first looked at it,' replied Dixon. 'But what he's actually done is the bridge game. He's just used the blank paper of the sudoku to write his answers.'

'Michael Allam played bridge.' Jane frowned. 'So what?'

◆　◆　◆

Charlesworth and Potter appeared at the top of the stairs at five o'clock on the dot, both of them leaning back against the banister at the top of the atrium, arms folded, the incident room falling silent.

'Thomas Fowler and George Sampson were bridge partners,' said Dixon. 'The card game, that is.'

'How d'you know, Sir?' asked Sarah.

'George told me.'

'I thought he's got dementia?'

'Long story.' Dixon glanced at Charlesworth and Potter, catching them nodding at each other. 'Michael Allam spent his days doing the bridge puzzles in *The Times* and, as we know, Deirdre Baxter spent a good deal of her day on her iPad playing bridge online on a website called . . .' He looked at Louise.

'Bridge Base dot com,' she said. 'It's in the report from High Tech.'

'My guess is that Michael Allam and Deirdre Baxter were bridge partners,' continued Dixon. 'Given that they knew each other through work.'

Potter and Charlesworth were already on their way back to the top of the stairs, a smile from Potter all he was going to get, for now.

'It's a reasonable assumption,' continued Dixon. 'And we're going to proceed with that as our principal line of enquiry for the time being. It connects all four of our victims.'

'Cards?' Wevill was looking at the Devon team one by one. 'No one's mentioned that to us in any of the interviews as a possible motive.'

'I didn't say it was a motive; I said it was a connection. And did you ask them?'

'No, Sir.'

'There's a photograph, Sir,' said Louise. 'At Deirdre Baxter's house, on the sideboard in the dining room. Her with an older man holding a trophy. I thought at the time it was her late husband, because it was with her wedding photos, but what if it wasn't? What if it was Michael Allam and they'd won a bridge thing?'

'I'll get you the key to her house,' offered Jane.

'Right then, everybody, you know what needs to be done.'

'Speak to all those bloody witnesses. Again.' The voice was low and tight, and came from the Devon team as the briefing broke up.

'Bridge?' Jane asked, her voice just about carrying to Dixon over the hubbub going on behind them.

'He can't remember his own name,' replied Dixon, wistfully. 'But put a pack of cards in George Sampson's hands and he's transformed to another time and place.'

'I'll take Monty home in a minute. I only hung on for the briefing.'

'I won't be far behind you. I want to see that photo Lou was talking about, then there's a bridge club that meets at the community centre in Burnham every Tuesday at seven.'

'He looks very similar to her husband,' said Louise, shining the light on her phone at the silver-framed photograph of Deirdre Baxter and Michael Allam. 'Same height and everything.'

They were parked outside Deirdre's bungalow in Berrow, Dixon having collected the picture from the sideboard in the dining room.

'It's definitely Allam, though,' Dixon said, putting on his seat-belt. 'Can you make out what the trophy is?'

'No, it's engraved, but I can't read it. Hi Tech may be able to do something with it.'

'Somebody will recognise a trophy like that.' A huge silver cup with an ornate lid and handles, at least two feet tall, it had taken both of them to hold it up for the camera. 'Let's go and see what they've got to say for themselves at the community centre.'

Light streaming across from the swimming pool and community centre on one side of the road, pitch darkness from the old putting green on the other.

'We need to get the speed camera van along here,' said Dixon, watching cars racing past, despite the zebra crossing further along, by the vet's.

The community centre had been recently painted, a fresh white that seemed to glow in the streetlights. A posh house once, the gardens lost under the car park. The curtains were open, revealing several tables of four people, all holding playing cards.

Swim club training in the pool next door, the usual cries of children playing replaced by a whistle and a man shouting.

'It's a pay and display,' said Louise.

'It'll be free at this time of night,' replied Dixon, placing the blue light on top of the Land Rover, just in case.

They were greeted by an empty table just inside the door, names on a clipboard and cash sitting in an open tin box. It wasn't long before they were spotted, though; possibly the youngest man in the room – apart from Dixon – laying his cards face down on the table and getting up.

'Five pounds each, to include tea and biscuits,' he said. 'We're always glad to see new members.'

The sight of a police warrant card wiped the welcome from his face unusually quickly.

'You need to do something with this cash, Sir.' Dixon gestured to the open tin box. 'We could've had that and gone before you'd looked up.'

The man closed the lid, turned the key and tucked the box under his arm. 'You're quite right, of course, but I'm guessing you're not here to tell me that.'

'No, Sir,' said Dixon. 'And you are?'

'Lionel Woakes.'

'Do the names Deirdre Baxter or Michael Allam mean anything to you?'

'No, sorry.'

'Perhaps this photograph might jog your memory?'

Woakes took the photograph in his left hand, lifting his reading glasses which were on a cord around his neck and using them like a magnifying glass in his right. 'Never seen either of them before,' he said. 'When were they members?'

'We don't know that they were,' replied Dixon. 'At this stage, we're just trying to find anyone who knew them.'

'There are several bridge clubs in Burnham. We play every Tuesday evening here, and there's another at the tennis club every Tuesday and Wednesday afternoon. They might have played there. It's quite an elderly demographic these days, I'm afraid. It's a chance to get out of the house and see a friendly face for most of us. The younger lot seem to play online. How long ago were they playing?'

'We don't know that either, I'm afraid, Sir.' Dixon sighed. 'That photo can't be more than twenty years old.'

'Ah, well, I've only been here ten years or so.'

'Do you have membership records?'

'Somewhere.' Woakes grimaced. 'I computerised it all about eight years ago, so I'd need to find the old book. It was just a ledger, really, with scribblings in it. And I say *computerised*; it's just a spreadsheet.'

'They were local teachers,' continued Dixon. 'Deirdre Baxter at St Christopher's and Michael Allam at St Joseph's.'

'Doesn't ring a bell.'

Dixon looked over Woakes's shoulder at the various tables in the large room. He'd counted nine, so that made thirty-five other people who might know them.

Woakes got the message. 'We can break for coffee after this hand, if you'd like to ask everyone. We've got a good turnout tonight.' He smiled. 'Must be football on the telly or something. I'd better just go and finish my . . .' His voice tailed off.

Dixon had never understood bridge, exhausting his limited knowledge in the opening bids he had been playing with George Sampson earlier that afternoon. 'One no trumps' – whatever the hell that was supposed to mean. He could make sense of no bid, or one heart even. It was like another language; he understood the odd word here and there.

'Do you play bridge, Sir?' asked Louise.

'I walk my dog.'

'Yeah, it's a bit beyond me too.'

People began getting up from their tables and heading towards the tea and coffee laid out on a table at the back of the room.

Woakes clapped his hands. 'Everybody, we have a couple of police officers here this evening. They'd like you to look at a photograph and see if you recognise the bridge players pictured.'

Tea and coffee seemed to be a higher priority.

'I'll go and stand behind the table with the photo,' said Louise.

'Keeps the mind agile.' Woakes appeared at Dixon's elbow with a cup of tea in one hand and a biscuit in the other. 'You should try it.'

'I have more than enough to keep my mind agile, Mr Woakes.'

'Of course you do. Sorry.' He took a sip of tea to hide his embarrassment. 'Is it about that woman who was murdered in Berrow?'

'It is.'

'And that's her in the photograph?'

'With, we think, her bridge partner.'

Louise was leading an elderly lady to an empty table on the far side of the room, holding her elbow and carrying a cup and

145

saucer for her. 'Sir, this is Agnes Harrington,' she said, when Dixon approached. 'Agnes knew Deirdre and Michael.'

The old lady looked up at Dixon, her eyes trying to focus on his face. 'I saw you earlier on the television, didn't I?'

'When I was asking anyone who knew Deirdre Baxter or Michael Allam to get in touch with us as a matter of urgency, perhaps?'

'I didn't think it would be relevant.' Agnes shrugged her apology. 'After all, I haven't seen either of them for, what, twenty years or more.'

Dixon sat down opposite Agnes, conscious that Louise was glaring at him. 'Start at the beginning.'

'I knew Deirdre through golf. We played in the ladies' section at Burnham and Berrow for several years, and then we started playing bridge. There was a group of ladies who'd play in the afternoons, after we'd done eighteen holes. I was hopeless at it, really, but Deirdre took to it. She taught maths and it suited her, at least that's what she said.'

'When was this?'

'The early nineties, maybe. I haven't played golf since the millennium – my ankles, you know – so it must've been before that.'

Agnes may have been in her late eighties, but her mind was still sharp enough. Maybe there was something to this bridge game? Her eyes burned brightly, even behind the bottle-top glasses.

'I tried bowls,' continued Agnes, 'but I couldn't get on with it, so started coming here to play bridge competitively. Deirdre did the same, but got very good, very quickly. She started playing with Michael Allam, I remember.' She picked up the framed photograph. 'That's a photograph of them holding the Somerset County Bridge Union Pairs Cup. 2003 I think that was. They went to the West of England Congress at the Winter Gardens in Weston-super-Mare. All over the place, they went.'

'Did you know Michael Allam?'

'I met him here when I joined and we played together once or twice, but I was nothing like good enough for him. I was driving the poor fellow mad. That's when he started playing with Deirdre. She was younger than me, and I think they hit it off in other ways too, if you know what I mean?'

'Spell it out for me, Agnes,' said Dixon.

The old woman turned to Louise. 'Must I?'

'I'm afraid you must,' replied Louise.

'Michael was married and they were having an affair, a sexual relationship, as well as being bridge partners. Weekends away in hotels at bridge tournaments; you don't need to have a vivid imagination.' Agnes picked up the biscuit from her saucer and took a bite. 'Then it all came crashing down around them,' she said, spraying crumbs across the table.

Dixon waited.

'Solicitors got involved and it was really nasty for a time,' continued Agnes. 'I don't remember what happened after that, I'm afraid.'

'Solicitors got involved with what?'

'Their win in the County Finals qualified them for the Regionals, but they were banned by the Somerset County Bridge Union.' She looked at Dixon over her glasses. 'Complaints were made,' she said, her voice flat. 'So they applied to the court for an injunction, the ban was overturned, and off to the Regional Qualifier they went. There was no real evidence, just gossip. All very unpleasant.' The old lady took a sip of tea. 'I don't think any of this lot here will remember it. Most of the old members have gone now.'

'Why were they banned?' asked Dixon.

'Cheating.'

'And did they cheat?'

'The Deirdre I knew would never have cheated, no. They didn't need to anyway; they were that good.'

'How were they supposed to have done it?'

'A series of signals to each other during the bidding phase. I know it does happen when some pairs get carried away. It's fiercely competitive, bridge, you know. We may look like a bunch of old fuddy-duddies to you, young man, but this is do-or-die stu—' She caught herself. 'Probably the wrong phrase in the present situation, I suppose.'

'What signals?'

'Hold the cards low for a poor hand, high for a good hand, scratching an ear or an eyebrow. It's just a matter of working it out in advance. Coughing is another one, like that *Who Wants to Be a Millionaire* case. At the bigger tournaments they had people watching for it, and now they use cameras. I never saw Deirdre after that. She changed bridge partners – married the new one, I think – started playing somewhere else; never to the same standard. I don't think she could face people after all the scandal.'

'So, let me make sure I understand this correctly,' said Dixon, watching Louise scribbling in her notebook. 'Complaints were made that Deirdre and Michael cheated in the County Finals and they were banned from the Regional Qualifier as a result?'

'Yes.'

'They instructed a solicitor.'

'Someone from Taunton, I think.'

'It went to court, they were granted an injunction, reinstated and allowed to compete at the Regional Qualifier?'

'That's right.'

'Did they win?'

'No.'

'So, who made this complaint?'

'The pair they beat in the County Finals,' replied Agnes. 'Sounded like sour grapes to me. I thought so at the time and I still do.'

Hunches were best followed, and he had nothing to lose. 'I don't suppose their names were Thomas Fowler and George Sampson, by any chance?' asked Dixon.

'Yes, that's them; from Yeovil way, I think. I'd not come across them before, but then I wasn't *on the circuit*, just a social player. Sore losers, they were, though. The whole episode was really sordid.'

Chapter Seventeen

'What's this when it's at home?' asked Dixon. He was staring at a plate on the kitchen worktop, a knife and fork neatly placed either side of it. Leaves, a tomato, grated cheese.

'I made you a salad,' replied Jane.

'A salad?'

The lights were off in the living room, only the top of Jane's head visible over the back of the sofa. Monty's tail too, hanging over the arm. The dull glow of a black and white film the only illumination in the whole cottage.

Dixon flicked on the kitchen light.

Yes, it was a plate of salad, with a bottle of low-fat salad dressing.

'I thought I might take Monty out for a walk in a bit.'

'I've done that. I was home early, don't forget; walked him up the lane and made you supper.' She paused the film. 'It's going be lovely when I go on maternity leave. I'll be able to do this every night, then we can really get your blood sugar levels under control.'

And suddenly all became clear.

'Have you eaten?' he asked.

'There wasn't enough salad for me, so I had to have a curry. I used the last of the mango chutney too.'

The crafty sod. He might not be able to see her grinning, but he could hear it in her voice.

'I got a tin of red salmon to go with your salad tomorrow, but I forgot the beetroot,' continued Jane. 'D'you like tinned salmon?'

Rub it in, why don't you?

'Yes, lovely.' He shuddered to himself as he pushed Monty on to the floor and sat down next to Jane on the sofa. She turned away, trying not to laugh, probably.

'D'you want me to start the film again?' she asked.

'No, it's fine.'

Oddly enough, Monty was showing an interest in Dixon's salad, although he might just have been after the cheese. He was sitting next to Dixon, his muzzle resting on the edge of the tray. '*Et tu, Brute?*' he muttered, pushing the dog away.

'Did you want to have that chat about me going on maternity leave now or later?' asked Jane, looking pleased with herself.

'Now,' replied Dixon, through a mouthful of lettuce and cucumber.

'Right, well, I'm not going yet, and that's that. It'll drive me round the bend sitting at home all day. I'm not due for another three months.'

'What's the time?'

'They've stopped serving food at the pub,' said Jane, trying not to sound smug. 'I'll go when I'm good and ready. All right?'

'If that's what you want.'

Jane reached over and took a pinch of grated cheese off Dixon's plate, dropping it on the floor for Monty. 'Right, well, I'm glad we've got that sorted out,' she said, with a note of triumph. 'I'll bung you a curry in the microwave.'

Brighton Rock. Jane was working her way through his collection of old black and white films.

'Did you get anywhere at the bridge club?' she asked, from the kitchen.

'They were Somerset county champions in 2003, made it through to the Regional Qualifier, and then got banned for cheating.'

'There's your motive, right there,' Jane said, her sentence punctuated by the slam of the microwave door.

'I doubt it.'

'Really?'

'They took it to court and got an injunction; were reinstated and still went to the Regional thing. And their accusers were Sampson and Fowler, apparently.' Dixon shrugged, not that Jane would see it from the kitchen. 'I could understand Deirdre Baxter and Michael Allam having a grudge against Sampson and Fowler because they accused them of cheating, or Sampson and Fowler having a grudge against Deirdre and Michael because they cheated them out of the county win. But who's going to be killing all four of them?'

'Three.'

'Only his dementia saved George Sampson.'

'Here,' Jane said, handing Dixon a beer. 'We got George's medical records and the diagnosis is confirmed.'

'I never doubted it for a minute,' he replied, snapping open the can. 'I've played bridge with him, remember?'

'So, where does that leave us?'

'Closer.' A swig. 'Anything else would be far too much of a coincidence.'

'We don't believe in those.'

'We don't.'

'Mark's got some fairly good shots of the car,' said Jane. 'On traffic cameras at Wells, then again on the M5 at Burnham going south. You can't see the driver, though. The number plate's been cloned too, which is a pain.'

'What is it?'

'A Fiat 500. The little jelly mould thing. We've spoken to the owner of the cloned car; she lives in Bristol and has only just got back from ten days away skiing. She's coming down to Express Park to make a statement tomorrow.'

'Where was her car while she was away?'

'Airport parking,' replied Jane, placing a tray in Dixon's lap, Monty taking more of an interest now. 'We checked with them and it didn't move the whole time she was away. Mark got someone to go over there and look at the CCTV to make sure. Strange how they managed to find just the right car to clone, though.'

'Not really.' Dixon was waiting for his curry to cool down a bit, the sauce still bubbling. 'You just go to Facebook, join the relevant owners' club group and wait for someone to post a picture of their lovely car that's an exact match for yours. Then find an unscrupulous garage with the right machine to copy the number plate.'

'There are plenty of them about,' said Jane. 'So what happens now?'

'We dig a little deeper into this bridge thing and see where it takes us. It's the only thing we've got that connects them all.' He hesitated. 'Did you really take Monty for a walk?'

'No, not really.' Jane smiled. 'I knew you'd want to.'

'We need to find out who leaked the exhumation to the press too.'

'My money's on Dean Wevill. I'm keeping an eye on him, but he gives me the creeps.'

Chapter Eighteen

Small world, thought Dixon, turning into the visitors' car park at Oxenden Hart solicitors the following morning. Jane had been asleep by the time he'd got back from his walk with Monty, and had gone before he'd woken up in the morning; nothing if not conscientious.

'It's the incident room manager's job to be first in and last out,' she had said.

He had tried pointing out that it was staffed twenty-four-seven, to no avail.

'I need to debrief the night shift before they go off duty.'

It was a fair point that had ended the discussion when he caught up with her at Express Park.

'Are you all right, Sir?' asked Louise. She was sitting in the passenger seat of Dixon's Land Rover, watching him staring at the revolving doors. 'Have you been here before?'

'Funny you should ask that,' he replied, sliding out of the driver's seat.

Floor to ceiling windows, a huge atrium with palm trees in giant pots, *automatic* revolving doors; the staff car park full of electric cars plugged in to chargers.

His Land Rover would have looked out of place, even if he didn't.

The receptionist recognised him, her face turning the same colour as her red blazer.

Warrant card this time. 'Detective Superintendent Dixon to see Mr Page,' he said, his voice taut. 'And it's urgent police business, so if you'd be kind enough to ask him not to keep me waiting half an hour this time.'

'Move on,' Jane had said. And he had been doing his best, but some things brought it all roaring back. His arrest for murder; job interviews at law firms. Beneath his sunny disposition, he was still seething.

Louise sat down on one of the red leather sofas, looking at Dixon with her eyebrows raised as far as they would go.

'I came here for a job interview,' he said, his voice hushed. 'When I was on leave. It was a vacancy for a newly qualified corporate finance solicitor.'

'You'd have loved that.'

'This fellow, Page, kept me waiting in reception nearly half an hour, so I walked out.'

'Good for you,' said Louise, shaking her head. 'Sounds to me like he did you a favour.'

'Maybe he did.'

'Certainly did us a favour.' She picked up a newspaper from the glass coffee table, idly glancing at the headlines.

The receptionist replaced the telephone handset nervously. 'He apologises for keeping you waiting and says he'll be down in a few minutes.'

Dixon had heard that before and wasn't having any of it. He walked over to the reception desk slowly, silently counting to ten, just as his anger management counsellor would have advised if she had been there instead of in the incident room. 'Either he comes down now,' said Dixon. 'Or I go upstairs and arrest him for obstructing a murder enquiry.'

'You really want me to tell him that?'

He nodded, slowly, menacingly, then listened to her repeating what he had said, word for word.

'It's that same police officer you kept waiting all that time when he came for a job interview,' she added, her eyes fixed on Dixon.

He couldn't quite make out what was being said on the other end of the line, but 'Oh, shit' carried plain as day.

Perhaps he was enjoying the moment a little too much?

Am I, bollocks.

The sound of running, then a door next to the lifts burst open.

'I'm so sorry,' said Page. He was doing up the top button of his shirt and straightening his tie, his suit jacket draped over his arm. 'I'm sorry about before too. I did ring the recruitment agent that afternoon, but they said you'd changed your mind.'

'The recruitment agent was being diplomatic, I think, Sir,' replied Dixon.

'Quite.'

'Forget it.'

'Thank you.'

Maybe Dixon would too; one day.

Page looked at the receptionist.

'Interview room four is free,' she said. 'Would anyone like a coffee?'

Red carpet, a round glass table, a pot of free pens in the middle, one of those folding cardboard calendar things emblazoned with the Oxenden Hart logo. It felt a bit like a Bentley dealership: 'If you have to ask, you can't afford it.'

Dixon waited until Page closed the door behind them.

'We're investigating the murders of Deirdre Baxter and Michael Allam,' he said. 'Clients of yours, I understand.'

'Yes, they were. A while ago now, back when we were in Hammet Street, in the town centre. That was even before the merger. I was a litigator back then – managing partner now, for my sins.'

'Do you still have the file?'

'That would've been destroyed long ago, I'm afraid. We keep litigation files for fifteen years then they go off to be incinerated.'

The smell of the coffee just about made it over the receptionist's perfume when the door opened. Even the mugs had the Oxenden Hart logo on them. 'There's milk and cream,' she said, before beating a hasty retreat.

'We've got three dead and one person visited by our killer, but not killed. All were bridge players,' said Dixon. 'And my understanding is that all four of them were parties to the litigation.'

'Allam and Baxter against the Somerset County Bridge Union and' – Page frowned – 'Sampson and Fowler. You never forget the names of some files. Actually it was a very interesting case. Lucrative too. Certainly made a change from the usual landlord and tenant, neighbour disputes and stuff like that. Glad to be out of it, to be honest.'

'How did you get the case?'

'Pure luck, really. I think they just picked us at random and I was prepared to see them quickly, so they came in.' Page was sorting through the sugar bowl, looking for a lump that was the right size. 'They were good players and had won the Pairs Cup at the County Finals. Then they were accused of cheating and it all got rather nasty. There was no proper investigation, and the Somerset County Bridge Union turned up at Deirdre's house and took back the trophy. Just like that. A letter arrived the next day by recorded delivery telling them they were banned for life.'

'And it was Sampson and Fowler who made the allegations?'

'Yes. They were the runners up. You can imagine it, can't you?'

'What did you do?'

'The first thing I did was to write a letter before action to the Bridge Union telling them that unless the ban was withdrawn immediately and their win reinstated, we'd be applying to the court for an injunction. There'd also be an action for damages and costs. A libel action too, because it had found its way into the newspapers.' Page was stirring his coffee. 'I got witness statements from Deirdre and Michael – several other players too. Got no reply from the Bridge Union, so we applied to the court. We instructed a silk from Bristol – a QC as they were back then, no expense spared – and the injunction was granted. They were reinstated and went to the Regional Qualifier as part of the Somerset Pairs team.' A sip of coffee. 'Mind you, it must have been a difficult trip because Sampson and Fowler were also on the team.' He chuckled at the thought. 'I'd love to have been a fly on the wall.'

'Were any of the defendants represented at the hearing?'

'The initial injunction was against the Bridge Union and they were represented. A solicitor from Yeovil, from memory, and they instructed junior counsel from Exeter chambers. Our QC made mincemeat of him and the injunction was granted. It was after that, when it became a claim for damages, that we joined Sampson and Fowler as additional defendants. After all, they were the ones making the libellous allegations.'

'Was there any evidence that your clients had cheated?' asked Dixon.

'Not that I could see. There was certainly nothing apart from the witness statements from Sampson and Fowler, and they were pretty vague. Suggestions of signalling, coughing, touching ears and noses, that sort of stuff.' Page was watching Louise scribbling notes. 'The sort of stuff you do naturally when you're concentrating hard, our QC said, and the judge agreed.'

'What happened after that?'

'Well, we were busy getting the case ready for trial, getting witness statements in place. We'd applied for disclosure of the Bridge Union's documents, which turned up some minutes of a meeting the day after the County Finals when they imposed the ban, but that was it, really. I suspect they just felt they had no alternative once the allegations had been made, but there should have been a proper investigation *before* such drastic steps were taken.'

Dixon had finished his coffee and placed the mug back on the tray. 'How did the case finish?' he asked.

'Well, that's the funny thing. They went off to the Regional Qualifier and when they came back they instructed us to discontinue.' Page looked disappointed, even after all this time. 'All parties agreed they would pay their own costs; Sampson and Fowler were separately represented by then, so that's three sets of solicitors' fees, counsel for us and the Bridge Union. It was a bit of shame, to be honest. It would've been a belter of a trial. I think Deirdre and Michael would've won too, and so did our silk, but we did as we were instructed, agreed an order for discontinuance with no order as to costs and that was that.'

'How much were your fees?'

'About fifty thousand, all told, including counsel's fees and VAT. Michael and Deirdre would've split it between them, I suppose, but it was still a hell of a lot of money to walk away from. We told them they might well win if they pressed on, but they were adamant. We had counsel's opinion too, and he said they had a strong case.'

'Was there an apology?'

'No, although it had been reported in the press that the ban had been lifted and that Deirdre and Michael had been reinstated. You know what the local press are like for gossipy stories. We had another a few years ago, allegations of cheating at Taunton Vale Golf Club; that ended with a withdrawal of the allegations and an apology, but you should have seen the local rag. I think it even got in the nationals – the tabloids, you know. Clickbait more than anything.'

'Have you acted for Deirdre or Michael since then?'

'I certainly haven't, but the firm may have done. Would you like me to check?'

'Yes, please.'

Louise used the opportunity to drink her coffee, which looked as if it had gone stone cold, a film of something floating on the surface like an oil slick. 'Bitter,' she said, through gritted teeth.

'Hideously expensive, no doubt.'

'Still horrible.'

Dixon was watching through the glass walls of the interview suite, Page leaning over the receptionist's computer.

'We did a new will for Deirdre about five years ago, and it looks like a colleague went to see her recently about a lasting power of attorney,' offered Page, when he reappeared in the doorway. 'And some conveyancing for Michael. Seems he moved to Sidmouth and we did the sale of his old place and purchase of the new one.'

'Thank you,' said Dixon, standing up.

Page was blocking his exit, his hand outstretched. 'Look, I'm sorry about before, the interview. I wouldn't want you to think that's the way we usually treat people at OH.'

'Of course not, Sir,' replied Dixon, hoping his smile looked sincere.

'I take it you changed your mind about leaving the police?'

'I did.'

'Our loss, their gain. And between you and me, I can't really see you as a corporate finance solicitor.'

'I'll take that as a compliment,' replied Dixon.

'Believe me, it was meant as one.'

Chapter Nineteen

'Here,' said Dixon, sitting back in the driver's seat of his Land Rover. 'Have a pen, courtesy of Oxenden Hart.' He'd already put three in the glovebox.

'Thank you, Sir,' replied Louise, grinning.

'Did you speak to someone at the County Bridge Union?'

'There won't be anybody there until this afternoon, but they gave me the contact details for the tournament director at the County Finals that year. Lives on the Blackdowns at a place called Clayhidon.'

One junction down on the M5, Louise took her chance in the car. 'Are you sure about this bridge thing?' she asked. 'I mean, they settled the litigation twenty years ago.'

Dixon had known it was coming. The last time Louise had questioned his judgement, he'd been flying by the seat of his pants, a whole major investigation team following little more than a hunch. Not that he'd told anyone except Jane, of course. But that was the SIO's job, to make the difficult decisions and record them in the Policy Log so he could be blamed later.

The Policy Log. That would need updating before Charlesworth ambushed him again.

'What else is there?' he asked.

'There's the car, the Fiat 500,' replied Louise.

'Mark's working on that.'

'The person dressed as an occupational therapist.'

'And what else could we, or should we, be doing about that?' asked Dixon. 'That we aren't doing already?'

'Nothing, I suppose. It's not as if we've got a big team either. Calling it a "regional task force" may make it sound bigger, but there are fewer people than last time for the graffiti thing. Killing students must be more important than killing old people.'

Louise had a point, and it was one that had occurred to him, not that there was much he could do about it either way. He reached into the back of the Land Rover, picked up the road atlas and dropped it in her lap.

'I've got it on my phone,' she said, taking the hint. 'It's on the road between Clayhidon and Hemyock.'

A bungalow, as it turned out, with a front garden that looked as though it hadn't been touched in years; the rotting wooden bench was collapsing under the weight of the branches of a fir tree. A conservatory at the side of the house, where the garage should be, not that there was a car in the drive, anyway.

A ramp up to the front door and a hand rail. Key safe too. Bridge seemed to be the preserve of the elderly.

An old man was sitting in the conservatory, a blanket over his legs tucked down beside the wheels of his chair. He was gesturing to the front door and shouting, 'It's open.'

Dixon waved, a cat escaping when he pushed open the door.

'Your cat's got out,' he said. 'Is that all right?'

'Yes, fine,' replied the old man. 'He's next door's anyway, but they never seem to feed him, so he comes here.'

'Mr Wilkinson?' asked Louise.

'And you'll be the police. I do remember our conversation. It was only this morning.'

Dixon perched on the windowsill, his back to the glass and the sloping concrete driveway leading down to his Land Rover, which he'd left across the drive.

'Some oaf has parked across my drive, otherwise you could have pulled in,' said Wilkinson, the glint in his eye telling Dixon the old man knew full well whose car it was.

'We wanted to ask you about the bridge County Finals and the year it ended in a court case. You were the tournament director, I think,' he said.

Wilkinson laughed quietly to himself. 'I remember it well, although the complainants didn't have the bottle to speak up at the time. They said nothing to their opponents, or to me; never asked for an auction to be reviewed by the tournament director, which is their right. They just went to the local press the following day. Frankly, I'd have banned *them* for life, but the union had other ideas.' He curled his lip. 'Some bright spark kept saying, "Justice had to be seen to be done."'

'And was it?'

'It was to the extent that those two who were banned ended up being reinstated, but they had to go to court. I gave a witness statement to their solicitor. I remember it well. Nothing was drawn to my attention during play and I can recall no irregularity, or even a suggestion of impropriety being made until the following day.' The old man was clearly seething at the memory. 'And that's the best place for newspapers, in my opinion,' he said, gesturing to a cat's litter tray in the corner of the conservatory.

Dixon was getting close, he could feel it, but how and why were beyond him. Nothing for it, but to keep digging.

'Were you involved in the Regional Qualifier?' he asked.

'Not that year. I used to go as a referee – not as the tournament director you understand – but we were away on a cruise that year. The Icelandic fjords; jolly nice it was too.'

'Can you remember who competed for Somerset?'

'The two accused of cheating were there, and their accusers, oddly enough, but I can't remember who else. The team varies – sometimes it's two pairs, sometimes three, and once we sent four pairs, from memory. It depends.'

'On what?'

'I couldn't honestly tell you now. It's changed anyway, I think. You'll need to ask someone at the Bridge Union.'

'Do you recall what happened to the court case?'

'It settled, I think. Rumour had it that there was a payoff, but I'm not sure.' Wilkinson gave an embarrassed shrug. 'You can imagine what the rumour mill was like. It was the talk of bridge clubs countywide for years. If it isn't any more, that's only because those of us who remember it are either dead or dying.'

'Have you seen the news recently?' asked Dixon.

'Don't watch the news, don't read the news. I don't even have a television that works. I had the licence people here snooping only the other day.'

'Deirdre Baxter and Michael Allam, the two who were accused of cheating—'

'I remember the names, now you come to mention them.'

'—have both been murdered,' continued Dixon. 'As has Thomas Fowler, one of their accusers. The other has dementia, which we believe saved him. Do you know why—?'

'Someone might have put them out of their misery,' interrupted Wilkinson. 'No, I don't know, but I wish someone would do the same for me.'

◆ ◆ ◆

. . . those of us who remember it are either dead or dying.

'The Somerset Bridge Union doesn't have an office, as such,' said Louise. 'They play twice a month at Woolavington Village Hall and there's a committee that meets at the hon. sec.'s house in Creech St Michael.'

Dixon was already heading north on the M5.

'His name's Frank Dolan and he lives at 3 Old School Cottages. Part of the old school, I expect,' mumbled Louise, busy scrolling on her phone.

Dixon could feel a valuation coming on.

'The one next door's on Rightmove for two-seventy.' She looked up to check Dixon was listening. 'Three bedrooms – small, mind. Looks nice.'

All he needed was Donald Watson and he could get a valuation of the household contents as well.

Dixon parked next to the 'Residents Only' sign in the small car park twenty minutes later, the rest of the journey having been spent in silence.

The water butt by the front door made an interesting feature in the gravelled front garden; paving slabs for stepping stones, a shed all but hidden under a clematis. The rose growing up the wall could've done with a prune too. A sloping roof with wonky tiles and Velux windows. It would've made a nice village school.

Dolan saw them approaching through the kitchen window and opened the door before they reached it. 'Come in out of the rain,' he said. 'Wilko rang me and told me you were coming.'

'How long have you known Mr Wilkinson?' asked Dixon.

'Thirty years. We played together for a while, but then he got involved in refereeing.'

Corduroys, a shirt and pullover; he'd even put a tie on for their visit. Ex-military, judging by the choice of prints on the wall.

The lounge/diner at the back of the cottage – Louise had tried to show Dixon the floor plan of next door on her phone – was more of an office with a sofa in it, French windows opening into a small courtyard area at the back.

Two desks, a computer with two screens, four filing cabinets, printers, piles of magazines, even a large photocopier against the back wall.

'I had to downsize when my wife went into a care home.' Dolan's voice was tinged with sadness. 'Ended up here and the office rather took over.'

'How long have you been honorary secretary?' asked Dixon, once Louise was seated on the sofa with her notebook at the ready.

'Fifteen years. I was chair before that, membership secretary before that; treasurer too. I think I've done the lot over the years. It'll be life president next, then a coffin.'

'It looks like a full-time job.' Dixon was standing by Dolan's desk, watching emails flashing up on the computer, a large spreadsheet open on the other screen that looked like competition results.

'It is, really. I get paid my expenses, but that's it.' Dolan shook his head. 'It keeps me busy, keeps me going, I suppose.'

'And what does it involve?'

'Well, we don't have a membership secretary any more, or a treasurer, so both of those jobs for a start. I'm competition secretary too, and that takes up most of my time: keeping track of the various leagues, pairs, teams of four, Swiss pairs. Then there are the trophy competitions, interclub competitions; updating the website, minutes of the committee meetings.' Dolan was standing in the French windows, watching the rain hammering down on his patio. 'What the bloody hell else am I going to do at my time of life? A widower, with no children.'

The wall above the filing cabinets was covered in framed photographs, mainly of Dolan presenting trophies to various bridge pairs and teams. And there it was: 2003, the trophy being presented to Michael Allam and Deirdre Baxter, both beaming at the camera, enjoying the moment, before the allegations of cheating started to fly.

'I was going to point that one out,' said Dolan, noticing Dixon staring at the picture. 'They made a fine pair. Deirdre a maths teacher, and I seem to recall that Michael had been an engineer before he took up teaching.'

'Can you tell me what you remember about the court case?'

'I knew George Sampson and Thomas Fowler well enough, I suppose. They were the losing finalists who made the cheating allegations and you could've knocked me down with a feather, to be honest. I was there, refereeing, and you've spoken to Wilko, haven't you. He was there as tournament director, and neither of us spotted anything untoward. Then, all of a sudden, Sampson and Fowler are crying "cheat". It had never happened before and it's never happened since either.'

'You suspended Deirdre and Michael?'

'The committee met the following day and we felt we had no choice, to be honest, once the allegations had been made. The press had picked it up and we needed to be seen to be taking it seriously. We took advice from the English Bridge Union and they confirmed it was within the rules to do so, so we did it.'

'And you defended the court proceedings?'

'We didn't feel we had a lot of choice about that either, so we instructed a local firm to deal with it.' Dolan sat down on his office chair and spun around to face Dixon. 'I was fairly relaxed about it, though. I took the view that the court was the appropriate forum to decide these matters, and if a judge overturned the ban, then so be it. And he did, meaning that off they went to the Regional Qualifier at the Palace Hotel, Torquay. Michael, Deirdre and their accusers.'

'Were you there?'

'I was, refereeing, although not matches in which the teams from Somerset were competing.'

'How many teams were there?'

'We sent three pairs actually.'

'Do you remember anything unusual happening?'

Dolan was stroking his grey beard with his left hand. 'You mean apart from the fire?'

Dixon waited.

'The ballroom burned to the ground on the Saturday night. Three people were killed; one of the competitors – from Cornwall, I think – his daughter and her little baby. The whole hotel had to be evacuated, and I remember standing out in the road watching the fire engines. There were people everywhere, milling about. It was chaos. Turned out it was arson in the end, and the bloke got a life sentence. Quite right too.'

'Did you see Michael or Deirdre during the fire?'

'Not that I recall. It was a huge hotel and some people were evacuated on to the golf course behind it. I suppose it depended on where you were staying in the complex. There used to be the terrace, then a nine-hole par-three course for residents to potter about on out the back. I had a go once, with Deirdre on the first afternoon; hired some clubs and off we went. She was bloody good.'

'You said *used* to be?'

'It's been knocked down for houses now, I believe. The whole place. Not as a result of the fire. The ballroom was rebuilt and we took the Regional Qualifier back there again a couple of years later. We used the Winter Gardens in Weston once, I think. That was for the rescheduled last day about a month after the fire. Then the Riviera Centre in Torquay for a couple of years, then back to the Palace Hotel.' Dolan had drifted off, deep in thought. 'I can remember the smell as if it was yesterday; the flames climbing high into the sky, the noise, blue lights everywhere, people screaming, trying to move cars out of the car park, would you believe it. As if that mattered.'

168

'Where were you when the fire started?' asked Dixon.

'In my room, so I was left standing out in the road in my pyjamas and dressing gown. It must've been ten or so. It had been a long day and I was due to be refereeing the first match on the Sunday morning. There were people everywhere. A huge crowd had gathered on the far side of the road to watch the fire, and I remember the hotel staff had terrible trouble trying to call the roll. It was horrible, really. The hotel was down a slope, so from the road you were almost looking down on it. The ballroom off to the right, huge pine trees behind it; you could see them starting to burn too.' Dolan was gesturing with his arms, laying out the geography. 'Behind and to the left as you looked at it was the leisure centre, which was untouched, and the main part of the hotel was all right, as well. It was just the ballroom and the rooms above it. Gas bottles in the kitchen, apparently.'

'Did you see the Somerset teams later that night?'

'No. I didn't see them again until the reconvened last day at the Winter Gardens about a month later. I was bit disorientated that night, ended up on someone's sofa in the flats opposite. Nice couple, they were. They even took me home the next day. We still exchange Christmas cards.'

'Did you speak to Michael and Deirdre at the Winter Gardens?'

'Not about the fire, and they seemed to have lost interest in the bridge, to be honest. Several pairs didn't turn up at all; only the few who had been in contention to qualify for the nationals, really. Michael and Deirdre were going through the motions, you might say; Sampson and Fowler too. And the other pair didn't turn up at all. It was odd, come to think of it.' Dolan was opening and closing the top drawers of the filing cabinets one by one before pulling out a file and flicking through it. 'Yes, I thought so,' he said to himself.

Dixon was doing his best to stay patient. He glanced down at Louise, her pen hovering over her notebook.

'Yes, look at this. None of the three pairs that went to the Regional Qualifier that year ever competed again as far as I can see. Certainly none of them made it through to the County Finals together again. It looks like they just stopped playing competitive bridge.'

'We know that Deirdre started playing with a new partner and ended up marrying him,' said Dixon.

'Maybe he wasn't any good at bridge, then,' replied Dolan. 'Or maybe the litigation and all the nastiness that went with it was too much for her?'

'What about Sampson and Fowler?'

'There's no record of them competing together again either.' Dolan was turning the pages of the ring binder. 'There's George Sampson reaching the County Finals three years in a row after that, but with a new partner. No mention of Thomas Fowler, I'm afraid.'

'What about the other pair?' asked Dixon. 'You said Somerset sent three pairs to the Regional Qualifier.'

'No record of them competing again at all,' said Dolan. He closed the file and turned to his computer, scrolling through a spreadsheet on the screen on the left. 'Not current members, either. I can give you the addresses I've got for them, but they might be a bit out of date, I'm afraid.'

Chapter Twenty

'Judith Bolam died in 2012,' said Louise, as Dixon accelerated along the main road towards Martock. 'Jane's going to speak to the daughter, but she lives in France. According to the electoral roll, Geoffrey Pannell still lives in Martock at the same address. He must be knocking on a bit now, though.' Her lips were moving as she did the maths in her head. 'Yeah, he'll be eighty-nine.'

'Get uniform over there now to do a welfare check,' said Dixon. 'Tell them to stay with him until we get there.'

'Yes, Sir' – her phone to her ear.

'It's got nothing to do with fucking bridge at all. Something happened during that fire and I want to know what it was.' He was talking out loud, ignoring Louise's telephone conversation.

She turned away, her left hand blocking her other ear. 'Sorry, I can't hear . . .'

'There's a reason why those teams never played together again and it's not that litigation. In fact' – he thumped the steering wheel – 'it's probably the same reason why they settled it and went their separate ways.'

Louise rang off. 'There's a patrol car on the way now.'

'Something happened at that Regional Qualifier, something to do with that fire.'

Two patrol cars were parked in the lane outside the small cottage on the edge of Martock, dog walkers standing under umbrellas on the opposite side of the road, neighbours leaning over the garden fence. The streetlights were on, drizzle falling on the officers as they looked in Geoffrey Pannell's front windows.

Dixon parked next to the patrol cars, blocking the lane, Louise jumping out of the Land Rover before it had come to a stop, warrant card at the ready.

'No sign of life, Sir,' said a uniformed sergeant Dixon didn't recognise. 'A neighbour has rung the daughter and she's on her way down from Bath. Said she'd be at least an hour and a half.'

Louise had squatted down and was looking through the letterbox. 'It's got one of those bloody brush things on it. Can't see a thing.'

A solid uPVC door, brand new by the looks of things; the type with a barrel lock and latches all the way down. There was no easy way through that. 'What's round the back?' asked Dixon.

'Kitchen door's wooden, Sir,' replied the sergeant, recognising the gist of the question. 'With a pane of glass. Probably bolts top and bottom. We haven't got a battering ram, though, I'm afraid.'

Dixon followed the path around the side of the cottage, picking up a stone urn on the way and emptying the mud in it on to the flowerbed. Flat bottomed, it looked much like a goblet; good grip, and ideal for breaking in.

'Like I said, though, Sir,' said the sergeant, following him, 'the daughter's on her way with a key if we can wait a bit.'

'We can't,' replied Dixon. He stopped in front of the back door, kicking the bottom of it with his toe. 'No bolt there anyway.'

'Usual protocol would be to wait, Sir,' said the sergeant, trying again.

'Somerset sent three pairs to the Regional Qualifier for the English National Pairs Final in 2003. One of them has dementia, four are dead – three of them murdered – which makes Mr Pannell last man standing.'

'And I have a horrible feeling someone's beaten us to him,' said Louise. She was standing on the edge of the small lawn, shining the light on her phone at the back door.

'Here, let me, Sir,' said the sergeant, taking the plant pot from Dixon. 'This bit of wood should come out easily enough.'

It was an old door, a wooden frame with a pane of frosted glass making up the top half and a wooden panel the bottom half, a cat flap cut into it. The sergeant swung the pot like a battering ram at the top corner of the wooden panel, pushing it inwards easily enough. Another hit in the top left corner and he was able to push it back on to the kitchen floor. Then he felt for a key in the lock. 'I'll have to climb in. Give me a sec.'

Dixon handed him a pair of latex gloves.

'Oh, right, yes, of course. We don't get a lot of that sort of thing down this way. Easy to get out of the habit.' Down on all fours now, the sergeant crawled through the hole in the door and stood up. 'There's a key on a hook.'

The door swung open.

'Just me,' said Dixon. He'd put on a pair of latex overshoes and was snapping on a pair of gloves. 'If it's a crime scene, the fewer the better.'

'Yes, Sir,' replied the sergeant, stepping out into the rain again.

'And if the daughter arrives, for God's sake don't let her in unless and until I say so.'

'Shall I let the other two lads go?'

'Not yet. We may need them for house to house.' Dixon flicked on the torch on his phone; touching a light switch might smudge a fingerprint, even in latex gloves.

No food bowl for a cat, so the flap was probably redundant. The kitchen was clean and tidy, the small dishwasher open a crack.

He opened the door into the hall; a flight of stairs on the left, new handrails either side, so Pannell might well be mobile. There had been no key safe by the front door, so he must have let his killer in. Best not to jump the gun, the old boy might just be asleep, although the banging at his back door should have woken him up, possibly. It didn't bode well.

Left into the dining room, living room on the right, door ajar.

The top of a head was visible over the back of an armchair, a faint glow coming from a Calor gas fire, the bottle running empty, a blue flame flickering at the base of the ceramic firebricks.

The television was off, curtains closed. Dixon could hear voices outside in the lane.

He shone his torch down at the figure slumped in the chair.

No finesse this time. No attempt to cover their tracks.

The knife was buried in the man's chest up to the handle, clean through the breast pocket of his shirt. Eyes closed, he looked relaxed, hands down by his sides, palms open.

Two mugs were sitting on a coffee table, the tea in one untouched, the other empty.

The armchair opposite Pannell had been pulled forward a few inches.

If he was a betting man, Dixon would have gone for drugged then stabbed, the killer far too smart to drink from their own mug and leave a DNA trace. *Her* own mug, if house to house turned up sightings of that OT again.

I'll make us a cup of tea, Geoffrey.

Dixon could hear it now.

Dead a while too, which made it the night before, probably. The OT struck after dark and Pannell had been dead longer than an hour, Dixon knew that much.

A quick glance around the room by the light of his torch. Several trophies in a corner cabinet, the usual photographs: wife and family, cats and dogs, holidays. A photograph of Pannell and a woman being presented with the Somerset County Bridge Union Pairs Cup, a label underneath dated 2002, the year before Michael Allam and Deirdre Baxter had won it. The woman was probably Judith Bolam, only spared a violent death by a heart attack.

He stepped back out into the drizzle. 'Stabbed,' he said, quietly. 'We'll need the road closed both ends. Let's get Mark and Sarah over here too; it's early enough to do a full house to house tonight. Doorbell camera or dashcam footage, usual stuff. We'll need Scientific and the pathologist from Yeovil, whoever that is.'

'I'll ring Hari Patel.' Louise was fishing her phone out of her coat pocket. 'We were too late then?'

'Twenty-four hours too late would be my guess.'

'Stabbed, though?'

'We've got the press conference to thank for that.' Dixon was watching uniformed officers clearing the lane of passers-by. 'No need to try and hide it any more, once they knew we were on to them.'

'Colonel Mustard, in the sitting room, with a knife.'

Dixon sighed. The pathologist from Yeovil Hospital had got there first and seemed to think he was a bit of a comedian. Either that or he was trying to lighten the mood.

'Do we wait for the crime scene manager?'

'We do,' replied Dixon.

'I'll be in my car, in that case.'

Uniformed officers had ushered the neighbours back inside their houses and cottages; the dog walkers had been moved on too. The lane was blocked at both ends by patrol cars, one of them reversing to allow a Scientific Services van through.

Another car appeared at the top end, and Dixon watched the animated conversation before a uniformed officer came jogging towards him. 'The daughter's here, Sir,' she said.

'A detective superintendent?' was the only response to his warrant card. 'What the bloody hell's a superintendent doing here? What's happened to my father?'

'Let's sit in the back of this patrol car, shall we?' said Dixon. 'Constable, see if one of these neighbours of Mr Pannell's would be kind enough to make Mrs West a cup of tea.'

'Yes, Sir.'

'There's no need to bother with that,' said Dixon, when Mrs West began putting on her seatbelt in the back of the patrol car. 'We're just sitting here to get out of the rain and for a bit of privacy.'

'Oh, right.'

'There's no easy way to say this, Mrs West, so I'll just come straight out with it.' He turned in his seat to face Pannell's daughter. 'I'm afraid your father's been murdered.'

'How? Why?' She started to cry, as quietly as she could.

'The pathologist hasn't been in yet, I'm afraid, but I can tell you that he's been stabbed.'

'Who would do such a thing? An old man, sitting in his chair.'

'You may have seen on the news we're investigating a series of murders, and all of the victims were members of the Somerset bridge team that went to the Regional Qualifier in 2003. There was a fire at the Palace Hotel, Torquay, which was the venue for the tournament.'

'I do remember that,' said Mrs West, dabbing her eyes with a tissue. 'I was at uni and was home for the holiday. Dad was really into his bridge. Good at it too. He was county champion the year before, I think it was, and that qualified him and his partner for the regionals the following year. Something like that anyway. His bridge partner was a woman and that was always a source of tension between my parents, if I'm being honest. Weekends away in hotels, you can imagine what my mum thought.'

'Was anything going on between your father and his bridge partner?'

'I don't think so.'

The car door opened and a mug of tea was handed in, first to Dixon, then across to Mrs West. 'Betty at number 6 says you're welcome to sit with her when you've finished, if you want to get out of the rain,' said the uniformed officer, before closing the car door.

'Can't I go in the house?' asked Mrs West, turning to Dixon.

'It's a crime scene, I'm afraid, and it'll be tomorrow before Scientific have finished. Do you know Betty?'

Mrs West nodded. 'I suppose he could have been having an affair,' she said.

'With Judith Bolam?'

'That's her. You never really know what your parents are getting up to, do you? You see old people and you tend to forget they were young once, getting up to much the same stuff we get up to these days.'

'Did he say anything when he got back from the qualifier?'

'Not really. There'd usually have been a row, a few plates broken and what have you, but I don't remember any of that. He did mention the fire, and we'd seen it on the news anyway, of course, but after that, nothing. He never played bridge again either, which was odd now I come to think of it.' A sip of tea. 'I bought him a book of bridge puzzles that Christmas, but I don't think he did any of them. He never touched it; cancelled his membership of the bridge club. There's an address book somewhere and he'd put a line through all of his bridge contacts. All of them. Never sent so much as a Christmas card to any of them again.'

'And he never said what happened during the fire?'

'Not to me.'

'Did your mother ever mention anything?'

'No.'

'I don't suppose your father kept a diary or anything like that?'

'Not as far as I'm aware. If he did, he never showed it to me. I do remember some photographs, though. He had one of those old cameras where you took the film into Boots to get it developed, although he used to send them off somewhere by then, I think, and get them back in the post.'

'Photographs of what?'

'The fire.' Mrs West was watching Scientific Services setting up a gazebo in her father's front garden, the scene lit by an arc lamp. 'It was a green wallet thing, with photos in it; I'm sure there were some of the fire. I wouldn't be surprised if he destroyed them, though. I remember he got very upset when we were watching the news and it said three people had been killed.'

Chapter Twenty-One

Dixon saw the clipboard first, the pathologist waiting patiently under the gazebo to be allowed into the cottage.

'I can't let you in as well. Sorry,' said Hari Patel to Dixon as he approached. 'There are too many people in there as it is. They haven't even got the stepping plates down yet.'

'Who's the senior scientific officer?'

'Donald Watson.'

'I need a word with him.'

'You'll have to wait until he comes out.'

'I've been in there already.'

'What?'

'I found the body.'

Hari was scribbling on his clipboard. 'You still can't go in,' he said.

Dixon turned to the pathologist. 'Would you be kind enough to ask Donald to come out here?'

'Of course.'

'And I need a time of death, please. It would be useful to know if he was drugged before he was stabbed as well. It looks like it to me, but it may give the daughter some comfort to know he was out of it when he was killed.'

'I'll see what I can do, but that will almost certainly have to wait for blood tests.'

Watson appeared a few seconds later, walking on the plastic sheeting in latex overshoes. 'Keeping us busy this time,' he said.

Dixon didn't take the bait. 'The daughter tells me there should be some photographs, the proper ones, printed and in a green paper wallet like the old days. My parents have got boxes of them at home.'

'I know what you mean.'

'There are some pictures of a fire at the Palace Hotel, Torquay.'

'I'll keep an eye out for them.'

'Let me know straight away if you find them.'

'I'll scan them and email them over to you.'

The pathologist had appeared in the doorway behind Watson, and they both stepped to one side to allow an officer to lay stepping plates along the length of the hallway. 'I can see why he was stabbed and not strangled, in case you were wondering. He's had a laryngectomy. Cancer probably. They remove the larynx and he breathed through a hole about here.' He was tapping a spot just below the knot of his tie. 'Dead about twenty-four hours, I'd say, and I can't confirm whether or not he was drugged without a tox screen, I'm afraid.'

'The fire had been on. Did I mention that?' asked Dixon.

'No.'

'It was just running out of gas when I got in there at five-seventeen.'

'Marvellous,' muttered the pathologist, disappearing back inside the cottage.

'That coincides with what the neighbour that side says.' Louise was standing under the gazebo behind Dixon. She had been helping with the house to house and looked soaked through. 'About five o'clock yesterday, a visit from someone, she didn't see who, just heard the doorbell go. Nothing since then and she hasn't seen Geoff all day, not that that's altogether unusual.'

'Anything else?'

'Mark and Sarah are here. They've got someone down there with a doorbell camera so they're having a look at that.'

Dixon's phone was buzzing in his pocket and had been for some time; a persistent buzzing. Someone was leaving it ringing until it cut off, then hitting redial. Over and over.

He slid his phone out of his inside jacket pocket and looked at the screen. Eight missed calls.

All from Jane.

'Must be something going on. Jane's been trying to get hold of me.'

Then Louise's phone rang. 'Hi Jane,' she said. 'Everything all ri—?' She looked at Dixon, her eyes wide. 'Yeah, he's here. Hold on.'

Dixon reached out for the phone, a sick feeling in the pit of his stomach. Whatever it was, it wasn't good. That much was clear from the look on Louise's face. 'What's up?' he asked.

'My father's had a heart attack.'

It hadn't taken long. Louise had said she'd get a lift back with Mark and Sarah, the patrol car blocking the lane had reversed out of the way, and Dixon was on his way to Weston-super-Mare hospital. He hadn't even bothered to tell Jane to drive carefully because she wouldn't have listened; that much was clear from the engine noise in the background of their call.

Rod and Sue had adopted Jane at birth and hadn't batted an eyelid when she'd found her birth mother. Couldn't have been easy.

Not that the relationship had lasted long, Sonia dead from a drug overdose after only their second meeting.

The good that had come of it had been Lucy, Jane's half-sister. Rod and Sue had become grandparents to her, of sorts, which fitted because Jane behaved more like Lucy's mother than her sister.

Lucy was proof that things could go well, despite everything. In and out of care all her life, her mother an abusive alcoholic, and here she was, a police cadet about to sit her GCSEs.

Jane had come into her life at just the right time.

A heart attack. The poor old sod. Not always fatal these days; it did mean one thing though. They'd need to get a wriggle on and marry sooner rather than later if Rod was to walk Jane down the aisle. It had been postponed once already, although everyone had understood the reason.

Jumbled thoughts popping in and out of his head like the wisps of fog hanging over the rhynes as he raced across the Somerset Levels, lights on full beam.

The whole bridge team of six was accounted for now, all three pairs either dead, murdered or suffering from dementia. Surely that would be an end to the killing?

And what *had* happened during that fire?

Plenty of time to worry about that tomorrow. Louise, Sarah and Mark could handle it in the meantime.

He parked in the car park outside the Accident and Emergency Department, next to Jane's VW Golf, Monty standing on the driver's seat, his front paws up on the steering wheel.

Through the swing doors, walking confidently, with his warrant card in his hand, he pretended not to notice the receptionist tapping on the glass screen to attract his attention. Through the security doors as someone else was coming out, then he walked along the line of cubicles, the curtains drawn, until he recognised the voices inside.

'How is he?' he asked, through the gap in the curtains.

'I'm fine,' said Rod, his voice mumbled behind an oxygen mask. 'They've got me wired to all these bloody machines.' Patches had been stuck to his chest, a cannula in the back of his hand; there was even something clamped on the tip of his index finger.

Dixon glanced at the line moving across the screen, the blip coinciding with a loud bleep.

There were few people Dixon would trust with his dog, but Rod was one of them. Said it all, really.

Sue was sitting next to Rod, holding his other hand. 'It was a mild one, mercifully,' she said. 'He'd been overdoing it in the garden. The doctor reckons he's been very lucky.'

Jane was sitting on the end of the bed, her eyes fixed on the screen.

'You shouldn't have bothered coming, Nick,' said Rod, holding his mask away from his mouth. 'I'm sure there are other places you need to be. I'll be fine. These two will see to it.'

Dixon stepped forward, clasping Rod's right hand in his, careful not to dislodge the sensor on his fingertip. 'You need to tell her, Rod. And you need to tell her now.'

It was definitely a Land Rover coming along the lane; Dixon recognised the headlights. They'd swapped car keys so he could bring Monty home in Jane's car. It could be her, he thought. Either that or someone out lamping. He'd heard several shotgun blasts as he'd wandered along the lane, following Monty's white coat in the moonlight.

'Why didn't you tell me?' would be her first question, and he was ready for that one. There'd be some tears too, but no chance of a medicinal gin and tonic.

Pub was closed anyway.

The Land Rover stopped and Jane got out, leaving the engine running. She ran over to the farm gateway where Dixon was waiting with Monty and put her arms around his neck, hugging him tight, her chest heaving as she sobbed.

'How is he?' he asked, rubbing her back with the palms of his hands. He'd been doing a lot of that lately; carrying a baby was back-breaking work, it seemed.

'They're keeping him in for a few days, but he's going to be all right, I think. I was there when the consultant came round; low risk of another one, apparently.' Jane was rubbing her eyes. 'He was digging in the garden – a vegetable patch, would you believe it? The silly sod never knows when to stop.'

'Have you eaten?'

'Oh no, you don't get out of it that easily.' She leaned back, Dixon's arms still tight around her waist. 'How long have you known?'

'He told me when I went to see him about the wedding.'

'You didn't go to see him about *the wedding*; you went to ask his permission to marry me.'

'I'm old-fashioned, so shoot me. And he appreciated the gesture.'

'He did, but that was months ago and you never said anything.'

'It wasn't my place. He wanted to tell you on your wedding day; it's a father and daughter thing. I did say I'd tell you if they left it too late.'

'All these years I thought they only adopted me because they couldn't have children of their own.'

'And all the time they could, but *chose* you instead. That's quite something when you think about it.'

'Yeah, it is.' Jane reached down to stroke Monty, who was jumping up at her. 'It'll take me a while to get my head round it.'

'Take as long as you want. You're entitled to compassionate leave.'

'You crafty—' She thought better of it, catching herself mid-sentence. 'I said I'd visit him in the evening, *after work*. They understand only too well what we've got going on, even if you don't.'

'I'm not sure I do – yet, anyway.' Dixon opened the back door of the Land Rover, allowing Monty to jump in. 'I thought about Valentine's Day. Will he be well enough to walk you down the aisle by then?'

'You just try and stop him.' Jane grinned. 'I'll ring Jonathan in the morning, see if he can squeeze us in. He did say he'd do his best when we had to cancel last time.'

'The function room at the Red Cow is free,' said Dixon. 'I checked. Managed to catch last orders too.'

'I bet you haven't eaten. And you've got an early start in the morning. You're due at Torquay Police Station at nine.'

Chapter Twenty-Two

'It's a building site.'

'A very big building site,' replied Dixon. He was standing with Louise on the pavement outside what had once been the Palace Hotel.

'I came here yonks ago with my parents,' she said. 'I must have been nine or ten, maybe. There was some family "do" on – you know how it is. The leisure centre was over there.'

A service road cut through the middle of the site, houses under construction on the far side.

'It was lovely; a big pool, squash courts. We had a great time.'

The main site had been hidden behind green-painted wooden panels covered in a multitude of signs and stickers: the name of the builders, hard hats must be worn, no admittance beyond this point – the usual stuff. The circus was in town too, the posters faded and torn at the edges, so probably dated from last summer.

Dixon ducked under the barrier and stood at the top of what had once been the drive, presumably, the road sweeping down in a gentle curve to the grand entrance, the edge marked by red and white interlocking crash barriers and wire fencing.

'This is what it used to look like,' said Louise, holding her phone in front of Dixon, the screen filled by the huge hotel, painted a similar shade of green to the wooden panels now hiding the desolate scene from the locals.

Vast piles of rubble were all that was left of it.

Some grey, some red.

Four men wearing hi-vis jackets and yellow hard hats were standing at the bottom of the access road, smoking. They glanced at Dixon and turned away, gawpers a familiar sight, probably.

'And this is the ballroom,' said Louise. 'It would have been laid out with tables and chairs for the bridge thing, though.'

Huge chandeliers hanging from an ornate curved ceiling, balconies overlooking a highly polished dance floor, red velvet curtains, a stage at the far end.

'Sad, isn't it?'

Dixon spun round to find them being watched by a dog walker standing at the barrier.

'It's been like this for a couple of years now,' she continued. 'An eyesore, it is, when you consider what it once was.' Jeans and a green coat, an umbrella in one hand, two small terriers in the other. 'Are you from the builders?'

'I'm afraid not.'

'Shame. I'd like to give the useless lot a piece of my mind.'

'Do you live locally?' asked Dixon.

'Those flats over there,' she replied, gesturing to the other side of the road.

'How long?'

'Twenty-five years.'

'So, you remember the fire in the ballroom?'

'That was terrible,' she said, grimacing at the memory. 'It was the next day before they put it out. And the smell. The smell was the worst part; it lingered for months. It was worse when it rained, for some reason. The ballroom was rebuilt, though, and it all went back to normal. For a while.'

'What's happening to the site now?'

'It was derelict for a couple of years, then it was bought by investors and the demolition took another couple of years. They got planning permission to build houses on the leisure centre bit, and the idea was that the proceeds from that would pay for the hotel to be rebuilt. Grand plans, they had. It was going to be five-star, no expense spared, luxury spa, rooftop bar, conference centre, you name it. The jewel in the crown of the English Riviera, they called it – huge bloody fanfare, there was. But it's no longer financially viable, apparently.'

Dixon waited. He'd obviously touched a raw nerve and she was building up a head of steam.

'Now an application's gone in for more houses instead; sixty-seven of them.' She scowled at Louise. 'You're not from the planning department, are you?'

'No, sorry.'

'They're a useless bunch of—' She stopped herself mid-sentence, glancing at Dixon's Land Rover, the hazard lights flashing. 'Who are you then?'

Dixon had been wondering when she would get around to that. 'Police.'

The woman hesitated, unsure whether she could or should ask the obvious question.

'We're looking again at the ballroom fire,' he said, putting her out of her misery.

'He's due out soon, the bugger who started it. It said so in the *Torbay Gazette*. On licence, or whatever it is they call it.'

'Did you give a statement at the time?'

'Yes, but there wasn't anything I could say, really. I watched it from my window; never saw how it started or anything like that. First I knew about it was the sirens and flashing lights. He admitted starting the fire, so what bit of it are you interested in?'

'It's an unrelated case,' replied Dixon. 'Four victims, all of whom were here for the bridge tournament going on in the ballroom. We're just exploring whether there might be a connection with what happened that night.'

'I remember there was a bridge thing going on.' Her dogs were sitting down on the wet pavement, waiting patiently to continue their walk. 'But I don't think it had anything to do with the fire, as such. It was a waiter; he'd been sacked and was getting his own back, and it all got a bit out of hand.'

A cheery wave and a 'Good luck' over her shoulder and she was gone.

'Show me that photo again,' said Dixon, turning back to Louise.

Green, with white detailing around the windows, four storeys, the ballroom off to the right, pine trees curving around behind it. A figure in a top hat and tails visible by the grand entrance, waiting to greet guests. It was a scene from a bygone age.

Now it was just rubble and abandoned building materials, delivered before they'd changed their minds about building the new hotel, probably; piles of breeze blocks wrapped in plastic, sections of huge concrete drainpipes, rusting steel girders.

Even the terrace had been torn up, the remains of the golf course behind it evidenced only by several flat sections where the greens would have been.

'Makes a sorry sight,' said Louise. 'In more ways than one.'

'The Palace Hotel Ballroom,' said Dixon. 'It sounds like something out of *The Blues Brothers*.'

◆ ◆ ◆

'Where are you supposed to park?' asked Louise. She was looking all around while Dixon waited at a set of traffic lights outside Torquay Police Station.

189

He'd been round the one-way system twice already, looking for on-street parking, but finding none. There was no visitors' car park either.

'One way of keeping people away, I suppose,' he said, watching a vehicle waiting at the electric gates to the staff car park at the side of the station. 'Those gates are even slower than ours. We can nip in there when she's gone.'

A dog van was turning out while he put the blue light on the roof of his Land Rover, the light slowing the approaching jobsworth long enough for Dixon to get his warrant card out of his pocket.

'Someone said you were coming. Just give me a shout when you're leaving, Sir, and I'll let you out.'

'Thank you.'

'We were told to ask for Superintendent Allott,' said Louise.

They were kept waiting long enough to work out how to use the coffee machine, before being shown into a vacant interview room, a large cardboard box sitting on the table.

'There's the main bit of the file, Sir,' said a tall officer, his shirt untucked. 'And there are eight more boxes downstairs.' He hadn't bothered to introduce himself either. 'Take as long as you want. The super will be along in a few minutes to have a chat.'

'Thank you.' Dixon had questions, but there was no point wasting his breath just yet.

'No questions for him, Sir?' asked Louise, when the officer had gone.

'He'd have been at school when the ballroom went up in flames, Lou.'

Louise opened the box and took out several bundles of witness statements, dropping them on the table. 'No shortage of witnesses,' she said. 'All the hotel guests, staff, local residents. It'll take days to wade through this lot.'

'See if you can find the arson investigator's report and the defendant's interviews,' said Dixon.

'They'll let us copy them, I expect.'

'Don't bother with that. We'll be taking the file with us.'

'Really?'

Two loud knocks, then the door opened. 'Detective Superintendent Allott.' Hand outstretched. 'I see you've found the coffee machine.'

'I thought it was chicken soup,' replied Dixon, putting on his best chatty, amenable self.

'Tastes a bit like it, I'll give you that.'

'Are there any officers left who were involved in the original investigation?' he asked, gesturing to the box that Louise was still rummaging through.

'Only me,' replied Allott. 'I was a DC back then and it was pretty much my first case in Devon; spent the whole time taking statements from people who'd seen nothing relevant, if I remember rightly.' He sat down at the table and leaned back in the chair, his hands behind his head. 'It was an open and shut case, really. We nicked the bloke at the scene, he confessed – the information he gave fitted with the arson investigator's assessment – and that was that. Life with a minimum of eighteen years, which was a bit light perhaps, but what can you do?'

'Who was the SIO?'

'DCS Campbell, although he wasn't a chief super back then, just a super.' Allott checked his watch. 'Retired now; he'll be on the beach with his dog, and then, come eleven o'clock, you'll find him in the Paignton Club, playing snooker. In the meantime, you're welcome to use the photocopier next door.'

Here we go.

'We'll be taking the file with us,' replied Dixon. 'After all, we're working together on a regional task force, aren't we? I know that both chief constables are keen to see collaboration, and all that.'

'Yes, but—'

'Not just that we are collaborating, but that we're being seen to be collaborating.'

'No, but—'

'And it's not as if there's any suggestion of anything amiss with the original Devon and Cornwall investigation. Merely that what happened that night is behind the motive for these killings.'

'I'm still not sure I can let the file go.'

'Well, you're not, are you? It's staying within the regional task force, of which Devon and Cornwall currently represents half.'

Allott looked nervously at Louise. 'Could we have the room, please?' he asked.

Dixon stifled a sigh. Another one watching too much American telly. He was tempted to ask Allott if he wanted a coffee, just to see if he said, 'I'm good.'

'Look,' said Allott, when Louise closed the door behind her. 'Our ACC is nervous about bad publicity for us.'

'Our ACC's a bit like that. I think it's in their job description.'

'There was a lot of unpleasantness in the town in the aftermath of the fire and he's really keen to see that's not raked up again. Particularly with what's going on at the site. And Rodwell's due out any day now.'

'Is there something I need to know?' asked Dixon.

'Not specifically. It just never looks good for a force when an old case is being picked apart, whatever the reason.'

Dixon got the distinct impression Allott was lying about something, or hiding something. 'I've got four murders, and the only time the victims' paths crossed in the last twenty years was at that bridge competition. All I can say is, I'm going to go over it, and I'm going to do that whether you let me take the file or not.'

Allott was sucking his teeth, running his tongue under his top lip, the movement exaggerated by his moustache. Then he reached forward and pushed the box across the table towards Dixon. 'Take it,' he said. 'I'll have the other boxes brought up. Read Rodwell's first interview, the one I conducted. He went "no comment" to the others after that.' Allott stood up and turned for the door. 'And you didn't hear that from me.'

Chapter Twenty-Three

'A green Barbour and a black lab, Allott said.' Louise was standing on Paignton seafront, her eyes scanning along the beach; not that there was much, the tide almost up to the sea wall, cramming the dog walkers into a strip no more than five yards wide.

Dixon had parked on the double yellow lines and was reading Rodwell's police interviews; three in total. He'd flicked through the second and third, all answers 'no comment', even to the question asking him to confirm his full name for the tape.

A solicitor had been present, which was the main difference. 'My client has made his position clear and will not be answering any more questions.'

So, to the first interview, conducted the evening after the fire, once the arson investigator had given his preliminary findings and the death toll had been confirmed.

'Do you want a coffee?' asked Louise, leaning in the driver's window. 'That stuff at the station tasted like shit. There's a stand over there and we've got ten minutes.'

'Thanks.'

'We can go and wait in the car park at the Paignton Club. I can see it from here, at the end of the promenade there.'

He flicked through the interview while Louise wandered across the green to the coffee stand on the far side. Dixon had never been good at speed reading, but the document ran to sixty-one pages, the interview lasting over two hours, and he only had ten minutes before his meeting with retired DCS Campbell. Talkative, was Sean Rodwell – at least to begin with – some answers running to over half a page of A4; DC Allott, as he then was, reluctant to interrupt him. And why would he?

If they want to talk, let them.

DC Allott: Three people died in a fire you started because you'd been sacked, Sean. Seventy-two-year-old John Compton, his thirty-six-year-old daughter Miriam Hudson, and her son, Patrick. Patrick was three months old.

Rodwell's answer ran to two pages of A4. And he hadn't even been asked a question that time.

'He's here, Sir,' said Louise. She was standing by the Land Rover, a coffee in each hand. 'I've just seen him going—'

She stopped herself, noticing Dixon was reading something. 'Sorry,' she said, tipping her head, trying to read it through the window of the car.

He took a deep breath, closing the document before folding it in half lengthways and slotting it into his coat pocket.

'Let's go and see what retired DCS Campbell has got to say for himself, shall we?'

Campbell was hiding behind a broadsheet newspaper in the bay window, a coffee on the table in front of him. The bar was deserted, the door open to the kitchen behind it, the clattering of plates and glasses – the familiar sound of a dishwasher being loaded.

It was a grandstand view, waves lapping against the sea wall outside.

There were worse ways to spend your retirement, thought Dixon. Walking a dog on the beach, playing snooker. He moved the cue from the seat next to Campbell's leather armchair and sat down.

Sleeping at night might be a bit more of a problem.

No movement from behind the newspaper, not even a curious glance around the side; Campbell knew who they were and why they were there.

Dixon slid the transcript of Rodwell's police interview out of his coat pocket and dropped it on the table in front of Campbell. The newspaper moved, a shaved head peering around it.

'Every single thing Rodwell said in that first interview was the truth,' said Dixon, matter of fact. 'How he started the fire, where he started the fire, it all corresponds exactly with the arson investigator's findings.'

Campbell folded his paper slowly and placed it on the table, covering the interview transcript, then he took off his reading glasses, slotting them into the top pocket of his jacket. 'I know where you're going with this. We looked at it at the time, of course we did, but there was no evidence to support his version of events. None whatsoever.'

Louise was trying to catch up. She wouldn't be able to; she hadn't read the interview.

'D'you know how many witness statements we took?' Campbell was gathering steam and volume. 'Hundreds, and not a single witness mentioned it.'

'Were they asked?'

'Of course they were bloody well asked. Don't you come in here questioning my investigation, you little—'

'We'll be asking them again,' interrupted Dixon.

Campbell was doing his best not to bristle, and was managing it, after a fashion. 'Look, I understand you've got a job to do. I know that all four of your victims were at that bridge tournament, but you have to understand it from my side. I was SIO in a major investigation, one of the biggest we've had in the bay, with hundreds of witnesses, three dead, and a known arsonist who confessed to starting the fire.'

Louise was still none the wiser, her frown taking on a look of permanence.

'Two dead and one missing, to be technically correct,' said Dixon, firmly.

'The evidence from the pathologist was quite clear on that.' Campbell sat up, taken aback for a second. 'The body of a three-month-old child in a fire of that intensity, burning for that length of time' – he threw his arms in the air – 'there'd be nothing left. All that bollocks in Rodwell's interview was just him trying to absolve himself of blame for the child's death. He could live with killing two adults but not a baby. That was too much even for him.'

Dixon picked up the transcript and began reading from the interview. '"I stayed to watch the fire. It started in the corner of the kitchen area at the back of the ballroom. It's not used for cooking, just keeping stuff warm for the buffet lunches, so there are gas bottles and hot plates. I'd stuffed a newspaper in a toaster and disconnected the gas. There was a flicker through the window, then the gas bottles went up, the fire alarms went off and it was chaos, people running everywhere, shouting and screaming. I was in the trees behind the ballroom, watching the fire spread along the wall inside. That would've been the velvet wallpaper. The windows blew out, sending bits of glass right across the golf course. I felt bad about that because there were people being cut and I could see blood. I never meant to hurt anyone, I really didn't."'

'I know what it says,' protested Campbell, taking his chance when Dixon drew breath.

'"There were groups of people out on the terrace, staff trying to usher them out on to the course. It was like the bridge teams were sticking together, that's what I thought at the time, but it might have been families as well. Someone had a clipboard and was trying to take a roll, ticking people off as they shouted over the sirens. That's when I saw it. There was a group of six, one of the bridge teams – I'd served them lunch in the ballroom that day – standing at the end of the terrace. Four men and two women, and I remember one of the women was carrying a baby. It couldn't have been hers because she was too old, late sixties or early seventies, and you said the only other kids in the hotel were toddlers and have been accounted for. It was screaming and crying on her shoulder, then another woman ran up to her and took it off her. I don't know whether it was a boy or a girl, to be honest, I couldn't see at that distance, couldn't hear what was being said, but this woman took it and disappeared into the crowd further along the terrace. She had short, dark hair – mid-thirties, maybe – and was wearing a red coat. Look, I accept entirely that I killed the woman and her father, but the baby isn't dead.'"

'He was lying.' Campbell was breathing deeply, his eyes squeezed shut. 'He knew if he went to prison labelled a baby-killer he was in deep shit and he was trying to lie his way out of it.'

'That baby would be twenty-one now,' said Dixon.

'So, what, you think he's come back for revenge on the bridge team that gave him away that night?' A tremble had crept into Campbell's voice. 'That's ridiculous.'

'What if . . . ?' asked Dixon, watching Campbell ask himself the rest of the question. Answering it too, judging by the look on his face.

'That baby died in the fire. We spoke to every single bridge player there that night, all of the tournament staff, referees, the tournament director, everyone, and not one of them saw a thing. And, like I said, according to the pathologist, there'd be nothing left of a baby in a fire like that.'

'Did you speak to the baby's father?'

198

'That was, without a doubt, the most difficult conversation I ever had to have in my thirty years on the force.' Campbell's eyes glazed over. 'To tell a man who's just lost his wife and son in a fire, that the man who started that fire is alleging his son was carried off into the night by some mysterious woman. You can imagine it, can't you? I had to tell him though. Rodwell pleaded not guilty to the murder of the boy and it would have come out at the trial. He'd have been watching from the public gallery, for heaven's sake. In the end, there was no trial. The CPS dropped the third charge and Rodwell pleaded guilty to the other two. Not in the public interest, they said. Imagine having to explain that to the boy's father, on top of everything else.'

'Was he there that night?'

'No. His wife had brought their newborn son down to see her father at the Palace Hotel. He might even have been playing bridge, I can't remember, but Will Hudson had taken their daughter to see his own parents in Wales, from memory. The daughter was two, I think.'

'And how did he react to Rodwell's story?'

'Not well. The family weren't short of a bob or two and they engaged the services of a private investigator, who interviewed all the witnesses. There was no secret about who they were; all the players at the bridge thing were listed on the English Bridge Union website, but he didn't turn anything up either. There was nothing on the CCTV, before you ask. We checked it all – car parks, the leisure centre, all of it.'

'There are some discs in the box,' said Louise.

'There you are, you can check for yourselves. There was a journalist too, made a nuisance of herself investigating it. There were a couple of articles in the local rag, and she had some podcast thing, but she never came up with anything that wasn't pure speculation.

That child died in the fire, I'm telling you.' The tremble had gone from Campbell's voice, but so had the certainty.

'Did you check with the Registrar of Births, Deaths and Marriages?'

'Yes. And with Social Services.' Campbell glanced up at the bar where a man was waiting, snooker cue in hand. 'There were no recorded deaths of three-month-old babies, apart from young Patrick Hudson, registered that year or the year before. No bereaved mother looking to replace her lost son. We checked and double-checked.'

'The coroner registered his death?'

'Eventually, there was an inquest, after we'd exhausted all lines of enquiry. The coroner arrived at the same conclusion we did: Rodwell was lying and the boy was dead. The only real doubt was exactly how he died, so it was an open verdict; and let me tell you, I sleep soundly at night. Now, if you'll excuse me,' Campbell said, standing up, 'my snooker partner is here.'

Dixon waited until Campbell had gone, listening to the footsteps on the stairs, an exchange just carrying over the noise of the dishwasher.

'Who was that?'

'Police stuff, you know how it is.'

'Unfinished business?'

'Not as far as I'm concerned.'

Louise had snatched the interview transcript off the coffee table and was reading the passage Dixon had read aloud. 'What if he survived and he's out there somewhere?'

'Think I'm barking up the wrong tree this time?' asked Dixon.

'No, Sir.'

'If you accept Rodwell's version of events is true, and every-thing else he said in that interview is, then the bridge team lied about the baby. And they've paid for it with their lives.'

◆ ◆ ◆

They had crossed the border from Devon into Somerset before Dixon spoke again.

'Have someone meet us at Deirdre's bungalow with the keys.'

Louise had known better than to interrupt his train of thought, reaching for her phone that was charging on the centre console of the Land Rover.

'Yeah, we're about half an hour away,' she said. 'No idea.' Then she rang off. 'Someone will meet us there.'

Dixon was deep in thought; he could feel the heat, smell the smoke – standing on the hotel terrace, the ballroom on fire, people milling about, sirens, blue lights, a group standing together, one of the women holding a baby.

Snatched? Really? How could you possibly *plan* that?

Unless Rodwell had started the fire deliberately to provide cover – a diversion, opportunity.

But there was no guarantee the opportunity would arise anyway, even in the confusion presented by a fire.

No, opportunity was close, but wasn't quite the right word.

Opportunistic; that was much better.

Campbell had said he slept soundly at night. Maybe he did, but Dixon doubted very much he would tonight.

Blue tape – 'Police Line Do Not Cross' – had been entwined in the steel gates at the bottom of Deirdre Baxter's drive, one end shredded and fluttering in the prevailing January wind; the tape on the gate at the bottom of the garden path ripped off by the wind and tangled in a rose bush.

Someone had been in; footprints in the flowerbed. The postman, probably, given that the tape on the front door had been pulled away from the letterbox.

A patrol car turned into the far end of Parsonage Lane, the unmistakable figure of Nigel Cole behind the wheel, no doubt enjoying the peace and quiet without Sarah.

'I was on my way home, Sir,' he said, pulling up adjacent to Dixon's Land Rover and winding down the window, a set of keys in his outstretched hand. 'You wanted these?'

'Thanks, Nige.'

'D'you want me to come in with you?'

'No, that's fine, you go home.'

Dixon had the key inserted in the lock before Louise asked the obvious question. 'What exactly are we looking for?'

'You should know. You found it.'

'Did I?'

She followed him into the utility room, the internal door to the garage standing open. Then he opened the car door and slid into the passenger seat. He opened the glovebox with his left hand, reached in with his right hand inside an evidence bag and took out the baby's dummy, turning the bag inside out as he did so.

It was a well-practised routine, as any dog owner could testify.

'We need to get this off for DNA testing,' he said, sealing the bag and handing it to Louise.

Chapter Twenty-Four

Dixon had been at Express Park for over an hour when he spotted Charlesworth's car turning into the visitors' car park at the front of the building. The floor to ceiling windows had their uses.

'What does he want now?' asked Jane.

'I'm guessing he's had a call from his opposite number at Devon and Cornwall and wants me to tread carefully.'

'I've never known you do that.'

'Neither's he, but he's got to go through the motions, I suppose.'

Jane grinned. 'You stomp.'

'Thank you, Sergeant.'

'You're welcome.'

'How's Rod doing?'

'Better, I think,' replied Jane. 'I'll be off to see him in a bit. He's coming home tomorrow.'

'Did you speak to Jonathan?'

'He can't do us in Brent Knoll on Valentine's Day. It's a Saturday and it's been booked up for yonks, so we could do either Friday the thirteenth in Brent Knoll or Valentine's Day at Berrow church. That's free, apparently, and he can get us a special dispensation or something.'

'Berrow it is, then.' His phone was buzzing in his pocket. 'The crafty sod's sent me a text message.' It was a new tactic that made dodging an ambush impossible. '"Deborah and I are in meeting room two. Thank you,"' he said, reading aloud.

'He doesn't actually ask you to go.' Jane was trying to be helpful. 'It's just a statement of fact, isn't it?'

A fair point, but the alternative wasn't exactly inviting, and he'd been putting it off for an hour already. A phrase involving the devil and the deep blue sea sprang to mind; it was either a meeting with Charlesworth and his entourage or the father of the baby boy. Campbell had said his meeting with him had been the most difficult of his career, and Dixon's was unlikely to be any easier.

Perhaps a cosy chat with Charlesworth might not be so bad after all?

Louise intercepted him as he weaved his way through the workstations towards the stairs. 'These are the witness statements the Torquay lot took from the Somerset bridge team at the time,' she said.

'Do they mention the boy?'

'There's a paragraph in each where they say they didn't see a child at all, at any point during the fire, so they must've been asked the question.'

'And lied.'

'Unless it was a different bridge team.' Louise gave a nervous shrug. 'It could've been, which would mean all this has nothing to do . . .' Her voice ran out of steam; taken the point as far she dared, possibly.

The thought had occurred to Dixon, but if right, that would make it the mother of all coincidences.

Charlesworth was standing on the landing outside meeting room 2, his eyes fixed on the top of the stairs, waiting for Dixon to appear. He gave a smug grin, pleased with himself that his new tactic had worked.

Blocking his number was the obvious answer.

'Come in, Nick,' said Charlesworth, his arm extended much like an usher's at a wedding. 'I've got Andrew Yeend here, the Devon ACC.'

An ambush good and proper then.

'We'd like an update on the investigation, if you've got a minute,' continued Charlesworth. 'And I know that Andy has some concerns.'

Deborah Potter was looking concerned too, and Vicky Thomas, the press officer, but then she always did. It would've been standing room only, if Charlesworth hadn't got an extra chair from somewhere.

'The boy is dead,' said Yeend, a strident edge to his voice. Oddly loud.

Dixon wasn't sure who he was trying to convince. 'Whether he is alive or dead, it remains a possible motive for these murders and will be explored on that basis.'

'We had a lot of trouble with the father,' continued Yeend. 'And you're opening a real can of worms for us here. There was litigation over the decision to close down the investigation. He applied for judicial review of the inquest verdict, employed a private detective, and there was lots of bad publicity for us. It dragged on for years.'

'Frankly, I don't blame him. The man had lost his wife and son.'

'In a fire. And I would remind you that the pathologist's report—'

'I've read it.'

'No trace of the boy's body was ever found, and we were being told that was entirely to be expected in a fire of that intensity. The arson investigator said so, and the pathologist.'

'And they're both quite right, of course,' said Dixon. 'There is another explanation for that, though.'

'That he wasn't there,' said Potter, slightly surprised that she'd said it out loud.

'Tell me about the baby's dummy,' said Charlesworth, turning to Dixon when he'd finished glaring at Potter.

That hadn't taken long. Dixon had only updated the Policy Log twenty minutes ago.

'We found it in the glovebox of Deirdre Baxter's car, and it's being tested for DNA.'

'What are the chances of that?' scoffed Yeend.

'It's the same car she had at the time, and probably drove to the Palace Hotel for the bridge tournament. It's been sitting in her garage for the last twenty years without moving, so who knows?' replied Dixon. 'It's unlikely, I'll give you that. Are you suggesting we shouldn't check it?'

'Of course not.'

'Is the father's DNA on the system?' asked Potter.

'No.'

'Good luck getting that,' said Yeend.

'He's a suspect, isn't he?' replied Dixon. 'So, if he doesn't volunteer it, I get a warrant.'

'A suspect?'

'Someone has killed the Somerset bridge team. It could be the father out of revenge because he thinks they were complicit in the abduction of his son. It could be the son himself, come back to exact his revenge. Either that or they're being silenced for some reason.'

'Silenced?' Yeend was glaring at Charlesworth now.

'Why else leave George Sampson alive?' Dixon folded his arms. 'There's no need to kill him, is there, no need to silence him, because he's got dementia.'

'So, what happens now?' asked Charlesworth, clearly keen to move the conversation along.

'We're revisiting all of the witnesses to the fire and asking them specifically about the baby boy. We've got the CCTV to go through, and I'm going to see Sean Rodwell at his halfway house in Weston in the morning.'

'Oh, that's bloody marvellous, that is.' Yeend was seething now, his teeth gritted. 'He lied, and the CPS fell for it in the end. They dropped the charge. And we did all this at the time. We had posters up, it was even on *Crimewatch* for heaven's sake; a woman with a red coat carrying a baby, and no one came forward. No one.'

'All right, Andrew,' said Charlesworth, his tone conciliatory. 'I really don't think there's any suggestion here that Devon and Cornwall got anything wrong, that there were any gaps in the investigation or anything like that. That's right, isn't it, Nick?'

'Yes, Sir,' replied Dixon. 'I've got the statements the murder victims gave at the time. They were clearly asked the question and, if Rodwell was telling the truth, they must have lied. It explains perhaps why they went their separate ways after the fire; none of the pairs ever played bridge together again competitively.'

'And Devon and Cornwall are part of the regional task force looking at it again, aren't they?' Charlesworth was looking at Yeend, pleading almost.

'I understand that, David. I'm just concerned how it's going to look for us if it turns out the boy was alive all along and we didn't find him.'

'What do you say to that, Nick?'

'There's not a lot I can say to that, Sir. Whether he's alive or not is a question of fact. It might be a PR disaster for Devon and Cornwall, but there's not a lot I can do about it. I'm sure you wouldn't expect interforce *collaboration* to extend to covering it up.' He gave an apologetic shrug. 'If you'll forgive me, shit happens.'

◆ ◆ ◆

'I've always fancied one of these,' said Louise, admiring the display of hot tubs from the passenger seat of Dixon's Land Rover as he drove into the small industrial estate on the edge of Glastonbury. 'Look at the size of them. Some are as big as small swimming pools.'

No doubt there'd be a comment about a hot tub adding value to a house. Dixon braced himself.

'Good selling point too.'

It was a meeting Dixon had been dreading, even before Campbell's comment about his own encounter with the boy's father all those years ago. No doubt the fire still burned brightly, even with the passage of time.

William Hudson had moved on by all accounts. He had married again and had two children with his new wife – Dixon never ceased to be amazed by the information people gave away freely on Facebook. There was even a post on what would have been Patrick's birthday each year; a picture of the baby boy, 'gone but not forgotten'.

'Let's not forget, first and foremost, he's a suspect in the murders of four people and we're going to need chapter and verse about where he was at the relevant times.' Dixon was saying it out loud more for his benefit than Louise's. 'A DNA sample too.'

'Are you going tell him about the baby's dummy?' she asked.

'Yes.' Dixon parked outside the hot tub showroom, only one other car in the car park. 'We need to see if Patrick had one the same.'

A man sitting at a glass desk glanced at them through the windows, quickly turning back to his computer; a young couple in a beaten-up old Land Rover, hardly the stuff of a hot tub sale late on a rainy Thursday in January.

'Probably thinks we're a pair of tyre-kickers,' said Louise. 'No one's spoken to him yet.'

Tall, smartly dressed in suit trousers and a shirt, open at the neck, a jacket slung over the back of his chair. It had been a conscious decision to catch him at work, just before closing, away from his new wife and family. If he was going to talk freely about his old life, then it was best done away from the new.

'Let's get it over and done with,' said Dixon, opening the driver's door.

Hudson Spas; Campbell had said the family were not short of a bob or two.

They were through the glass doors before he looked away from his computer again, appearing surprised that they were ignoring the hot tubs.

'William Hudson?'

'Who wants to know?' He swung round on his office chair.

'Police, Sir,' replied Dixon, warrant card at the ready. 'Is there anyone else who could watch the showroom while we talk?'

'What's it about?'

'Patrick.'

Dixon let that hang in the air for a moment, watching the blood drain from Hudson's face. He stood up, slowly, breathing heavily through his nose.

'I'll close up,' said Hudson, walking towards the door. 'There's no one else here and January isn't exactly our busiest time.' The clack of his heels on the tiled floor echoed around the showroom. 'I saw you on the television – on the news – didn't I?' he asked, his question punctuated by the click of the lock. 'You're investigating those three murders; elderly people in their own homes. What's that got to do with Patrick?'

'It's four now, actually, Sir, and all of them were members of the Somerset bridge team that competed at the Regional Qualifier at the Palace Hotel, Torquay.'

'They were there the night of the fire?'

Dixon nodded, slowly.

'They were *the* bridge team Sean Rodwell talked about in his interview?'

'We're working on that assumption.'

Hudson dropped back down on to his office chair. 'So, what Rodwell said was true all the time. It has to be. Why else would someone want to kill the bridge team?' He slammed his fist down on the desk. 'I knew it. All the time I knew Patrick was alive. Do you know where he is?'

'No, Sir.' Dixon swallowed hard. 'But, if he's out there, we'll find him.'

'I'll get on to Copeland again. He was our private investigator, perhaps he can help you.'

Time to grasp the nettle. 'We have to look at possible motives for the murders of the bridge team, and one motive that we need to explore is revenge.'

Hudson stifled a laugh. 'Me, you mean?'

'We'll need you to account for your whereabouts at the relevant times. We'll also need a DNA sample.'

'Fill your boots.' Hands raised in mock surrender. 'Treat me as a suspect if you must, but I've got nothing to hide. I just want to know where my son is. I think I'm owed that, after all this time.'

Dixon gestured to Louise and left them to it – she had come prepared, the dates in her notebook and a DNA kit in her pocket. He pretended to watch the rain pouring down the windows, when actually he was watching what was going on in the reflection. And listening.

'If I was going to do that, I'd have done it long before now,' said Hudson, an air of resignation in his voice. 'There was a time, perhaps, before Sally and the girls came along.'

Swab under the tongue and around the inside of his cheek.

'Thank you, Sir,' said Louise.

'I suppose you'll need to talk to Sally?'

'We will, Sir.'

'She'll verify everything I've said. And you're welcome to speak to anyone at the Rotary Club do that night.'

'And you've heard nothing from Patrick?' asked Dixon.

'Of course not.' Hudson's face darkened, lines digging deep into his forehead. 'You're not suggesting Patrick might be killing . . .' His voice tailed off, the thought too horrible to contemplate.

'He would be twenty-one now.'

'Yes, but he'd make himself known to me, to his sister, before doing something like that, surely?' Hudson was leaning back in his chair, staring at the ceiling. 'It doesn't make sense.'

'What were your wife and son doing at the hotel that night?'

'They'd gone to see Miriam's father. Her parents lived on Scilly and he was over for the bridge thing, so she took Patrick to meet his grandfather and stayed a couple of nights in a room just along the corridor. I should have gone, but I took our daughter to see my parents in Llandudno. Freya was two and I could cope with her on my own, just about.' Hudson stood up and started pacing up and down. 'Miriam would have seen to it Patrick was safe, handed him to someone on their way out – on the fire escape even – and then gone back to get her father. Their bodies were found together, in the corner of what was left of his hotel room. Everything I know about Miriam fits with what Rodwell said in his interview. I said that time and time again to Campbell and his cronies.' Hudson spun round. 'Have you met him?'

'We spoke to him this morning, Sir.'

'The bloke's a stubborn fool.'

'From what I can see the question was put to all of the witnesses.'

'Only to refute what Rodwell was saying. There was no real attempt made to find my son. All they were interested in was pinning three murders on him instead of two. Our private investigator spoke to the witnesses and it'd been a throwaway question: "You didn't see a baby, did you?" and then it becomes a whole paragraph in their statements.'

'Did Mr Copeland find anyone who'd seen Patrick on the veranda when he reinterviewed the witnesses?'

Hudson was visibly deflated by the question. 'No,' he said, reluctantly.

'What did Miriam take with her for the weekend?' asked Dixon.

'You got children?'

'On the way,' replied Dixon. 'Three months to go.'

'You'll find out then, soon enough. The usual stuff – bottles, nappies, changes of clothes, toys. One bag for her and three for him. I helped her load the car.'

'Did Patrick have a dummy?'

'He'd just started teething so he had one, yes. It helped calm him down; it was blue with a cartoon fox on it.'

Louise must have given it away; Dixon had done his best poker face.

'Have you found his dummy?' demanded Hudson, looking from one to the other.

'We've found a baby's dummy that matches that description in the glovebox of Deirdre Baxter's car,' replied Dixon. 'Mrs Baxter was a member of the Somerset bridge team at the Palace Hotel that night and was found murdered last Saturday. It's being tested for DNA now, but I have to tell you a result is unlikely after all this time.'

Tears had started to roll down Hudson's cheeks. 'She bloody well lied. All this time, my son was alive and she lied. They all must have done, the whole team.' He looked up at Dixon, fighting to keep his composure. 'Why?'

Chapter Twenty-Five

'That could've been worse.' Louise broke the silence. 'I thought he took it rather well. I'd have . . . well, I don't know what I'd have done if it had been Katie.'

'Grief is a brutal business,' replied Dixon. 'It can do terrible things to people. And make people do terrible things.'

'I just hope to God it's not the son behind these killings, because I'd hate to have to break that news to him. *We've found your son, but he's going down for four murders.*'

'Let's get his alibis checked.'

'Freya, the daughter, lives in Taunton,' said Louise. 'So we could call in on Dr Poland on the way if you want. I emailed him the pathologist's report earlier, like you asked.'

'Let's do that.'

The Pathology Department had closed, the reception in darkness, so Dixon followed the flowerbeds around the back, just enough light coming from the orthopaedic department opposite. Lights were on inside the lab, a green figure looming large in the frosted windows.

Dixon tapped on the glass.

'Who is it?' Poland's voice.

'Nick.'

'Fire escape.'

Poland had removed his apron, gloves and mask before he opened the fire escape door, although blood was still smeared on the sleeve of his smock. 'They still haven't fixed this,' he said, closing the door behind them and lifting the lever. 'We'll go in my office. I've got a grim one on the go in there.'

'The Ilminster bypass again, is it?' asked Dixon.

'The A37 this time.'

'You free on Valentine's Day?'

'It's already in the diary,' replied Poland, grinning. 'Jane texted me, not that it's really the bride's job to organise the best man.'

Dixon glanced into the lab through the open door of Poland's office.

'Go and have a look, if you want,' offered Poland, knowing full well he'd be ignored.

'Did you have a look at the stuff Lou sent over?'

'Heat-induced changes in the infant skeleton are a bit of a specialist subject of mine,' said Poland. He had opened the top drawer of the filing cabinet and taken a bottle of Scotch from behind the files. 'Fancy a nip?'

'We're on duty, Roger.'

'Of course you are, sorry.' Poland looked confused, wondering why that had never been an issue before, probably. 'Let's cut to the chase then, shall we?' He picked up a mug from his desk and drained the dregs of a cold coffee before pouring himself a whisky. 'I can't disagree with the pathologist's findings. And I've never met the fellow, so can't comment on his competence, either; he's long since retired too.'

'I can feel a "but" coming on.'

'But I am surprised by them.'

'Go on.' Dixon had perched on the windowsill, leaving the one chair in front of Poland's desk for Louise, who was making notes.

'It was certainly a high-intensity fire. That much is clear from the photographs of the mother and her father. We're soft tissue and bone, basically, and the body fat acts as fuel. In an adult, the bone has calcified and will survive a fire in one form or another. Even the local crem has to crush the bones so we get ashes to scatter, but in a baby it's different.' Poland drained the whisky in one go before putting the bottle back in the filing cabinet, talking over the clang of the drawer. 'The bones are soft, and calcification doesn't start until about three months after birth, so it's a reasonable assumption there'd be nothing left in a high-intensity fire.'

'I'm still waiting for this "but".'

'In my experience – and I have some, sadly – a mother in that situation will do everything she can to try to shield her baby from the flames, and if she does that, the likelihood is that something of the child's body will survive underneath the mother's body. *Survive* is the wrong word in that instance.' Poland grimaced. 'Something of the baby's body will remain, possibly even fused to the mother's body by the fire. Here, there's nothing.'

'So, she didn't have her baby with her?'

'Possibly not is the best I can say, I'm afraid.'

'Is there anything else in the photographs?'

'Not really. Our muscles contract when we burn, so it's difficult to read too much into the pose. The mother and her father were together, in the corner of the hotel room, embracing, which makes it less likely she had her baby with her, unless they were both trying to shield him, but then you'd expect some remains, as I say.'

'We spoke to the boy's father and he said his wife would've done everything she could to get their son out, and then gone back for her father.'

'And the bloke who started the fire said in interview he saw a group on the terrace holding a small baby,' said Louise, her voice wobbly. 'Sorry, I keep thinking what I'd do if it was me and Katie.'

215

'Whisky?' mouthed Poland.

'Best not,' replied Louise, forcing a smile.

'All right then, Roger,' said Dixon. 'You're in the witness box, under oath. Where's the baby?'

'It's possible he died in the fire, but based on my past experience, I'd say it's more likely she got him out.'

◆ ◆ ◆

'That explains why the CPS dropped the charge,' said Dixon, turning the key, pausing while his diesel engine rumbled into life. 'A pathologist for the defence saying that in the witness box, and there's your reasonable doubt. A jury would never have convicted Rodwell of killing the boy in the fire.'

'Drop the charge, accept a plea to the murders of the mother and her father.' Louise shook her head. 'Case closed.'

'Let's go and see if Freya thinks her little brother died in the fire.'

'She's in one of the new houses over at Monkton Heathfield.'

A crescent of townhouses off one of the interminable number of new roundabouts; Dixon had lost count.

'Number twenty-seven,' said Louise. 'Must be that way.'

Odd numbers to the left, evens to the right.

Three storeys, built in blocks of three; upstairs to the living room, judging by the sofa and the flicker of the TV screen visible in the first-floor window. A small car parked in the drive, child seat in the back.

'She's got a son,' said Louise. 'There was a picture on Facebook. She's called him Patrick.'

A nice touch.

The front door opened before Dixon had a chance to ring the bell, a young man stepping out into the darkness. 'I was just leaving,' he said, narrowly avoiding a collision with Louise in the entrance porch. A glance at their warrant cards. 'She's expecting you. Upstairs, in the kitchen.' And then he was gone, across the grass in the middle of the crescent, the lights flashing on a car on the far side.

'They never build these new developments with enough parking,' said Louise.

It hadn't bothered Dixon, leaving his Land Rover across the drive. No, what bothered him was that he recognised the young man, but couldn't place him. It would come; all in good time.

'Miss Hudson,' called Louise, from the bottom of the stairs.

'Up here.'

Long, straight black hair, black leggings and a white T-shirt spattered with food; a small child sitting in a high chair banging a plastic spoon on the tray in front of him.

'My father rang, said you'd want to speak to me about the fire.'

'Who was that just leaving?' asked Dixon.

'Oh, you met Jos?' She was warming something in a microwave, keeping an eye on whatever was inside through the Perspex window. 'He's my ex-boyfriend. Jos Hope-Bruce. His family owns the Oake Cider Farm. Well, he does, actually.'

And there it was. Behind the temporary bar at the wassailing.

'Is he your son's father?' asked Louise, pulling a face at the child waiting not so patiently for his pudding.

'No. *He's* not part of our lives any more, and we're fine with that.' She was emptying the contents of a plastic tray on to a small plate, blowing on it. 'Look, I was only two at the time of the fire, so I'm not sure how much help I can be. I don't even remember my mother or my brother, I'm sorry to say. I have images in my head, but I don't know whether they're real memories, or I've just picked them up from family photographs.'

'What d'you think of Sean Rodwell's statement that he saw a group of people on the terrace, during the fire, holding a baby? He said he thought it was one of the bridge teams.'

'I know my dad wants to believe it. He's always thought Patrick was alive, somewhere.'

'You don't believe it?'

'Never have. I'm not saying I'd have felt it in my bones, or anything daft like that. I just don't think he's alive. I thought my dad was moving on as well, to be honest, and now we've got you lot dragging it all up, opening all the old wounds. He could really do without it, especially if it comes to nothing. He's struggled with his mental health and I really don't want this to tip him over the edge. Again.'

'We've got four murders to investigate, all of them members of the Somerset bridge team that was there that night.'

'I understand that. I'm sorry, I just don't want my father having another breakdown, that's all. I'm not sure Sally could cope with it, either.'

'Tell me about Sally.' Dixon was walking around the open-plan first floor, pictures printed on to canvas mounted on the wall; all of Freya's young son, none of her brother.

'I was just grateful he met *someone*. It was about ten years ago, and they got married, making her my stepmother. Then two sisters came along; half-sisters I suppose, to be technically correct, but it's never felt like that. Later on, I moved out, got pregnant, and Dad lets us live in one of these. He bought the whole block of three off plan. The other two are rented out.'

'What are your earliest memories of the aftermath of the fire?'

'Dad obsessing about it. It was all he ever did. I was dragged to meetings with a private detective; I can remember his grubby little office in Paignton, up a side street. Sitting outside the Palace Hotel in the car. We'd do that for hours at a time. I think Dad was hoping my brother would come back, for some reason; that he was still in the area. We even checked into the hotel a couple of times and stayed in the rebuilt bit. I can remember swimming in the pool. And the dining room, playing in the ballroom – the new one.' Her eyes glazed over. 'I never felt as if I was enough. There was always something missing. And there was, obviously.'

'Did he ever talk about your mother?'

'All the time, but it was always about how brave she was, about how she'd have seen to it Patrick was safe, and that she'd have gone back for her father, my grandfather. There's a photo somewhere of him holding me in his arms, but I can't remember meeting him, can I?' She wiped away a tear. 'I can't remember my mother, let alone my grandfather. Just photos, that's all I've got.'

'And later?'

'After Sally came along she got the brunt of it; nearly split them up in the beginning, but he just kept it inside – eating away at him, it was. He started drinking, had a breakdown, but then the girls came along and he seemed to settle. Then when I called this little one Patrick, Dad seemed to move on.' She sighed. 'God knows what will happen now.'

'We have some formalities we need to deal with, if that's all right,' said Dixon, with an apologetic smile.

'Dad warned me,' replied Freya, rolling her eyes. 'We're suspects.' Her voice was loaded with sarcasm, not that Dixon could blame her for that. Her father was more realistic, but the idea that a woman who was two at the time of her brother's disappearance would kill four members of a bridge team in revenge was a bit of a stretch, perhaps. That said, the one witness thought the mysterious OT was female.

Louise stepped forward, notebook in hand.

'I won't really have an alibi, as such. I'll have been here with him,' Freya said, gesturing to her little boy.

They went through the dates, one by one.

'That Saturday I went out with a friend, so she'll vouch for me, and there'll be the babysitter as well.'

Then the DNA swab.

'How long have you known Jos?' asked Dixon.

'About three years. We went out for a while, but it wasn't to be.' She was feeding her son, most of the stewed apple ending up down the boy's front. 'Have you got children?'

'Louise has a four-year-old,' replied Dixon. 'Mine's on the way.'

'If Patrick's out there, you will find him this time, won't you? I'm not sure my father will survive another disappointment. His marriage to Sally certainly won't.'

Chapter Twenty-Six

'Find him this time,' muttered Dixon, his voice just carrying over the diesel engine as he accelerated up the on-slip on to the motorway.

'The Devon and Cornwall major investigation team twenty years ago was three times the size of our regional task force,' said Louise. 'And they were at it for three years.'

'Four.'

'Four years. Plus there was that private detective reinterviewing everybody.'

'It might be useful to speak to him.'

'I'll see if he'll come to Express Park, save us flogging down to Paignton.'

'They both seem fairly relaxed about being suspects in four murders.'

'Maybe they know they didn't do it?' Louise was dialling the private detective's telephone number.

'Maybe they think we can't catch them,' replied Dixon. 'We've got no forensics and they've got alibis. Sort of.'

He drifted off while Louise spoke to the private detective, lights flashing by on the southbound carriageway as he drove north. No mention of a baby in the witness statements from the Somerset six – *don't start calling them that, for God's sake; if the bloody press got hold of it* – but then that might be expected if they'd put their heads together and decided to lie about it; to forget about it.

But then there was no mention of him in *any* of the witness statements. Surely someone else must have seen a baby on the terrace? Pandemonium it certainly must have been: smoke swirling, gas bottles exploding, sirens, blue lights, screaming, flying glass. Maybe everybody had just been too busy saving themselves?

And they could be forgiven for that.

He'd forgotten to ask William Hudson where he'd gone to school, but then the investigation had moved on from that with the murders of Thomas Fowler and George Sampson anyway.

'Simon Copeland,' said Louise, ringing off. 'Said he can be at Express Park for seven.'

'Good.'

'William had been on to him already, he said, so he was expecting a call.'

'We're going to need to be careful,' said Dixon. 'We're investigating four murders, and looking at the fire at the Palace Hotel as a possible motive for those murders. That's all. Charlesworth will tell us it's not our job to find the boy.'

'What do you tell him if he tries that on?'

'Find the boy, find the killer.'

'And if the boy really is dead?'

'Then it's likely to be revenge and we're looking at the father.'

'He seemed genuine, I thought.'

'Some people are accomplished liars,' said Dixon. 'They get a lot of practice.'

◆ ◆ ◆

DS Wevill cut a lone figure, leaning against the worktop, waiting for the kettle to boil. He was looking at something on his phone, but then most people seemed to spend most of their time doing that these days, thought Dixon. He wondered how long it would have taken the Devon ACC, Yeend, to start throwing his weight around after their meeting. And how many times that day Wevill had been contacted by Superintendent Small.

Dixon could hear the conversation playing over in his head as he walked up the stairs: *Keep an eye on things, Deano, and let us know . . .*

Gits.

He was sure it was Wevill feeding information to that journalist too. If he could remember, he'd let slip some crap and see if it popped up in print.

'Jane's gone to see her dad,' said Sarah. 'He's home early, they discharged him this afternoon. Said she'd stop off at your cottage to feed Monty on the way.'

'Thank you,' replied Dixon, sitting down at a computer, intending to update the Policy Log. Hoping something else might pop up, suitably urgent, that meant he didn't have to.

'We've got people out checking alibis, and you'll find additional witness statements from the bridge players on the system,' said Mark. 'Fire brigade who attended the scene too, hotel staff. It's going to take a while with a team this size.'

'Find anything on the cameras?'

'Only the cloned Fiat. No clear image of the driver.'

Dixon saved the changes to the Policy Log, his phone buzzing on his desk within seconds.

Charlesworth.

He could imagine it – *Well done, good work, you're sticking your neck out, tread carefully*. He decided to save the ACC the bother, dropping his phone into his jacket pocket, careful not to answer the call by mistake. Voicemail was a wonderful thing.

'There's a Mr Copeland in reception asking for you,' said Sarah, her head appearing over the top of Dixon's computer.

'Where's Louise?'

'Gone home,' replied Sarah. 'You told her to go and get some rest.'

'You are claiming your overtime, aren't you?'

'I wasn't, but Jane insisted. She's got the forms.'

'Good. Grab a notebook then, and let's go and see what Mr Copeland has got to say for himself.'

He didn't look much like a private detective, but then American telly hadn't done them many favours. Grubby little men in dirty raincoats, cigarettes sticking out of the corners of their mouths. Thomas Magnum was different, of course, with his flowery shirts and Ferrari, but Copeland didn't fit either stereotype.

He looked more like a bank manager, back in the days when banks had managers, with a touch of the Private Walker about him, perhaps, although that may have been the moustache.

'Ah, the SIO himself,' said Copeland, when Dixon opened the security door. 'I saw the press conference on the television. So, it's true then?' He was clutching a thin file tightly to his chest. 'Will Hudson rang me, said you might be in touch.'

Dixon gestured to the three doors standing open at the far end of the reception area. 'Pick an interview room.'

Sarah closed the door behind them.

'Five members of the Somerset bridge team are dead, four of them murdered.'

'Who's last man standing?' asked Copeland. He clearly understood the gravity of the situation and was trying to contain his excitement.

'George Sampson,' replied Dixon. 'We believe our killer visited him, but left him alive because he's in the advanced stages of dementia.'

'I always thought that lot were hiding something,' said Copeland. 'They were the only ones who refused to speak to me. Everybody else was happy to go over it again – even though they couldn't add much to their police statements, if anything – but I could never persuade any of the Somerset team to cooperate. And they all said pretty much the same thing, that they'd given detailed statements to the police and had nothing to add.'

'You think their refusal was coordinated?'

'Definitely. They'd put their heads together and agreed what they'd say. They even used much the same language.' He sighed. 'So, they were Rodwell's bridge team, were they?'

'It's a line of enquiry.'

'Five years of my life I spent on this case, on and off.'

'Were there any flaws in the original police investigation?'

Copeland appeared surprised by the question, raising his eyebrows above his horn-rimmed glasses, albeit fleetingly. 'Not really, if I'm honest. They did everything you'd expect. Took statements, asked the question of everybody.'

'And what d'you think happened to Patrick Hudson?'

'He was taken.' No hesitation, no room for doubt. 'Tucked under a red coat, off across the golf course to the coast path and gone. There was a gate on the far side of the trees that took you out on to Anstey's Cove Road, then another path into the trees on the far side. It's no bloody wonder nobody saw anything. Dense woodland, it is.'

'A local then, who knew the area.'

'Unquestionably. Then you can go in either direction on the coast path – north to Babbacombe or south towards Hope Cove and the Wellswood area. Anybody out and about would've been watching the fire.'

Copeland had placed the thin yellow file on the table in front of him face down, hiding the label, and was turning it as he spoke.

'Have you spoken to Sean?' he asked.

'I'm seeing him tomorrow morning.'

'You develop a good bullshit detector in this line of work, and I thought Sean was telling the truth about the woman in the red coat. Days I spent, out on the coast path, talking to anybody and everybody, asking if they remembered seeing a woman in a red coat. In both directions too, where the path drops down to Babbacombe beach and further south.' He inhaled deeply through his nose, then turned the file over. 'And eventually I found a witness.'

He slid the file across the table to Dixon.

'Did you go to the police with this at the time?'

'They weren't interested. I took it to Campbell and he said the witness was unreliable. You can keep that,' he said, when Dixon picked up the file. 'It's a signed witness statement.'

'Why unreliable?'

'She was known to police. A drug addict, sex worker, alcoholic; multiple convictions. Campbell said she'd probably read about it or heard it somewhere – the woman in the red coat – it had been in the papers and come up at Rodwell's trial too, so it had made national news. I'm not daft, I know Campbell had a point, but he could and should have spoken to her.'

'Where is she now?'

'Dead. She was found on a bench at Babbacombe Downs; drug overdose, accidental according to the coroner.'

'When?'

'Long time ago, maybe twelve years?' Copeland was watching Dixon closely. 'I know what you're thinking, but there was nothing suspicious about it. It was just a matter of time for her, sadly.' Copeland stood up. 'Where is Sean these days? He was supposed to be out soon.'

'At a halfway house.'

'He really is out then.' Copeland pursed his lips. 'I went to see him several times and always found him frank and open, to be honest. They sacked him; eating leftover food was the reason given, but that was an excuse, I think. Sean was just a disgruntled employee who started a fire out of revenge and it got out of hand.'

'Killing two people.'

'He never intended to hurt anyone.' Copeland gave a lopsided grin. 'You said two, not three.'

'I did.'

◆ ◆ ◆

Jane's text had arrived in the nick of time.

Eaten with mum and dad. There's plenty in the freezer. Jx

He'd been halfway up the hill with Monty when he got the message, but made it with five minutes to spare – the Red Cow stopped serving food at nine.

Fish and chips, a couple of beers, and he was stretched out on the sofa when Jane arrived home just before midnight.

'How is he?'

'He's fine, I think,' replied Jane. 'I got them one of those pulse oximeter things that you stick on your finger, and Mum won't let him take it off. She's even banned him from watching the football; he gets too excited. She's going to drive him round the bend.'

'At least it's January so he can leave the bloody garden alone.'

'She's locked his tools in the shed and hidden the key.'

'Pleased to hear it.' Dixon sat up, watching Jane fending off Monty in the kitchen. 'It was gone eight before Sarah went home. She is claiming her overtime?'

'She wasn't, but I made her fill in the forms.'

227

'What d'you think of that fellow Wevill?'

'I don't trust him. He keeps going out to take phone calls in the car park. The rest of the Devon lot are fine,' replied Jane. 'Hard workers, but he's a tosser.' She lowered herself on to the sofa, one hand in the small of her back. 'I'm beginning to think there are two in there,' she said, rubbing her abdomen. 'What's that you're watching?'

'It's an old Sherlock Holmes with Basil Rathbone.' He flicked off the TV, plunging the living room into near-darkness, only the streetlights outside finding their way in through a gap in the curtains, a harsh white light from the new LED bulbs. 'Will you fit into your wedding dress?'

'Mum's going to let it out a bit.' Jane was talking over a yawn. 'So, it's all about this baby boy?'

'Patrick Hudson.'

'I spoke to Roger and he's right about a mother shielding her child from the fire. I know I would.'

'I know you would too.'

'I forgot to mention, the solicitor rang me today and we exchanged contracts on this place. I knew you wanted to go ahead, so I told him not to bother ringing you. Completion is set for the Friday before we get married.'

'The thirteenth?'

'I'm not superstitious.'

'I noticed that, when we were setting the wedding date,' said Dixon.

'Finish this case before then and we might get a honeymoon. I'm not supposed to tell you, but Dad was talking about booking us something as a surprise.'

'He does know I haven't got a passport, doesn't he?'

'And that you won't go anywhere without Monty. I'm to let him know, and he'll find us something in the Lakes.' Jane leaned

228

over, her head resting on Dixon's shoulder. 'I'm almost too tired to go to bed.'

'I'll carry you up the stairs,' he said, sitting up. 'It'll be good practice for carrying you over the threshold.'

'God, you are old-fashioned, aren't you?'

'Is that such a bad thing?'

'I'm not saying *obey*. Love, cherish, till death us do part, all of that, but not *obey*.'

Chapter Twenty-Seven

Charlesworth's text message arrived while Dixon was waiting for Louise the following morning.

> *We can't justify police protection for Sean Rodwell. Tell him to stay in the halfway house at all times. He'll be safe there.*

It had been worth a try, but the response was inevitable, perhaps, Charlesworth following it up with a second message.

> *If revenge was the motive, Rodwell would be dead already. After all, he's been out of prison and accessible for two weeks.*

It was a fair point, although it hadn't become public knowledge until recently.

The bridge team had been silenced; killed to prevent them telling the truth about something. That much was clear from the fact that George Sampson had been left alive. And that something could only be that they had indeed handed young Patrick Hudson to the mystery woman in a red coat on the terrace of the Palace Hotel during the fire that fateful night more than twenty years ago.

If that was right, then there was no need to kill Rodwell. He hadn't been believed back then, and without the bridge team to back him up, there was no chance he'd be believed now. He'd be a lone voice, crying in the wind; assuming he decided to speak up, anyway. He could be forgiven for avoiding the limelight like the plague.

That said, revenge remained a powerful motive, and the killer might just be biding his or her time.

Dixon tapped out a reply to Charlesworth.

On your head be it.

He thought better of it, hitting the Delete button instead of Send. Then tapped out another to Jane.

Can we cross check the guest lists against the statements taken. Look for anyone at the hotel that night who didn't give a statement. Nx

The chances were slim, but if the abduction of Patrick Hudson had been opportunistic, as it must surely have been, then the woman in the red coat had had another reason to be there that night.

A dinner guest, possibly. No hotel asked the names of all diners when taking a dinner reservation.

Another text to Jane:

Check leisure centre members too. Ta

Dixon was almost hoping Louise would be late when the barking started. Seconds later, a knock at the door.

'We'll take your car,' he said, opening the front door of the cottage.

'We're not taking him with us, are we?'

'I'll pick up the Land Rover and him on the way back.'

The halfway house was just another house in the street. No signs, or fences to keep anyone in or out. Dull grey stone with bay windows, the front garden paved over for parking; a police patrol car fifty yards further along – Dixon had organised it anyway.

Mercifully, there was a space for Louise to park.

'Shall I go in there?'

'I would,' replied Dixon.

'I know you would.'

The front door flew open. 'You can't park there!'

Warrant cards at the ready.

'You can put those away, please. We like to be unobtrusive around here, for obvious reasons.'

'We've come to see Sean Rodwell,' said Dixon, his voice hushed – being unobtrusive, as instructed.

The man's eyes were darting from side to side; checking for neighbours snooping, probably. 'He's in. Top of the stairs, first door on the right.'

The front room with the bay window.

Nice.

Rodwell was lying on the bed, shoes on, watching breakfast television. He'd have done much the same for the last twenty years, and old habits die hard.

Louise sat down at the table in the window and took out her notebook, Dixon standing at the end of the bed between Rodwell and *This Morning*.

'I smell coppers,' said Rodwell.

'No, you don't. There might be a *look*, Sean, but there isn't a smell.'

'What d'you want?'

'Nice room.'

'They keep this one for the lifers out on licence.'

'How long have you been here?'

'Since I got out. I'll be here six months, I expect. I would've gone home after that, but my mother's dead.'

'Aren't you supposed to be getting a job, integrating into society?'

'I've got a couple of interviews lined up. Got a plumbing qualification on the inside.' Rodwell was leaning back on his pillows, his hands behind his head. 'Look, what d'you want exactly, or are you just here to pass the time of day?'

'We're investigating the disappearance of Patrick Hudson,' replied Dixon. A little white lie, but it had the desired effect.

Rodwell sat up. 'Disappearance?'

'You said in your first interview you saw him with a bridge team on the terrace.'

'That's right. An older woman was holding him and she handed him over to the woman in the red coat.'

'Describe the bridge team.'

'There were six of them, all around the same age, sixty or so, maybe older; two women and four men. I was watching from the trees on the far side of the golf course, so it was difficult to see what they were wearing. The lights on the terrace had gone off, so they were in silhouette – almost – and then there was the smoke. There were people running about, screaming.'

'How far away were you?'

'The trees curved around and it was only a pitch and putt, so they were seventy yards from where I was. No more than that.'

Dixon slid a photograph out of his coat pocket, the one of Deirdre Baxter and Michael Allam holding the county bridge trophy. 'Do you recognise these two?'

'Yes, that's them, and that's the woman who was holding Patrick. Definitely. It's the hair. I'd been on lunches that day and had served them a buffet at the back of the ballroom.'

'Tell me exactly what happened when the baby was taken.'

'They were standing at the end of the terrace, waiting to get to the steps down to the gardens, and from there on to the golf course. There was a lot of people being evacuated that way. A woman in a red coat, it had a hood that was up, ran up to them, said something to the woman with Patrick and then she handed him over.' Rodwell had gone back in time, deep in thought, his eyes glazed over. 'Then the woman in the red coat ran along the terrace, behind the crowd, and I lost sight of her at the far end. She went behind some big bushes at that end of the rose garden.'

'Did she look like she knew where she was going?'

'Oh, yeah. She made a beeline for the trees at the far end of the terrace. There's a path through the trees and then it's out on to the road that runs around the back. She knew full well where she was going all right.'

'What did the bridge team do then?'

'I lost sight of them in the crowd. I reckon they'd have followed everyone else, down the steps and out on to the golf course.'

'What did you do after that?'

'I decided I'd seen enough and was walking home along the Babbacombe Road when your lot picked me up. I'd been sacked that afternoon and was top of the list of suspects, apparently.'

'Why were you sacked?'

'Eating leftovers, they said, but the head chef had it in for me and it was a way of getting rid of me without paying notice.'

Rodwell sighed. 'If only the bloody bridge team had said something about the boy.'

'It wouldn't have made any difference to your sentence.'

'I suppose not, but there's the family. His father came to see me in prison, but there wasn't a lot I could tell him. And I got what I deserved. His wife and father-in-law died thanks to me.' He was sitting with his legs over the side of the bed now, his elbows resting on his knees. 'Why now though?'

'The bridge team are dead.'

'Which ones?'

'All of them, except one who's got dementia. One died of a heart attack in 2012, the other four have been murdered.'

'Fuck me.'

'And you're sure there's nothing else you can tell us about that night?'

'There was a private detective. Had the same name as that bloke from The Police – the rock band, you know. Copeland, was it? He was brought in by the boy's family and I tried to help him as best I could. He said he'd found a witness who saw the woman in the red coat.'

'We know about her,' replied Dixon.

'Where is she?'

'Dead.'

'All I can say is, that boy didn't die in the fire. I accept entirely that his mother and grandfather did, and I've done my time for that; there's not a day goes by that I don't regret what happened. But Patrick Hudson is out there somewhere. He'll be, what, twenty-one by now?'

'Well, if you think of anything else, you let me know,' said Dixon, handing Rodwell a business card.

'Acting detective superintendent? Bit young, aren't you?'

'I thought all police officers were supposed to look younger these days.'

'Yeah, right.'

'Look, there's a strong possibility that revenge is the motive, Sean, and if that's right then you're at risk, so I have to advise you to remain in the halfway house at all times. It's for your own safety, you understand, just until we've got this thing cleared up.'

'And how long's that likely to be?'

'As long as it takes,' replied Dixon. 'I've arranged for the local lot to keep an eye on you, and don't forget your curfew.'

Louise closed her notebook and headed for the door, Dixon close behind her.

'There was something else,' said Rodwell. 'The woman who had been holding Patrick bent down and picked something up after she'd handed him over. She went to give it to the woman in the red coat, but she'd gone, so she put it in her pocket. I never saw what it was.'

'It was the boy's dummy, Sean. She'd kept it in the glovebox of her car.'

Chapter Twenty-Eight

'Two things,' said Jane, when Dixon appeared by her workstation at Express Park. 'There's a DNA match on the baby's dummy. They managed to get some saliva off it, apparently, and it's a match with Patrick. One in a billion. It's definitely his.'

'They had his DNA on the system?'

'Off a hair brush. It was taken at the time for identification purposes, just in case.' Jane stood up. 'The other thing is there's a DC from Torquay waiting to see you. She won't talk to anyone else and she's been here ages, so I put her in the canteen, the table in the corner.'

'She looks like she's hiding.' Dixon was standing in the doorway of the canteen a few moments later.

'Who from, I wonder.'

'Let's find out.'

The woman cut a crumpled figure, hunched over a mug of coffee, a ripped-open chocolate wrapper on the table in front of her; lunch, probably. She had her back to the door, the collar of her coat pulled as far up as it would go, greying hair tied back.

Jane pulled out the chair next to her. 'He's here,' she said, smiling as she sat down.

'Can I get you another drink?' asked Dixon, to break the ice as much as anything; the woman looked as if she was about to burst into tears.

'No, I'm fine, thank you.'

'What can I do for you?' he asked, sitting down opposite her.

Strong perfume, and too much of it, to mask the tobacco, the tell-tale lines in her top lip left by years of pulling on cigarettes. Fake tan, possibly. If it wasn't, she'd spent too much time on a sunbed.

'It's more about what I can do for you,' she said, hesitantly.

'This is DC Tremayne from Torquay,' said Jane.

'Kaye, please.'

'Kaye it is then.' Whatever was coming, Dixon knew it was likely to be important enough for her to be terrified at the prospect of being found out.

'I'm on my day off,' she said. 'If my guv'nor found out I was here, he'd string me up. Is there anywhere I can have a smoke?'

'Top deck of the car park,' replied Dixon. 'This way. There are some Devon officers in the incident room, though. From Sidmouth.'

'They won't recognise me, that's fine.'

Once through the security door, they squeezed down the side of Dixon's Land Rover, trying to ignore the barking from inside.

'Whose is that?' asked Kaye, leaning back as far as she could, even in the narrow gap between the car and the wall.

'Mine,' replied Dixon. 'He's a pussycat, really.'

Bloodshot eyes were lit up by the flicker from Kaye's lighter, the cigarette bouncing around in the flame as she tried to light it in the breeze whipping around the corner of the car park. Then she reached into a shopping bag and took out a bundle of papers. 'I did a bit of photocopying,' she said, handing the bundle to Dixon. 'It might be connected, it might not, but I thought you ought to know about it. The powers that be decided it was unconnected to the original investigation and have kept it quiet for fear of opening old wounds. There was some early press coverage, but none since then. No press conferences, nothing.'

'Press coverage of what?' asked Jane.

Dixon would have asked himself, but he was trying to look at the documents in his hand in the dim glow from the fire exit sign over the security door. Not that he was having much luck.

'Workmen on a building site in Wellswood uncovered the remains of a dead baby.' Kaye flicked her ash over the wall into the darkness below. 'It was scrubland behind the houses off Ilsham Marine Drive and they got planning permission for two houses. Builders were in, clearing the land, levelling it. It's on the market now as two building plots. We made all the usual enquiries, but came up with nothing.'

'Is there a pathologist's report?' asked Dixon.

'A baby boy, not less than two months old, not more than four, buried between twenty and twenty-five years ago.'

'Have you got DNA?'

Kaye nodded. 'A partial profile. There wasn't a lot left of him, to be honest, and the bloke on the digger did well to spot it. The soft tissue had gone, most of the bones too, just the knuckle ends of the long bones where they'd started to calcify, or ossify, or whatever it is.' She was shaking her head now, the plume of smoke from the cigarette in her mouth weaving skyward. 'I know what you're thinking, but we checked it against the Hudson sample and there was no match. There was a bereaved mother, though, somewhere.'

'What else was there?'

'I've copied the photos for you,' replied Kaye. 'A red babygrow with a cartoon fox on the chest and a teddy bear. So fucking sad.'

'No appeals for information, nothing?' demanded Jane.

'Nope.' Kaye shrugged. 'We had a team on it to begin with. Spoke to everyone living in the vicinity in that time frame. We checked all births registered back then and everyone's accounted for. We checked with local midwives, hospitals, doctors. There's no cause of death, don't forget, so it's never been treated as a murder investigation. All but closed now. I'm the only one still working on it.'

'And what are you doing?' asked Dixon.

'Nothing, to be honest. The file sits in my filing cabinet; other things take priority. You know how it is.'

'When's the inquest?'

'It was opened and adjourned for police enquiries and I haven't been back to the coroner yet, so there's nothing fixed.'

'What about DNA testing?'

'Like I said, it was a partial profile, so the best we could hope for was a parental or sibling match. Everybody living in the area at that time was tested and they all came back *inconclusive*. Nothing came up on the database either.'

'How far is this from the site of the Palace Hotel?'

'Not far at all. Ten minutes' walk, maybe, along the coast path. The bit of scrubland is accessible off the coast path too.'

Dixon was flicking through the bundle. 'Is this everything?' he frowned. 'Can't be, surely.'

'Not everything. Just what I thought was going to be of most use to you. I'll get in deep shit for this, you know, and if I'd been caught smuggling that lot out . . .' Her sentence was punctuated by the click of her lighter as she lit another cigarette. 'Not that I give a toss, to be honest.'

'When was the body found?' Dixon thought he knew the answer to that question, but asked it anyway.

'The builders found the body at the beginning of September, and we were doing the DNA testing October and November.' Kaye smiled. 'That's what you want to know, isn't it?'

'It is.'

◆ ◆ ◆

'She's gone,' said Jane. 'I told her if they give her a hard time she's to apply for a transfer to Avon and Somerset. She won't, though. She's only a year off retirement.'

Dixon was back in the canteen, flicking through the bundle of documents.

'Why are you skulking in here?' asked Jane.

'Keeping out of the way of the Devon lot for the time being. We'll need to find a way of making it look like we found it under our own steam, rather than landing Kaye in the shit.'

'It's connected then?'

'Thomas Fowler was killed not long after the initial press coverage, and the community DNA testing started. Even if it wasn't in the press, it'd have been all over social media.'

'And we don't believe in coincidence.' Jane was eyeing up Dixon's cheese and onion baguette. 'Don't you want that?'

'You finish it.' Most of the grated cheese had spilled out into the cellophane wrapper, leaving only red onion in the baguette. Nice.

'I'm eating for two, remember,' Jane said, picking up the flakes of cheese one by one.

Dixon looked up. 'The partial DNA profile from the dead baby and Patrick Hudson's DNA don't match. Shame, but then that would've been too easy.'

'Kaye's right about a bereaved mother. It has been known.'

'No real press coverage was a mistake. And when a police officer's first thought is covering his or her own arse, something's gone badly wrong.'

'You need to remind Charlesworth of that.'

'I do. Regularly.' Dixon slid the documents into a cardboard file and stood up.

'Where are you going?' asked Jane.

'Torquay.'

◆ ◆ ◆

'Bloody hell, it doesn't get much posher than this,' said Louise. She was sitting in the passenger seat of Dixon's Land Rover, her lunch finished, the crumbs swept on to the floor and the wrapper stuffed in the door pocket. 'That one must be well over two million. Look at it.'

Dixon didn't bother.

Ilsham Marine Drive. Trees on the right, down to the cliff edge, the sea beyond; houses on the left, unusually large ones with high gates at the bottom of private drives, the houses themselves visible further up the hill, affording them grandstand sea views from balconies and terraces.

'It's further round,' Dixon said. 'Before we get to Richmond Close, on the right.'

'I must start doing the lottery again.'

Dixon parked across two corrugated iron gates where the road swung around and away from the tree-lined cliff edge on his right, a gravel track beyond visible through a gap in the gates cut for the padlock and chain. The 'For Sale' board had helped.

'The estate agent said he'd meet us here at two-thirty,' said Louise. 'He's only five minutes away, down in Wellswood, he said.'

'You did tell him we weren't here to buy anything?'

'Yes, Sir.'

'Sorry, I was doing a viewing over at Babbacombe.' The suit was climbing out of a Mini emblazoned with estate agency logos.

'They're good-sized plots.'

242

Dixon turned away, cringing to himself as Louise turned property developer.

'How much are they?' she asked.

'One-point-one each.'

'Just for the plot?'

'With full planning permission.' The agent was rummaging through a set of keys. 'Five bedrooms, double garage and an indoor pool. Good-sized gardens too, with sea glimpses.'

Dixon turned around, looking for the sea.

'It's in that direction, from the upstairs windows and the top of the garden,' continued the agent. 'There are balconies and you could put a summer house up there to make the most of it.'

'You did tell him we weren't buying?'

'Yes, Sir.'

The chain slid out of the padlock, the gate swinging open to reveal a gravel track, the building plots marked out beyond with wooden stakes and white tape.

'What are the houses on the left?' asked Dixon.

'That's the back of Richmond Close. And those over there are part of Ilsham Marine Drive.'

'And out the back?'

'That's owned by the council. It's part of the coast path and there's a seating area. The coast path used to come through here, but they've moved it to the other side of those houses. It was only a hundred yard section.'

Both plots had been cleared to bare earth and levelled, the whole area enclosed in brand new wood panel fencing.

'What did it look like before it was cleared?'

'It was very overgrown, trees and brambles mainly. Kids used to play in here; sometimes you'd get druggies, people living in tents, hidden in the bushes. There was even an old shelter in the middle someone had built out of bits of this and that – pallets and old sections of fence.'

'Could you move about without being seen?'

'Oh, God yes. It was woodland, basically, and very overgrown, as I say.'

Dixon was weaving in between the puddles, his hands thrust deep into his coat pockets. 'Who owned it?'

'A local developer bought it off the family when the owner died,' replied the agent. 'He lived in the bottom corner of Richmond Close and bought it years ago just to stop it being built on, I think. Anyway, when he died, the family moved on and sold the land.'

'And the house?'

'Yes, that was sold last year. Probate held it up a bit, you know how it is.'

'Where were the baby's remains found?'

'That corner, I think.' The agent was gesturing to the far side of the plot, furthest from the sea, close to the back of the houses in Richmond Close. 'About there,' he said, when Dixon was standing on the spot.

Not that there was anything to see except bare earth, neatly levelled by a digger, a new fence and planting beyond; evidence that the residents of Richmond Close weren't entirely happy with the idea of new neighbours. Most had opted for leylandii.

The old fence was still there, oddly enough, the new one having been built just inside the boundary, a gap of no more than a few inches between the two.

'They've all got back gates,' Dixon said, dropping back down and brushing his hands together. 'Not much use now though.'

'Yes, I think they used to use it as a bit of a dumping ground,' replied the agent. 'Grass clippings and stuff like that. Garden rubbish.'

◆ ◆ ◆

'Drive round and park in Richmond Close,' Dixon had said, getting on for half an hour ago.

Louise had resisted the temptation to sigh loudly. She hadn't commented on the houses either, which was unusual. Modern, timber clad, conservatories, front lawns open to the road; Dixon had never understood that. Large blue hydrangeas, pine trees and conifers, the lines of leylandii at the back just getting going.

He had been working his way through the results of the DNA testing done by Torquay police the previous October and November, just before someone started killing the bridge team. All the local residents had dutifully complied, according to the spreadsheet. Past residents too; DNA had been taken from those fortunate enough – or unfortunate enough, depending on which way you looked at it – to live in Richmond Close covering the entire five-year period given by the pathologist. 'Been in the ground between twenty and twenty-five years.'

That said, Dixon was only really interested in the residents at the time of the fire at the Palace Hotel.

And there it was, or rather there they were.

14 Richmond Close.

DNA sample taken: 3 Nov.

Result: Inconclusive.

Sample destroyed at subject's request: tick.

Louise must have spotted the smile creeping across Dixon's face. 'It's easy to see what happened,' she said. 'Baby dies, bereaved mother buries his body on that waste ground and then snatches poor Patrick Hudson the night of the fire. As you said, opportunistic. A straight swap. Who's going to know with a baby at three months?'

'The father.'

'There'll be a reason why he didn't.' Louise frowned. 'I wonder why the Torquay lot didn't get a parental match when they did the DNA testing, though?'

'That's easy,' replied Dixon. 'When she was asked to provide a sample, she sent her son along to give it.'

Chapter Twenty-Nine

A gravel drive curved away to a red-brick pile, not that Louise would call it that. It could have been an office in a different setting, with blinds at the windows rather than curtains, and without the Virginia creeper, perhaps. It was growing up the wall of the octagonal living room that overlooked ornate gardens sloping down to a terrace, where an outdoor swimming pool was hidden under a cover.

No garage, which seemed odd for a property of this size, and it certainly wasn't a cottage, despite the name.

Louise drew breath.

'Don't say it,' said Dixon, not really needing a valuation.

Even the gravel looked new, and he'd be picking it out of the tyres of his Land Rover for weeks.

'Can I help you?' The woman had appeared from around the side of a single-storey extension on the left, a long dining table visible through the window. Dixon had quickly lost count of the chairs.

Mid-fifties, waxed coat, wellies, gardening gloves, a pair of secateurs in one hand and a large tub of rose clippings in the other.

More vehicles had turned into the drive behind Dixon: a patrol car, followed by Mark and Sarah if all had gone to plan. He didn't turn to look.

'What's going on?' asked the woman, her voice shrill. 'Who are you? And why are the police here?'

'Shall we go inside?' asked Dixon. 'Unless you want your neighbours to overhear.'

'We don't have any neighbours.'

'In that case, we'll do it right here. Mrs Diana Hope-Bruce, I am arresting you on suspicion of the abduction of Patrick Hudson. You do not have to say anything, but it may harm your defence if you do not mention when questioned something which you later rely on in court.'

First the secateurs, then the large tub fell to the ground, rolling on to its side, scattering leaves and clippings on the gravel.

'Anything you do say may be given in evidence.'

Her head bowed, breathing heavily through her nose. Then she looked up, fixing Dixon with piercing blue eyes. 'You know, it's almost a relief, after all these years. Let's get it over with.' Hands outstretched in front of her, wrists together ready for the handcuffs.

◆ ◆ ◆

The shouting had started in the back of the patrol car, the mention of Scientific Services and the search team setting her off.

'There's a lot of highly confidential business documents in the office. Commercially sensitive.' Dixon slammed the rear passenger door, reducing the volume a bit. 'The filing cabinets are locked. You do not have my permission to break them open.'

The uniformed officer in the driver's seat tried his best to calm her down, in the end driving off mid-sentence.

'And I don't want muddy boots on my carpet—'

Dixon could see why. They were white, a sure sign there was no dog in the house – two life-sized bronze statues of Afghan hounds either side of the fireplace in the dining room didn't count. He'd been expecting something to pounce when he opened the back door.

White leather furniture, white tiled floor, white walls; it looked more like a dentist's surgery.

'What are we looking for, Sir?' asked Sarah, following Dixon and Louise into the hall.

'There's a bloody cinema through here,' said Mark, using his phone to illuminate a room with no windows. 'There's even tiered seating like you get at the bloody Odeon.'

'She's been arrested on suspicion of abduction, so anything relevant to that. She's also now our prime suspect in the murders of the bridge team.'

'I'll brief Scientific.' Louise was watching through the window as a large van pulled in next to Dixon's Land Rover.

A woman's most treasured possessions would be kept in her bedroom. He wasn't an expert on women by any means, but he knew that much.

'This must be her handbag,' said Sarah, holding up a black leather bag in a latex-gloved hand. 'It's got her phone in it.'

Mark was looking out of the back window. 'There's a pond and a swimming pool,' he said. 'Best not get pissed and muddle them up.'

'Shut up, Mark.'

'Yes, Sir.'

The master bedroom was more of a suite; bigger than the whole of the ground floor of Dixon's cottage. A walk-in wardrobe and dressing room, marble tiled wet room, a vast bed.

'That's one of those sleigh beds,' said Sarah. She had been following Dixon, so quietly that he hadn't known she was there. 'I've always fancied one of those.'

The dressing room turned out to be a treasure trove of family photographs, lined up in small frames on a shelf under her mirror.

He saw it in the mirror first, on the wall behind him, spinning round to look at it closely.

A white box frame with a black and white photograph of a baby boy, and a handprint. 'Welcome to the world, Jos Blake Hope-Bruce, aged 2 weeks, born 2nd June, 6lb 13oz.'

Dixon lifted the frame off the hook and placed it in an evidence bag being held open for him by Sarah.

'We'll be able to match the prints, won't we, Sir?'

'If I'm right, then we won't. The baby who made that handprint is long dead, sadly.' He sighed. 'Not much of a welcome to the world.'

◆ ◆ ◆

'Bravo, Nick.' Charlesworth and Potter were standing on the landing, outside the canteen. 'We're in meeting room two, if you've got a minute?'

'I haven't really, Sir,' replied Dixon. 'The custody clock's ticking and we haven't interviewed her yet.'

'No, of course. So, you've found the woman in the red coat?'

'She's downstairs now, with her solicitor.'

'She must be prime suspect for the murders too,' said Potter. 'It can't be a coincidence that the killings started when the baby's remains were found, can it?'

'No, it can't.'

'They gave a DNA sample when Torquay did their testing, though, surely?' asked Charlesworth. 'Failure to provide a sample would've been a red flag.'

'The son provided the sample,' replied Dixon, trying to edge past them in the corridor. 'But then he's not part of the Hope-Bruce family, is he, so there was no match. He's Patrick Hudson.'

'You're sure about that?'

'We'll be doing a fresh DNA test to make sure, Sir. The sample he gave at the time was destroyed at his request.'

'How on earth did she ever think she'd get away with it?'

'Well, she has done for over twenty years,' replied Dixon. 'But I suspect the truth is far simpler. She never thought about it. She was a bereaved mother, out of her mind with grief, and she just snatched Patrick without thinking about the consequences at all.'

'She'll bloody well have to think about them now.'

'Yes, Sir.'

'Did she kill her own son?' Charlesworth curled his lip. 'That's the next question, isn't it?'

'I'll be running it past Roger Poland, but the Torquay pathologist couldn't come up with a cause of death from the few bones that are left, so it's unlikely we'll be able to prove that one way or the other. She may have shaken him, or smothered him, or it may have been a sudden infant death. Unless she tells us, we'll never know.'

'Have you told the boy's father?'

'Not yet, Sir. I want to be sure before we do that.'

'You'd best get on with it then, hadn't you.'

Dixon managed to squeeze past the crowd in the corridor, jostling for position in the video suite. Two screens, both showing the interview room, a woman sitting next to a man in a suit. Diana Hope-Bruce, the mysterious woman in the red coat, had drawn a crowd, most of them Devon and Cornwall officers shuffling silently into the back of the room, as if Charlesworth and Potter didn't know what was going on behind them.

It was something of a departure for Dixon, opting for interview room one, where suspect and interviewing officer sat side by side, the digital recorder on a table in front of them. His style was confrontational, he'd been told that enough times in the past, and a table between him and the suspect was usually a welcome buffer. Not this time.

This time was different.

It was about a woman and her dead baby, and the desperate act that followed.

At least to begin with.

The interview room layout was still designed by an idiot, one who had never conducted a police interview, almost certainly, but this time it might have its uses.

Louise dealt with the formalities.

'This interview is being audio and visually recorded on to a secure digital hard drive. Identify yourself for the recording, please.'

The elbow in Dixon's ribs meant it must be his turn.

A solicitor he didn't recognise, but then he'd driven up from Torquay, so that was hardly surprising. A privately paying client and all that.

'When I arrested you, Diana, you said it was almost a relief after all these years. What did you mean by that?'

'What d'you think I meant?' Sharp, and more of a retort than a question.

The answer was stating the obvious, perhaps, but that was exactly what he wanted her to do.

He waited.

'I meant it's a relief that the secret is finally out.' She shook her head. 'That I don't have to hide it any more, always looking over my shoulder.'

'What secret is that?'

'My husband was working overseas at the time and I had an affair that resulted in a pregnancy. I told no one, least of all my husband, feigned illness so that none of my friends or family became suspicious when they didn't see me for a few months. I gave birth

252

at home – didn't register it, before you ask – and then just as I was about to put him up for adoption I found him dead in the bed next to me one morning. I panicked, and buried him on the waste ground behind the house.'

She'd even managed to force some tears. It was an impressive performance.

Some of it was true, of course; the bit about burying him on the waste ground, but the rest . . .

'I know I should have said something at the time, but my husband would've found out about the affair, and, like I said, I panicked.'

'When was this?'

'About twenty-five years ago.'

Right at the limit of the pathologist's estimate for how long the baby's body had been in the ground. A nice touch.

'Tell me about Jos, then.'

A deep breath, busy picking the varnish off her fingernails and dropping it on the floor. 'Jos came along a couple of years later. Something must've gone wrong during my home birth and I couldn't conceive, so he was the result of an unwanted pregnancy; a friend of a friend. It was an informal thing, we never adopted him or anything, but that explains why the DNA didn't match when he did the test.'

So many holes, it was difficult to know where to begin. Even her solicitor was shaking his head.

'Let's start at the beginning then,' said Dixon, trying to stay patient. 'Who did you have the affair with?'

'I'd rather not say.'

'Not really an option, I'm afraid, Diana.' Dixon had turned on his chair to face her.

'His name was Giles Hancock. He was the tennis coach at the Palace leisure centre.'

'And how long did this affair last?'

'About a year, until I found out he was at it with several other women at the same time.' She sneered. 'I suppose he thought it was part of his job description.'

'Where was your husband at the time?'

'Robert was in Jeddah. He was in the oil business, working for Shell, and spent a lot of time in Saudi. Then his father died and he came back to take over the cider farm.'

'How often did he come back when he was in Saudi Arabia?'

'Every six months usually.'

'So, how were you able to hide the pregnancy from him when he came home?'

Silence.

'The best estimate is that the child was between two and four months old, and you'd have been pregnant for nine months. How is it that he didn't notice?'

Picking at the skin now, tiny flecks of blood appearing at the base of her nails. 'He didn't always come home, maybe he didn't at all that year. I don't remember.'

I'd be telling a client of mine to go 'no comment' right about now, thought Dixon.

'Let's say he came home when you were three months pregnant, he could be forgiven for missing that perhaps, but on his next visit, six months later . . . ?' Dixon let that hang in the air.

Even Diana's solicitor was starting to fidget. Time to end the charade, before her solicitor stepped in.

'You see, there's no record of you giving birth twenty-five years ago, but as you say, you kept that secret and told no one.'

'I did.'

'But there is a record of you giving birth to a healthy 6lb 13oz baby boy twenty-one years ago.'

Louise placed a file in Dixon's outstretched hand.

'These are your hospital records,' he said. 'Robert wasn't there, by all accounts.'

No reply.

'Still in Saudi? We can check the dates easily enough.'

'Yes.'

Dixon held the box-framed photograph and handprint in front of her, moving it lower when she looked down at her feet. 'And this is a picture of your son, isn't it? We've got a partial DNA profile, but this gives us his handprint too, doesn't it? Welcome to the world, it says.'

'I'm sorry.' Diana started to shake.

'I think it's time we—'

Dixon wasn't having that. 'Sorry for what?' he said, interrupting her solicitor.

'He wouldn't stop crying. All night and all day, he just wouldn't stop. I was at the end of my tether with it. I tried everything to make him stop, sitting up, leaving him. In the end I snapped and I shook him, and shook him.' Sobbing now, her face hidden in her hands. 'He went quiet, so I put him down in his cot. Then, when I went in the next morning, he was cold.'

'So, you panicked and buried him on the waste ground behind your house?'

'Yes.'

'What happened after that?'

'Robert was due back from Saudi and he was expecting to see his son. I was drinking, walking out on the coast path. I was intending to jump off the cliff, I think. It seemed the only way out. Then I saw the hotel on fire and went to see what was going on. We spent a lot of time there, were members of the leisure centre, so I knew the area well.'

Diana was breathing heavily now, her eyes fixed on the ceiling, tears streaming down her cheeks.

'There were people milling about on the terrace, being evacuated, and I noticed a group at the end of the terrace; older people, and there'd been a bridge thing going on, so I guessed they were players. One of the women was carrying a baby, so I took my chance. I didn't have a lot to lose at that point, did I?'

'What did you do?'

'I ran over to them, told them the baby was my nephew and that I'd look after him.' Diana turned to face Dixon; a look of surprise, if anything. 'She just handed him over to me. It was like someone was giving me a second chance, so I just ran.'

'Did the woman say anything to you?'

'Nothing at all.'

'What happened when Robert came home?'

'Nothing, really. He was delighted to meet Jos, his baby boy.'

'And you never told him?'

'Never. He didn't need to know, and he never knew.'

'It was a road traffic accident,' said Dixon.

'He was a motorcyclist; had a Honda Fireblade he used to go out on. Someone was doing a three-point turn on the A39 and that was that. Killed instantly.'

'What about the publicity, the hunt for the missing child. Did he never suspect anything?'

'He was back in Saudi for most of that, and it soon died down.'

'Does Jos know?'

'No. And I'd rather he didn't, if there's any way we—'

The solicitor placed his hand on Diana's arm. 'There isn't, Diana. We did talk about that.'

'Didn't Jos think it odd when you asked him to give the DNA sample?' asked Dixon.

'Why would he? We were asked to provide an immediate-family sample and he's part of the family.'

'All right, Diana, let's move on,' said Dixon. 'Does the name Deirdre Baxter mean anything to you?'

The hand on the arm again. Not a good sign.

'No comment.'

'Deirdre was a member of the Somerset bridge team at the Regional Qualifier that night at the Palace Hotel. Deirdre has been identified as the woman who handed the baby boy to you.'

'Who by?' demanded her solicitor.

'Sean Rodwell.'

'A convicted murderer and arsonist.'

'Deirdre was found dead in her home, strangled,' continued Dixon, not that he was going to get anywhere. 'In fact, all six members of the Somerset bridge team there that night are either dead or suffering from dementia; four of them have been murdered.'

'No comment.'

'Where were you on the night of—'

'My client has provided me with details of her whereabouts for the relevant dates. I have them here,' said her solicitor, 'and am instructed to pass them to you at the conclusion of this interview.'

'Someone has killed four elderly and defenceless people in their own homes, Diana. Who d'you think that might be?'

'No comment.'

'Someone taking revenge perhaps?'

'No comment.'

'Jos?'

'Don't be ridiculous. Why would he do that?'

'Because they gave him away. To you.'

'That boy wanted for nothing. And he doesn't know anything about this, anyway.'

'To silence the bridge team, perhaps?' Dixon tried an understanding smile, now he'd got her talking again. 'Were you being blackmailed?'

'Certainly not.'

'Only, the killings started after your son's remains were found on the building site. A bit of a coincidence that, don't you think?'

'I have advised my client to answer no further questions in relation to this matter,' said the solicitor, closing his notebook. 'She has given a full and frank admission in relation to the death of her son and the abduction of Patrick Hudson. She has also provided her alibis for each of the murders, *in writing*.' He took a firm grip of her wrist.

One more question. It was worth a try. 'I'm assuming you know Jos, or Patrick I should say, was in a relationship with his sister, Freya?'

A sharp intake of breath, a firmer grip on the wrist.

Startled, she mumbled, 'No . . . no comment.'

Chapter Thirty

It was either back past the video suite or out of the security door and into the rain. The crowd had dispersed, not that he minded the audience; it saved another briefing if everyone knew anyway.

Charlesworth was still there, though, waiting in the doorway to pounce.

'You got all that from her sending her son to do the DNA test?' he asked, springing out into the corridor in front of Dixon.

'It makes perfect sense when you put the two cases together.'

'I'll let my oppo know. At least Devon and Cornwall will be able to put that one to bed,' Charlesworth said, triumphantly. 'Nice to know we sorted it out for them. When are you going to tell the Hudson family?'

'When we've got the DNA results.'

'The revelation puts them in the frame for the bridge team murders, so you'll need to tread carefully.'

'We will, Sir. We'll need another sample from Jos to compare against the sample we have from Patrick, but Diana's sample is already at the lab for comparison to the remains found on the waste ground. If it's her child then we're halfway there on that, at least.'

'Rather you than me.'

'Thank you, Sir.'

'It's a bit late, isn't it, Sir?' Louise was sitting in the passenger seat of Dixon's Land Rover, looking at the time on her phone.

'He's going to be wondering where his mother is, or the woman he thinks is his mother anyway, so we need to break the news to him and get a DNA sample.'

'I've got a kit.'

Lights were on inside Lynch Cottage; there were even lights outside on the grass, pointing up at the house, and more twinkly lights entwined in the creeper growing up the walls. It would have made a lovely photograph for estate agent's particulars.

A figure was moving about inside, wearing a white T-shirt and shorts, a phone clamped to his ear. Ringing his mother, probably, her phone with High Tech by now.

'I'm not sure which is worse,' said Louise. 'Telling someone a loved one is dead, or telling them they've slept with their sister.'

'That's a conversation for another day,' replied Dixon. 'I want no mention of the Hudson family until it's confirmed. The last thing we want is him charging round there.'

It turned out the shorts were boxers, although that didn't stop Jos answering the door. He looked slightly embarrassed when he saw Louise, taking a moment to recover his composure, but not before Dixon had used the uncertainty to invite himself in.

'I'll just go and put some trousers on.'

Jos returned a few moments later, clutching a piece of paper. 'Maybe you can tell me what this is all about? I found it on the kitchen table.'

'I can tell you exactly what that is, Sir,' replied Dixon, without looking at the document. 'It's a search warrant that was executed at this property earlier today.'

'A search warrant?'

Dixon was still standing in the hall, looking at himself in the huge mirrors, multiple versions of himself disappearing into the distance, wondering what a psychologist would make of it. It felt like a metaphor for something.

'Look, what's this all about?' demanded Jos. 'And where the bloody hell is my mother?'

'Is there somewhere we could sit down, perhaps?' he asked.

'In the kitchen.'

Mercifully Jos didn't spot that they knew the way. He perched on a bar stool, his arms folded tightly across his chest.

'Mrs Diana Hope-Bruce is currently in custody at the police centre at Express Park, Bridgwater.' Dixon was choosing his words carefully, making sure he didn't refer to Diana as 'mother'; watching for Jos's reaction would be even more important. 'She has been arrested on suspicion of child abduction, and will remain in custody until such time as she is charged and brought before a court.'

'Child abduction?' Jos straightened. 'What child?'

'You.'

'Me? That's bollocks. What evidence have you got?'

'She's confessed.'

'Confessed to abducting me?' The blood drained from Jos's face. 'Abducting me from who?'

'There's no easy way of saying this, so I'll just speak plainly,' said Dixon. 'Roughly around the time you were born in Musgrove Park Hospital, Diana gave birth to a boy in Torbay Hospital. That boy died and his remains were found buried on the area of waste ground behind your old house in Torquay. You remember she asked you to give a DNA sample for testing?'

'There was no match though.'

'There wouldn't have been, *to you*, but there would have been to her, which is why she asked you to give the sample. When the boy

261

died, she abducted you to take his place. It was an opportunistic thing, she didn't plan it; the opportunity presented itself and she took it. The man you know as your father, Robert Hope-Bruce, was overseas at the time and none the wiser. He returned from Saudi Arabia and there you were.'

'I can't get my head round this.' Jos had his hands pressed to the side of his skull, squeezing hard. 'Abducting me from who?'

'I'm afraid we can't tell you that until it's confirmed by DNA and we've spoken to them. In the meantime, is there someone we can call?' asked Dixon. 'Someone who could come and sit with you?'

'No.'

'I can arrange for a family liaison officer if that would help.'

'No, thank you.' The initial sadness was slowly being replaced by anger. 'What did you find when you searched this place?'

'We recovered some documents from the office.'

'That explains the filing cabinets.'

'And the framed photograph and handprint on the wall in Diana's dressing room,' replied Dixon. 'Ideally, we'll be asking you for a handprint for comparison purposes.'

'It's not my handprint, you mean? Not me in the photo?'

'Possibly not. Diana didn't confirm it one way or the other in interview.'

'You'll be wanting my DNA too, I suppose?' asked Jos.

'The sample you gave before was destroyed, at your request,' replied Dixon.

'You need to give me some time to process this.'

'I should also tell you that Diana is a suspect in the murders of four members of a bridge team; they are, or were, the people from whom she took you. They'd been entrusted with your care, albeit temporarily, and she persuaded them to hand you over.'

'Four murders? No way.' Jos stood up sharply, sending the metal-framed bar stool clattering across the tiled floor. 'Whatever you say, she brought me up and she's still my mother as far as I'm concerned. Am I under arrest?'

'No.'

'Do I have to give a DNA sample or my handprint?'

'No, you don't. I'd need a warrant.'

'In that case, I'm not doing anything to help you build a case against her. I don't care what she's done. And first thing in the morning I'll be speaking to my solicitor. Until then, I'd like you to leave me alone, please.'

Chapter Thirty-One

'You've done it again, haven't you?' Jane sighed. 'How many times have I told you? I don't care what time it is, just come to bed.' She was standing on the rug in the living room, her hands on her hips, looking down at Dixon stretched out on the sofa. 'I really don't mind being woken up. I'd much rather that than you sleeping down here.'

He yawned. 'I didn't want to wake you.'

'You always say that.' She reminded him of a primary school-teacher towering over a naughty child.

'My leg's gone numb.'

'That's probably because Monty's been using it as a pillow.' Another sigh, louder this time. 'I'll put the kettle on.'

'What time is it?' asked Dixon, rubbing his leg, Monty unceremoniously turfed on to the floor.

'Quarter to seven.'

It was still dark outside, the glow from the streetlights creeping around the curtains.

'How's Rod?'

'He's all right.' Jane was in the kitchen, dog biscuits dropping into a tin bowl sending Monty running in. 'He's insisting on coming to the stag do; won't be able to drink though.'

'Good. He can keep an eye on me.'

'When is it?'

'The Saturday before. Roger's been on to the place in Lynmouth and it's fine. He'd postponed it rather than cancelled.'

'Did you ask him about the baby's remains?' Jane's voice was increasing in volume, rising above the boiling kettle. 'Can he confirm what she said in interview?'

'He said he's not a bloody clairvoyant, which is a fair point. I never thought he could, to be honest. All he can say is the original pathologist's estimate of the baby's age at death is correct, but then the label in the babygrow says three to six months, so that's hardly rocket science.'

'Do you believe her?'

'Why would she confess to killing her baby if it wasn't true? She could've said it was sudden infant death and we couldn't have disproved it. She'd still have been in the frame for preventing lawful burial and the abduction of Patrick, but there'd have been no manslaughter charge.'

'We need to think about getting some baby clothes,' said Jane, appearing in the doorway with a mug in each hand.

'Can we leave it until this case is over?'

'Yeah.'

'We've still got four murders. We may have got the motive, but we've got precious little else.'

'Well,' said Jane, handing Dixon a mug, the sound of a dog bowl being pushed around a tiled kitchen floor in the background. 'Sarah and Mark have been doing a bit of work on the key safes that may interest you.'

◆ ◆ ◆

'Thomas Fowler, Deirdre Baxter and Geoffrey Pannell all had key safes on their front doors, so I was wondering how the killer might have known the codes,' said Sarah. She was sitting at a workstation, looking up at the small crowd gathered around her desk. 'I got their call records – they all had landlines, most people do at that age – and all of them received a call from a mobile phone number in the days before their deaths.'

'The same mobile number?' asked Dixon.

'No, a different one each time. The numbers weren't in any of their address books. I checked,' continued Sarah. 'So, I was working on the basis that someone had phoned them. Some people might be persuaded to give out their key safe code to an OT for a prearranged visit, or leave the door on the latch even.'

'How did they get their phone numbers?' asked Jane.

'They're all in the phone book,' replied Sarah. 'Directory enquiries, the phone book's online.'

'A powerful argument for being ex-directory if ever I heard one.'

'The mobile phones were burners, only live for long enough to make the calls, but we traced them,' said Mark. 'You authorised it, Sir.'

'Did I?'

'You did,' said Jane, nudging his elbow.

'Triangulation places the calls in an area south of Taunton,' continued Mark. 'There are base stations at Hillfarrance, Bishop's Hull, a couple along the A38 there. And it looks like the calls were made from the Oake Cider Farm.'

◆ ◆ ◆

'Go in hard.'

It was an instruction he'd given to enough people, enough times. Blue lights, sirens wailing; that would set the tone. A few uniformed officers milling about while he asked his questions would put most people on the back foot.

Oake Cider. It wasn't quite what Dixon had been expecting. His first experience of a cider farm had been cycling out from school in Taunton to an old scrumpy place at Ashill. Cloudy, and sold by the gallon; he woke up the next day back at school and never did know how he got there. Happy days, before he was diabetic – cider was far too sweet for him now.

This was very different. A huge barn off to the right of the visitors' centre and shop, vast oak vats, miles of chrome piping. A cider bar too.

Beyond all of that was a factory, a lorry reversed up to the loading bay, a forklift truck stacking pallets inside with golden-coloured cans wrapped in plastic; all of it screened from the road by a line of trees. Steel and glass from the ground up, offices on the second floor, judging by the figure watching from the window.

Jos Hope-Bruce. Or rather Patrick Hudson, to give him his proper name.

Dixon had been before, for the wassailing, but that had taken place at an old barn on the far side of the orchards, all nine hundred acres of them.

'That's the new canning plant,' offered Mark. 'Caused quite a kerfuffle when the planning application went in.'

'What the bloody hell's going on?' The man was walking towards the patrol cars, their lights still flashing. Dixon had intended to make an entrance and it seemed to have worked.

'Police, Sir,' he replied, warrant card at the ready. 'We're here to see Jos Hope-Bruce.'

'I'm his uncle Malcolm. Is there anything I can do?' He was wearing a shirt and tie beneath his white lab coat, an image of a large red apple embroidered on the top pocket. 'We had a shoplifter a couple of days ago, but I can't imagine you're here for that.'

'No, Sir.'

'Well, he's in the office, if you'd like to follow me.'

The conference table was long and made of glass an inch thick. Dixon waited with Louise, while the uniformed officers, Sarah and Mark, had a look around outside. He could see Mark from the first-floor window, marvelling at the acres of orchards stretching away to the far horizon. Half a chance and Mark would be nipping in the shop.

'He's on his way,' said the uncle. 'It's quite a sight, isn't it.'

Lines and lines of trees, all of them pruned to the same size, the same distance apart, a dusting of snow on the ground.

'We buy in a lot of apples too,' continued the uncle.

'Why haven't I seen your cider in a pub?' asked Dixon.

'We export most of it. The farm's been in the family for five generations and we're sort of hoping it'll stay that way. Anyway, do let me know if you need anything.'

'Thank you,' replied Dixon, turning back to the window just in time to see Mark walking back to his car with a carrier bag in his hand.

He recognised the solicitor before the glass door opened, the same one who had been advising Diana Hope-Bruce – not terribly well, as it happened – and had sat in on her police interview.

'Here we go,' said Louise, sitting down at the conference table, notebook at the ready.

The solicitor waited until Jos had closed the door behind them. 'I have advised my client not to answer any of your questions at the present time,' he said.

Dixon watched Jos sit down at the head of the table and fold his arms.

'He is not prepared to give a DNA sample, nor will he give his fingerprints or a handprint, for that matter.' The solicitor was watching Dixon closely. 'I know what you're thinking, Superintendent, but there is no conflict of interest that prevents me from acting for both Diana and Jos. If a conflict does arise, then Jos understands that I will have to decline to act for him further. Now, do you have any evidence of wrongdoing on his part?'

'I am investigating the murders of four members of the bridge team from whom Diana Hope-Bruce abducted your client as a baby. Three of those victims had key safes on their front doors. They were telephoned in the days before their murders, presumably to get their key codes. The calls were made from mobile phones, and mast data places those calls as having been made from the vicinity of this farm.' It was the best Dixon could do. He knew what was coming and braced himself.

'Do you have any evidence that those calls were made by my client?'

Bollocks.

'No.'

'Then they could have been made by anybody.'

Time to light the fuse and retreat to a safe distance. 'Diana Hope-Bruce has confessed to abducting your client from the bridge team and I am seeking a DNA sample merely to establish whether or not that is true.'

'Jos has already made it clear to you, has he not, that he will not assist you, in any way, to build a case against his mother?'

'It's important for Jos to know sooner rather than later,' said Dixon. 'Because it's entirely possible that he's in or has had a romantic relationship with his sister, Freya.'

'Freya is my sister?' Jos jumped up from the table. 'No way, that can't be right.'

'Are you the father of her child?' asked Dixon, tightening the screw a little.

'No, I'm not. She was with someone else to begin with. This just can't be fucking right. I loved her, for fuck's sake, and she loved me!'

'If what Diana says is true, then it is right, Jos.' Dixon was shifting from one foot to the other. 'But what concerns me more than that, frankly, is that someone is murdering elderly people in their own homes in the most brutal fashion imaginable. Up close and personal.'

'That is no concern of my client,' said the solicitor. 'Sit down, Jos, if you will.'

Jos was typing a message on his phone, holding it in both hands, his thumbs moving at speed across the screen. 'We met at a college disco. I was at boarding school and hated it, so my mother took me out and I went to Richard Huish Sixth Form College. Freya was in the year above me, but there was a connection . . .' His voice was running out of steam. 'What are the fucking chances of that?' He was still typing, trembling, the phone shaking; deleting and retyping the message, hissing under his breath.

'Your client is a suspect, and if he refuses to cooperate you will no doubt tell him what conclusion we are likely to draw.'

'The only conclusion I draw from his refusal to cooperate is that he is being properly advised.'

'We'll have a look around on the way out, if that's all right,' said Dixon, stalking towards the door.

'There's a tour starting at eleven,' said the solicitor, with a smirk. 'Tickets are fifteen pounds each.'

Chapter Thirty-Two

'Do you think he ever sells any of these hot tubs?' asked Louise.

'Not in February, no,' replied Dixon. 'Did we get the company search back?'

'Small company accounts, so they tell you bugger all, really. It's owned by William and his wife, Sally. She's the company secretary as well.'

The hot tub on the grass outside the showroom was on, steam rising into the cold and miserable winter morning. Lights were on inside, a lone figure sitting at a desk.

'We still haven't had a DNA test to confirm it,' said Louise, the palm of her hand on the door.

'We're not likely to get it now, are we?' Dixon gritted his teeth. 'We've got her confession, so that'll have to do.'

'You again,' said Hudson, when Louise pushed open the door. 'Let me lock up. We shut at one on a Saturday anyway.' He locked the door and then flicked a switch on the wall, turning off the hot tub outside. 'I'll put the cover on it on the way out.'

'I'm pleased to tell you, Sir, that we've made an arrest for the abduction of Patrick.'

'Who?' Hudson spun round, eyes wide.

'A Mrs Diana Hope-Bruce. Her own baby had died, sadly, and she's confessed to abducting your son on the terrace of the Palace

Hotel. It happened much as you thought, oddly enough; she saw a group of older hotel guests during the fire, a woman among them holding a baby, ran up to them and convinced them the boy was her nephew, so they handed him over.'

'Where is he now?' Hudson had sat down at his desk in the middle of the showroom, breathing heavily. 'Have you found him?'

'Yes, we have, but this is where it gets a bit tricky, I'm afraid. His name now is Jos Hope-Bruce.'

'Not Jos who was seeing Freya?'

'I'm afraid so, Sir.'

'Oh, for God's sake.' He puffed out his cheeks. 'She's going to love that.'

'Do you know how they met?'

'I'm sorry,' replied Hudson, 'you'll have to give me a minute.' He was wiping the tears from his cheeks with his shirtsleeves.

'Take your time,' said Dixon.

'All this time, I knew he was alive, I just knew it. And now I find out I've known him for a year without even knowing he was my son.' He frowned. 'I should have felt something, surely? There should have been some connection, some father and son thing. Freya clearly felt something for him, although there'll have been nothing sisterly about that. Does she know?'

'We told Jos this morning, so I'm guessing he's told her by now,' replied Dixon.

'I ought to go and find her. She'll be in bits.'

'A few questions before you do. How long has Freya known him?'

'They met at Richard Huish, so that'll be four years ago. She was with someone else back then, so they only got together a year or so ago, and it only lasted a couple of months, I think.'

'And they'd never met before that?'

272

'No. Freya was nearing the end of her second year of sixth form when Jos started, and she left four years ago. He wasn't there that long before his father died – a year maybe – so he left to go and work at the cider farm. Then Freya met him again at a pub in Taunton about a year ago, as I say. They were both free agents then and decided to give it a go. I'm not sure it was too serious.' He caught himself, taking a sharp intake of breath. 'God, I hope it wasn't, for both their sakes.'

◆ ◆ ◆

'Did we check his alibis?' asked Dixon. He was sitting in his Land Rover, watching Hudson hastily covering the outside hot tub.

'They checked out,' replied Louise. 'The Rotary dinner, and his wife confirmed the other dates, although she was out for Geoffrey Pannell's murder. She went to a Pilates class and he was at home alone with the kids.'

'How old are they?'

'Five and seven. Neighbours didn't see him leave, if that's what you're thinking, and he was able to confirm what he watched on the telly; even had an invoice for one of the *Mission Impossible* films. I can't remember which one, but we've got a statement.'

'What about his mobile phone?'

'Never left the house.'

Dixon wasn't entirely sure why he even bothered asking that last question. Anyone with half a brain who was up to no good would leave their phone at home, surely? There was enough true crime on the telly these days. 'Anyone with a Netflix subscription is a bloody forensics expert,' as the chap from High Tech was so fond of saying.

'What about calls?'

'Nothing you wouldn't expect to see – Freya, his wife, stuff like that.'

'Well, somebody's killing these old people.' He turned the key; much harder and it would've snapped off in the ignition.

The drive back to Express Park was endured in silence, Dixon taking the opportunity to admire the view across the Levels towards the Sedgemoor battlefield as he drove along the A39 – until the vision of a blood-soaked scythe popped into his head.

'Everybody's still out and about,' said Jane, when they appeared in the incident room. She had been populating the whiteboards with photographs from Facebook.

'We're still waiting for Jos and Freya's call records,' said Mark. 'I've got Diana Hope-Bruce's, but there's nothing there.'

'What does she drive?'

'An Audi, and the dashcam's gone to High Tech,' replied Jane. 'We got a charging decision from the Crown Prosecution Service. Manslaughter, child abduction, and there's a new offence of concealment of a body. We're going to charge her in a bit, if you want to be there?'

'You can handle it.'

'We'll be keeping her here until Monday morning, when she goes to court.'

Been there, done that.

Every now and again the memory flashed into his mind; rarely lingering these days, thankfully.

'Where's Sarah?'

'I don't know,' replied Mark. 'She went out about half an hour ago and I've not seen her since.' He shrugged. 'I tried ringing her, but there's no reply.'

'And she didn't say where she was going?'

'There's something else you need to know,' said Jane, ominously. 'We had a call from the halfway house and there's no sign of Sean Rodwell, apparently. He went out last night to get a takeaway and hasn't been seen since. It puts him in breach of his licence conditions, so the local lot in Weston are keeping an eye out for him.'

'They were supposed to be doing that already.'

Chapter Thirty-Three

It had been a long day, up to his neck in pig shit. He was beginning to think Rural Crimes wasn't such a good deal after all, although it was regular hours. No punch-ups in Bridgwater at pub-kicking-out-time on a Saturday night either, unless he needed the overtime. Every cloud, and all that. His shifts were his own choice too – basically, he could come and go as he pleased – a reward, of sorts, for facing down that bloke with the crossbow. That, and the commendation, of course, which was nice. His wife had framed it for him and it was on the wall at home, taking pride of place in the downstairs loo.

Nigel Cole had spent too long in the shower, and too long looking at himself in the mirror. He was reaching that age when things were just starting to sag, ever so slightly. Maybe he'd go back to playing rugby? The police fielded a veterans' team. He gave a silent snarl at the mirror, tapping his dental implant with a fingernail. Best not.

'I'm not having my bloody teeth knocked out again.'

An early shift today, which gave him the afternoon off to watch the rugger. Or at least it should have done.

'There you are, Nige. You couldn't do me a favour, could you?'

He recognised the voice, silently cursing the unisex changing rooms. There really was nowhere to hide.

Thankfully, his towel was wrapped tightly around his waist. A glance over his shoulder in the mirror and there she was, dressed like a CID officer in a navy blue two-piece suit and white blouse; a younger version of the chief super already – Deborah Potter's *mini-me*. A future chief constable almost inevitably; Nick Dixon was right.

A regional task force, at your age. It isn't natural.

One hand on the towel, just to make sure, he turned around. 'What?' he asked, knowing he would regret it. His answer should have been 'Sorry, I've got a train to catch,' but he knew that whatever it was, the silly sod would do it on her own if he didn't go with her.

'Could you come with me?' asked Sarah. 'There's a barn I need to check.'

'Couldn't one of your new colleagues go with you?'

'I should have checked it when we were there this morning, and I don't want them to know I didn't. I was with Mark Pearce and he was too busy in the shop, buying cider.'

That sounded about right. 'Give me a minute and I'll throw some clothes on.'

'Shall I bring my car around to the front?'

'We'll go in mine.'

◆ ◆ ◆

'This is fun. What is it?'

'A BMW M3.'

'How many miles has it got on the clock?'

'More than me,' replied Cole.

'Beats my Ford Fiesta,' said Sarah. She sounded almost apologetic, but then that was only right and proper. It was the first

Saturday of the Six Nations and he was going to miss the opening game.

'When you're chief constable, you'll have a chauffeur-driven car.'

She blushed, and he immediately felt guilty for shutting down the conversation like that. She brought out the worst in him, she really did, but then that was probably because she was everything he wasn't, and he knew it. She didn't, but he did.

Twenty-five years a police constable, promotion never even discussed at performance reviews. He wouldn't say he was bitter, just mildly pissed off perhaps. Besides, he'd done his fair share of detective work on the major investigation team for the crossbow killings. Nick Dixon's bagman, no less. It had been fun, but it wasn't for him. He was 'plod', through and through.

And he knew what *they* said about him. 'A good man to have by your side when the shit hits the fan,' and that was fine by him. He might even have it on his gravestone.

'I'm sorry,' he said, after a while. 'Just ignore me. You'll go far, you really will. I'm just jealous.'

'Thanks, Nige,' Sarah said, with a warm smile.

'Where is this place, then?'

'It's on the far side of the orchards, about two miles from the visitor centre.' Sarah had a satnav app open on her phone and was following the route on the screen. 'I did look at it on Google Earth.'

'And what are you expecting to find?'

'Nothing, hopefully.' She was holding the phone to her ear, listening to the voice giving directions, the volume turned down. 'Take the next right,' she said. 'It's a narrow lane. Then fork left after a while. The barn's on the left after about another mile or so.'

Signs had been tied to the bare willow branches of the hedge on the nearside: 'Oake Cider Farm Wassailing', and a big arrow pointed straight ahead.

'Looks like we can just follow these arrows,' said Cole.

'In one thousand feet you will have reached your destination,' said Sarah, sliding her phone back into her coat pocket.

Cole slowed, the sound of the tyres splashing through the puddles now drowned out by the growl of the engine.

'That must be it there,' said Sarah, pointing to a pair of closed five-bar gates on the nearside. 'Where are we going?' she asked, turning in her seat as Cole drove past.

'It's gravelled in front of the gates, so we'll find somewhere to park down here and walk back.'

It was either a gateway or a passing place in the single-track lane, but it would do. Cole wasn't planning on staying long. He let Sarah out and then parked tight to the hedge, walking silently back along the lane, dodging the puddles.

The gates were padlocked, a sturdy chain wrapped umpteen times around the frames where they met in the middle.

'Up and over,' said Cole, holding the gate steady while Sarah tried to avoid the single strand of barbed wire along the top. At least she wasn't wearing heels.

A large gravelled area, bordered by railway sleepers, lines of apple trees stretching away up the slope towards another hedge. The barn was off to the right, red brick and thatched, the double doors padlocked.

Wooden benches and tables were slowly rotting on a lawned area in front, a fire pit on the far side of that.

Sarah was peering in the windows of the barn, her hands cupped around her eyes, shielding them from the reflection.

'Can you see anything?' asked Cole.

'There's some strange wooden thing, and some huge oak vats. I suppose they're oak. Lots of barrels too.'

'Let me have a look.' He was looking through the same window, towering over Sarah. 'That's a cider press. Funny that, finding a cider press on a cider farm.'

'There's an upstairs,' she whispered. 'We need to get in there, really.'

'Why are you whispering?'

'In case there's anyone here?'

'Then they can bloody well let us in, can't they.' Cole stepped back. 'Hello! Hello!'

'We haven't got a warrant.'

'We don't need one if they let us in.'

'And what if they don't?'

'Then they've got something to hide and we go and get a warrant.'

'You make it sound so easy.'

Cole followed Sarah around to the back of the barn, each window giving a view of the same cider press and oak barrels, albeit from different angles. It was an odd contraption: two giant wooden screws at either end of a beam, a barrel underneath to catch the juice when the beam was screwed down to crush the apples. No doubt the canning plant two miles away had a more modern version.

Several pallets of gold and pink cans wrapped in plastic were gathering dust at the far end of the barn; other cans had been opened, the contents poured down a drain in the floor, and then dumped in a green wheelie bin that looked out of place in the otherwise antique barn.

'There's nothing here,' said Cole.

Back round the front of the barn now, still dutifully following Sarah, he leaned on a five-bar gate and looked out across the orchard beyond to a fork in the farm track. 'I'm guessing left will take us across the orchards to the visitors' centre,' he said, following the line of light bulbs in the apple trees, the cable sagging in the gap between the branches. 'Where does the right track take you?'

Sarah was dragging a map across the screen on her phone, following the farm track – virtually at least. 'There's another barn,' she said. 'Let's go and have a look.'

'Bloody marvellous.' Cole was making no effort to hide his irritation. 'I'm so glad I asked.'

Trudging now, stepping over the puddles and the fresh tyre tracks in the mud. The dusting of snow that had fallen that morning had long gone; he'd got covered in it on that pig farm, but it had melted by the time he'd left Express Park at the end of his shift. He tapped Sarah on the shoulder. 'These tracks were made after the snow melted.'

'How can you tell?'

'I just can, all right. I am the Rural Crimes team, after all.' Cole shook his head. 'They're dry, where the tyre has compressed the water out of the mud.'

Sarah kept going, much to Cole's disappointment.

'There it is,' she said. 'In those trees. The track continues on, so presumably it goes out to the road further down.'

Tiptoeing now, although he wasn't entirely sure why. Sarah was, so that must be it.

The barn was set back from the track, an old post and rail fence around the front, the gate long gone, only the iron hinges left sticking out of the post. More fresh tracks had come in from the other direction too; come and gone, if the mud splash pattern was anything to go by.

Two large barn doors, a padlock hanging open from the latch on one of them. It was smaller than the other barn, single storey, with a tiled roof that was covered in moss; damp from the overhanging trees.

'It's not locked.'

'I can see that,' replied Cole.

Sarah opened the door slowly, trying not to stand on the tyre tracks leading into the barn. The door swung easily, coming to rest against the small grass bank that Cole was standing on. She blinked, her eyes trying to adjust to the darkness. 'There's a car, up on blocks,' she said.

'What is it?'

'It's got a cover on it and the wheels are off. It's not going anywhere.'

Cole had stepped over the tyre tracks and was opening the left-hand door, allowing more light to flood into the barn. 'It looks like an old moggie to me,' he said. 'Judging by the shape.'

'What's a moggie?'

'A Morris Minor. Classics, they are, these days.'

A black cover, elasticated; it had been hooked under the bumper front and back.

'Would a Morris Minor have alloy wheels?' asked Sarah. She was shining the light of her phone at the stack of four wheels piled up behind the car.

'Probably not.'

'It looks very much like a Fiat 500 to me, and our occupational therapist drives one.'

Cole knew that. He'd been reading the intranet since the incident at the bungalow in Berrow.

Sarah unhooked the cover at the back of the car, the elastic pulling tight and dragging it clear of the rear window. 'There's no number plate either.'

She shone her light at a bench against the back wall, where several number plates were stacked in a pile, alongside a screwdriver and four screws. 'There are loads here,' she said. 'All different registration numbers.'

'Best not touch,' said Cole. 'We'll need to get Forensics over here.'

Sarah was dialling a number on her phone, but stopped abruptly, her eyes wide and fixed on something behind Cole. He spun round, seeing the gun butt swinging towards his head – it was definitely a gun butt.

Then it all went black.

Chapter Thirty-Four

Last call on a Saturday. Louise had taken a long overdue afternoon off, so it was Jane in the passenger seat grumbling about his parking, baggy coat done up to hide her bump. Monty was grumbling too, but that was aimed at another dog being exercised off the lead on the far side of the grass area in the middle of the crescent.

'Off the lead on a public road,' muttered Dixon.

'I think we've got more important things to be worrying about, don't you?'

He would have parked across the drive, but someone had beaten him to it.

'Is that his?' asked Jane.

Red, with the unmistakable badge.

'Let's hope we don't get involved in a car chase,' said Dixon.

'His monthly insurance payment must be more than I earn.'

A twenty-one-year-old in a Ferrari. It didn't bear thinking about.

It was Dixon's turn to grumble. 'I'm in the wrong business.'

'You've always known that.'

Double-glazed windows, but the sound of a baby crying still carried to the pavement. It was something he would need to get used to, if such a thing was possible.

'She'll know by now, if he's here,' said Jane.

'I want to talk to her alone, so we'll need to get rid of him somehow.' There had been movement in the upstairs window, but he rang the bell anyway.

'Is it true?' asked Freya, opening the front door. 'Is he my brother?'

There were tears, but Dixon would reserve judgement on whether they were genuine or not.

'Jos has so far refused to give us a DNA sample,' replied Dixon.

'So he might not be?'

'He is, according to Diana Hope-Bruce. And she should know.' He took his chance and stepped in through the open door.

'We're upstairs,' she said, closing the door behind them.

'Do I need my solicitor again?' demanded Jos, when Dixon appeared on the landing.

'We've come to talk to Freya, actually,' replied Dixon. 'So, you're free to leave.'

'I'll stay.'

'Let me rephrase that then.' Dixon was looking along the mantelpiece, fake and over an electric fire. There wasn't even a chimney. 'Go.'

'I'd rather he stayed,' said Freya. She had followed Jane up the stairs. 'How far gone are you?' she asked.

'Six months.'

'Is he the father?' she asked, nodding in Dixon's direction.

'Yes.'

'Oh, God. I was joking, sorry.'

Her son was sitting in a high chair, trying to feed himself with a plastic spoon.

'How old is he?' Jane knew the answer to that one, but was making polite conversation; something in common, and all that.

'Eighteen months.'

'And you called him Patrick.' Jane was leaning over the high chair now, brushing the baby's hair back off his face. 'I thought that was nice.'

'Thank you.'

'Named him after me.' Jos's voice was loaded with venom.

'It's nobody's fault, Jos,' said Freya.

'Yes, it bloody well is. My mother's, or the woman I thought was my mother.' He stood up, walked over to the mantelpiece, picking up a framed photograph. 'That's my real mother.' He handed the picture to Jane. 'And that's me she's holding in her arms. Me and Freya were in a relationship for six months, and I've only just found out; all along, I was shagging my sister, for fuck's sake.'

It was an unfortunate turn of phrase, albeit accurate. 'You couldn't have known,' said Dixon.

'There was a connection. We felt it when we first met at college – I did anyway – and the spark was still there when we bumped into each other again at Zinc. Remember?' Freya was smiling at Jos; a sadness to it, though. 'I was footloose and fancy free then, so I made the first move; grabbed your hand and pulled you on to the dance floor.'

'I was too shy, apparently,' mumbled Jos. 'What I actually thought was that you were still with someone.' He gestured to the boy in the high chair, now being fed by Jane, a dollop of something indescribable dripping off the spoon. '*His* father.'

'Sorry,' Jane said. 'I'm just getting a bit of practice in.'

'Be my guest,' replied Freya.

Dixon knew what she was really up to; they'd been on the same training course. It was called empathy – putting the interviewee at their ease. 'Was it serious, your relationship?' he asked.

'I thought so,' replied Freya.

Jos took a deep breath, reached into his jacket pocket. 'I'd bought a ring,' he said, a little black velvet box sitting in the palm of his hand. 'I was going to ask her to marry me, but my mother went nuts when she found out. I know why now. You might as well have it, to remember me by.'

'You're not going anywhere, Jos. You're still my brother.'

'I wanted to be your husband.'

Not quite the same, thought Dixon. And somebody was going somewhere; he just didn't know who yet.

'Look, I'm going to go,' said Jos. He stopped in front of Dixon. 'I suppose I ought to ask how my mother is, but right at this moment, I don't give a shit.'

'She'll be appearing before the magistrates at Taunton on Monday morning at ten.'

'I might turn up. If I can be bothered.'

'And she remains a suspect in the murders of the bridge team.'

'So do I, I suppose?'

Dixon stood in the French windows, overlooking the Ferrari in the drive below. There was a loud growl when Jos started the engine, very different to the rumble of a Land Rover.

'What did your father think of Jos when he met him?'

'He liked him,' replied Freya. 'He had the usual reservations, I suppose. I'd had my fingers burned once – badly – and then this flash lad in a Ferrari is on the scene, but Dad liked him. Gave him a lecture about driving carefully.' Another sad smile. 'You can imagine it, can't you?'

'I can,' said Jane. 'Although mine rolled up in an old Land Rover, with his dog on the passenger seat.'

'Did your father give any indication that he knew who Jos was?' asked Dixon.

'He'd have said something if he did.' Freya frowned. 'He's hardly going to let me get involved with my brother if he knew, is he? Jos's mother went nuts, but Dad was fine about it.'

'What about when you were growing up?' Jos had left the ring box on the mantelpiece; replaced the picture of his mother too, slightly out of line, so Dixon reached up and nudged it into its original position. 'Do you remember much about the hunt for your brother? Your father never gave up, did he?'

'Not to begin with,' replied Freya. 'But it gradually faded into the background when he met Sally and got married again. He still had that private detective on the case, but that stopped when Olivia came along. She wasn't well and he became totally focused on getting her through that. She's fine now, though, so all's well that ends well.'

'Did you ever ask him about the search?'

'I didn't have to. He never talked about anything else in the early days. He never hid anything from me. My brother was gone and I had to get used to it. My mother was gone too, and the worst part is I don't really remember her at all. That was harder than losing my brother.' She grimaced. 'That sounds a horrible thing to say, doesn't it?'

'Understandable, for a girl of that age.'

'Definitely,' said Jane.

'You lost your mother?' asked Freya.

'It's complicated.'

'A text from Mark,' said Dixon, handing his phone to Jane as he was driving.

'"You really need to see this, Sir",' she said, reading aloud. 'Bang goes an evening in the pub.'

'What did you think of Jos and Freya?'

'If they were a couple, I'll eat my hat. And yours.'

'You didn't see her face when he took the photograph off the mantelpiece?' asked Dixon.

'No, why?'

'There was a bottle of eye drops behind it; no better way to make it look as though you've been blubbing. He must've seen it and taken them when he put it back. It wasn't there when I was straightening the picture.'

'They just didn't seem natural together, to me.'

'Well, they wouldn't be, would they? Not after the revelation that they're brother and sister.'

'I suppose not.'

'How would you feel if you found out I was your long lost brother?'

'Sick.'

'Really?'

'I'm carrying your child.'

'And if you weren't?'

'I'd still feel sick.'

'There was no hint of that, was there?'

'Lou said she wasn't entirely happy with the father either,' said Jane. She was watching the cars flashing by on the opposite carriageway, the sets of headlights few and far between.

'He knows we're looking for his son, so I would've expected his first question to be "Have you found him?" Instead we got, "You again."'

'We've been here before, haven't we? And last time it was because the person knew damn well where the child was.'

Dixon was turning into the visitors' car park at Express Park. 'The thought had crossed my mind,' he said, idly.

'It would be a hell of a coincidence, wouldn't it?' Jane knew what she was doing, a hint of mischief in her voice. 'First they meet at college, and then again at Zinc.'

They were walking across to the side entrance when Dixon spotted Dean Wevill on the ramp, waiting for the electric gates of the staff car park to open.

'Give me a minute, will you.' Then he walked across to the bottom of the ramp, flagging down Wevill as he was turning for home.

'Off back to Devon?' he asked, when Wevill wound down the window.

'Yes, Sir. Back on Monday morning now, I'm afraid.'

'It looks like we've found a second set of remains on that building plot in Torquay,' said Dixon. 'Do you live anywhere near there?'

'Not really, I'm in Exmouth.'

'Only the dig's starting in the morning and I need someone to go along and keep an eye on it.' He waved his hand. 'Not to worry. I can find someone else.'

'A second set of remains?'

'An adult female, aged thirty or so. There's hair and teeth so we should get a name soon enough.'

'I can go if you—'

'No, it's fine. Have a good weekend.'

'What was that all about?' asked Jane, when Dixon jogged back across the car park.

'Just baiting a trap.'

◆ ◆ ◆

'What was it I need to see, Mark?' asked Dixon, approaching the one occupied workstation in the incident room, the glow from the computer screen the only light on anywhere.

'The filing cabinet in Diana Hope-Bruce's home office,' replied Mark, looking away from the screen. 'There's a box of documents on the desk there. I've fished out what looks the most important to me, but I'm no lawyer, so I thought you'd better have a rummage.

There's a Memorandum of Understanding and all sorts of other stuff.'

'Understanding of what?' asked Dixon, watching the footage on the screen.

'It looks like the cider farm has been or is being sold. That's what it looks like to me anyway,' replied Mark. 'One hundred and twenty million quid.'

'Funny nobody's mentioned that before,' said Jane.

'Have you heard from Sarah?'

'Not yet. I've left a couple of messages, but her phone's switched off. There's still no sign of Sean Rodwell either, but uniform are aware.'

Dixon was staring at the computer screen, watching the traffic camera footage, a Fiat 500 entering a roundabout on the A303. The clip had been edited and was rolling on a loop, the same car entering the same roundabout over and over again. 'That's Sparkford.'

'The night Thomas Fowler was murdered,' replied Mark. 'What d'you notice about it?'

'There are two people in the car.'

'Can't get a good look at them, I'm afraid. Give me a sec.' Then he paused the film. 'That's as good as it gets. You've got to remember the cameras are really just after the number plate. That's plain as day, but cloned.'

Driver and passenger sideways on, hooded coats or hoodies; either way, their faces were obscured.

'Everybody knows the cameras are there these days,' offered Mark.

Jane flicked on a desk lamp while Dixon opened the box and pulled out a lever arch file, white plastic and emblazoned with the Oxenden Hart logo; a label on the spine: 'Acquisition of Oake Cider Farm Ltd by Diagent Plc – Disclosure 1'.

'Imagine having to go through this lot,' said Jane. 'Corporate finance lawyers must lead dull lives.'

Dixon resisted the temptation.

'The Memorandum of Understanding is in a plastic document wallet. I slotted it down the side,' said Mark.

It ran to three pages, but was the starting gun on a transaction that would take months to complete.

'How much d'you reckon this lot would cost?' asked Jane. 'In fees, I mean.'

'That's only one box,' said Mark. 'There are six more downstairs.'

'Cost?' Dixon pursed his lips. 'About two hundred and fifty thousand. And four lives.'

Chapter Thirty-Five

'All right, clever clogs,' Dixon said. 'What's the most important thing about that document?'

Jane was sitting in the passenger seat of the Land Rover. 'You still haven't told me where we're going?'

'Oake.'

'Who lives there?'

'Malcolm Hope-Bruce, Jos's uncle.'

The converted mill was visible from the other side of the bridge in the middle of the village, illuminated by lights on the lawn; even the old waterwheel immaculately restored and lit up for all to see.

'I've never understood that,' said Jane, idly. 'Lighting up your house like that. What's the bloody point? And think of the electricity bill.'

'We've got a streetlight outside ours that does it for free.'

Several cars were parked outside the house, more lined up down the drive, so Dixon pulled in off the lane and left his Land Rover blocking them all in.

'They must have guests,' said Jane. 'One family couldn't have all these cars.'

'You still haven't told me what's important about the Memorandum.'

'What?'

'The date.' Dixon reached up and rang the doorbell. 'It's dated three weeks before the baby's remains were found in Torquay.'

The large oak door opened slowly. 'I'm guessing you're not here for the wine and cheese?' asked Malcolm, recognising Dixon in the light.

'No, Sir,' replied Dixon.

'We're having a bit of a fundraiser for the local Conservatives. Wine and cheese, a raffle, that sort of guff, you know.'

'Might we have a word in private?' asked Dixon. 'We'll try not to take up too much of your time.'

'Yes, of course. Follow me.'

A hall table made an imaginative use of the millstone. At least it wasn't turning. The flagstone floor was original too. Voices in the room to the left, a gathering visible through the open door, guests with a glass in one hand and a plate in the other, large windows overlooking the millstream behind.

Malcolm was tall, a fully paid-up member of the red corduroy brigade, wearing a check shirt and tie; late forties, maybe – the younger brother, almost certainly.

'My wife can hold the fort for a while. They're her cronies, really,' said Malcolm, opening the door to his office. 'Now, how can I help? I still haven't found out what you were doing at the cider farm. Has it got anything to do with Diana's arrest?'

'I'm afraid there's very little I can tell you at the moment, Sir,' replied Dixon.

'Surely not. She's my sister-in-law.'

'I do need to ask you about this, though.'

Malcolm flinched at the Memorandum of Understanding in Dixon's outstretched hand. He turned away, deliberately refusing even to touch it. 'Where did you get that?'

'During our brief conversation in the car park at Oake this morning,' continued Dixon, 'you made a remark that seems very interesting in the light of this document. You said the cider farm had been in your family for five generations and you were hoping it would stay that way. You said much the same at the wassailing.'

'It's a family company, always has been and always should be. All of us want it to stay that way, except our majority shareholder.' He sat down in a leather office chair, behind a large desk with matching leather inlay, and lit a cigar. 'My brother, Robert, was the eldest, then there's my sister, and I'm the youngest. My father, in his infinite wisdom, decided to leave the eldest child the majority shareholding, so instead of leaving us one-third each, he gave fifty per cent plus one to my brother and basically twenty-five per cent each to me and my sister. It's the *plus one* that gave my brother control of the company. Father's thinking was that it would avoid disagreements if one of us had outright control.'

'What happened when your father died?'

'Robert was in Saudi Arabia, so he came home to run the company. I was operations director, and I'd been working at the cider farm since I left school – but, no, he came home and took over.' He left the cigar balanced on the edge of an ashtray, the plume of smoke gradually fizzling out. 'In fairness to him he did a good job. We'd been bottles only up to that point, but he decided cans were the way forward, then we expanded into exports, and now almost all of our production is for the overseas market. The new canning plant was his brainchild too, and the day it was opened he was out on that bloody motorbike of his, and bang. Dead.'

'And now Jos is the majority shareholder?'

'Appointed himself chairman and chief executive when he turned eighteen. I'm still the operations director, though, and my sister is the finance director.'

'What does Jos know about the cider business?' asked Dixon. A deliberately leading question.

'You might well ask.' Malcolm flicked the ash off his cigar. 'He didn't even complete his A levels. I was hoping he'd go to university and do business studies, or something like that, but it wasn't to be.'

'Your brother's will left his shares to Jos rather than his wife?'

'Diana was well provided for, and it was inheritance tax efficient.' Malcolm shrugged. 'The company shares were eligible for business property relief and the rest went to Diana under the spouse exemption, so there was no inheritance tax to pay at all.'

Dixon was standing with his back to the fireplace, not that the wood burning stove was lit. He'd already looked at the photographs: children at various ages, playing sport or on stage at the school play. Some of Malcolm skydiving. It seemed he owned a glider too.

'What about the approach from Diagent?'

'They'd been sniffing around for years. Ever since we started exporting in earnest, I suppose. We've got a healthy turnover and we're an attractive proposition for them. Profitable, and the deal would open up new markets for their other products. They're exclusively beer, wines and spirits, so it would be a good fit.'

'But you're against it?'

'I am. And my sister is. There's no way my brother would've gone for it, either, and my father would turn in his grave at the very thought. It's a family business. Always has been. We employ forty people, and they're as much a part of the Oake family as we are.'

'You'll do quite well out of it, though, surely?'

'That's not the point. I do quite well enough as it is, thank you. I don't need the money, or want it for that matter, but my sister and I don't seem to have a lot of choice. Jos is the majority shareholder and he's decided the sale is going ahead. We took legal advice on it, but short of going to court, there's nothing we can do. And even if we fought it, we'd probably lose.'

'I'm guessing there are drag-along rights in the Articles of Association in that case?' asked Dixon.

'He can drag us along with him – kicking and screaming – if the company is being sold; force us to sell our shares to the buyer whether we want to or not. If we wanted to fight it, we'd have to prove it was unfairly prejudicial to the minority shareholders, and we were advised we'd be unlikely to succeed. The provision has been in the Articles since before we became shareholders, so . . .'

The door opened, a head appearing. 'Are you coming back to the party, darling? Eddie is about to make his speech, then we're going to do the raffle.'

'Give me a minute.' Malcolm stood up, waiting until the door closed behind his wife. 'Eddie is our parliamentary candidate,' he said, rolling his eyes. 'He's a nice chap, but thick as two short planks. Don't quote me on that.'

'How advanced is the sale?' asked Dixon.

'Very. And it's been conducted in absolute secrecy up to now – negotiations, everything. Nobody outside the family knows, so I'd be grateful if this was treated in the strictest confidence.'

'The staff don't know?' asked Jane.

'Especially not the staff, and if the press got hold of it before the official announcement is made, I dread to think what might happen. It'll need to be very carefully managed. There are people coming down from Diagent's PR company on Tuesday. There are all sorts of confidentiality clauses in the contract, as you might imagine. It's a bloody nightmare, really. There'll be hell to pay with the staff when they do find out.'

'When is completion?'

'Monday. The team from Diagent and their lawyers are travelling down from London in the morning, and there's a meeting in the boardroom at Oake starting at midday. Disclosure first and, all being well, completion after that. I'm told it will go on for as long as it takes and it could be a late night.'

'One hundred and twenty million,' said Dixon.

'That's the figure in the Memorandum of Understanding,' replied Malcolm, edging his way towards the door. 'It's since been tweaked a bit, so it's sixty million in cash, and the remainder in shares in Diagent Plc. There are earnouts and share options too. I'm going to remain as operations director, so actually it'll make very little difference to me on a daily basis, it's more the principle of the thing I'm struggling with. A twenty-one-year-old boy decides we're going to sell the family company and there's nothing I can do about it.'

'Are you angry about it?'

'No, I'm not angry. I wouldn't say I was angry. More fucking livid, if you'll pardon my language.'

Chapter Thirty-Six

He was aware of the pain first. A dull ache from the left side of his forehead, radiating across the top of his skull. A searing pain behind his eyes too; he hadn't had a headache like this since that fist fight at the rugby club when he lost his front tooth. Concussion, he'd been diagnosed with, and there'd been no painkillers known to man that had touched it for days.

Eyes still closed, Cole was listening to the sound of running water behind him – in a drainpipe, possibly. Listening *for* anything else.

His arms were behind him, the feeling slowly returning, but he couldn't move them. They were tied at the wrists; it felt like cable ties to the back of a chair. Legs too, cable ties at the ankles. Tight, cutting in.

Sitting upright at least.

He tried to open his eyes, but they felt as if they were glued shut. Congealed blood, if the taste in his mouth was anything to go by.

He ran his tongue over his front teeth; both still there. Small mercies.

He raised his shoulder as high as he could, turned his head, trying to wipe his eyes on his coat. Grimaced, unable to reach.

'Is that you, Nige?'

A soft voice; female. He recognised it from somewhere.

Think!

'It's me. Sarah.'

Then it all came roaring back. The barn, the car, the gun butt. The pain suddenly sharper too.

'I'm sorry I got you into this.'

'Where are we?' he asked.

'We're in a cellar,' she replied, her voice wobbly. 'Under the barn.'

'Who?'

'I didn't see his face. He was wearing a zombie face mask.'

'Why can't I open my eyes?'

'You've got a big gash in your forehead, over your left eye, and the blood's run down. You've been unconscious for ages, although I can't see my watch and he's taken our phones. There's a small window and it's dark outside. God knows what time it is; middle of the night, I reckon.'

'Describe this cellar to me.' Cole was blinking furiously, trying to force his eyelids apart.

'There's not a lot down here,' replied Sarah. 'You're sitting opposite me, about ten feet away. We're both on wooden chairs. There are some cider bottles in boxes against the wall to your left, a small cider press in the corner behind me, a workbench on the far side of the cellar off to your right; and one of those dresser things behind you, the things people line up their plates on.'

'I know.'

Cole tensed his legs and lurched forward, his chair moving an inch or so. 'Where's the door?'

'Behind you and to the right, in the corner. There's some steps and a door at the top. I heard it lock when he left. There's a light switch top and bottom.'

'What did he do to you?'

300

'He hit me with the shotgun. I woke up tied to this chair, like you. He was gone. I've almost got my right hand free, but I must've taken the skin off my thumb.'

'Is it cable ties?'

'Big white ones.'

'Did this bloke say anything?'

'Nothing at all,' replied Sarah. 'He hit you bloody hard, then he dragged you down the stairs. Are you all right?'

That explained the pain. Everywhere was hurting now.

'There's something else you need to know,' continued Sarah. 'Behind you, at the base of the dresser thing, there's a dead body. I think he's dead anyway. He hasn't moved the whole time I've been sitting here, and there's a lot of blood on the floor next to him. Looks to me like he's had his throat cut.'

She was keeping her composure remarkably well for a probationer. Cole was about to lose his, but Sarah seemed unflappable.

'Do you recognise him?'

'No, never seen him before. He's lying in the foetal position, right behind you, hands tied behind his back; must've been there when we arrived. Definitely had his throat cut.'

And there it was, in one sentence, the fate that awaited them. Cole could see it, even if Sarah couldn't. The man had probably been sitting on the same chair before he'd been killed.

Think, for fuck's sake!

'He took our phones, you said.'

'Yeah, he did,' replied Sarah.

'That means they'll have pinged masts near here, so as soon as someone realises we're missing and checks, they'll come looking and find us.' Cole wasn't entirely sure who he was trying to convince, Sarah or himself. And whoever it was would realise that too, and come back to clean up the mess.

'My mum will be doing her nut,' said Sarah. 'I usually ring her if I'm going to be late.'

'My wife the same,' said Cole. 'I'll never hear the last of it.'

'It's raining now.' He could hear her chair creaking as Sarah turned in her seat. 'I can hear it hitting a tin roof outside,' she said.

His right eye was opening now, just, although the lashes were still matted together with blood. Dark shadows emerging from the darkness, a shape in the faintest glow from the tiny window just beneath the ceiling. He tried to turn and look over his shoulder, but couldn't see anything at all of the dead body behind him.

It was going to have to be the cider bottles. Lurch over, one hop at a time, fall over backwards on to them, hoping the chair broke the glass and a splinter didn't take an artery with it. Then he'd have to feel for a shard of glass in the darkness and cut himself free.

He really should have told her he had a train to catch, but then she'd be down here all on her own.

'Where exactly were these cider bottles?'

'Against the wall to your left. There are three boxes, lined up.'

'In front of me, level with me or behind?'

'The middle one is level with you. Why? What are you going to do, Nige?'

Chapter Thirty-Seven

'What time is it?' Jane's head was on Dixon's pillow, her eyes closed.

'Just before six.'

A long, slow sigh. 'And what's his problem?'

Monty was sitting on the end of the bed staring at the gap in the curtains, tipping his head from side to side, growling softly.

'There's a car outside.'

'Tell him it's a road, there are bound to be cars outside.'

A loud knock on the front door of the cottage, and Monty was gone, paws thundering down the stairs. Then the barking started.

'Who the hell is that at this time in the morning?' hissed Jane, rolling over. 'We didn't get to bed till gone two, for heaven's sake.'

Dixon picked up his phone; four missed calls and four texts. All from Louise. 'It'll be Lou,' he said, trying to see through the gap in the curtains as he pulled on a pair of jeans.

The knocking on the door only stopped when he switched on the landing light.

'Come in, Lou,' he said, opening the front door on the way to the kettle. 'What's going on?'

She was squeezing past Monty, who was still grumbling. 'There's no sign of Sarah,' she said. 'And Nigel Cole's missing too, apparently. No one's seen them since yesterday afternoon and we've got his wife and her parents at Express Park. Out of their minds they are.'

'Any sign of their phones?'

'Mark put a trace on them and they're both at the Premier Inn at junction twenty-four. The Bridgwater Gateway, or whatever it is.'

'And we've tried ringing them?'

'Loads of times. They're not answering.'

'Get someone over there now to pick them up.'

'Nigel and Sarah?'

'Their phones,' replied Dixon. He had abandoned the kettle in the sink and was heading for the stairs. 'They'll have been dumped somewhere in the grounds, close to the building. The bar area, even. Get them to look at the CCTV as well, see if they can see who dumped them.'

Jane had appeared on the landing, rubbing her eyes. 'Did I hear that right – Nige and Sarah are at a hotel together?'

'Their phones are, which tells me they're in deep shit.'

It was slow going; about an inch at a time. And if he lost his balance and fell over, he'd never get back up.

The cable ties were biting into his ankles and wrists, but at least his feet had been left in contact with the ground when he'd been tied to the chair. That gave him some leverage, off his toes.

Shifting his weight, lurching to the left, the sound of the wooden chair legs scraping across the concrete floor the only real evidence that he'd moved at all.

It was pitch dark, so he couldn't see where he was going; he just had to keep moving, hoping to find the boxes of cider bottles in the darkness.

He had managed to turn, although it had been a sixteen-point turn that had taken too long and too much out of him, but at least he was lurching forwards now, feeling for the boxes that should be in front of him now with his toes.

'How are you getting on?' asked Sarah, her voice a faint whisper.

'Slowly.'

'What if he comes back?'

'We'll worry about that when the time comes, shall we?' Cole's sentence was punctuated with another scrape of the chair legs on the concrete floor. 'How far away were these bloody bottles?'

'About eight feet.'

He was moving an inch or so with a good heave, so what was twelve eights? Too bloody many and his head hurt far too much for maths calculations.

The rests between lurches were getting longer too. It was all taking too long.

'What's twelve times eight?' he asked.

No reply.

'Sarah, what are twelve eights?'

'Ninety-six.'

'Are you all right?'

'My head hurts. He hit me with the shotgun. I feel a bit dizzy, to be honest. And I think I'm going to be—' Then she vomited.

'Keep talking to me, all right,' demanded Cole. 'You must keep talking to me.'

'What about?'

'What sport do you play?'

'I used to play rugby,' she replied.

'I played rugby. I was a second row.' Another lurch. 'Do we have a women's team?'

'There is a police team, but this was touch rugby when I was at school. I was on the wing.'

'What about football?' asked Cole. She was far too young to be taking a blow to the head from a gun butt. Dizziness and vomiting were signs of concussion; a bleed on the brain and she'd be dead within hours.

'I tried football, but they always put me in goal.'

Another lurch, the scrape of the chair legs, but there was the sound of rattling glass bottles this time. He flicked out with his toes to make sure.

'You've reached the bottles?' Sarah asked, hesitantly.

'I have.'

'Oh God, Nige. What if the glass cuts your wrists?'

'You let me worry about that,' he replied. And he was worried about it, but then with a dead body lying on the ground behind him, throat cut, he knew what was in store for them. It was a chance he had to take; their only chance. Sarah's certainly – she needed to be in a hospital and she needed to be there sooner rather than later.

He began lurching to the right, feeling for the end of the line of boxes with his toes. Adrenaline pumping now, no rest between lurches.

It was now or never.

He turned slowly, the chair hopping round an inch at a time, until the boxes were behind him.

'Here goes,' he muttered.

A deep breath, then a final lurch, over backwards.

◆ ◆ ◆

It had been worth a try, but Jane wasn't having any of it. 'Of course I'm bloody well coming,' she had said, firmly.

The lights were on in the reception area at Express Park, three figures inside. Dixon recognised Nigel Cole's wife, sitting with her head in her hands. The other two – Sarah's parents, presumably – were pacing up and down. A uniformed officer was sitting at the reception desk, which would usually be closed at this time on a Sunday morning. He'd even switched on the coffee machine for them.

The side entrance would avoid awkward questions and, more importantly, save time.

'I reckon Nige is getting his leg ov—'

'Shut up, Mark,' said Dixon.

'Yes, Sir.'

The incident room was deserted apart from a small crowd gathered around Mark's workstation; several uniformed officers, including Chief Inspector Bateman.

'Nigel Cole's shift finished at two yesterday afternoon,' said Bateman. 'Then we've got them on CCTV leaving in his car about forty minutes later. Now they're at a bloody hotel together.'

'That's what we're supposed to think,' said Dixon. 'Our killer is forensically aware, according to Donald Watson. Now we find out he's phone signal aware too. Trace it back, Mark. Where were the phones before that?'

'Give me a minute.'

'You haven't told his wife and her parents they're at a hotel, have you?' asked Jane, glaring at Bateman.

'I did mention it, yes. I was trying to reassure them they were safe and well.'

'Let me explain it to you in words of one syllable,' said Dixon. 'Their phones have been left there to make it look as though they are there and all is well. They are not. They are in deep shit.'

'Yes, Sir.'

It felt odd, Bateman calling him 'Sir'. Only twelve months earlier Bateman had outranked him.

'How the bloody hell do I explain that to them?' he asked.

It was a good question, and one that Dixon would worry about later. 'Tell them nothing for now.'

'I'm not sure which is worse, anyway,' said Jane. 'His wife thinking Nigel is sleeping with someone else or that he's dead.'

'Oh, God.' The blood drained from Mark's face. 'When we were at the cider farm yesterday she was wittering on about this barn on the far side of the orchards. Wanted to check it out, she did, but it was about two miles away and I wasn't going over there. There wasn't time anyway; we weren't there long enough and we didn't have a warrant either. I reckon she went to check that barn and took Nigel with her. Looks like that's where they went from here.'

Cole landed with a crash, the sound of breaking glass underneath him. He braced himself for the pain, but there was very little – some from his arms, but nothing from his wrists or hands. He waited, knowing only too well that wasn't always a good sign when it came to cuts from glass; there'd been that twerp outside the Carousel with a broken bottle, and that window when he'd been breaking into a house in Edithmead for a welfare check.

There was definitely blood running down his left wrist, he could feel it now, but nothing from his right. Not yet, anyway.

Feeling with his fingers for a piece of broken glass.

'Are you still there, Sarah?' he asked. 'Talk to me.'

No reply.

Then he found what he was looking for. A shard of glass, curved, going to a point. He had picked it up in his left hand before transferring it to his right.

Maybe four inches long, thick too, from the neck of a bottle.

Now to start the cutting. Not easy with his hands behind him, cable-tied to the chair at the wrist. It hardly mattered that it was dark, because he couldn't see what he was doing anyway.

There was more blood now too, making the glass slippery.

Find the base of the cable tie. If he could do that, then he could cut it without hitting flesh.

A sawing motion at his wrists in the dark with a piece of glass. He kept telling himself he'd been in worse scrapes and had always got out, but actually that was bollocks, this was the worst by far. Not that he'd tell her that.

'Sarah?'

Nothing.

Fumbling in the dark with the piece of glass between the fingers of his right hand, whatever it was he'd found with it felt solid, rather than soft like flesh, so he started cutting; no more pain than before either, so maybe he was cutting the cable tie rather than his own flesh.

He'd soon find out.

Somebody must be looking for us by now, for fuck's sake.

The sawing motion was taking the point of the shard into his left wrist, right where his watch would have been, if he'd been wearing it. That surely meant that he was cutting the plastic of the cable tie? It didn't feel like wood.

Then his left hand came free.

He flexed his fingers, despite the pain, relieved that all seemed to be in working order.

What now?

Feet next, then get yourself stood up.

He transferred the shard of glass to his left hand, then began sawing at the cable tie fastening his left ankle to the chair, quickly kicking out and straightening his leg, rubbing his thigh and calf muscles, the piece of glass between his teeth.

Fucking cramp now.

Reaching down to his right ankle was a bit more of a stretch, but he made it and was soon massaging his right thigh.

'I've done it, Sarah. I'm free.'

A groan was all that came from her direction.

He rolled off the boxes and on to the floor, before standing up, the chair dangling from his right wrist by the remaining cable tie, which was soon cut.

Rubbing his wrists now, wiggling his fingers. Whatever he'd been hacking away at in the darkness, it hadn't been tendons, at least; not that he'd ever been much of a pianist. There was a lot of blood though, he could feel it. Smell it.

He was holding the piece of glass between his teeth, only too aware of the need to keep it. Cutting tool no longer. It was now a weapon.

He crept forward in the darkness, feeling his way with his foot, moving towards where he knew Sarah was sitting. What little light had been coming in through the small window had gone when it had started to rain, but he had his bearings, after a fashion, from her detailed description of the cellar.

His toe hit something soft and he reached out, feeling for her.

She was slumped over, her hands tied behind her, just as his had been.

'Sarah.'

Unresponsive. His hands on both shoulders now, shaking her gently. 'Sarah.'

Then he heard an engine, the cellar illuminated just for a second as the car swung around and parked behind the barn.

Chapter Thirty-Eight

Just before dawn on a Sunday morning. A wild ride on deserted roads, even in the middle of Taunton; Dixon in the passenger seat of a pursuit vehicle travelling at over one hundred miles an hour, Jane, Louise and Mark crammed in the back – they'd still have been out on the M5 in his Land Rover, so it was worth the rollercoaster ride.

An officer was standing resolutely in the middle of the road by the time they arrived from Express Park.

'Armed Response are going in now, Sir,' he said.

Dixon was out of the pursuit vehicle, climbing into the driver's seat of the patrol car blocking the lane. 'Where's the bloody handbrake in this thing?' He was looking for a lever down beside the seat, but there wasn't one. Handbrake off and the car should just roll out of the way.

'I can't let you through, Sir,' protested the officer.

'Let me, Sir,' said Mark, shoving the uniformed officer out of the way. 'There's a button.'

Once through the roadblock they were speeding down the single track lane, high hedges on both sides, at a modest sixty miles an hour this time, blue light switched off.

'This is as far as I can get,' said the traffic officer behind the wheel, the lane in front of them blocked by a line of ambulances, vans and cars.

'Thanks, mate,' said Mark, his hand on the driver's shoulder.

Squeezing between the vans and the hedge, dead branches coated in frost clawed at their coats, the occasional rotten blackberry still hanging on for grim death. The dead of winter, they called it; only two things going for it – ice climbing, not that he did that any more, and deserted beaches.

The dead of winter.

Please, God, no.

Two large five-bar gates were standing open, a heavy chain on the ground just visible in the first light of dawn.

'I can't let you go any further, Sir,' said Inspector Watts, the senior Armed Response officer.

Another one calling Dixon 'Sir'. The last time their paths had crossed they'd been the same rank. This was going to take some getting used to, although Dixon had more important things to worry about.

'They're going in now, although we've had a look with a drone and can't see anything.'

'Armed police!' The shout came from the barn, figures creeping along the wall at the front, crouching low, the movement visible through the hedge.

'We'll never get through the barn doors, but there's a door at the far end that'll take a battering ram,' said Watts.

Jane was crouching behind Dixon, then came Louise and Mark.

Two crashes, wood splintering, shouts of 'Armed police!' coming from inside the barn now. Dixon braced for the gunshots.

'Clear!'

More officers emerged from the darkness opposite the barn, behind arc lamps now illuminating the front.

The radio on Watts's body armour crackled into life. 'There's no one here, Guv.'

'Fuck it,' muttered Dixon. 'Check for a cellar,' he said, turning to Mark and Louise behind him.

'They'll have done that,' snapped Watts.

'Check it again. They're here somewhere, they must be.'

'Unless they really are in the hote—' Mark thought better of it.

'Jane, stay here and find out if we've found their phones yet, will you.'

A sharp intake of breath, about to protest, but it never came. Perhaps that conversation about eating for two, sleeping for two and taking risks for two had done the trick?

The barn doors were standing open by the time Dixon received clearance to go and have a look for himself, lights on inside now.

It had been open the night of wassailing, the ancient cider press the centrepiece of a small museum of sorts. This time there were pallets of cans wrapped in plastic, stickers with red crosses and 'Quality Control' on them. Some had been emptied down a drain and dumped in a recycling bin on wheels.

'Shocking waste,' said Mark, quietly.

Trestle tables leaning against the wall, stacks of chairs; Dixon even noticed two old toasters on the side. A wooden ladder led to a mezzanine floor.

'It's clear, Sir,' said an Armed Response officer, spotting him about to start the climb. 'There's nothing up there.'

Watts had followed him into the barn. 'We've been through every door and there are no trapdoors in the floor. I'm sorry, Sir, but there's no one here.'

A sharp kick at the gravel sent stones flying across the seating area outside, clattering into the sodden wooden benches and tables. Dixon was watching the ambulances and vans turning off the lane and into the car park. It seemed only yesterday he had parked there for the wassailing, flames from the fire pit rising into the darkness, the smell of mulled cider, people milling about everywhere, Roger queuing at the bar.

It was much the same scene now, arc lamps replacing the flames perhaps. And the people were carrying guns. The Portaloos had gone too.

'We've found their phones,' said Jane, appearing at Dixon's elbow. 'They were behind a sofa in the bar area. We're checking the CCTV now.'

'What about the families?'

'Still at Express Park,' replied Jane. 'Reception will be opening to the public in a bit, so I told them to put them upstairs in the canteen.'

Dixon was leaning on the five-bar gate, looking into the gloom beyond, a fork in the farm track fifty or so yards away. 'What's down there?' he asked.

'Orchards,' replied Jane. 'That's where we went to bless the apple trees. You escaped that, I seem to remember.'

'Yeah.'

'And where do the tracks lead to, I wonder?' Jane was dragging a map across the screen on her phone. 'That one goes off across the orchards to the canning plant,' she said, pointing to the left fork. 'And that one goes back to the road about half a mile further along. Wait a minute, what's that?'

'Switch it to satellite view.'

'There's another barn, in the trees, about five hundred yards down there, on the right.'

Dixon was already astride the gate. 'Tell Watts and then wait here,' he said, jumping down on the far side just as a muffled gunshot sent a flock of wood pigeons into the dawn sky.

◆ ◆ ◆

Feeling his way in the darkness. Cole knew where the chair should be and had seconds to find it before the door to the cellar opened. His only chance was to be seated again before the light came on and hope his captor didn't notice the broken glass.

Or the blood.

Legs cramping, but it was easing; tiptoeing forwards, feeling with his feet, his hands waving from side to side in front of him.

Whatever was going to happen would happen quickly now. He'd have to make his move before the cable ties lying on the ground gave him away. He'd never find those in the darkness.

Keep left a bit, away from the broken glass. He'd avoided treading on any up to now – or at least he thought he had – and now would not be a good time to start.

Then his left foot touched something on the floor in front of him, the sound of wood scraping on a concrete floor.

The chair.

He leaned forwards and picked it up, facing it in the direction he'd come from, back towards where Sarah was sitting.

Was dying.

Sitting down now, moving his legs into the same position they'd been in, or as near to it as he could get them, heels back to the chair legs, his muscles twitching, cramping again. Hands behind him, the shard of glass in his right.

Eyes closed, head bowed, just as the cellar door opened.

Footsteps on the stairs. Heavy; male, possibly. He'd soon find out.

The light came on.

Cole opened his eyes a fraction, hoping it was masked by the blood matted in his eyelashes; he listened to the footsteps moving across the concrete floor towards Sarah.

Tall, dark clothes, zombie mask.

The single light bulb above Sarah was covered in cobwebs and dust, much of the cellar still in darkness. He could hardly make out the broken glass himself, which might buy him a few seconds.

Cole was able to watch the figure cross the cellar, pausing to leave something leaning against the workbench as he went past, before standing behind Sarah, lifting her head and letting it fall back to her chest.

He turned his head, ever so slightly, spotting the shotgun, perhaps three paces to his right.

Moving before he had a chance to think it through, he lurched to his right, throwing the shard of glass at the man, who ducked behind Sarah. Cole was relieved his legs were taking his weight, moving where and when he asked them despite the pain and the cramping; hoping, praying it would last.

He snatched up the gun and turned to face his captor, flicking off the safety catch, trying to ignore the blood on his hands and arms.

'Drop the knife!'

His captor was standing behind Sarah, her head pulled back in his left hand, a knife to her throat in his right. 'Put down the gun or I kill the girl.'

Cole knew he was going to do that anyway. It was what he'd come back for – to finish the job. 'She's not a girl,' he said, his voice tight. 'She's a police officer.'

It must be loaded. Cole was holding the stock tightly in his left hand, squeezing the blood out from between his fingers. 'What the fuck is this all about anyway?' he asked.

'You don't know?'

'I just came with her,' replied Cole.

His captor gave a sarcastic laugh. 'Sixty million quid.'

'And who's this on the ground behind me?'

'His name's Sean Rodwell. He started the fire that killed my wife.'

Sean Rodwell was a familiar name, now Cole had started reading the intranet.

'Drop the gun, or I kill the girl.'

'You're going to do it anyway,' said Cole, oddly calm now.

Fuck that.

Then he pulled the triggers.

Both barrels, squarely in the chest, their captor slammed back into the wall of the cellar behind Sarah, his lifeless body sliding down into the darkness.

Cole's legs buckled. He dropped the gun as he fell to the ground, crawling towards Sarah now, tears streaming down his cheeks. He pulled himself up, lifting her head to the light, trickles of blood coming from shotgun pellets that had hit her in the face and neck.

Birdshot cartridges, the spread enough to have caught her at that range. It was a chance he'd had to take.

He picked up the shard of glass that was lying next to her chair and began sawing at the cable ties; first her ankles, then reaching around to the back and freeing her hands. Sarah slumped forwards into his arms.

He lowered her gently to the ground, cradling her head in his arms, and started to sob.

◆ ◆ ◆

Dixon was fifty yards ahead of the Armed Response team, sprinting along the track, ignoring the shouts from behind.

'Stand down, Superintendent!' Watts, playing it by the book, as usual. 'Armed officers must secure the area.'

He slowed as he reached the barn. The double doors were open, a Fiat 500 up on blocks, wheels off. A door was open at the side, stairs down, a shaft of light coming from a cellar below, no doubt the source of the gunshot.

Taking the stairs two at a time, Dixon ran down into the gloom below.

Cole was sitting on the concrete floor, his legs stretched out in front of him, Sarah's head in his arms. He looked up. 'She's dead, Sir,' he said. 'I had to shoot him and I hit her as well. He was going to slit her throat.'

Dixon picked up the shotgun and moved towards the body lying against the wall behind Cole, flicking on the light on his phone.

Both barrels squarely in the middle of the chest. There was no coming back from that.

He used the gun to move the zombie mask to one side.

Git.

'There's another one over there, Sir,' mumbled Cole. 'Sean Rodwell, apparently. He hasn't moved all night, I think he's dead.'

'Armed police!' A shout from the top of the stairs.

'3275 Superintendent Dixon. I have the gun; the area is secure.'

Then he leaned over Cole, shining the light on his phone in his face. A gash to the forehead, hair matted with blood, hands and arms cut to ribbons. 'Let me take her,' he said, softly.

'I killed her, Sir.'

A blow to the back of her head, her neck and collar soaked in blood; several shotgun pellet holes, blood trickling down her face and neck. But bleeding was a good sign, Dixon knew that much. He pressed his fingers to the side of Sarah's neck, feeling for a pulse.

'Let her go, Nige,' he said. 'She's alive.'

Chapter Thirty-Nine

Dixon was standing in the middle of the track, watching an ambulance picking its way between the puddles and ruts as it headed back out to the lane with Sarah in the back; on a stretcher, her head secured in a brace, oxygen mask clamped over her mouth. There was a doctor on board, and the air ambulance was standing by at Musgrove Park to take her to Bristol if need be. Jane had insisted on going as well – to keep her company, more than anything.

Nigel Cole was sitting in the back of the other ambulance, having his various cuts and lacerations bandaged before being taken to hospital. He had insisted his head injury was no worse than he'd had before around the blind side of a scrum, but his speech was slurred, so concussion it was, whether he liked it or not.

A convoy of Scientific Services vans was approaching along the lane from the other direction, Hari Patel and his clipboard walking alongside.

Charlesworth had appeared on the scene too, dressed in jeans and a pullover. Still, it was Sunday morning and he did live just up the road.

'Thank God you found them,' he said. 'Will she live?'

'Yes, Sir. She'll live. The doctor thinks so, anyway.'

'Someone needs to go and tell their families. They're still at Express Park. Would you like me to—?'

'I'll do it, Sir,' replied Dixon.

'William Hudson.' Charlesworth shook his head. 'Revenge then? I'm told Sean Rodwell's in there as well.'

'That was certainly revenge. I'm not so sure about the rest.'

'And what's this I hear about a second set of remains on the Torquay building site? It's the lead story on the *Torbay Gazette* website.'

'There is no second set of remains, Sir. That was a trap I set for Detective Sergeant Dean Wevill. He's been tipping off journalists; you'll recall we had a welcoming committee waiting for us at the exhumation.'

'I'll deal with him,' said Charlesworth, firmly. 'So, what happens now?'

'I'd like you to see to it that Nigel Cole is awarded the George Medal, Sir,' replied Dixon. 'Despite being seriously injured, he threw himself on to a box of glass bottles in a successful attempt to free himself from his bonds. He was then able to tackle William Hudson, killing him just as he was about to murder Police Constable Sarah Loveday. If ever an officer deserved a medal.'

'I'll go and sit with him in the ambulance.'

'He's very shaken up, but I don't think he knows it yet, Sir.'

'There'll need to be an IOPC investigation into the shooting, you do know that?'

'It will exonerate him. I have no doubt about that.'

Dixon left Louise and Mark at the scene and hitched a ride in an Armed Response vehicle going back to Express Park. The area at the front of the station was a hive of activity; blue lights flashing, sirens wailing as cars and vans raced off towards Oake.

Dixon noticed three figures standing in the window of the canteen, watching all the comings and goings. Jane's text message hadn't helped, arriving just as he'd stepped out of the car:

*Doctor had to relieve pressure on her brain. Craniectomy
in the back of the ambulance. Leaving for Bristol now. Jx*

Upstairs, a canteen assistant was just unlocking the doors.

'Keep them locked,' he said, pushing past the small queue and squeezing in the door.

'We open at ten on a Sunday.'

'Not today, you don't.'

'Have you found them?' Nigel Cole's wife was the first to summon up the courage to ask, probably still thinking her husband was having an affair.

'Yes, we have,' replied Dixon. 'They were being held captive in a cellar south of Taunton. Both of them are alive and on their way to hospital.'

'Alive, but not well?' Sarah Loveday's father – must be.

'Sarah received a blow to the head. The doctor was able to relieve the pressure on her brain in the ambulance and she's on her way to Bristol for surgery as we speak.'

Sarah's mother was listening intently, but didn't seem to be taking it all in.

'Is someone with her?'

'Detective Sergeant Winter went with her in the ambulance and is going to Bristol with her in the helicopter.'

'Helicopter?' If she hadn't understood the seriousness of it until then, she did now, the tears starting to roll slowly down her cheeks.

'What about Nigel?' asked Cole's wife.

'Concussion, multiple cuts and lacerations. He's on his way to Musgrove Park.' Dixon tried a reassuring smile. 'I'm arranging for cars to take you all to the relevant hospital as soon as you're ready to leave.'

'Are you Nick Dixon?' asked Sarah's mother.

'Yes.'

'She wants to be a CID officer, just like you, when her proba-tion's finished.'

'She will be. She's a very fine police officer; far better than she knows.'

◆ ◆ ◆

Two cars, one going south to Taunton, the other north to Bristol. Dixon watched them leave from the floor to ceiling windows.

So many questions and few answers. Yet.

Charlesworth had thought it was all over, and perhaps it was? If revenge had been William Hudson's motive and he'd killed all of the victims, then possibly. A forensic examination of the Fiat 500 was the first step, and a flatbed lorry had already arrived at the barn to take it away.

There could be little doubt that Hudson had killed Sean Rodwell, but what about the bridge team? One stabbed, so possibly that one, but three of them had been strangled in their own homes by a female occupational therapist with small hands.

Perhaps not, then.

And it wasn't just about revenge. Hudson had said that much to Cole in the cellar. It was about money – sixty million quid.

All this, and it came down to money.

Several of the Devon and Cornwall officers were sitting in the incident room, but no sign of Dean Wevill, although he wasn't due in until Monday morning.

'The search team have arrived at Hudson's place in Glastonbury, Sir,' said one. 'His wife's in and they're parked around the corner. Do you want them to go in or wait for Scientific?'

'Wait. And his wife doesn't leave until I get there. If she tries, stop her.'

'We seem to have lost our sergeant, Sir,' said another officer, with an apologetic shrug. 'Is there anything you'd like us to do, or shall we continue working our way through people at the Palace Hotel the night of the fire?'

'I need a file,' replied Dixon. 'Joanne Lucking. Drug overdose. She was found on a park bench on Babbacombe Downs. The coroner's file too, if you can get hold of it on a Sunday.'

'Yes, Sir.'

Dixon ignored the quizzical look and headed for the stairs.

Half an hour to Glastonbury, through the drizzle, his dog for company, Monty only jumping over on to the front passenger seat when Dixon switched off the engine. That was the time-honoured signal.

It didn't look much from the road; a rather grubby double-fronted property in need of a coat of paint. Now would be the time to do it, thought Dixon, the huge wisteria growing up the corner pruned back to bare stems. The paved area was overgrown too, even in winter.

He had picked up the search team and a Scientific Services van on the way, the convoy parking across the driveway, blocking in an estate car with the boot up.

Dixon was walking down the side of the property, a uniformed sergeant at his elbow, when a woman appeared carrying a suitcase.

'Mrs Sally Hudson?' he asked, warrant card at the ready.

'Yes.' She straightened up, seeing the uniform and the warrant at the same time. 'Is it Will?'

'Could we go inside?'

'Er, yes, of course.' She slammed the boot of the car.

The back of the property offered a very different perspective. Large bay windows overlooking a lawn and walled garden. Maybe there was money in hot tubs, after all? That was Dixon's only real interest in property – what it could tell him about the people who lived there.

A child was sitting at the kitchen table, playing a game on an iPad.

'Go to your room, Olivia.'

Dixon waited until Sally Hudson closed the door behind her daughter. 'Mrs Hudson, I'm afraid I have some bad news. Your husband, William, is dead.'

She leaned back against the kitchen sink and folded her arms. 'Did he kill himself?'

'No,' replied Dixon. 'Perhaps you might like to sit down?' he asked, gesturing to a kitchen chair.

'I'm fine standing up.'

If that's the way you want it.

'He had taken two police officers hostage at gunpoint and was holding them in a cellar just south of Taunton. One of them was able to get free, and in the ensuing struggle, your husband was shot and killed.'

She nodded, slowly.

'Had he not been killed, then I would have been arresting him for the murder of Sean Rodwell, whose body was found in the cellar. Is that a name known to you?'

'I know who Sean Rodwell is, yes.'

'It doesn't seem to have come as much of a surprise that your husband is alleged to have murdered him.'

'It isn't. He talked about nothing else for years.'

'I have a search team outside, and we're going to be searching this property, as you might imagine. Is there somewhere you can go?'

'I was going to my sister's anyway,' replied Sally. 'I was just loading the car.'

'Can I ask why?'

324

'I've had enough. Enough of his lies, enough of Sean bloody Rodwell and that sodding fire. This place is on the market; one-point-five million, and it'll just about cover his debts.'

'He talked a lot about the fire?'

'He talked about nothing else.'

'Were you aware that a woman has confessed to the abduction of William's son, Patrick, the night of the fire?'

'No. Did Will know?'

'He found out yesterday.'

'And he knew where Patrick was?'

'He did.'

'He never said a thing to me. Bloody marvellous, after everything he put me through.'

A free-standing kitchen, quarry tiled floor, range. You could be forgiven for thinking there really was a lot of money in hot tubs. 'Tell me about his business.'

'You'd better speak to his accountant. All I know is he hadn't made a profit for at least five years, but then he never made much of a profit before that. There was a family trust or something that bailed him out. Cost of living crisis, I suppose. People aren't going to be spending out on luxury items like that, are they? I tried to tell him, but he wouldn't listen. I think he sold six last year, he said. And that was *all* year. Then the rent on that fancy unit kicked in after the initial rent-free period, and we were borrowing against this place just to keep the business afloat – or stop it sinking so quickly, I should say.'

'What about his rental properties?'

'Bought them off plan, mortgaged up to the hilt, and look what's happened to interest rates. The rent he gets doesn't come close to covering it. Bankruptcy was inevitable, and he knew it.' She was standing with her hands on her hips. 'I'm going to have to go back to work. I had hoped to wait until the girls were a bit older, but needs must.'

'What do you do?'

'I'm an occupational therapist,' replied Sally. 'There's a training course I'll have to do when I go back, to get up to date, you know. I thought part-time would do, but it looks like I'm going to need the money.'

'Do you still have your uniform?'

'No, it's gone. Somewhere. I don't know. I was going to pack it, but it's not there. Maybe Will chucked it out?'

'You gave your husband an alibi for each of—'

'I didn't lie, if that's what you're getting at.'

'Is there life insurance?'

'I wish.'

Officers were filing in through the open back door; Scientific Services officers too, carrying aluminium cases and arc lamps.

'What exactly are you looking for?'

'Does your husband have an office at home?' asked Dixon, ignoring Sally's question.

'Follow me.'

Weaving between uniformed officers opening drawers and cupboards in the hall sideboard, and into a room with a red-brick fireplace and wood burning stove, built-in shelves either side. A desk too, and a filing cabinet.

An upright piano was standing against the wall opposite the window, photographs in silver frames lined up along the top. The photographs were different from the others on display; older, some in black and white.

'I'll leave you to it.'

'Who are the people in these photos?' asked Dixon, before Mrs Hudson could make her escape.

'His family from before we met.' Her arms were folded tightly across her chest, her left hand pointing as she spoke, before being tucked in each time. 'That's his first wife, Miriam. That's Freya and Patrick, before he was snatched, obviously. That's Miriam with her father; he died with her in the fire. And that's William's parents; they'd both died before I met him.'

'Did you ever meet Freya's ex-boyfriend?'

'Which one? Not the shit who got her pregnant?'

'Jos.'

'She never brought him here. It wasn't serious, I don't think, and it certainly didn't last that long.'

'Is she seeing anyone now?'

'Not that I know of.'

'What was your relationship like with Freya?'

'She was the typical resentful kid at first, but she soon got used to me. I like to think we got on. Why, has she said something different?'

'Not at all.'

'She was ten when I met her father, so just the wrong age, really. But we got there in the end. And she loves her sisters, I think. Babysits from time to time, or at least she did. I hope she still will. Does she know her father is dead?'

'There's a family liaison officer with her now.'

'Look, I wouldn't want you to think it was all bad. He could be lovely, and it was great to begin with. Then the girls came along and he was over the moon. The last six months, though.' Sally sighed. 'It all seemed to come roaring back. Patrick and the fire. The anger, resentment, anxiety; the drinking. I've been there, done that, got that T-shirt, and I wasn't going through it again, not now the girls are of an age they understand what's going on.'

◆ ◆ ◆

327

He could be lovely.

It wasn't something Dixon would tell Nigel Cole or Sarah, if she ever regained consciousness. Jane's text had arrived while he'd been talking to Sally Hudson.

Sarah gone into surgery. Doctors optimistic. Brain – the shotgun pellets will have to wait. Fingers crossed. Jx

He tapped out a reply that started an exchange of messages, typing as he walked:

Her parents are on the way. Nx

They're already here. How's Nige?

In surgery. I was going to see him, but it'll be a few hours. Some of the cuts are v deep.

Where are you?

On the beach.

Jane would understand. Even Charlesworth and Potter were starting to get the hang of it.

A sandwich from the petrol station, a bar of chocolate stuffed in his coat pocket just in case, and he left his car at the top of Allandale Road, setting off towards the lighthouse.

'No tennis ball today,' he said, holding his hands towards Monty so the dog could see they were empty. Monty turned away in disgust, sniffing the lines of seaweed instead.

Five murders.

Some good forensics from the Fiat 500, all being well, but at what cost?

Dixon had only just buried one colleague, and the idea of another funeral sent shivers down his spine. The bloody idiot, going off to search the barn like that. That said, it was difficult to be too cross with her because Dixon would have done exactly the same thing – probably gone on his own, come to think of it – and he could guarantee Jane would remind him of that just at the wrong moment, when he was giving Sarah a good ticking off.

That was quite something Cole had done. Pitching over backwards on to glass, both wrists exposed like that. It could so easily have gone the other way. And then firing the gun in the sure and certain knowledge Sarah would be hit as well; only four or five pellets as it turned out, but, God willing, she'd never let him forget it.

Dixon had spent ten minutes with Cole in the back of the ambulance and knew the enormity of what had happened was still to hit him. He'd be off work for a while, then there'd be counselling. Not to mention Dixon's stag do.

'I hope to God I'd have had the courage to do that, Nige.'

Cole had grinned, congealed blood between his teeth. 'A good man to have by your side when the shit hits the fan.'

'There's nobody else, Nige,' Dixon had replied. 'Nobody.'

Dixon would return the favour, being by Cole's side for the police conduct investigation.

Coincidences.

The case was riddled with them. He slid his phone out of his jacket pocket and googled the definition. He thought he knew what it meant – everybody thought they knew what it meant, but what did it *really* mean?

A remarkable concurrence of events without apparent causal connection.

It was hardly a coincidence that two teenagers living in the same area might meet at sixth form college. Hardly a coincidence that a brother and sister might feel some connection to each other too. It had happened before. But there were plenty of other coincidences.

He sat down on a piece of the old sea defences.

. . . *apparent* causal connection.

And there it was.

Assume nothing was a coincidence, and the whole sorry mess dropped into place; everything – every single thing – suddenly made sense.

Yes, Hudson had taken the chance for his revenge on Sean Rodwell, but it all boiled down to money in the end.

Sixty million quid.

Chapter Forty

'I wasn't expecting you,' said Jane, looking up. 'I was going to get a taxi home.'

'How is she?' asked Dixon. He sat down next to her in the waiting room; empty chairs around the wall, a coffee table in the middle with a jumble of magazines.

'I'm guessing she's out of surgery,' replied Jane, dropping a magazine back on the pile. 'Someone came and got her parents, presumably to speak to the consultant.'

'How are they doing?' Dixon was eyeing the coffee machine, wondering whether he could face powdered crap.

'Surprisingly' – Jane hesitated, searching for the right word – 'collected. She knew the risks, but was determined to be a police officer, come what may.'

'I dropped Monty off with your parents. Rod's looking better.'

'He's got to wear a thing that records his heartbeat for a couple of days, but he seems fine.'

'You'll be able to spend more time with him when you go on maternity leave,' said Dixon, idly.

'I know. I've been thinking about that.'

'You said you'd go when this case finished.'

'When's that likely to be?'

'Tomorrow.'

Jane knew better than to ask. She'd find out when he was good and ready. 'Any news on Nige? Last I heard he was in surgery.'

'He's out now and doing fine, according to his wife. He's going to need a bit of plastic surgery at some point, but that's it. Should be home tomorrow or the next day.'

'Counselling too, I expect.'

'You know Nige,' said Dixon, trying to make light of it. 'It's nothing a good game of rugby won't fix.'

'Yeah.'

Footsteps in the corridor outside, Dixon and Jane standing up as one when Sarah's parents shuffled into the waiting room, her father holding her mother up by the looks of things, both sobbing uncontrollably.

Jane snatched the box of tissues off the window ledge.

'You needn't have come,' said Sarah's father, forcing a smile. 'I know how busy you must be.'

'It's fine.' Dixon was resisting the temptation to ask.

'We'd like to meet Nigel Cole,' said her mother. 'Would that be possible?'

'I'm sure it would,' replied Jane. 'He's out of surgery and I'm sure he'd be delighted to meet you both.'

'He saved Sarah's life, and we'd like to thank him.'

Her father swallowed hard. 'The surgery went well and we're being told she should make a full recovery; the scans look good and they don't think there's any permanent damage.'

'Where is she?' asked Jane.

'She's in intensive care for the time being. They're going to keep her in a medically induced coma until the morning and then bring her round.'

'We can offer you a lift home—'

'We're going to stay, thank you,' replied Sarah's mother. 'They're finding us a room somewhere, so we can be here when they wake her up.'

'You will let me know.'

'Of course.' Sarah's mother had clasped Jane's hand. 'You go, you'll need some sleep yourself. Just thank you for being there for her.'

◆ ◆ ◆

'You're on speakerphone, Lou.' Jane was sitting in the passenger seat of Dixon's Land Rover holding his phone in front of him as he drove south on a deserted M5, lights on full beam.

He eased off the accelerator and flicked the windscreen wipers to intermittent, to cut down the background noise.

'What's going on, Lou?' he shouted.

'The Fiat 500's gone off to the lab, but Scientific still say they'll be at the barn until the end of tomorrow. There's an occupational therapist's uniform in the boot of the car, and a can of petrol, so I reckon he'd come back to finish them off and then he was going to take the car somewhere and torch it.'

'Any sign of Jos?'

'Not yet, and his phone's switched off.'

'What about his father's will?'

'I've got a copy, like you asked. Do you want me to scan it and email it?'

'Yes, please,' replied Dixon. 'Did you get a chance to look at what Sarah was working on before she went off with Nige?'

'She was doing family trees.'

Of course she was.

'Hang on to the papers and let me see them in the morning.'

'Will do.'

'What time is Diana Hope-Bruce up before the magistrates?'

'Ten; court one.'

'What about the bank statements I asked for?'

'The request's gone in, but it's a Sunday don't forget. We'll follow them up with calls in the morning,' replied Louise. 'How's Sarah? We're all on the edge of our chairs here.'

'She's going to be all right, they think,' replied Jane, turning the microphone towards her. 'The surgery went well and the scans are showing no signs of permanent damage.'

'Thank God for that. Nige is going to be all right too, apparently.'

'We know.'

'Go home, Lou,' said Dixon. 'Who else is there?'

'Mark,' replied Louise. 'I think he feels a bit guilty he didn't check the barn with her when we were over there yesterday.' Louise was whispering, her voice just carrying over the engine noise, despite being on full volume.

'Tell him to go home and get some sleep. And I suggest you do the same.'

Jane rang off. 'Are you going to tell me what this is all about then?'

'Money.'

'Not revenge?'

'Sean Rodwell was revenge. Will Hudson killed the man who started the fire that killed his wife.' Dixon took a deep breath. 'Not sure I blame him for that, either.'

'After all this, it comes down to money. Four murders.'

'Five. You're forgetting the poor sod on the park bench in Torquay.'

'You'll never prove that after all this time.'

'Not without a confession.'

Chapter Forty-One

It had been one of those nights, his mind racing, tossing and turning; trying not to wake Jane up. At least he didn't have Monty curled up on the end of the bed, although he might have taken him out for a walk if the dog had been there.

Now he was sitting in the corner of the small canteen area at Taunton Magistrates' Court, reading the research Sarah had been doing before she'd slipped out to check the barn.

Family trees – incomplete, sadly – but she'd been on the right track. Before anyone else too.

A bright kid.

'All parties in the case of Diana Hope-Bruce to court one, please.'

Dixon obeyed the tannoy, catching the crown prosecutor in the waiting area outside the court; the same crown prosecutor who had been there the day of his own appearance before the magistrates.

'You're the officer in the case of Diana Hope-Bruce?' asked the prosecutor, his face flushed.

'I am,' replied Dixon.

'Look, I hope you don't think—'

Dixon raised his hand, silencing the prosecutor mid-sentence. 'If you'd objected to my bail application it might be different,' he said. 'But there are no hard feelings. None at all.'

'Thank you.' The prosecutor looked relieved. 'And you've been promoted, I see,' he said, examining the identity card dangling on a lanyard around Dixon's neck, although that was more to avoid making eye contact, possibly.

'Don't remind me.'

'What about Diana Hope-Bruce, then? Clearly a flight risk, it seems to me.'

'She won't flee. There's too much at stake.'

'She's charged with the manslaughter of her three-month-old baby, concealment of a body and child abduction, so we would ordinarily resist a bail application as a matter of course.'

'Don't,' replied Dixon. 'A condition of residence will be fine. Reporting daily to Taunton police station, and surrender of her passport too, but I want her out – need her out.'

'If you say so.'

It had been a short hearing, the magistrate even giving him a cheery smile. It was the same one who had granted him bail and she clearly remembered him, but then it wasn't every day a detective chief inspector was up in front of the magistrates on a murder charge.

Happy days.

He could almost laugh about it now. Almost. But not quite.

News of the hearing had reached Express Park before he had, the result being Charlesworth and Deborah Potter lying in wait, Charlesworth springing out of the open door of meeting room 2 like a trapdoor spider.

'In here, if you've got a minute, Nick.'

He had, as it happened.

'What's this I hear about Diana Hope-Bruce getting bail?' asked Charlesworth, closing the door behind Dixon, loudly enough to convey his displeasure. 'We didn't object to bail being granted, I'm told.'

'We didn't, because we don't, Sir,' replied Dixon.

'She's clearly a flight risk,' said Potter, chewing her reading glasses; it was becoming a habit.

At least there was no press officer hovering this time.

'I disagree. It's certainly not in the public interest to remand her in custody. And, besides, I need her out and about.'

'I've had my opposite number from Devon and Cornwall on the phone, bending my ear about Sergeant Wevill and the mysterious second set of remains,' grumbled Charlesworth. 'Stirred up a bloody hornets' nest in Torquay, that has.'

'It was one of their officers leaking information to the press, Sir. Anyway, the article had gone from the website when I checked, and the local rag can easily print a correction.'

'That's what I tell him, is it? He says the information came from us.'

'Tell him to tighten up his recruitment process and be a bit more careful who he promotes.'

'That's your suggestion, is it?'

'I'm quite happy to tell him myself, if that would assist, Sir,' said Dixon.

'That won't be necessary, thank you.'

He thought not.

'Good news about Sarah Loveday,' offered Potter. 'She's come round and is talking, even had something to eat.'

'Nigel Cole's going home later too,' said Dixon.

'I said I'd go and see him this afternoon.' Charlesworth smiled. 'The chief con has approved an application for a George Medal, which is quite something if Cole gets it.'

'He deserves it, Sir.'

'So, where does all this leave us with this case, Nick?' asked Potter. 'You can pin Sean Rodwell's murder on William Hudson easily enough, but what about the other four, the bridge team?'

'There are five murders, actually,' replied Dixon. 'But whether we're able to bring a charge for all of them is up for grabs at the moment.'

'Sorry,' said Charlesworth, a frown etched deep into his forehead. 'Are you saying you know what's gone on?'

'I know exactly who has done what, to whom, when and why. Whether or not I can prove any of it is another matter.'

A set of reading glasses slid across the table. 'Are you going to tell us?' asked Potter.

'It's about coincidences,' replied Dixon. 'The case is riddled with them, but if you strip them out, accept there was a causal connection between all these events – that everything happened for a reason – then it all drops into place.'

'The relationship between Jos and Freya, you mean? It turning out they were brother and sister?'

'That's hardly a coincidence that. They both live in the area and met at sixth form college. Nothing unusual there. Nothing unusual that a brother and sister felt a connection either. If they didn't know they were brother and sister they might very well have confused it for something else. No, the biggest coincidence – the elephant in the room – was Diana Hope-Bruce being at the Palace Hotel the night of the fire.'

'You said that was *opportunistic*?'

'It seemed reasonable, and it was a means of explaining away the coincidence, but there was a causal connection all along. She was there for a reason. The evidence from Sean Rodwell was that he saw her approaching Deirdre Baxter along the terrace, which means she was at the hotel already.'

'Doing what?'

'Well, that becomes clear if you accept that what she said when she approached Deirdre and took the baby boy from her was true.' Dixon stood up, turning for the door. 'It was a throwaway line and she never imagined in her wildest dreams we'd take it seriously; she dressed it up as a lie to get Deirdre to hand the boy over, but it was true. All along it was true. The fire's raging, blue lights flashing, people milling about everywhere, alarms blaring, and she runs up to Deirdre and says, "He's my nephew. I'll look after him."'

Chapter Forty-Two

'You can't go up there.'

'I think you'll find we can.' Dixon was standing in the foyer of the canning plant at Oake Cider Farm, looking up the glass staircase to the mezzanine floor above while he waited for the police officers to file in behind him.

Louise, Mark, Jane and several in uniform. They were mainly there for their bodycams, Dixon not expecting any trouble. Live footage of the arrests might be useful; *anything you do say may be given in evidence* and all that.

The only slight fly in the ointment was the glass walls of the conference room, heads turning as the uniforms appeared at the top of the stairs, two of them following Mark and Louise to the other door at the far end of the corridor.

Most of the seats were taken at the long table. Diana Hope-Bruce and Jos sitting one side with their legal team, opposite five from Diagent Plc, a couple of directors – finance and the chief executive would be usual for a deal of this size – and their solicitors, pinstripe suit jackets slung over the backs of chairs revealing starched shirts and red braces. It looked like an organised crime squad meeting.

Malcolm Hope-Bruce was there too, sitting at the far end with two women; one must be his sister, Penny, and the other their own solicitor.

Dixon had attended several completion meetings on the sale of companies during his time as a trainee solicitor, and this one looked no different: boxes strewn on the floor, the table all but covered in open lever arch files. Long, drawn out and extraordinarily boring affairs, often going on until the early hours of the morning. Perhaps he'd be doing them a favour, livening this one up a bit?

And shortening it.

He recognised none of the lawyers from Oxenden Hart, but then they'd be from the corporate team and he'd never got to meet them. He hadn't even bothered to look at their website when he'd been applying for a job – such was his enthusiasm, or lack of it.

'You can't come in here. This is a private meeting,' said the older man, standing up. The head of department, probably. A deal of this size was big for any law firm and would merit his presence.

Dixon walked slowly around the table to where Jos was sitting, the young man turning in his seat to look up at him. 'I'm going to use your proper name,' he said. 'Patrick Hudson, I am arresting you on suspicion of fraud. You do not have to say anything, but it may harm your defence if you do not mention when questioned something you later rely on in court.' Dixon paused, listening for any reaction in the room – watching Diana – but there was none. 'Anything you do say may be given in evidence.'

Jos stood up, glaring at Diana, pleading. 'My name is Jos Hope-Bruce. Tell them!'

'Who is Patrick Hudson?' demanded Malcolm. 'Is this anything to do with the incident down at the barn?'

'We made full disclosure of the police incident,' said the head of department, leaning across the table towards the legal team on the other side. 'What we know about it so far, anyway. It was being used as a bolthole by a man alleged to have committed several murders; he held two police officers captive for a time, but I believe the incident ended satisfactorily and there is no connection with the cider farm.'

'Actually, there is,' said Dixon. 'The whole thing is *about* the cider farm, and the man killed was your father, Patrick. William Hudson.'

'So you say.'

'A DNA test will settle it.'

There would come a point when Diana had heard enough, but Dixon clearly hadn't got there yet.

'Hang on a minute,' said Malcolm. 'If you're Patrick Hudson and not Jos, then you don't inherit the shares, you're not the majority shareholder in the company – never have been – and can't force us to sell it.'

The legal team from Diagent Plc were taking a real interest now, one even taking shorthand notes.

'My father left me those shares.'

'He didn't, I'm afraid, Patrick,' replied Dixon. 'His will is quite clear; he left them to *my son* Jos. And you're not his son Jos.'

'I was as far as he was concerned.'

'He may have thought you were, but only because of a cruel deception on the part of his wife, Diana, who is charged with the manslaughter of Jos, the concealment of his body on waste ground behind her house in Richmond Close, Torquay, and the abduction of you to take his place.'

All eyes in the room turned to settle on Diana Hope-Bruce, sitting almost at the head of the table, but not quite, her head bowed.

'His son Jos was dead,' continued Dixon. 'And his testamentary intention was quite clear. Clause twelve of his will is an administrative provision: *references in this my Will to children and/or issue shall*

342

not include adopted or stepchildren. That means bloodline only, and you're not of his bloodline.'

'Is that true, Diana?' demanded Malcolm.

No reply.

'Jos was three months old at the time,' continued Dixon. 'And died at his mother's hand before his father, Robert Hope-Bruce, ever clapped eyes on him. By the time he returned from Saudi Arabia, Jos had been replaced with you, Patrick, and he was none the wiser.'

'The gift in Robert's will fails in that case,' said Malcolm, clapping his hands. 'And he left the shares to me and Penny in the event that Jos died before him. I'm sorry, ladies and gentlemen, the deal's off. Oake Cider is a family company and it's bloody well going to stay that way.'

A single glance from Dixon was enough to wipe the glee from Malcolm's face. 'As you now know, Patrick, you were snatched from a bridge team standing on the terrace of the Palace Hotel during a fire in the ballroom. Your real mother, Miriam, and your grandfather died in that fire, and four members of that bridge team have since been murdered. You are also to be investigated in connection with those murders.'

'Wait a minute.' Diana jumped up, two uniformed officers moving quickly to flank her. 'He knows nothing about this; any of it.'

'About what?'

She took a deep breath, then slumped back down into the chair. 'I killed them. The first three, anyway. Will killed the last one – stabbed him.'

'Don't say anything, Mum.'

'I'm not your mum, Jos. He's right. Your real name is Patrick Hudson.'

343

Dixon looked at Jane and nodded in Diana's direction. The room hushed, listening to Jane arresting her for the murders of Deirdre Baxter, Michael Allam, Thomas Fowler and Geoffrey Pannell.

'We'll also be looking again at the deaths of Joanne Lucking and your husband, Robert,' said Dixon.

'My brother was murdered?' Malcolm again.

'Who's Joanne Lucking?' asked Diana.

'She was found dead on a park bench on Babbacombe Downs,' replied Dixon. 'The official cause of death was accidental drug overdose.'

Diana was watching Dixon, shaking her head. 'We employed a private detective to see if there were any witnesses and he found some druggie who'd seen me running along the coast path with a baby in my arms. So, she had to die. I gave her the fatal dose and sat with her while she injected it; watched her drift off. It was quite peaceful, really.'

'Who's *we*?' Patrick's hands were handcuffed behind his back now, a uniformed officer holding each arm.

Dixon placed two framed pictures on the table in front of Diana. 'This is a photograph of your parents that we found in your dressing room. And this a photograph of William Hudson's parents we found at his house.'

She looked ready to deny it, but crumpled. 'Yes. He was my brother.'

'If he was your bloody brother, how come I never met him until I was going out with Freya?' demanded Patrick.

'No one could know,' replied Diana. 'We talked on the phone, met in secret. The two sides of the family had never met, so it was easy enough.'

'So, when you ran up to Deirdre Baxter on the terrace and said, "He's my nephew, I'll look after him," you were telling the truth?' asked Dixon, handing the framed photographs back to Jane.

'It was a couple of days after Jos died and I'd gone for a drink with Miriam. She was at the hotel with her father, who was in the bridge thing. It was a longstanding arrangement and I couldn't get out of it, so I told them Jos wasn't well – sniffles or something – and I'd get a babysitter. When I got there the fire was raging and this group of people was standing on the terrace with Patrick, so I took him off them. The woman said Miriam had handed him to her on the fire escape, gone back for her father and not reappeared. I told her the baby was my nephew and she gave him to me. The police came knocking the next day. They knew I'd not long given birth, so I told them he was mine. What else could I do? I'd killed my own baby.' Diana was breathing heavily, her chest heaving. 'All hell broke loose after that, what with the hunt for the missing child. Then Will came to see me maybe a week later. He'd have recognised Patrick straight away, so I told him what had happened, about Jos and everything. I'd have gone to prison. My own beautiful baby boy. I shook him, and shook him . . . he just wouldn't stop crying . . .'

Dixon waited while she gathered her composure.

She gave a long, slow shrug. 'Will was going to have enough trouble as a single parent as it was, without a baby on his hands – Freya was only two – and I'd have probably ended up looking after Patrick anyway, so he decided to let me keep him. It was either that or watch his sister go to prison. And then there was what we could offer Patrick . . . money was no object.'

'Fucking Harrow,' sneered Patrick. 'I hated it anyway.'

'The private detective and the campaign to find him – it was just a smokescreen,' continued Diana, lost in her own thoughts. 'We knew where he was the whole time. All we had to do was get to the bridge team before the police did, which was easy enough. The teams were listed on the bridge union website and Somerset was the only team of six with four men and two women. Will spoke

345

to them one by one, assured them Patrick was safe – he was the boy's father after all – offered them some money and that was that. They kept quiet; told the police they had no recollection of seeing a baby that night. Will was protecting me, bless him. He'd always done that, but that's another story I'll not repeat in front of all these people.' She closed the lever arch file in front of her and slid it into the middle of the table. 'If it had come out that Patrick survived the fire then I'd have gone to prison for killing Jos. And the CPS had dropped the charge against Rodwell relating to Patrick's death, so we weren't even perverting the course of justice, Will said. It was a private family arrangement, and nobody else's business.'

'What about my brother?' asked Malcolm.

'That was an accident, it really was,' replied Diana. 'But it gave us an opportunity. As far as the rest of the world was concerned, Patrick was Robert's son, so he inherited half the company. I'd been helping Will financially; not the most astute of businessmen to say the least, but this was thirty million in cash we're talking about if this deal went through.' She clenched her fists. 'Then the piece of waste ground behind our old house was sold and builders found Jos's body. It all started to unravel after that.'

'You took a bit of a gamble sending Patrick to take the DNA test, given that he was Jos's cousin,' said Dixon.

'What choice did I have? We were told it was only a partial profile, so I thought he was less likely to be a match. I'd have stood no chance. Sending him seemed like the perfect answer, and it worked.'

'I'm guessing it was Thomas Fowler who got in touch, wanting more money, seeing as he was the first to die.'

Diana's eyes narrowed. 'I thought I'd got away with it, once they buried him. It had to be you, didn't it, and not the Torquay lot. Will had them wrapped around his little finger.' She gave a self-pitying sigh. 'We'd paid the bridge team off and the private detective couldn't get them to talk. They were still denying all knowledge of Patrick surviving the fire, so we thought we'd be all right. Then the call came. Fowler had seen the report of the baby's remains in the paper, put two and two together, and demanded to know if they were connected. He didn't really *know* anything, but then he didn't need to; all he had to do was ask the question. Or tell the police about Patrick and leave them to ask the question; that's what he threatened to do. He wanted more money, said he was going into a care home and needed it for that. I was wearing Sally's OT uniform and the silly old sod let me in before he realised who it was. Died surprisingly quickly, come to think of it. They all did.'

'Why not just pay him off again?' asked Dixon.

'We didn't have any money to give him at that point. I tried reasoning with him – said if he could wait just a few months – but he wouldn't.'

'Were the others blackmailing you as well?'

'No, but Will said we couldn't take the chance. By then there was too much at stake, and we'd got away with it once already. The slightest suspicion that Jos wasn't Jos and that shit would've demanded a DNA test.' Diana jabbed her finger at Malcolm. 'We couldn't risk the sale of the company falling through; losing all that money.'

'I really don't think you should be saying any more, Mrs Hope-Bruce,' said her corporate lawyer. 'Not until you've spoken to someone in our crime team.'

'I've got my own solicitor, thanks, and in for a penny, in for a pound,' she replied. 'Anyway, it's a bit late now.'

'So, Freya really is my sister.' Patrick was wrestling with the officers holding his arms. 'Why didn't you just say that instead of coming up with all that crap about her not being suitable? She was just a gold digger, you said. That's fucking priceless, that is.'

'I was trying to protect you.' Diana looked up at Dixon, her eyes welling up. 'He really didn't know about any of this. Neither did Freya. Sally didn't even know we'd taken her old uniform.'

'And Will killed Sean Rodwell?'

'He thought the game was up by then and wanted to make damn sure he got him before it was too late. He was watching the halfway house in Weston when Rodwell came out, and he grabbed him. I told Will it was over and we should just come clean, but there was no stopping him by then. Then that silly girl and her colleague came sniffing around the barn. He was under so much pressure and he just flipped, I think. I hadn't been able to give him any more money since my husband died, and his business was going under. Again. This deal was his last chance. It's why he insisted on killing the last bridge player. I said the game was up by then, you were on to us, but he did it anyway. Are they all right, your two colleagues?'

'They'll live,' replied Dixon.

'I'm sorry, for all of it. You do what you think is right at each turn and, before you know it, there's no going back.'

Chapter Forty-Three

'Are you sure you want to do this?'

Jane was holding a bunch of flowers in both hands, trying to shield them from the rain. 'We've come all this way. And you've got the key from the estate agent now.'

Dixon inserted it in the lock and turned it, the chain dropping to the ground. Then he pushed open the gates, ignoring the barking coming from his Land Rover behind him.

'Aren't you going to bring him?'

'Not with all this mud,' he replied. 'He can have a run on the beach when we get home.'

He wasn't sure whether it was tears or raindrops rolling down Jane's cheeks as they picked their way across the mud. There were plenty of boot prints, the ground floors of the two houses marked out with tape ready for building work to start, a 'Sold Subject to Contract' notice stuck at a jaunty angle across the 'For Sale' board at the entrance.

'Where was he buried?' asked Jane.

Dixon had read the witness statements from the builders and looked at the photographs, and knew roughly where it was, although the site looked very different now. 'It was about here,' he said, gesturing to the ground at his feet. 'That was the house they lived in.'

'Poor little mite.' Jane leaned over and placed the flowers on the ground, the rain hitting the cellophane wrapper with that familiar pit-pat.

'You've left the price on them,' said Dixon.

'Does it matter?'

'I suppose not.'

'Everybody seems to forget this poor little lad. He was only three months old.' Jane took Dixon's hand and squeezed it. 'The first victim.'

'Eight people dead, and it all started with little Jos Hope-Bruce.'

'Yeah.'

'C'mon, let's go home.'

'Can we just stand here for a minute?' Jane's hands were resting on her abdomen, feeling for a kick, possibly. There'd been a lot of that lately.

'Of course we can,' replied Dixon, although he'd have brought his brolly from the back of the car if he'd known.

'Did you get a charging decision out of the CPS?' she asked.

'Diana's been charged with five counts of murder, to add to the manslaughter and concealment of a body. That includes Geoffrey Pannell's murder, even though her brother wielded the knife – it was part of a joint enterprise. They've dropped the abduction, though; she had parental consent all along.'

'What was that story about her brother protecting her?'

'Their father.'

'Enough said.' Jane sighed. 'What about Patrick?'

'There's no evidence he knew anything about it, just like she said, so he's off the hook. Got enough to be worrying about, mind you, although Diana is giving him the house and what money she's got, so he won't be short of a bob or two.'

'It's the least she could do.'

'It's not as if she's going to need it where she's going, and the chances of her ever getting out are pretty slim. She might well get a whole life order.'

'Good.'

'It's Sally I feel sorry for. She's going to lose the lot, and her and her girls are going to be homeless. Freya too, when their houses are repossessed.'

'Freya will go and live with her brother, I expect,' said Jane. 'Only not as a couple.'

Their feet were starting to sink into the mud, rivulets trickling across the building plot from the raised ground behind. 'A bit of drainage work to be done, I think,' muttered Dixon.

'I spoke to Deborah Potter this morning. Told her I was going on maternity leave, effective immediately.'

'What did she say?'

'Good luck.' Jane turned for the Land Rover, Dixon following her. 'Sarah's doing well. Her mother rang me; said she might even make it to our wedding.'

'What are you doing about your girls' night out?' He was stepping over the rainwater that was now leaving wide tracks in the mud, Jane splashing straight through them in her boots.

'Cancelled it. It's not as if I can have much of a party when I'm six months pregnant, and there'd only be me and Lou anyway. My mother won't leave my father at the moment.'

'Don't forget Lucy.'

'She's only sixteen, so she can't drink.'

'You lucky sod. Roger's still insisting on this piss-up he's organised at a hotel in Lynmouth. He's only gone and invited Charlesworth as well.'

Jane made no attempt to stifle her chuckle. 'I think I'd rather spend a night in the cells.'

351

'Nige's hands will still be bandaged, so he said he's going to drink through a straw.'

'Sounds like a riot.'

'I'll think of something.'

Dixon closed the gates, replacing the padlock and chain. 'Where to now?' he asked, climbing into the driver's seat.

'Home.'

'I've just got to drop these keys in on the way.' He stopped across the entrance to Richmond Close, looking up at what had once been the Hope-Bruce family home at the far end. A new family in residence – cars in the drive, a child's bicycle on the lawn, lights on inside; oblivious to what had gone on there, hopefully. 'Do you ever think we spend too much of our lives gazing into the abyss?'

'It's who we are,' replied Jane.

'It'll be interesting to see if you feel the same when you've had a few months away from it.'

'So, what are you saying?' She frowned. 'That you want to go back to the legal profession after all?'

'What was it Nietzsche said about monsters?'

'I know that one,' replied Jane. 'Something about he who fights monsters becoming a monster themselves. That won't happen to us.'

'You can guarantee that, can you?'

Author's Note

It is astonishing to me that the series is still going, ten years and fourteen books on, but it is entirely thanks to the many readers who have followed Nick, Jane and Monty from the outset, who follow on social media and continue to cheer them (and me) on. Thank you all very much, and for reading *From the Ashes*. I do hope you enjoyed it!

There are a great many people who have contributed to *From the Ashes* along the way and to whom I would like to take this opportunity to record my grateful thanks.

First and foremost, my wife, Shelley, whose support and encouragement remain invaluable. Shelley's willingness to drop everything and read the manuscript on a daily basis never ceases to amaze me.

To my dear friend and harshest critic, Rod Glanville. Thanks, Rodders!

To David Hall and Clare Paul, whose encyclopedic knowledge of Somerset (and Land Rovers) is always freely given and gratefully received.

To my developmental editor, Ian Pindar, and the team at Thomas & Mercer, in particular Sammia Hamer, Victoria Haslam and Eoin Purcell. Thank you!

From the Ashes was another trip down memory lane for me, back to my school days in Burnham-on-Sea in the seventies. It is funny the things that stick in the mind, although I cannot now recall whether the story about the girl falling off the stage and breaking her neck really happened. It may have been a ghost story that the older pupils used to terrorise the younger ones. If there is anyone out there who knows, please get in touch via my website.

I would also like to apologise to any girl from St Christopher's whose toes I trod on during the ballroom dancing lessons. Yes, they really did happen!

I have fond memories of the Palace Hotel too, and even played the little nine-hole golf course behind it many years ago. Sadly, it really is now just a building site, and at the time of writing, the plans to build a new hotel on the site have been shelved.

My late father even used to play bridge in the community centre in Burnham-on-Sea.

Writing is an oddly personal affair!

Damien Boyd
Devon, UK
November 2023

About the Author

Damien Boyd is a solicitor by training and draws on his extensive experience of criminal law, along with a spell in the Crown Prosecution Service, to write fast-paced crime thrillers featuring Detective Inspector Nick Dixon. Find out more at damienboyd.com

Follow the Author on Amazon

If you enjoyed this book, follow Damien Boyd on Amazon to be notified when the author releases a new book!

To do this, please follow these instructions:

Desktop:

1) Search for the author's name on Amazon or in the Amazon App.

2) Click on the author's name to arrive on their Amazon page.

3) Click the 'Follow' button.

Mobile and Tablet:

1) Search for the author's name on Amazon or in the Amazon App.

2) Click on one of the author's books.

3) Click on the author's name to arrive on their Amazon page.

4) Click the 'Follow' button.

Kindle eReader and Kindle App:

If you enjoyed this book on a Kindle eReader or in the Kindle App, you will find the author 'Follow' button after the last page.